BROKEN GHOSTS

For Barbara, who took me to Wales,
and the people of Pwllpeiran and Cwmystwyth,
who welcomed me when I arrived.

Light breaks where no sun shines;
Where no sea runs, the waters of the heart
Push in their tides;
And, broken ghosts with glow-worms in their heads,
The things of light
File through the flesh where no flesh decks the bones.

'Light Breaks Where No Sun Shines' – Dylan Thomas –
from *18 Poems* (1934)

1

2023

No matter how many times she comes back, the house always looks wrong. Like a badly fitted false tooth, it's too modern compared to the buildings on either side. The windows don't match; the roof tiles are a different shade of grey; the harling has fewer cracks than the neighbours', even if there are more this year than last. None of the houses in this quiet cul-de-sac are the same any more, although she remembers a time when they were. A generation has come and gone, multiple owners making their small marks of difference, but the buildings are all essentially the same. Same shape, same dimensions, same size.

Except the one in the middle.

She sits in the car, unsure whether she has the strength of will to climb out, get closer. The view intermittently blurs and clears as the windscreen wipers sweep away the lightest of smirrs. There is no one left in this little community who would know who she is now. No one who would understand why that one house in the scheme is not like all the rest. On the passenger seat beside her, the bunch of flowers seems unnecessary, even a little vulgar. What would people think if they saw her placing it beside the low wall that separates the front garden from the pavement? How long would they stay there after she left? Why does she even keep coming here, year after year?

Survivor's guilt, they call it. Although really it's more complicated than that. She survived, it's true. But the alternative would have meant she survived too. And there would be no need to come here every year, sit in her car and stare at a house she never lived in. That's what she tells herself, at least. And sometimes she almost believes it too.

Movement to one side is a twitch in the curtains of the house two doors down. She's been noticed now, and no doubt someone will be calling the police soon enough. It's that kind of place, a Neighbourhood Watch roundel pinned to the nearest lamppost. She checks the clock on the dashboard, is five minutes enough? More than enough, she's sure. It's not as if anyone's going to take her to task for her lack of respect. Nobody told her to come here, after all.

She starts the car, turns awkwardly in the narrow space of the cul-de-sac. As she glances in the mirror, for a moment the blurred image is lit with red from the brake lights and the scene takes on a hellish feel. As if that oddly ill-fitting house is ablaze. The thought has barely enough time to catch her breath before the rear wiper clears it away. Still, it sends a shudder through her, and she reaches for the button to turn up the heat a little.

She shouldn't have come here. Time, surely, to put this annual pilgrimage behind her. As she checks the traffic before pulling out onto the Edinburgh road, she see the flowers still in their cellophane, lying on the passenger seat. Cheering and colourful, they'll look nice in her living room, brighten the place up a bit for a change.

2

1985

The train clattered over worn tracks, noisy and slow and packed with far too many people. Normally Phoebe would expect the carriage to be colder at this time of year, but this one seemed to have stored all the heat missing from all those other trips she'd made in her twelve years. She stuck a finger in the collar of her blouse, scratched at her neck and felt sweat trickle down her back. At least she'd managed to nab a seat, unlike half of the school trip.

If they'd been on the train they were meant to catch, it would have been fine. But Morag Carstairs and her gang had decided a trip to the National Museum was too boring and bunked off to go shopping or something. By the time they'd been rounded up and given a pointless stern lecture by Mrs Erskine, the whole group was an hour late. When they'd finally reached Waverley Station it had been chaos, thanks to faulty points, whatever they were. No trains out to Fife for hours, and two teachers trying to keep a bunch of increasingly fractious twelve-year-olds in check. When the trains had started running again, four hours after they should all have been home, the rush to fit five times as many people into each carriage as it was designed to hold had been brutal. Good luck to any ticket inspector trying to work his way down the aisle.

On balance, Phoebe didn't mind the delay too much. She'd bought herself a Mars Bar and a bottle of Irn-Bru, found a bench and slipped her headphones on. She loved to watch people come and go, make up stories about their lives. There was so much going on in the bustling, chaotic station she could have sat even longer. After all, the alternative was an evening in her room, on her own, flicking through copies of *Smash Hits* and wishing she was old enough to go out unsupervised and hang out with her friends. As she stared through the dripping condensation on the glass at the slow-moving darkness outside the train, it struck her that this noisy, sweaty, smelly place was far preferable to the strained silence of home.

The train stopped everywhere, its cargo of squashed passengers slowly leaking away with each new station. By the time they'd pulled out of Markinch, there were enough seats for everybody. With an exaggerated gasp of relief, Jen slumped into the seat beside her, squeezing up against Phoebe far more than was strictly necessary.

'What you listening to, Feebs?'

'Nothing.' Phoebe slipped off her headphones and hung them round her neck, picked up her Walkman. 'Batteries ran out an hour ago.'

'You're weird, you know?' Jen stared at her, frizzy brown hair tumbling over her eyes. It stuck out at odd angles with the static from her fake fur-lined hood and whatever material the seats were covered in.

'Stops people bothering me. Mostly. Creepy guy over there was staring at both of us all the way to Kirkcaldy.' Phoebe gestured to the far side of the carriage and a set of four seats now occupied by Morag Carstairs and her gang. Of course Morag took that moment to look up, scowling like she always did. For a moment Phoebe thought the girl might come over and make something of it, but apparently everyone was too fed up and tired even for that. There'd be words at school in the morning though. No doubt about that. No one could hold an unwarranted grudge like Morag.

'Ugh. Makes my skin crawl just thinking about it.'

Phoebe might have asked Jen whether she was talking about the creepy guy or Morag and her gang, but the train had begun to slow now, approaching Cupar and home.

Gathering up her things, Phoebe followed Jen and the rest of their group of pupils and teachers out onto the cold night platform. The young and the old trudged up the stone steps to the road and headed their separate ways or stumbled across the car park to waiting cars and anxious parents. At the far corner, she spotted the familiar shape of Mrs Dalgliesh's dark-coloured Range Rover, twin wisps of steam curling up from its exhaust pipes. Jen's mum at least was on time.

'You want a lift?' Mrs Dalgliesh wound down the window to speak to Phoebe as her daughter climbed in on the other side.

'Thanks, Mrs D, but Dad's going to pick me up. Mrs Erskine said she spoke to them.'

Mrs Dalgliesh smiled at her. 'OK, hen. You take care now.'

With a low rumble, the car pulled away, Jen waving from the passenger seat as if they would never see each other again, rather than both being in school the next morning. Phoebe stood alone in the car park, hands shoved in her coat pockets against the chill. A couple of taxis moved off, then quiet fell upon the town. She looked up the road in the direction her father would come, seeing nothing. Maybe she should have taken Mrs Dalgliesh up on her offer. Chances were her dad had fallen asleep in front of the telly, and Mum would be in bed long since.

Phoebe took a deep breath and noticed for the first time the faint smell of smoke on the breeze. Chilly enough for people to be lighting their fires. She hunched her shoulders, shoved her hands deeper into her coat pockets in search of warmth, and began the walk home.

The first police car was silent. Whistling past her at twice the speed limit, it disappeared round a bend in the road with a slight chirp of tyres. Phoebe paid it little heed.

The second police car had its lights flashing, and flipped on its siren as it passed, jolting her out of her reverie. It was then that she noticed the smoke again, only this time it wasn't the sweet smell of burning logs. This was more like that time Dad forgot to put the fire-guard in place and a spark flew out onto the carpet. Burning hair too close to the barbecue.

A fire engine roared past and Phoebe quickened her pace. All these vehicles were going the same way as her. Flickering movement caught her eye. She looked up to see the cloud base, low now, swirling with orange patterns and dark, dark smoke. Someone's house was on fire and it was horribly close to where she lived. She needed to get home and let her parents know she was all right.

She ran the last few hundred yards, rounded the street corner and launched herself up the hill towards the end of the little cul-de-sac. Another police car sped past, followed by an ambulance, and then Phoebe started to see people. Some dressed in night clothes, others in dark blue uniforms, they milled around in the road like a street party for oldies. All of them had their backs to her; all stared at the inferno straight ahead.

The noise hit her like a jet fighter from Leuchars, roaring overhead. Only it didn't quieten, didn't fade into the distance at supersonic speed. Phoebe pushed through the people, all of them too fixated on the fire to notice her. She needed to get closer, had to get home.

'Keep back, love. It's too dangerous.' A firm hand clasped her shoulder, stopped her in her tracks. She looked at it, not quite understanding what was going on, followed the length of the arm up to a shoulder, then a face. Dark shadows strobed blue and orange in the light from the police cars, the glare from the burning house.

'But I've got to get home.' She pulled against the strong hold.

'Home?' The policeman bent down to her level and she could see sweat from the heat of the fire beading on his cheeks and forehead. 'Where you live, then, love?'

Phoebe pointed beyond the fire engine, towards what looked like a wall of flame. Her house, her home, her parents. There was something not right in her mind, and she couldn't think what it was. Some huge thought that she couldn't quite form.

'In there.'

3

It was stupid really, but all she could think of was the poster they'd been shown at school as part of fire awareness. A melted plastic clock in a pile of rubble and ashes and the caption 'I didn't check the battery because I didn't want to wake the children.' As if that made any sense at all. She knew the fire alarm at home worked fine. The batteries were fresh, and the system was wired to the mains. She can remember all too well dad's delight in setting off the kitchen alarm and hearing all the others ring throughout the house. State of the art, he was dead chuffed with it all.

Now he was just dead.

Phoebe sat at the front of the church. There were two coffins in front of her. That had to be a bit weird, didn't it? She'd not been to a lot of funerals; Jenny's gran last year was the only one she could think of. But normally you would bury one at a time. Two took up too much space in front of the altar. There wasn't enough room to get them down the aisle side by side. And who decided who was to go first; Mum or Dad?

Mum or Dad. They were in those wooden boxes. Not ten feet away. Phoebe fought a perverse urge to open them up, look once more on the faces she had known all her life. She wanted to ask them what they were doing, how they could leave her without even saying goodbye. But she couldn't move, numbed by it all.

People stood and sat around her, up and down like some fair-ground ride. Music came and went, hymns, readings. None of it meant anything. Phoebe glanced sideways at the people in the front row. There was Jenny, her oldest friend, eyes puffy and wet, a handkerchief clutched in her pudgy hand. Mr and Mrs Dalgliesh were still alive, and looked very serious, dressed in black. To the other side, a man she barely remembered. Mum's older brother, Uncle Louis. As he stared unblinking at the coffins, Phoebe thought she maybe understood something of what was going on in his head. But then he wiped at his eyes with his hand, and a single tear trickled down his cheek. His Adam's apple bobbed up and down as he swallowed his grief, as if his stomach would know what to do with it any better.

Phoebe turned her attention back to the priest, though his words seemed to be in a foreign language. It sounded like English, but she couldn't for the life of her understand what he was saying. As if his accent was impenetrable, even though she knew he lived in the manse at the back of the church. The sights and sounds of normal life came close, but couldn't quite penetrate the cocoon that surrounded her. It was too big, this change that had swamped everything. She needed to hide from it, to run, to scream at the sky. She needed to cry, but the tears wouldn't come.

Why could she not she cry?

Phoebe stood by the church doors and watched as the two coffins were placed in separate hearses. Flowers removed, she had no idea which was Mum and which was Dad. Without much further cere-mony, the black-suited funeral attendants climbed in the front and both vehicles drove off. For a moment she panicked. Was she meant to be going with them? There had been talk of cremation, hadn't there? She wasn't sure. There had been lots of talk, lots of serious adult faces and words which she knew but whose meaning she couldn't quite understand. Nothing much stayed in her mind these days, or if it did it was lost in the fog. All she could see, all she could remember, was the wall of flame as it devoured her home.

'You OK, Phoebe?' The question came at the same time as she felt the gentlest of touches on her elbow. Looking round, she saw her uncle just behind her. He had crouched a little so as not to loom over her, although she was only a few inches shorter than him in the black leather boots she'd borrowed from Jenny.

'Shouldn't we be . . . I don't know . . . going with them?' She found herself pointing into the distance where the two hearses had long since disappeared. Dropped her hand to her side again.

'Do you want to? Or would you rather remember your mum and dad in happier times?'

Phoebe could only see her home on fire whenever she thought of her parents now, one of the reasons why she'd been trying so hard not to think of them at all. This day, with all these well-meaning strangers staring at her with those expressions of sympathy and terror, was exquisite torture.

'I just want it all to stop.'

Uncle Louis put his arm around her shoulder and pulled her into a gentle hug. Phoebe felt the awkwardness of it almost second hand. Everything was awkward right now, and the arrival of this man two days after the fire was the least of it. He wasn't a total stranger, after all. She'd met him plenty of times before. He'd visited maybe two or three times a year for as long as she could remember, although he never stayed for long. He was sixteen years older than her mum though, a different generation. Old enough to be Phoebe's grandad, really. And yet he was the only family she had now.

'You want to get out of here?' Uncle Louis gave Phoebe a light squeeze before he released her and stood up straight.

'But aren't we supposed to be going to . . .' She racked her brain for the name of the place where the wake was to be held, but couldn't remember, try as she might. That was more terrifying than anything, her inability to focus, to recall things. What if it never got better?

'Don't you worry about that. I've let Mrs Dalgliesh know you're getting a bit of air. It's not far, anyway. The walk'll do you good.'

Phoebe took one quick look back at the church and the milling people, nodded her head at her uncle. He crooked his arm, elbow out towards her. After a moment's incomprehension, she slid her own arm through the gap and allowed herself to be led away towards the street.

They walked in silence for a while, ignored by the people going about their everyday lives. None of them could know the trauma Phoebe had endured, why should they? Life went on, cruelly ignoring her plight.

'What's going to happen now?' she asked eventually. It was a question she'd not dared voice before, because she was fairly sure she knew the answer and really didn't like it.

'Now? We go to the wake, and a lot of strangers will shake your hand, express their condolences, maybe tell you some small thing about your mum and dad they remember. I'll not lie, it'll be hard, Phoebe. And there's no shame in crying, or just walking away. Bear with it though, if you can. Those people, their stories, will bring you comfort in the bleak days ahead.'

Phoebe stopped walking, slipped her arm out from her uncle's. His accent was soft, the emphasis of his words falling in strange places. He sounded a bit like her mum when she was agitated, but less manic. And he hadn't answered her question. Not really. He took another step before noticing she wasn't still with him. Stopped and turned.

'That's not what you meant though, is it.'

'I have no home.' Phoebe looked down at her feet, the black boots she'd borrowed from Jenny, the mourning outfit she'd borrowed from Jenny's mum. She'd dressed that morning in the spare room at the Dalglieshes, where she'd been staying since that fateful night. Everything she'd owned apart from the clothes she'd worn on the school trip had burned in the fire. 'I have nothing.'

Uncle Louis wrapped her in another awkward hug as her eyes filled with tears.

'There, there, Phoebe. It's OK. We'll get that all sorted in good time. But you've no need to worry about your things; we can get you new ones. And as for your home, well, you'll come and live with us. Your Aunt Maude and me.'

Phoebe pulled away, sniffed, wiped the tears as best she could on the long black gloves that made her feel like a goth. 'But you live in Wales. My life is here.'

Uncle Louis looked at the ground, the surrounding buildings, away along the street, anywhere but straight at her. Phoebe wanted to scream at him, but the same numbness that had held back her tears in the church made her silent and sullen here.

'I know,' her uncle said finally. 'And I know it's not fair. But it is how it has to be. You're only just twelve years old and I am your legal guardian. I have a responsibility, and even if I didn't, I would still look after you.'

'In Wales.' Phoebe tried to make her outrage felt, but in truth she was too worn down by grieving and this horrible, endless day.

'It's not so bad, really.' Uncle Louis gave her a half-smile, as if even he didn't really believe it. 'And it's not for ever.'

Nothing is, Phoebe thought. She shrugged reluctant acceptance, and followed her uncle to the wake. There wasn't much else she could do.

4

2023

The call comes in as she's crossing the Forth, heading south towards Edinburgh and home. A glance at the big screen on the dashboard gives only a number, not someone in her contact list. She almost lets it go, something for the voicemail to deal with for now, but then she recognises the area code. Aberystwyth. Strange she should get a call from there today of all days. She taps the screen to accept.

'Hello?'

'Ms MacDonald?' A female voice, young, uncertain. It's Doctor MacDonald, actually, but Phoebe lets that go. She has slowed, moved over to exit the dual carriageway without thinking. There's a supermarket nearby where she can stop. She will need to stop, she knows already. Only one person would call her from Wales with good news, and her number's in the phone's memory.

'Speaking.'

'Are you OK to talk?'

They always ask. Perhaps it's in some training manual or something. Or more likely they're just trying to ease themselves into what is going to be a difficult conversation.

'It's hands-free, I'm fine.' Phoebe slows for the roundabout, muscle memory working the controls while her mind races ahead. 'This is about Maude, I take it? Maude Jenkins?'

The pause gives her time to negotiate the roundabout, then slow down for the queue of traffic waiting to turn into the supermarket car park.

'It is, yes. I'm very sorry, but Mrs Jenkins passed in the early hours of this morning.'

'Ms Jenkins.' Phoebe can't stop herself this time.

'I'm sorry?'

'Ms Jenkins. Or Miss if you prefer. Maude never actually married my uncle. She'd have been Mrs Beard if she had, and she couldn't bear the thought of that.'

'I . . .' Another pause as the caller parses what she's been told. Is this a nurse? A police officer? Phoebe can't be sure. She hasn't introduced herself.

'I didn't catch your name.'

'Oh, I'm sorry. I thought I'd said. Angharad Fairweather. Police Constable. I'm one of the Family Liaison Officers working out of Aberystwyth.'

Angharad. Phoebe smiles at the name, remembering an Angharad who would never have been a police officer. She smiles at Constable Fairweather's accent too. It's been a while since she's heard that sing-song voice. Apart from Maude, of course, but that always seemed different somehow.

'I spoke to her just yesterday evening.'

'Yes, we have her phone here. That's how I got your number. She has you listed as emergency contact. She was your aunt, I understand.'

Phoebe pulls the car into a space, turns it off. No engine, everything's electric these days. How different from . . . 'After a fashion, yes. Like I said, she and my uncle never married. How . . . how did it happen?' Through the windscreen she can see shoppers pushing trolleys to and from the entrance to the supermarket.

Silent, industrious, they remind her of worker bees in search of nectar. Only these bees come empty to the hive and leave full.

'She passed in her sleep, according to the doctor. The home help found her this morning. From what I'm told she looked peaceful.'

Phoebe casts her mind back to their last conversation, just a few hours ago. Had there been any sign? No, of course not. Maude had been Maude, same as she ever was. Slower perhaps than in earlier times, but she'd never been quite the same since Uncle Louis had died. She'd wished Phoebe well, as she did every year on this particular anniversary. What had her last words been? Take care, speak soon. And now she never would.

'I'll have to come and deal with everything. She's no other kin. Where is she now?'

'In the mortuary at Bronglais. They'll be ready to release the body in a day or two. Have you far to travel?'

Have I far to travel? Phoebe almost laughs, and then she almost cries. 'I live in Edinburgh, but it's not so far really. I'll head down in the morning. Maybe tonight. Will I contact you when I get there?'

'That'd be great. You know where you're going?'

Phoebe assures the constable that she knows exactly where she's going. She even has a key to the house, although the last time it was locked is anyone's guess. They exchange relevant details and with a slightly more cheery 'bye' than perhaps she intended, PC Angharad Fairweather ends the call. Phoebe sits in the cocoon of her car, staring out at nothing as the news slowly sinks in.

Aunt Maude.

Dead.

On this of all days.

5

1985

Mr Stearn fitted his surname perfectly. His face was narrow, too tall really, as if it had once been normal but had been squeezed hard from either side. What little hair he had left clung to his shiny scalp in thin grey tufts, shaved almost to nothing. His eyes never blinked and his gaze never left her face except when it dropped to the thick folder lying open on his desk. Phoebe had met him before, most recently at the funeral of her parents, but unlike the many unnamed faces who had spoken to her that day, he had not gone on from the church to the wake.

'Terrible business, Miss MacDonald. Dreadful really. I'm so sorry for your loss.'

Phoebe sat in the uncomfortable leather chair feeling for all the world as if she were up in front of the headmaster. She'd been in this office once before, a lifetime ago when she still had a mum and dad. One of those great ideas, bring your child to work day. Perhaps it was fun if your dad made things in a factory, or drove a van, or even ran a shop like Mr Dalgliesh. But the offices of a small legal firm in a sleepy market town like Cupar wasn't the most fascinating of places to spend a day out of school. The most interesting thing Phoebe remembered was going to get lunch from the sandwich shop across the road. The heady responsibility of being in charge of the list, and a crisp twenty-pound note in her hand. And then there had been the hour she'd spent in this very office, being lectured by Mr Stearn about the importance of attention to detail. He'd told her she'd no doubt make a fine lawyer's clerk when she was older, maybe even a legal secretary. And that had been the moment she had known without a doubt which profession she wouldn't be pursuing.

'We need to discuss the matter of your father's will.' Mr Stearn's moment of compassion was over; now it was back to business. 'You are the sole beneficiary, of course. But it is to be held in trust until you reach your majority.'

'What's that mean, then?' Phoebe asked. Beside her, Uncle Louis shifted uncomfortably in his seat. She looked at him sideways, aware that he'd mentioned this when they had walked from the church to the hotel. She knew what was coming, even though her brain had tried its hardest to forget. To make it not so.

'It means when you reach the age of sixteen, Miss MacDonald.' Mr Stearn ran a long thin finger down the page in front of him, caressing the paper like a normal person might stroke a cat. 'In just under four years' time, in fact.'

'So what do I do 'till then?'

Mr Stearn looked down at his papers, then fixed Phoebe with a surprisingly sympathetic gaze.

'Until then you are the legal responsibility of your guardian.' Mr Stearn switched his gaze pointedly to Uncle Louis. 'He will look after you.'

'What, here?' Of course not. But she could still hope.

'No, Phoebe. We discussed this, remember? You'll be coming to live with us.'

'But this is my home. All my friends live here. What about school?'

'We do have schools in Wales, you know. And telephones. You

can keep up with your friends, and once you're settled they can come and visit.'

'Why can't I stay with Jenny? Her mum said she'd look after me.' It wasn't strictly true, but she'd been staying with them since the fire, and no one had complained so far. Phoebe heard the whine in her voice, like she was six years old and pestering her mum. The thought only made her more desperate.

'Because Louis is your uncle, your only remaining family, and also your legal guardian,' Mr Stearn said. 'It is his duty to look after you until you are of age, and he has indicated he is more than happy to do so. As co-trustee of your inheritance, I cannot go against your parents' wishes on this matter.'

'Inheritance?' Phoebe slumped back into her chair, her anger gone as swiftly as it had come.

'Of course. As I said before, you are the sole beneficiary of your parents' wills.'

'But everything was burned in the fire. There's nothing left to inherit, surely.'

Mr Stearn stared at Phoebe for a while, then pulled out a pair of thin spectacles and carefully placed them on his nose before returning his attention to the folder.

'Your father was a partner in this law firm, Miss MacDonald. He was not a wealthy man, but neither was he poor. He had savings and a few shares as well as a stake in this company. The house and all its contents are, as you so rightly pointed out, destroyed. They are not, however, worthless. An insurance claim has been lodged on behalf of your father's estate to cover the value of the house and its contents. Once that is dealt with you will have to consider what to do with the land upon which the house stood. My suggestion would be that you allow it to be sold for redevelopment, with the proceeds added to the capital held in trust for you.'

'I . . .' Phoebe began to speak, then realised she had nothing to say. Nothing made sense, and nothing would stick, apart from the one horrifying fact: she had no home here in Scotland any more.

'It's a lot to take in, I know.' Mr Stearn removed his spectacles and slid them back into the top pocket of his tweed jacket. Leaning forward, he tried to put on a friendly face, but it was clearly something he wasn't used to doing. 'Your uncle and I have already thrashed out a lot of the details. You'll be provided with an allowance for clothes and other items, and any major expenses can be discussed on an ad hoc basis. You'll not want for anything, rest assured.'

Except that the one thing she truly wanted, for none of this to have ever happened, was beyond the power of anyone to give. Not even dour old Mr Stearn. There was no fighting it, which was just as well, because she had no fight left in her. Phoebe swallowed back the grief as best she could, wiped her nose on the back of her hand like a toddler, sniffed once and accepted that she was going to have to leave the only place she'd known all her life. She would have to say goodbye to all her friends and move to live in another country.

Another world.

6

Phoebe could barely remember the journey from Cupar to Edinburgh. She'd not slept much the night before, up late chatting with Jenny, making plans, promising to keep in touch, all that and more. Breakfast had been dry toast and orange juice, followed by a hurried trip to the downstairs loo to bring it back up again. Jen's mum had taken her to the station alone, Phoebe's oldest friend too distraught to see her go in the end. Between the moment she had climbed into the back of Mrs Dalgliesh's Range Rover and the sudden realisation she was staring at the rapidly emptying platform of Waverley Station, Phoebe could remember little else. Presumably someone must have checked her ticket, as the red and white card had a hole punched close to one edge. She had no recollection of taking it from her pocket, let alone showing it to anyone.

Uncle Louis had said he would meet her on the concourse fifteen minutes before their train south was due to leave. He'd gone to Edinburgh the day after their visit to the solicitor. Something to do with publishers was all Phoebe had understood when he'd told her. She stood in front of the departure boards and looked around at the busy people. Where were they all going in such a rush? It was still early enough for commuters to be pushing and weaving through the throng, swinging briefcases like battering rams. This was the kind of life she had imagined for herself, once school was done and maybe university or college. She hadn't really decided what she wanted to do, who she wanted to be. Much of that hung on her exams, or at least they had done. Now? Who knew?

'Ah, there you are. Excellent.'

Phoebe turned at the voice, and saw Uncle Louis push through the throng. He had an old leather travelling bag in one hand, a shabby overcoat over the handles. Over the other shoulder hung what looked like the kind of school satchel Phoebe had always wanted when she was little, but now seemed unbearably twee. He put everything down as if to hug her, then seemed to think better of it. Glanced instead at her own small rucksack.

'You travel light,' he said, and Phoebe watched his friendly expression turn to one of utter horror as the words travelled from his mouth to his brain. 'Oh my god, Phoebe. I'm so sorry. That was utterly insensitive of me.'

'It's OK.' As she said it, Phoebe realised that it was. There wasn't much to laugh at these days, but a simple little error like that was more amusing than hurtful she found. 'I'd be travelling a lot lighter if it wasn't for Jenny's mum. I'll need to pay her back for this.'

She swung the rucksack off her shoulder, round and onto the other one. Half empty though it might be, it was still a weight. Mr Stearn the lawyer had mentioned an allowance, but so far Phoebe had seen nothing.

'Shall we go see if the train's here, then?' Uncle Louis heaved up his considerably heavier bag and shrugged the satchel back into place. He peered briefly at the departure board, then started to look around for platform numbers.

'It's this way.' Phoebe pointed, and then led him through the thinning crowd. The train snaked up a long platform, its sides streaked with dirt and wet with rain. Phoebe asked her uncle for the tickets, and there was an awkward pause while he went through his satchel and the top of his bag before finding them in the pocket of his overcoat. When he handed them over, she was surprised to find they were first class.

'I don't travel as much as I used to, but when I do, I like to do so in style,' Uncle Louis said as they walked the length of the platform to the front of the train. 'And besides, they give you more room in first class. It's easier to get some work done.'

First class was a far cry from the rattly old Sprinter trains Phoebe was used to. Their seats were either side of a table, facing each other and made of something that looked like leather. They were adjustable too, and Phoebe spent a while fiddling with the control on hers. By the time she'd settled herself comfortably, her uncle had stowed his bag and was staring at her with a slightly amused expression on his face.

'What?' she asked.

'Just thinking what Maude's going to make of you. She's very excited to meet you.'

'Maude?' The question was out before Phoebe remembered. Uncle Louis wasn't married, but he lived with a woman called Maude. Or 'that scarlet woman' as her father had always said on the very few occasions the topic had come up in conversation. Phoebe didn't think she'd ever met Maude, although it was possible she'd done so when she'd been an infant.

'Maude, yes. You remember her, don't you?' Uncle Louis screwed up his face in concentration for a moment, then shrugged it away. 'Maybe not. Your father never much liked her, so she kept away. And anyway, I only used to come north for writing festivals and the like. Maude's always been happier at home than mixing with the literary crowd. Can't say as I blame her, to be honest.'

Phoebe opened her mouth to say something, but couldn't think what. She was saved by the slight lurch of the train as it pulled away from the platform. How long was the journey? Like everything else she'd been told over the past week and more, she couldn't remember.

Her uncle checked his watch as they slid into the tunnel. 'On time. Good.' He flipped open his satchel and pulled out a notebook, fetched a pen from his jacket pocket. 'They'll be bringing the lunch trolley soon. Might see if I can get a little work done before then. Editors, eh? Never satisfied.'

Phoebe watched as he flipped through his notebook until he found a clean page and began writing. The look of concentration on his face was one she'd seen her dad make when he was utterly absorbed in something. No chance of conversation, then. Not that she'd have known what to talk about. She pulled out her Walkman, slipped her headphones over her ears. When she pressed play, the familiar gentle hiss eased away the noise of the train, and then Jim Kerr started singing to her. 'Don't You (Forget About Me)'. It seems weirdly appropriate.

Leaning back into her comfortable seat, Phoebe wished she'd brought something to read other than the most recent *Smash Hits*, which she and Jenny had already gone through from cover to cover. It was going to be a long day.

Rain began to spatter the windows of the train carriage as it pulled out of Birmingham New Street. Phoebe watched the station names change from unknown places like Telford, Shrewsbury and Welshpool to unpronounceable ones like Caersws, Machynlleth and finally Aberystwyth. And all the while the weather grew ever worse. Sitting opposite her, across a narrow Formica table, Uncle Louis had barely said a word all the way south, in turns staring out the window and scribbling furiously in his notebook. Now, finally, he snapped it closed and put it away in his satchel, checked his watch.

'On time again. The gods of travel must be smiling down on us.'

Phoebe dragged her rucksack from the overhead rack, despair at how little she owned threatening to engulf her again. Uncle Louis was already threading his way along the narrow aisle to the exit, quite oblivious to her plight. She hurried to catch up, and together they stepped out onto the wet platform. Across the tracks, a lone seagull sat on the roof of a low, boarded-up brick building and screamed at the grey sky. At least the rain had stopped, for now.

'I've got to go and see my accountant,' Uncle Louis announced as they stepped out of the station building onto a busy road. 'Your aunt won't be here to pick us up for an hour yet. You want to have a wander round the town and meet me back here?'

Phoebe peered across the road at the collection of sorry-looking pubs and houses. Directly opposite her, a chip shop was plying its greasy trade and the smell of burning fat filled the damp air. It occurred to her that her uncle's suggestion hadn't really been voiced as a question, and the thought of spending the time in an accountant's waiting room was even less inviting than wandering around an unfamiliar seaside town in the rain.

'I guess,' she answered.

'The sea's that way.' Uncle Louis pointed across the road. 'Most of the shops are that way too. It's not a big place, I doubt you'll get lost. See you back here at five.' And with that he was off.

Aberystwyth didn't improve much away from the station. Shouldering her rucksack, Phoebe wandered down a narrow lane with a name she wasn't even sure how to read, and found herself standing on what must have been the main street. Scaffolding partially obscured a bank; some overlarge pots were filled with what looked like a clever arrangement of dead flowers and cigarette butts; people milled around aimlessly, as if they were all as lost as she felt. A family marched past, dad leading the way like some doomed general. He was dressed in shorts and T-shirt despite the rain and chill wind, but might have been better off with a size or two bigger, given the way the fabric stretched taut over his belly. Two young children traipsed in his wake, looking as miserable as Phoebe felt, and his tiny wife followed along behind. Weighed down by a heavy holdall spilling beach towels and swimwear, her expression was one of utter despair.

Transfixed by the spectacle, Phoebe was about to step into the road and make good her escape, when a roaring noise made her look up. An old tractor battled its way down the street at what seemed a dangerously high speed. In the cab, high above the crowd, the driver bounced up and down on his seat as the great machine screamed along. Behind it, a large trailer showed the desperate woolly faces of sheep, peering through little slit-windows as they were taken to whatever fate awaited them.

Paying more attention to the traffic, Phoebe crossed the road and wandered down the next street. She was vaguely following her uncle's waved directions towards the sea. Not from any great desire to see it, but because it was the only thing he had mentioned about the town and so likely the most interesting. If a short arc of pebbly beach, populated by screaming, semi-naked children and their harassed mothers, yapping dogs, crows and seagulls was your idea of interesting, then this was obviously the place to be. Phoebe took one look at the long promenade, the kiosk selling ice cream, the tired façades of the tall terraced houses facing the sea, and moved on.

She found the castle more by accident than design, not realising what it was until she'd already walked through most of the ruins. It wasn't any more exciting than the beach, to be honest. Neither was the harbour, though she spent a diverted five minutes watching a tiny trawler battle against the swell as it approached the harbour mouth. When it didn't sink, she turned back towards the centre of town, glancing at her watch to see that she'd only managed to waste a half an hour.

The one thing Phoebe couldn't help but notice about Aberystwyth, apart from the fact that it ran Cupar a close second in the most dull town in Britain stakes, was that it had a lot of pubs.

Almost every street corner seemed to have a sign hanging over a half-open door, opaque windows etched with brewery names obscuring the drinkers within. Perhaps there was nothing else to do in town.

As she passed one, the door swung open, two figures stumbling out at such a pace she had to step into the space between two parked cars to avoid being knocked over. At first she thought they were drunk, but then she noticed the burly-armed man standing in the doorway, sleeves rolled up to reveal a mess of tattoos, an angry scowl on his face.

'And see you don't come back in here again,' he shouted as the two young men gathered their wits. For a moment Phoebe thought they might start a fight, but they restrained themselves to a few muttered curses and a rude hand gesture or two. The landlord ignored them, closed the door firmly and disappeared back into his pub.

'Well, that might've gone better, bro,' one of them said as the other lit up a cigarette. Waiting for them to move on so that she could get back onto the pavement, Phoebe saw now that they were twins. As they were coming out of the pub, she'd assumed them to be at least in their twenties, but she revised that down a few years now she could get a better look at them. Sixteen, maybe seventeen. Young enough to be still in school, although something made her doubt that they were. Certainly young enough to get thrown out of a pub.

'What you lookin' at?' The twin with the cigarette scowled at her almost as angrily as the landlord had at him. Phoebe backed away, but had to stop before she stepped into the traffic.

'Leave her, bro. Got better things to be doing than chatting up jailbait, right?'

The scowl eased a little as the twin took a long drag on his cigarette. Without looking around, he handed it to his brother, then exhaled his lungful of smoke in Phoebe's direction.

'Too skinny anyway. Put some meat on your bones and come see me some day, little snail.'

Her initial shock turning to anger now, Phoebe was about to give the two of them a piece of her mind, but the second twin slapped his brother on the shoulder, laughing like a whipped donkey. 'Little snail. That's good, bro. Like, the backpack's her shell.' They set off up the street, smoke from their shared cigarette drifting over the heads as they brayed identical laughs.

Phoebe stepped onto the pavement and set off in the opposite direction, not caring if it was the wrong way. Had she been in any danger from them? Probably not, but she was shaking all the same. What was this place she'd been brought to against her will? What else might happen to her?

7

2023

Everything is the same, and yet everything is changed. She slips the key into the lock, shoulders the half-stuck front door with an easy familiarity. Her feet echo on the stone steps as they spiral to the top floor and her tenement flat. She pauses at the first window, with its collection of house plants and view across the shared drying green to the distant Pentland Hills. Nothing is different from how it was when she left this morning, except for her.

The flat is as chaotically untidy as ever, the stuff of a lifetime hung from the walls, piled on the tables, dumped in the corners. Phoebe barely registers it as she drops her keys into her coat pocket and hangs it on the rack behind the door. There's a light flashing messages by the phone, but she'll deal with that later. First she needs a shower, then she'll have to pack a bag. But how long will she be away? No real way to know.

Somehow she finds herself in the kitchen, staring into the fridge at the bottle of wine. With a shake of the head, Phoebe closes the door. No alcohol, she needs to drive again. Soon as the car's finished charging.

Showered, her hair tied up in a towel, another pulled around her and tucked in tight, she pads back and forth in the bedroom picking out clothes for the trip. How long has it been since she last visited? Too long, and Phoebe knows why. There are so many memories tied to the place, so much sadness. And now there will be even more.

Bag packed, she surveys the fridge once more. This time it's with a view to what might go off in the next few days. Or weeks. She throws a few things into the freezer, a few more into the bin. That'll have to go out, too. The last leaves from a bag of salad, a hard-boiled egg, some cooked potatoes that still smell more or less OK, Phoebe puts together an almost healthy meal and eyes the bottle of wine again. It hasn't been opened, so she could leave it where it is. Or take it with her. Decisions.

It's getting dark outside as she makes herself coffee and finally goes back to the answerphone. It's what she's been avoiding all this time, and not just because there'll be a message on it from Angharad Fairweather asking her to call. That's been done and dealt with, it's the other messages she dreads. Or is it perhaps that there won't be any?

The machine is ancient, something the previous owner left behind when she bought this flat over twenty years ago. It uses actual tape, and there are dozens of old cassettes in the drawer under the hall table. If she went through them, she'd probably find messages from Aunt Maude, hear her voice once again. She'd hear Uncle Louis, too, and that thought brings an unexpected lump to Phoebe's throat that the news of Maude's death hasn't yet. She's even pulled the drawer open before she understands that she's stalling again. Pushing it gently closed, she reaches out and presses the play button.

'. . . the accident you were recently—' Phoebe hits the fast-forward button to the next message.

'. . . name is Constable Angharad Fairweather. I'll try your mobile number, but if you could give me a—' She fast-forwards again.

'. . . Feebs. Sorry I shouted at you like. Shouldn't have let my temper get the better of me, but, well . . . it's been a stressful few months. Hell, it's been a stressful couple of years, hasn't it? Don't really know where to start. Feel like we've been growing apart for a while now, and I know that's a cliché, but, well, it's true, isn't it? Anyways, I've thought about it a while and I can't see it working long term, you know? So, I think it's only fair if—'

The tape in the machine stops spooling as the cassette comes to an end. With a clunk, the play button pops up. Bloody typical. Still, it's more or less what Phoebe had been expecting. And though a part of her feels hollowed out, there's also a sense of relief. One less thing to worry about, at least for now. Sooner or later Clare will find out about Aunt Maude. At the very least, Phoebe will have to text her to say where she's gone. Perhaps Clare will try to use that as an excuse to open negotiations again. But right now, Phoebe doesn't have the mental energy. A bit of enforced separation will do the both of them good. Maybe it's time to draw a line under their long and bumpy relationship now.

A quick look around the flat to check things aren't switched on that don't need to be. Winter's passed, so it shouldn't be a problem leaving the heating off. Finally, Phoebe grabs her coat and bag, heads out of the door. As she turns to lock it, sees the familiar faded gloss paint, the brass handle and letterbox that could do with a polish, the welcome mat worn so thin it reads W E with a big space between them, it occurs to her that she should be more distraught. The last of her family dead, her girlfriend, partner, whatever of nearly two decades gone, shouldn't she be upset? Shouldn't she be feeling something, anything at all?

She shakes her head, twists the key to set the deadlock, sets off down the stairs and the start of a long journey with clear eyes.

She never was all that good at crying. And it's not as if this is the worst thing that has ever happened to her.

8

1985

Uncle Louis was nowhere to be seen when Phoebe returned to the station at a quarter to five. She'd overcome her initial shock at the confrontation outside the pub, and spent the rest of the time idly looking at clothes in the high street. She needed to buy stuff, but as yet Mr Stearn the solicitor had not come up with any of the money he had promised her by way of an allowance. The house insurance should have covered all her belongings, too, but again it was all in the hands of the lawyers. At least she had the clothes Jenny's mum had bought her.

Thinking of her friend, Phoebe looked around the station for a phone box. She should call Mrs Dalgliesh and let her know she'd arrived in Aberystwyth. It would be good to chat with Jen too. She found a phone close to the car park exit, pulled open the door and stepped inside. As phone boxes went, it didn't smell too bad, but it wanted change before she could place the call. Change Phoebe didn't have.

She'd known it would be that way, of course. And yet she'd still let herself hope. As she stepped back out of the phone box, all the pent-up frustrations and long-suppressed grief caught up with her at once. Tears filled her eyes before she could stop them, and she struggled to breathe over the lump that rose up in her throat. Phoebe slumped to the pavement, back against the stone of the station wall. She dropped her head into her hands as much to cover her embarrassment as anything, great heaving sobs racking her frame as the trauma of the past two weeks crashed in on her. An ambush far worse than her encounter with the twins could ever be.

And then there was a light touch on her shoulder, a voice quietly asking 'Phoebe?' She looked up through tear-smeared eyes and for an instant that was too painful to bear, thought she saw her mother standing over her, reaching out to comfort her. Phoebe sniffed, blinked her tears away as best she could, and saw with crushing disappointment that the woman wasn't her mother after all. About the same height, similar shape to her face, but her hair was silvery grey shot with a few darker lines, not mousy brown. Cut above the shoulders rather than long. Crow's feet wrinkled around her worried eyes and frowning mouth.

'You are Phoebe, aren't you? Of course you are. You look just like your mother. Did Louis leave you here and wander off? That's so like him.'

Phoebe sniffed back her tears, wiped her nose on the sleeve of her jacket and looked up again at the woman addressing her.

'Who . . . who are you?' she asked.

'Gracious me, girl. I don't suppose you'd remember. It's been a fair few years and you were only a wee thing then.' The still-unnamed woman put out a hand. 'I'm your Aunt Maude.'

Phoebe took the hand without thinking, and allowed herself to be hauled to her feet.

'Well, technically speaking not your actual aunt, since Louis and I never married. But that's no matter. Here, let me take that.' Maude fussed over Phoebe like a mother hen, smoothing at the creases in her collar and all but wrestling the rucksack off her back.

It seemed like years since anyone had fussed over her, and Phoebe felt the tears coming back, tried to will them away.

'Is this all you've got? I'd have thought a girl your age would have been weighed down with . . . oh, I'm sorry. That was thoughtless of me.' Aunt Maude touched Phoebe's shoulder again.

'Ah, I see you two have found each other. Good, good.' Uncle Louis lumbered into view. He embraced Maude with such uninhibited passion that Phoebe had to look away. Old people didn't behave like that, surely? And in public?

'Shall we get on, then?' he said after what seemed an indecently long time.

'Umm, Uncle Louis?' Phoebe asked.

'Phoebe?'

'It's . . .' Now that she had opened her mouth to ask the question, she found she was shaking almost as much as after her encounter with the twins. Something she wouldn't have thought twice about asking her parents, but now?

'What's the problem, dear?' Aunt Maude crouched down to her height. Not so far, but enough to help put Phoebe a little at ease.

'I really need some new clothes. I've barely anything to wear.' She held up her Walkman with one hand. 'And the batteries are dead. Can I get some new ones?'

'Didn't you get anything while you were in town?' He glanced at his watch. 'Everything will be closing by now.'

'I . . . I don't have any money.'

'Louis?' Aunt Maude asked. 'I thought you were going to sort that out while you were still in Scotland.'

Uncle Louis pondered awhile, his face creased in a frown as if he couldn't quite understand the concept. Then he beamed a wide smile. 'It's all in hand, Phoebe. Don't worry for now, eh? I'm sure we've something at home you can wear. We'll get you all kitted out once you've had a chance to settle in, shall we?'

★ ★ ★

If Phoebe had thought that Aberystwyth was a hopeless backwater of a place, the ride into the heart of Ceredigion made it seem positively cosmopolitan. Aunt Maude's ancient car didn't help matters, its engine screeching like a tortured cat as it struggled up the hills. The back, where she was sitting, had obviously been used as a storage locker for unwanted things, and the seats had a worrying damp greasiness about them. Quite what the smell was, she couldn't be sure, and neither did she want to dwell upon it for too long.

It was a far cry from Jenny's mum's Range Rover which had taken her to Cupar Station. Even her dad's old Saab had a certain class about it; but that was one more casualty of the fire.

'Is it far, your house?' she asked, aware that it made her sound like a needy child, but desperate for something to take her mind off her inevitable train of thought.

'Not far, no,' Uncle Louis said from the passenger seat. 'Twenty-five minutes, Maude?'

Peering through the windscreen and inch-thick spectacles, Maude didn't take her eyes off the road, but nodded very slightly and muttered something that might have been a yes. Phoebe slumped back in her seat, then wished she hadn't as clouds of unpleasant-smelling dust rose up around her. They'd already been going for twenty minutes, at least. To her, another twenty-five was a lifetime.

'That's the old silver lead mines over there.' Uncle Louis pointed through the window at what looked like a pile of rocks and an abandoned stone building. 'There's loads of them around here. Used to be big business.'

But not any more, it would seem. And not for quite some time.

The rest of the journey passed slowly by, with occasional interjections from Uncle Louis, almost inevitably about something that had just gone past. Although at the speed Aunt Maude was driving, Phoebe could usually turn around and get a good look. The coastal scenery gave way to rolling hills and then they were climbing up a steep-sided valley, dark regiments of pine trees marching towards the skyline in all directions. The road narrowed and lost its white line to a long stretch of tufty grass, pushing manfully through the ancient tarmac. Every so often passing places lured the unwary into roadside ditches, and at one point they drove under an old stone arch that seemed to have no purpose whatsoever. As if there had once been a huge castle here and the road builders had simply ignored its ruins. Phoebe had been about to ask, surprised that her uncle hadn't immediately offered an explanation for the strange site, but without warning, indication or a reduction in her already meagre speed, Maude turned off the road onto a potholed forestry track. The little car bounced and groaned through a dark tunnel of ancient trees, and finally emerged into a large clearing.

'Welcome to Pant Melyn,' Uncle Louis said. 'Our little idyll in the woods.'

The house was larger than Phoebe had been expecting. Her mum had always referred to it as a cottage, but the building they pulled up in front of was really quite substantial. Climbing plants rambled up most of the walls. Upstairs the tall, narrow windows rose into the steep-pitched roof in turret-like dormers; downstairs they reached almost to the ground, their sills at knee height. A neat little porch boxed in the front door like an afterthought.

'Come in, girl. It's going to rain, I think.' Aunt Maude stepped into the porch and pushed open the unlocked door. Uncle Louis steered Phoebe gently towards the house with a hand in the middle of her back.

'It'll be fine,' he said as if he had read her hesitance. 'You'll settle in fast enough.'

Inside, despite the large windows, the house was dark and cluttered. There was an odd, sweet smell about the front room with its overlarge fireplace and mismatched collection of furniture. Every available wall was taken up with bookshelves, piled two deep with more books than Phoebe had ever seen, even in the school library.

'I'll give you the quick tour, shall I?' Uncle Louis didn't wait for an answer, heading off into the depths of the house with a spring in his step. Phoebe was shown a bewildering collection of rooms, but failed to see a single television anywhere. They clambered up a narrow staircase, with more books lining the landing at the top. Uncle Louis pushed open doors, letting Phoebe look in on untidy bedrooms and bathrooms filled with ancient plumbing.

'That's Maude's room. Mine's over here.'

'You don't share the same room?' Phoebe asked.

'Not always, no. Maude says she can't stand my snoring when I've had a drink or two.' Uncle Louis grinned at what he obviously considered a great joke, then led Phoebe down a corridor that took them to the other end of the house. A narrow door opened onto a tiny bathroom that smelled like it hadn't been used in years, and just beyond it a set of bare wooden stairs led up into the eaves.

'We thought you'd be happiest up here. It's nice and quiet, away from everyone else.' Uncle Louis scrabbled up the steps, and Phoebe followed him through into the room beyond.

It couldn't have been more unlike her bedroom back home. Even before that had been reduced to a pile of rubble and ash. It was large, for one thing, and desperately gloomy. What light there was fought its way through a couple of iron-framed rooflights, low enough down the sloping eaves to give a view out onto the garden, the meadow and the forest beyond. A single bare light bulb cast a pathetic yellow light onto a wide bed, a tall wardrobe in dark wood, a chest of drawers and a scruffy-looking armchair. A rickety wooden desk sat under one of the windows, and beside it an old acoustic guitar propped up in a stand. Yet more books cluttered the shelves lining the low walls beneath the sloped ceiling. Under her feet, Phoebe saw an ancient, threadbare Persian rug, and where it didn't reach the walls, uneven floorboards.

'You like it?' Uncle Louis asked, dumping Phoebe's rucksack onto the armchair and raising a small tempest of dust.

'It's . . .'

'I know, stupid question.' Uncle Louis held up his hands in a gesture of defeat. 'This must be very hard for you, Phoebe. Christ, I can't begin to imagine. But it'll get better. Well, easier. Time really is the best healer.'

Phoebe stood in the middle of the room, numb. She couldn't think what to do next, didn't know what to say. That morning she'd woken up in her best friend's spare room. A fortnight ago she'd had a mother and father. Now she was in a different country, in a stranger's house, in a room full of someone else's belongings.

'Maude will have got the tea on. I'll go and see if she needs any help. Why don't you settle yourself in, eh?' Uncle Louis gave Phoebe a gentle pat on the shoulder, then clumped away down the steep wooden steps, leaving her all alone.

9

S unlight on her face woke Phoebe from dreamless sleep. For a moment she lay motionless, her brain a dozy haze, just enjoying the warmth and comfort. Staring up, she could see the angled shadows of the ceiling, and a long jagged crack in the plaster running from the ancient light fitting across to the door. That was wrong, wasn't it? There were no cracks in her bedroom ceiling. Come to think of it, her bedroom ceiling was flat, not angled. She rolled over, scrabbling for coherent thought, trying to work out where she was. Something went 'twang' and an uncomfortable lump pushed its way through the mattress and into her thigh. At precisely the same moment it all came flooding back on a wave of vertigo that left her dizzy and nauseous. The fire, the funeral, the journey by train from all she knew to a place of complete mystery. Two faces, her uncle and aunt, as strange to her as anyone here.

Stumbling out of bed, Phoebe managed to make it across the room, down the steep stairs and into the tiny bathroom without being sick, but only just. The remains of last night's supper looked slightly more appetising the second time around. She rinsed her mouth out, washed her face and stared at herself in the heavy glass mirror. Most of the silvering had leached from the edges, lending a slightly fairytale feel to the image that stared back. She looked gaunt, her dirty-blonde hair framing her pale face made her eyes

38

look like little black beads. All the puppy-fat chubbiness had gone from her cheeks and her pink hippo pyjamas hung from her frame as if she'd borrowed them from a much larger sibling, not her best friend. Nothing like losing both your parents in a house fire to suppress the appetite. Maybe she could patent it as the ultimate weight-loss plan.

Dressed in her only remaining clean clothes, Phoebe went downstairs. The house was quiet, no one about, and she wondered if her aunt and uncle were late sleepers or up with the lark. She knew next to nothing about them, she realised. Uncle Louis had written a famous book, she recalled, but that had been years ago – long before she was born. What did he do now? And what did Aunt Maude do?

A battered kettle sat by the old range stove, but Phoebe had no idea where the teabags lived, let alone the mugs. Looking around the cluttered and rustic room, she realised she couldn't even see a fridge. At Jenny's, where she'd spent the last fortnight, she'd known where everything was and never thought twice about helping her-self. It was like a second home to her anyway; she and Jenny had been best friends since before primary school.

'Morning, Phoebe. Sleep well?'

Phoebe looked up to see Uncle Louis emerging from a door-way on the far side of the kitchen. He wore a dark red velvet dressing gown not quite long enough to hide his shins and bare feet. His grey hair was tousled and unkempt in a manner her father would never have tolerated, and he yawned expansively as he shuf-fled over to the stove and put the kettle on.

'Coffee?'

Uncertain how things worked in this house, Phoebe nodded, although she didn't really like coffee, and would much have pre-ferred tea. Uncle Louis set about the kitchen, clattering open cupboard doors as if he, too, had no idea where anything was kept. Eventually he managed to find everything, just in time for the kettle to start boiling. The fridge, it turned out, was in the utility room leading from the kitchen to the back garden, although it took Phoebe a while to realise that the milk was in a china jug, not a plastic bottle with Wm.Low written on the side. She brought it back to the table and they both sat down.

'You want some breakfast?' Uncle Louis asked, then looked around the kitchen as if it were a foreign land to him. 'Not sure what there is, mind you. Maude makes her own muesli, but it's a bit like eating sawdust if you ask me.' He backed this up with a tiny conspiratorial wink.

'Toast?' Phoebe hazarded.

'Now toast I think I can do.' Uncle Louis leapt to his feet and set about his task. The bread was in a large earthenware crock, with a heavy wooden top that doubled as a breadboard. The slices he hacked off were only slightly thinner than the kitchen tabletop, and appeared to be made of much the same material. Phoebe was intrigued to see what manner of toaster could accommodate such enormous slabs, but Uncle Louis just opened the oven door and slid them in onto a wire rack near the top.

'Some butter to go on those, and some of Maude's honey. There really is nothing better to start off the morning.'

'Where is Aunt Maude?' Phoebe took a sip of her coffee, then wished she hadn't. Mum and Dad had both been heavy coffee drinkers, and she'd recently started trying it herself. This was not like the instant powder she was used to. It had a strange, bitter taste quite unlike anything she'd encountered before.

'Oh, she's probably out in the vegetable garden somewhere.' Uncle Louis pointed to the window and the bright sunny day unfolding beyond. 'Days like these are rare, so she likes to make the most of them. You could give her a hand once you've had your breakfast.'

Slathered in butter, the toast wasn't as bad as she had expected. Phoebe had to admit as she helped herself to a second slice that

Aunt Maude's honey was also very good. She noticed her uncle spoon a large lump of it into his coffee and decided to try that for herself. The resulting drink still tasted odd, certainly nothing like the Mellow Birds Mum favoured, but at least it was palatable. She would still have preferred tea, but wasn't quite sure how to ask. The simplest of things felt difficult now all the rules had changed.

'What am I going to do?' Phoebe asked, after she'd decided her uncle wasn't going to say anything.

'Well, you could help your aunt in the garden, like I said.'

'No. Well, I mean, aye. I can do that. But that's not what I meant.'

Uncle Louis frowned a while, the wheels in his head slowly meshing together. 'Oh, right. Well, what do you want to do?' was the best he could come up with.

Phoebe was tempted to say 'go home to my friends', but she knew that wasn't an option. And besides, she wasn't so bold or so rude. Instead she went with 'I don't really know. I don't know anything about this place, I don't know anyone. Is there anyone my age anywhere near here?'

Again, her uncle looked puzzled as the search going through his mind wrote itself across his round face. Eventually he smiled. 'There's Angharad, I guess. She works in the pub at the weekends. She'd be a bit older than you too, I guess. Maude'll know better than me, anyway. I'm a bit of a recluse, see?'

Phoebe wasn't sure if that was a question or simply the way her uncle spoke. Either way, it didn't bode well. Bad enough to be so far from her friends; she'd at least imagined she might be able to make a few new ones.

'What about school? I'm meant to be doing O Grades soon. Do they even do them down here?'

'Ah, yes. School.' The way he said it didn't fill Phoebe with confidence, neither did the naughty schoolboy look that crossed Uncle Louis's face. He was, she realised, pathetically easy to read.

'I am going to school, aren't I?'

'Well . . . how can I put this? There's a small problem.'

'Problem? What kind of problem?'

'Well, let me see. Wy ti'n siarad Cymraeg?'

'What?'

'Do you speak Welsh?'

'Of course not. I'm from Scotland.'

Uncle Louis gave her a little smirk. 'You're from Fife, I believe. Here's an interesting fact: the language they would have spoken there a millennia or so back would have been far closer to what's spoken in these hills now than the Gaelic of the Western Isles. Of course, there wouldn't have been any schools as you know them for you to attend.'

'Is there a point to this?'

'Sort of. The nearest school teaches almost entirely in Welsh. All the other pupils are native speakers, so you'd find it hard to fit in, and anyway you're a bit old for it, I think. The nearest English-speaking school's in Aberystwyth.'

Phoebe recalled the endless journey from the station out into the hills. Back home she'd always walked to school, and it had never taken more than ten minutes. But she didn't have a home any more, of course.

'Is there a bus?'

'Actually we discussed this before you came, Maude and me. We thought we'd give homeschooling a try.'

Phoebe was too stunned to say anything. She couldn't really think straight at all.

'It makes sense, if you think about it,' Uncle Louis continued. 'Like you said, you've been following the Scottish curriculum. So you'd find it hard enough to catch up with a Welsh school anyway.'

'I think they'd find it hard to catch up with me.' Phoebe focused on the one certainty she could find. Everyone knew that the Scottish education system was infinitely superior to any other in the United Kingdom. Possibly the world.

'Sorry. Of course you're right.' Uncle Louis drained his coffee and put the mug down on the table. 'But it's all academic . . .' he laughed at his unintentional and terrible pun '. . . for the next couple of months at least. Meantime I've written to the Scottish Education Board and they'll be sending us everything we need to know about the curriculum. Your old school's been very helpful too, and Maude's sounding out some of the locals for ideas. A lot of university types living round here. I do a bit of lecturing myself, you know.'

Phoebe slumped in her chair, head in her hands and elbows on the table in a manner her dad would have told her off for. Listening to her uncle, it was clear this had already been decided for her without anyone thinking of asking what she wanted. Was that how it was going to be here, then?

'Right, I'd better get back to work.' Uncle Louis stood up and tightened the belt around his dressing gown. 'You don't mind clearing the table, do you?' And without waiting for an answer, he strode across to the door through which he had entered, pulled it open and went in to the room beyond. Before Phoebe could see what lay inside, he had pulled it sharply closed.

There wasn't much left of her coffee, and what there was had started to congeal. Phoebe collected up her plate and both mugs, then spent a fruitless five minutes searching for the dishwasher. She even looked in the pantry and utility room, but apart from the fridge, the only remotely sophisticated piece of machinery was an elderly top-loading washing machine remarkably similar to one she'd seen in an exhibition on the 1950s. Finally admitting defeat, she took the crockery to the sink and washed it all up by hand.

Breakfast cleared, Phoebe sat back down at the kitchen table and wondered what to do. Her chat with Uncle Louis had left more questions than answers; she really didn't know how she was going to fit into this household, how she was meant to relate to this odd couple who were supposed to take the place of her parents but seemed old enough to be her grandparents. The thought of being home schooled made her even more depressed. She'd known that finding her place in a new school would have been hard, but at least she'd have been with people her own age.

A wave of homesickness swept over her, bringing tears to her eyes and that terrible lump back into her throat. She needed to talk to a friend, and there was really only one person who fitted the bill. Pulling herself up from her chair, Phoebe hurried out to the hallway, where she'd noticed an elderly phone the day before. A quick glance at the clock showed it wasn't too late to catch Jenny before she headed out to school. Lucky her. But as Phoebe reached for the handset, it occurred to her that she should probably get permission to use it, especially since she'd be calling long distance. She went back into the kitchen, hoping to find her aunt and ask her. There was still no sign of her, so she crossed the room to the door her uncle had used, knocked gently and pushed it open.

'Uncle Louis, I . . .' Phoebe stopped mid-sentence. The room was obviously her uncle's study, its walls lined from floor to ceiling with bookcases, all packed haphazardly with an uncounted mass of words. Boxes of papers turned the floor into an obstacle course best tackled when completely sober, or not at all; an elderly leather armchair might have been comfortable had it been possible to sit on it without being buried in an avalanche of falling box files and yet more books. Dominating the room was a large desk, positioned to face the door and piled high with yet more clutter. A chunky desktop computer sat in the middle, incongruous among all the ancient artefacts, and behind it sat Uncle Louis.

He looked up as soon as she opened the door, one hand going to the rim of a pair of half-moon spectacles perched on the end of his nose. For a moment there was an expression of such unbridled fury on his usually jovial features that Phoebe feared he might leap up and attack her.

She had seen a look like that once before, on her mother's face. Phoebe had been seven, and had wandered bored into the front room at home. She knew that the china ornaments in the glass-fronted cabinet were not toys, that they were priceless family heirlooms. She knew too that touching them was absolutely forbidden. But she was bored, and they were colourful. And there was a delicious guilty pleasure to be had in breaking the rules.

Afterwards she told herself that it was the shock of her mother coming into the room and discovering her that had made her drop the figurine. She could still see the little ballet dancer spiral a perfect pirouette to the hard wooden floor, feel the moment of dreadful certainty as it shattered into a million tiny pieces. She could still hear the shriek of despair and anger, such an alien noise to come from her mother's lips. And she well remembered the look of pure fury on her face. Seen here, now, that same expression on Uncle Louis, was the first time Phoebe thought of him as being in any way related to her.

Almost as soon it had come, the moment passed. Uncle Louis took off his spectacles with one hand, placed them carefully on top of the papers stacked on his desk, and let out a deep sigh.

'Phoebe. There are very few rules in this household. We won't make you go to bed before you want to, and we won't wake you up just because the day's started without you. As long as you contribute your share to the everyday chores that need doing, you're free to spend your time as you wish. I am happy . . . no, honoured to take on the task of raising you after the terrible tragedy that befell your parents. My dear little sister . . .' For a moment Uncle Louis seemed to lose himself to reminiscence, his eyes glazing over. Then he remembered what he had been saying and fixed Phoebe with a stern gaze.

'But there is one rule you must remember, and which I really should have mentioned when we got here last night. You can come into my study whenever the door is open. Whether I'm in here or not, it doesn't matter. But if the door is shut you must never open it. Never knock, and keep any noise in the kitchen to the absolute minimum. When the door is closed, it means I'm working. I must have absolutely no disturbance then, you understand?'

Phoebe felt a hot blush over her cheeks, her ears burning. All thoughts of phoning Jenny forgotten. 'I . . . Sorry . . . I didn't know . . . I—'

'No harm done this time.' Uncle Louis was back to his normal cheerful self. 'My fault for forgetting to tell you. How could you have known? But please remember, OK? Never open that door. Now. Why don't you go off and see if you can help your aunt in the garden.'

10

The lawn was slick with morning dew, great fat drops glistening at the tips of leaves and drooping flower stems to the ground as if in genuflection to the rising sun. Phoebe shivered involuntarily at the change in temperature from the house, but soon warmed up as the sunlight caught her. She stood for a moment just breathing the air and listening to the silence; it was like nothing she had ever encountered before.

Slowly sounds came to her. The distant call of birds, the rustling of trees in the breeze, a gentle trickling sound of water hidden away. And then the tuneless whistling of someone at work. Her aunt, no doubt. There were marks in the lawn where feet had wiped away the damp, heading in the general direction of the whistle, so Phoebe set off to see if she could be any help.

Before she had gone more than a half-dozen paces, Aunt Maude strode out of a gap in the hedge. She had a stout pair of gardening gloves on, secateurs in one hand and a wooden trug in the other. A wide-brimmed canvas hat protected her head from the morning sun and a calf-length pair of rubber galoshes kept her feet dry. But apart from that, she was stark naked.

Phoebe started to back away, hoping to hide herself and her embarrassment, but too late.

'There you are, Phoebe dear. I was beginning to think you'd sleep all day long.'

Phoebe stared, unable to say anything. Then she tried to look away, which just made things worse. She could feel the heat climbing up her neck, flooding her cheeks and the tips of her ears.

'Goodness me, girl. Don't tell me you've never seen a naked body before.' Aunt Maude bore down on her like a force of nature, and Phoebe couldn't help but stare inappropriately.

'There's nothing to be ashamed of in nudity,' her aunt said, and now she was standing very close to Phoebe. 'We came into this world naked, after all.'

'Umm . . .' Phoebe looked up at her aunt's face. Her normal head-down, avoid eye-contact posture was leading to too much embarrassment. 'Aren't you cold?'

Maude laughed. 'Of course not. It's a beautiful morning. There's nothing quite like the feel of the sun on your skin to make you feel young. You should try it some time.'

For a horrible moment, Phoebe thought she was going to be ordered to strip. It must have shown on her face, as Maude let out another snort of laughter.

'Deary me, you youngsters are so serious all the time. Come.' She took Phoebe by the arm and led her along a narrow path between two tall hedges, forcing Phoebe to come much closer to the naked woman than felt entirely comfortable. Her aunt smelled of earth and sun lotion, and small beads of sweat were collecting in the small of her back. Had her uncle known about this when he'd suggested she go out to the garden? A fresh wave of embarrassment flushed her face. Who were these strange people and why was she here with them?

The path ended at a large archway that opened onto a walled vegetable garden. Through the gate, gravel paths criss-crossed a vast area, all neatly squared off with beds full of a bewildering assortment of plants. Over on the far side, a white-framed greenhouse the size of a Wimpey home leaned against the red brick wall.

'Welcome to my little paradise.' Aunt Maude released Phoebe's arm so that she could raise her own in a mockery of prayer. 'All nature's bounty can be found in here.'

'It's . . . very big.'

'I know. Isn't it wonderful?' Maude strode off down the nearest pathway, stroking the plants, stopping every now and then to bend down and peer at something. Phoebe followed at a slightly more comfortable distance, although she would much rather have run back to the house and hidden in her bedroom.

'Do you know much about growing vegetables, Phoebe?'

'I grew some carrots once. At school.'

Maude beamed a great smile that made it almost possible to forget she didn't have any clothes on. 'Well, that's just perfect. Your uncle loves his carrots. Here.' And she trotted off to another corner of the walled garden. Phoebe had to look away as she bent down, and when she finally looked back, Aunt Maude held a bunch of tiny orange carrots with great fronds of feathery leaves sprouting from their tops. 'Try one.'

'But they're all covered in dirt.'

'Nothing wrong with a bit of dirt. Keeps you honest.' Maude brushed at the roots with her hand, as if that would make a difference to the heavy soil clinging to them, then shoved one in Phoebe's direction. When Phoebe took it, Maude broke the leaves off the top of another one and stuck it in her mouth, crunching loudly.

Phoebe looked at her own carrot, still covered in fine silt. It would be rude not to do the same as her aunt, she guessed, and yet that dirt was very real. Then again, so was the stare she was being given by a naked old lady, which made it very hard to think straight. She wiped at the carrot as best she could, snapped the stringy roots from the bottom and took a bite. Tiny pieces of grit scratched against her teeth, setting them on edge far worse than fingernails down a blackboard.

'Much nicer than anything you buy in a shop,' Aunt Maude said. Phoebe couldn't tell whether the smile on her face was genuine, or she was laughing inside at the silly little girl who was stupid enough to eat a dirty carrot.

'Lovely.' She surreptitiously spat the half-chewed remains into her hand while Aunt Maude's back was turned.

'Right, then, we'd better find you something to do.'

Under the watchful eye of her naked aunt, and the growing heat of the sun, Phoebe worked her way up and down rows of vegetables, slicing weeds off at the neck with something that was apparently called a hoe. It seemed to go on for ever, and she was soon dripping with sweat, caked with dirt. Her sole pair of trainers were ruined; one of only two pairs of jeans in need of a good wash. Her aunt's strange predilection for nudity began to make a curious kind of sense, although Maude herself was hardly breaking a sweat as she pottered around the plants with a pair of secateurs, stopping occasionally to make some comment on Phoebe's performance.

'Well, I think that's a profitable morning's work, don't you?' she said eventually. Phoebe's hands were beginning to blister, her arms aching. Her hair hung around her eyes like something dead, and she felt sticky all over.

'It's finished?' she asked, hopefully.

'Oh dear me, no. Weeding's never finished. Little buggers'll be growing again before you know it.' Maude smiled. 'But you can't work all day. Not in this sun. Sometimes a girl's got to have a little fun. Come on. We've just about enough time before lunch.'

She set off across the walled garden, but instead of going to the gate that would lead back to the house, Aunt Maude led them away towards the far side. Phoebe followed because she didn't know what else to do, exiting from the garden into a wild meadow beyond. A narrow path cut across the grass and into the woods, twisting through arrow-straight pine trees as they dropped down into the valley. After a while, Phoebe noticed a fork in the path, one way clearly well used, the other overgrown with brambles and bracken. Not far from the fork, she could make out what looked like an old stone bridge, covered in moss and ivy, its arch long-since tumbled away.

'Not that way, Phoebe dear.' Aunt Maude pointed her away towards the well-used path. 'The old bridge fell down before even I was born. Used to be you could jump across, if you were bold. When we were your age it was a bit of a dare. More stone keeps falling away every year though. You'd like as not be taking a swim if you tried now. And anyway, they built a nice new wooden bridge downstream. Much easier going.'

Less than a hundred yards further on, they came out in a clearing above a natural pool. Rocks rose above the water on both sides, a waterfall splashing down and foaming the surface. Further downstream, the rock gave way to a shallow sandy beach, before the river once more plunged into a steep-sided gorge.

Aunt Maude stopped at the bank where a flat-topped rock perched high above the water. She shucked off her boots and pulled off her hat and gardening gloves, then leapt into the pool with all the grace of a toad. Phoebe watched in horror as she disappeared under, invisible beneath the foam. The water itself was a dark peaty brown, hiding whatever menace might lurk beneath. She looked downstream, to where the current eddied around the beach and shallows, half-expecting her aunt's body to rise to the surface, face down and lifeless. Instead, a shriek of girlish laughter burst out from the opposite direction.

Phoebe turned to see where the noise had come from, and saw Aunt Maude's head bobbing above the surface beside the waterfall. She raised one hand above the surface and beckoned.

'Come on in. The water's lovely.' She ducked under again, came up standing under the cascade of water as if it were a shower. Phoebe shook her head, hugged her arms to her sides. There was no way she was going in there. It would mean stripping off, for one thing, and even the thought of that made her shiver with awkward embarrassment. Her aunt might not have a problem with naked-ness, but this wasn't the walled garden any more. It was public. Anyone might come by at any moment and see.

As if reading her thoughts, something rustled in the bushes behind her. Or at least Phoebe thought something did. She spun around expecting to see a person, but there was only foliage moving in the breeze. Over the sound of the waterfall, she thought she heard another girlish giggle. Only it didn't come from where Aunt Maude was busy washing her hair in the stream, but much closer. Almost by her ear.

'Who's there?' She spun around again, and at the same moment some bird wheeled and screamed overhead like a child crying. Phoebe looked up too swiftly, and before she knew what was hap-pening she was scrabbling at the edge of the rock. She briefly glimpsed Aunt Maude standing under the waterfall, white-spumed spray cascading off her head and shoulders like some bizarre sham-poo advertisement, and then she was falling.

The water hit her like a wall, knocked the wind out of her before it sucked her into its dark embrace. Her ears filled with a roaring noise. Panic gripped her as the world turned upside down. She was going to die here in this dingy little backwater, away from her friends. Well, at least she'd get to see her mum and dad again soon.

Strong hands grabbed her under the arms and hauled her upwards out of the water. Instinctively, Phoebe put her feet down, only to discover that the bottom was far closer than she had thought. Wheezing and coughing, she gasped for air as slowly the world righted itself and came back into focus.

'Mercy me, girl. It's more normal to take your clothes off first, before jumping in.' Aunt Maude stood in front of her, droplets of water rolling off her skin. Perhaps it was the wetness darkening the grey in her hair, or the look of mischief on her face, but she seemed much younger.

'I . . . I slipped,' Phoebe said, shivering slightly. The water was cold, but refreshing after the sweat of her morning's toil. And although her clothes clung to her like they were painted on, she felt wonderfully clean.

'Well, you're in now. Better make the most of it. I can recommend the falls. It really scrubs out your hair.'

Phoebe looked across the pool to the waterfall, spattering down from high above. She was already wet enough, standing up to her thighs in the cool water. The thought of wading or even swimming the distance, plunging herself in once more, was not appealing.

'The trick is to keep moving. That way you won't feel cold.' Aunt Maude let herself fall backwards into the pool, lying on her back so that the brown water made her skin look even more tanned. 'Get those wet clothes off and have yourself a proper swim.'

Clothes off. The thought of it sent another shiver of embarrassment up Phoebe's spine. She waded towards the beach and dragged herself out.

'I want to go home,' she said and realised that she really meant it. Not to the house half a mile away, but home to Scotland, to Cupar and the little cul-de-sac she'd known all her life. She wanted her mum and dad to be back, to laugh and smile and joke with her. She wanted to talk to her friends and plan a Saturday trip to Dundee, or even Edinburgh. She wanted things to be normal, and knew with a horrible wrenching in her gut that they never would be again.

'Here, it's all right. Just let it out.'

Without warning Phoebe found herself enveloped in a warm hug. She hadn't realised she was crying until that moment, but her aunt's touch sparked off a fit off sobs. She clung to the old woman as if her life depended on it, and for a while it didn't matter that she was naked, that she smelled of the river, that she was in so many ways a total stranger.

For now it was enough simply to be held.

11

Rain, persistent and heavy, greeted Phoebe on her second day in Wales. No gardening to be done, she found herself wandering from room to room in search of the television. It was a rambling place, this old house, much larger than she had at first thought, but one of these rooms had to have a telly in it, surely. There were radios, dotted around on window ledges and shelves. She had found a stereo system that played actual records, like the ones her dad kept neatly shelved in the living room and treated like some kind of religious relics. Or at least he had done until the fire had melted them all. She found a video camera in a room that looked like nobody had entered in years. As big as her head, it had a lens like a whale's eye, covered in a thick film of dust, but it gave her hope. If they had a camera, then there must be something to play back the recordings on. But she couldn't find it anywhere.

Aunt Maude was in the kitchen kneading dough when Phoebe slouched in, throwing herself into a chair at the large table, defeated. A parcel lay half-open in front of her, full of books. That just about summed up this strange house, really. Full of books. Nothing useful or fun. Just millions and millions of dry words.

'What have you been up to, girl?' Aunt Maude's tone wasn't exactly unfriendly, but she had a curious curtness about her.

'Just looking around.'

'If you're bored, there's plenty I can find for you to do.'

Phoebe fiddled idly with the edge of the parcel, pulling it this way and that without really thinking. Then she noticed the cover of one of the books inside, and tugged the whole package closer. There were six books in all, three copies each of a couple of romances. One was called *Love's Triangle*, the other *He Remembered My Name*.

'Muriel Baywater.' Phoebe voiced the author's name slightly louder than she had intended, caught out as yet more memories reminded her of how shitty life could be. 'Mum used to love her books. Don't think she had these ones though.'

Aunt Maude punched at the dough as if it had insulted her in a former life. 'They'll be new ones. Review copies, no doubt. Your uncle's publishers keep on sending him all manner of rubbish. There's a stack of that woman's purple prose a mile high. She seems to churn them out every other month.'

Phoebe turned one of the books over in her hands, feeling the weight of it. An image of her mother, curled up in an armchair, glass of wine perched precariously on the side, her attention focused entirely on the book in her hands. She had loved Muriel Baywater more than any other writer, though for the life of her Phoebe couldn't think why. If the cover was anything to go by, neither of these books was worth reading.

'Why don't you take those?' Aunt Maude said. 'Or if you don't fancy reading something that trashy, have a look on the shelves in the sitting room. I'm sure you'll find something interesting.'

'You want me to read? Like, a book?'

'What else would you do with it?'

Phoebe looked at her watch, then out the window where rain was coming down in sheets. 'I'd rather watch telly. Can't seem to find one though.'

Aunt Maude flumped the dough down onto the tabletop, flour billowing around it as she rubbed her hands together in what looked far too much like glee for Phoebe's comfort.

'I thought you'd have worked it out by now, Phoebe dear, what with all your stomping around the house and searching every room. Your uncle and I don't own a television.'

Phoebe looked up so sharply her neck cracked, sending a little jolt of pain down her spine and up into her brain, as if this was an impossible thing she was being asked to accept.

'You what?'

'We don't have a television in the house.'

'But you've got a video camera. I found it.'

'That old thing? I doubt you can still get tapes for it. Never worked terribly well when you could. Lou was given that when they made a documentary about the filming of his book.'

Phoebe slumped in her chair, realised she had clasped the books to her chest like some poor lovesick damsel. Waiting for her prince to come and rescue her from this cruel prison with no television. She put them back down on the table, the awful realisation of her predicament dawning.

'No telly.' It was too horrible to contemplate.

'You can't get a signal here in the valley anyway,' Aunt Maude said, as if that made it any better. 'Now why don't you give me a hand in the barn. There's a load of old flowerpots that need sorting and cleaning. Just the job for a grey day.'

Phoebe grabbed the books back off the table. 'I'm busy,' she said and stalked out of the kitchen. She stomped through the house, fuming at the regimented rows of books, piled high on every wall, clumped up the rickety wooden stairs to her bedroom and threw herself down on her bed, fighting back the tears and the urge to scream. It was all so unfair, and there was nothing she could do about it. Which was even more unfair.

The drumming of the rain on the rooflight soothed away her frustration after a while, or at least beat it into submission. She rolled over and pushed the pillows up, slouching against the bedstead. Across the room, more books leaned awkwardly into each other on a half-filled set of shelves, as if they too had been thrown into a situation not of their liking. Phoebe's hand hovered over the two books lying on the bed beside her. Decisions, decisions. Finally she plumped for *He Remembered My Name*, cracked the spine open and began to read.

She had to be called down to lunch, so engrossed was Phoebe in the tale of misfortune that was *He Remembered My Name*. Even then, Aunt Maude had to make the climb all the way to her bedroom door and knock twice. It was an age since last she'd so utterly lost herself in a book. Something she'd stopped doing . . . when? Round about the time she and Jenny and Charlotte had started catching the bus to Dundee on the weekends, maybe? Perhaps when she'd got more into music and clothes, experimenting with her look, trying to decide whether boys were worth the effort or not. Jury still out on that last one. Well, except Jim Kerr.

Uncle Louis was already at the kitchen table, a steaming bowl of suspiciously green soup in front of him, a plate of doorstop bread slices alongside it. He glanced at the book Phoebe still grasped in one hand, an eyebrow rising as he smiled at her.

'Muriel, eh? Wondered what was keeping you so quiet all morning.'

Phoebe placed the book down on the table, noting the box it had come from was still sitting at one end. 'Not much else to do.'

'Nonsense, Phoebe dear. There's always plenty to do. You young things just don't have the imagination.' Aunt Maude spooned soup into another bowl and put it down in front of her. Phoebe was surprised by the colour, but it smelled wonderful. Her stomach growled in anticipation, too.

'Do what? We're in the middle of nowhere,' she said.

'Well, you could go for a walk. Explore the woods.' Uncle Louis dunked some bread in his soup, shoved it in his mouth and chewed for a while. 'There's miles of tracks and paths around here, all manner of interesting things to see.'

Phoebe glanced out the window. The glass was wet with raindrops, but it seemed to have stopped falling from the sky, at least for now. The leaden colour of the clouds didn't inspire much confidence, and the sunny weather of *He Remembered My Name* was much more appealing.

'What sort of things?' she asked. 'It looks like nothing but trees to me.'

'Nothing but trees.' Uncle Louis put the bread back on his plate, picked up his spoon and then shook it in her general direction as if he were a teacher admonishing a particularly stupid pupil. 'There's history in this valley goes back thousands of years. People have been mining the hills and grazing animals on the moors since Roman times. Before that, even.'

'They're not here now though, are they.'

'Are they not? Haven't you seen them, Phoebe? Haven't you heard them?'

There was something in the way Uncle Louis posed the questions that made her shiver. He was normally so flippant it was hard to tell when he was being serious.

'What do you mean?' she asked.

'Well now.' Uncle Louis dropped the spoon into his soup with a 'ploip' noise, took up his bread once more. He tore off a chunk and shoved it in his mouth, chewing for a moment as if in thought. Then, without swallowing, he asked, 'Have you heard of Myfanwy's baby?'

'Louis, really. I—' Aunt Maude began to protest, but he waved her silent.

'No,' Phoebe said. 'Who's Myfanwy?'

'Well now,' Uncle Louis said again. 'Where to start? There's some say Myfanwy was the mine captain's daughter, some that she was just a scullery maid in the old mansion house down the valley.

It doesn't really matter now, does it. She was young, maybe your age. A bit older, but not much. Pretty too. The girls from this valley are all pretty, their daughters too.'

Phoebe blushed at that, hiding her embarrassment by taking a mouthful of soup. It was very good, even if she couldn't have said what it was made of.

'Now young Myfanwy, she caught the eye of the local lord. Geraint, his name was. Nasty man, but powerful. Rich too. He owned the land from the valley head all the way to Bont near the sea. All that silver dug out of the hills belonged to him. There's those would say all the people who worked on the land belonged to him too. So when he took a shine to young Myfanwy, well, there wasn't much anyone could do about it.'

'Wait. When is all this meant to have happened?'

'Oh, two, three hundred years ago? Who knows? But here's the thing, Geraint had his way with Myfanwy, but when he learned she was carrying his child, he threw her out of the house into the cold.'

'Why would he do that?'

'Well, I suppose he didn't want her to have any hold over him. Nasty man, like I said. And this was winter too. She tried to go home, but Geraint forbade her parents to help her or they too would be thrown out. From house to house she went and always it was the same. The people wanted to help her, but they knew if they did they would be next. Oh, they did what they could, they weren't completely heartless. A loaf of bread here, a block of cheese there. Maybe turn a blind eye for a day or two if she slept in the byre. But always there was the threat hanging over her, see?'

Phoebe wondered whether she'd not stumbled into one of Muriel Baywater's romances, although there didn't seem to be a happy ending anywhere. 'So what happened to her? She had the baby, I take it?'

'She did indeed.' Uncle Louis leaned forward again, brow

furrowed as he spoke. 'Out in the woods there, not half a mile from where we're sitting. She gave birth alone, on the riverbank, with the snow all around her. The poor child lived only long enough to let out a single wail before it died.'

'Oh.' Phoebe had quite forgotten her soup now, her bread untouched. 'And what of Myfanwy?'

'They found her the next morning, frozen stiff as a board, her dead child clasped to her lifeless bosom. They say when the air is still, you can hear the babe's cry to this day.'

A silence had fallen over the kitchen, only the low gurgle of the range cooker and the slow tock tock tock of the grandfather clock in the corner. Phoebe realised her spoon hung limply in her grip, halfway between bowl and mouth, and lowered it slowly back into the soup as her brain caught up with what had happened.

'You made that up,' she said, even though she was impressed by the story.

Uncle Louis shrugged expansively. 'It's what I do for a living, Phoebe. And besides, who's to say it isn't true? The woods are full of stories. Ghosts too. You just need to get out there and find them.'

12

2023

Chester Services is like another world in the wee small hours of the morning. Low clouds turned hellish by the arc lights from the nearby industry of Ellesmere Port lend everything an unreal glow. Phoebe hasn't stopped here in ages, but she needs to stop now. Her car needs to charge, and she needs coffee. Not like the mad young days of her twenties when she'd drive eight hours without a break. Scotland to Wales on her annual pilgrimage. When did that stop?

She orders a tall latte, extra shot of espresso to keep her going. Adds a couple of very expensive chocolate brownies to the mix before taking her haul back to the car. It's too bright in the service forecourt, the night people oddly loud. Retreating to the warmth of her personal space, she stares out the windscreen as the meter ticks slowly upwards. She should walk, stretch her legs before the last two and a half hours along increasingly narrow and twisted roads. Iron the kinks out of her back before the potholes hammer them in again.

Instead, she checks her phone. How easy it is now to be in touch with the world. Everything you need at your fingertips, and a great deal more beside. There's a temptation to log in to her socials, see what Clare's up to. But there have been no messages, no pleading texts. And it's the middle of the night. Clare will be in her bed. Alone, or maybe even with someone else.

The coffee scalds at first, but her tongue soon gets used to it. The first brownie is too sickly sweet for her to finish, but it gives her the boost she needed. The car's only a little over half charged by the time she's lost patience. Still, it'll be more than enough to get her to where she's going. And it's not as if Wales doesn't have electricity. Even in the wilds of Llancwm.

She turns on the radio as she leaves the service station and rejoins the last few miles of dual carriageway. Some worthy but dull professor lectures her about macroeconomics for half an hour before she gives up and searches for a music station instead. She should have loaded an audiobook, probably has something on her phone, but the thought of stopping for long enough to find it is too much. She's about to turn off the noise and enjoy her thoughts in silence when a familiar song comes on.

'Don't You (Forget About Me)' sounds different through the high-quality speakers built into the car. Even so, Phoebe can almost hear the gentle hiss of the old cassette in her long-forgotten portable tape machine. Jim Kerr's voice seems lower-pitched, the tempo a little less upbeat. But then she'd recorded the song from the chart show on her dad's ancient stereo system one bored Sunday afternoon. Hardly surprising that her cheap knock-off Walkman would be a little fast. She still knows every word, every note. How many times did she listen to it that long mad summer a lifetime ago? It had been her only link to the past, after all.

She's so lost in the memories, Phoebe can't understand why the next song to be played is not the one she'd recorded next on that old mix tape. It should be Madonna now, shouldn't it? Realisation dawns slow, her fatigue making her stupid. She taps the button to turn off the radio, shakes her head a little in an attempt to scare off the sleepiness. The last dregs of her latte are cold now, but she drinks them anyway and concentrates on the drive.

The roads are at once familiar and strange. She has driven them countless times before; she learned to drive on some of them. And yet little things have changed. Some new signs here, fresh road markings there. A roundabout where once there was a junction. Newtown has a bypass, which throws her for a while. But as she nears her destination and begins the slow, single-track climb into the mountains, so that old familiar feeling creeps back in.

The light creeps back in too, a pre-dawn glow washing out the car's headlight beam. Phoebe spots badgers, foxes, the occasional rabbit. And as the light grows, so she sees the familiar shape of the red kites as they wheel above the endless forest. Close now, she turns away from the sign to the village, carries on up the mountain road.

It's only as she swings off the tarmac and onto the forest track that she remembers her car is low to the ground and heavy with its enormous battery slung underneath. Something makes a horrible grinding noise as she picks a path around the worst of the potholes, and she is concentrating so hard on minimising damage she is at the house before she realises. It sits in the clearing, surrounded by ancient trees. There are no lights on, of course, but that in itself is not unusual. Phoebe pulls to a halt and turns off her car, stares through the windscreen at the place she once called home. Pant Melyn looks lifeless now, empty and without any soul.

Aunt Maude is dead.

13

1985

Phoebe hadn't fully appreciated how big the woods were until she took yet another fork in the endless paths and realised that she was utterly lost. Panic hadn't quite set in yet, but she could feel the beginnings of it, that ever so slightly queasy feeling in her stomach that was an oddly welcome counterpoint to her usual gloom and despair.

It had all started a couple of hours earlier. Breakfast that morning had been interrupted by a phone call. From the look on Aunt Maude's face after she'd finished speaking to whoever it had been, Phoebe knew it couldn't be good news. That had been confirmed when her aunt had announced that she and Uncle Louis had to go to Aberystwyth, and Phoebe couldn't come with them this time. When she had asked why, the answer had been as close to 'because I said so' as Phoebe could remember ever hearing from anyone since her seventh birthday.

'We'll be back by teatime, get yourself some lunch,' her aunt had said as she bustled a still-sleep-fuddled Uncle Louis out of the door and into the car. If she'd heard Phoebe's plaintive 'What will I do all day?' she had made no answer.

And so Phoebe had sat for a while in the kitchen, lost in her misery. Then she had tidied up breakfast despondently and moped around some more. Nothing the house had to offer interested her at all, which left little else to do but go outside.

She had found a pair of walking boots that almost fit, pulled on one of her aunt's old coats, and headed out across the meadow to the edge of the woods. She'd stopped at the rickety old gate not because anyone had told her not to go into the forest; quite the opposite, her uncle had even suggested she go explore it. More, it was the noisy quiet of the place, the dark shadows and slices of sunlight, the smells and the flashes of movement that had held her back. The sensory overload had made her think she was hearing voices, just too quiet to make out words, see things that might be people or might be ghosts, or might simply be her imagination playing tricks on her. And yet it wasn't so much frightening as overwhelming, and after a while her curiosity had grown strong enough to outweigh the unease. She had followed the paths where they took her. And now she was lost.

A shiver ran through her that might have been the gentlest of breezes finding its way down between the ranks of trees. Their roots broke up the ground into undulations like waves on a stormy sea, and low branches blocked the view beyond more than a few feet. Only the path itself was clear. She could either turn back or carry on.

Looking back the way she had come, she saw only darkness, but up ahead the way seemed clearer. An easy decision, she set off towards the light, and soon stepped out into a wide glade.

Phoebe didn't know much about trees, but she understood the majority of them in this valley in Wales were conifers of some form or another. They lined the path on either side, and now they edged the glade in an almost impenetrable wall, dark-needled branches stooping to the ground as if in genuflection to the one vast oak that grew at the centre. It was an oak, of that she was sure, but even so she found herself doubting it could be true. What was a single, ancient oak tree doing here, surrounded by all these younger pines?

It reached up to a pale blue sky dotted with clouds, and spread out in a leafy circle as wide as it was tall. Time had whittled away at its symmetry, a noticeable dent in one side where a large bough had broken, years ago by the look of it. Short grass and wildflowers grew in the shade right up to the ancient, gnarled trunk, and fat, lazy bees bumbled around in their endless search for nectar. Phoebe half expected to find a fawn curled asleep in the bowl between two roots. Instead, as she stepped into the cool air under the green canopy, she found a bunch of flowers had been placed there, stems neatly tied with a piece of orange twine.

Closer still, she could see that they were wilted, some petals turned brown, fallen to the earth to be reclaimed by the soil. Whoever had placed the bouquet, they had done it a while ago. But maybe not more than a couple of weeks.

The thought sent a shiver all over her. Phoebe stood up quickly, afraid of being seen even if she wasn't doing anything wrong. For a moment, the air around her darkened and she felt light-headed as the blood rushed to her feet. She put a hand out, touched the old bark of the trunk for support until everything settled again. And that was when she heard the voice.

It was quiet, female and young. Coming from the other side of the tree. Phoebe couldn't quite make out the words, or was it just that it was humming rather than singing? A slow, almost mournful tune she didn't recognise, she found herself drawn to it all the same. Letting her fingers trail along the rough bark of the tree, she slowly stepped around the trunk until she could see who it was.

On the far side, the canopy opened up where some time in the past a large branch had died. It looped down, bare of leaves, dipping at its lowest to a point a few feet higher than the top of Phoebe's head. The bark had been worn away there, which would explain why the branch was dead. Most likely generations of local children had swung from the tattered few frays of rope that hung there, blissfully unaware of the damage they were doing to the tree.

Beneath it, the grass grew longer, filled with wildflowers thriving in the sunshine. And there, sitting on the top of a low mound, facing away from the tree trunk, sat a girl.

'Umm . . . Hello?' Phoebe found she was still touching the old oak, as if she needed its reassurance that this place was real. Slowly, the girl turned, eyes searching what must have been gloomy darkness from her position in the sun.

'It's OK. You can come out. Won't bite you.' The girl's voice was soft, her accent local. From a distance, Phoebe couldn't make out much of her features, so reluctantly she let go of the tree and stepped out from under the canopy. As she approached, the girl stood up, revealing the two of them to be much the same height. Phoebe couldn't help noticing the girl's bare feet, and the old-fashioned floral dress she wore looked like something from the cover of one of her dad's folk albums. Her dirty straw-coloured hair framed a pale face with a thin nose and bright oval eyes, a gaze that darted here, there and everywhere. There was something hauntingly familiar about her, although Phoebe couldn't exactly say what. Perhaps it was that hair, much the same colour as her own only a lot grubbier.

'Hi. I'm Phoebe.' She held out a hand to shake, even though that felt weird. 'D'you live here?'

'What, here?' The girl looked past Phoebe, up at the tree, arms wide and shoulders shrugged to take in the whole glade. For a moment she looked serious, but then a grin like the sun split her face and she reached for Phoebe's offered hand, clasping it in both of hers. 'Just kidding with you, aren't I. Know who you are right enough. You're Lou Pant Melyn's niece. Come to live with him an' Maude. Nice to meet you, Phoebe. I'm Gwyneth.'

All this was delivered with such speed, the cadence of her speech so alien to Phoebe's ears, it took a while for her to catch up. She retrieved her hand, noticing as she did that Gwyneth's were grimy with dirt as if she'd been digging, and now some of that soil clung to her own fingers. The young girl ran the back of her hand across her face, leaving a smear that would have done a toddler proud.

'So what brings you up this side of the valley, then, Phoebe?'

For a moment, Phoebe couldn't remember how she had got to this strange place, let alone why. Then it came back to her, the miserable trudging along endless forest paths, walking as a way to keep her dark thoughts at bay. It occurred to her that she really wasn't sure exactly where she was, let alone how to get back.

'You know why I've come to stay with my uncle and aunt?' she asked, not sure how she felt about total strangers knowing that most horrible of things. Gwyneth ducked her head slightly in acknowledgement, her face sombre.

'Figured if you wanted to talk about it you would. Not my business otherwise. I'm sorry, mind. For what it's worth.'

Phoebe liked the sentiment. She didn't want to talk about it, although she was the one who had brought it up. She searched around for something to change the subject, lighted upon Gwyneth's bare feet.

'You lose your shoes?' she asked, inclining her head towards the ground. There was the slightest of mounds where Gwyneth stood, a gentle undulation that the grass and wildflowers all but obscured.

'Like the feel of the earth between my toes.' Gwyneth looked down at her hands, as if that was the first time she'd noticed them. 'And between my fingers too. Keeps me connected with the land.'

'You live around here, then?' Phoebe asked.

'In a manner of speaking. You could say the woods are my home.'

There was something about Gwyneth that Phoebe couldn't quite put her finger on. Her bare feet and muddy hands were odd, it was true, as were her old-fashioned clothes, but there was also something other-worldly about her. She seemed friendly enough, though. And she was the first person Phoebe had met since arriving in Wales who was close to her own age.

'You'll know the area pretty well, then.'

'Don't suppose there's a corner of this valley I've not visited at least once. I can show you the best bits, if you'd like.' Gwyneth glanced up at the sky briefly. 'But not today. It's going to rain soon, so you'd best be getting back to Pant Melyn. Unless you like getting soaked.'

Phoebe recalled her accidental dip in the stream the first time she'd visited it with Aunt Maude. Had Gwyneth been there? Spying on them? She shook her head slightly to dislodge the odd thought. Looking up, she saw that the little fluffy white cotton-wool balls had merged into a bank of dull grey cloud. The wind had picked up too, tugging at the tops of the pine trees and making the old oak rustle.

'I'm not sure what's the quickest way back,' she said, although in truth she wasn't sure what was any way back.

Gwyneth smiled that sunbeam smile again, reached out and grabbed Phoebe's hand, tugged her towards the edge of the clearing directly opposite where she had entered.

'Come on. I'll show you back to the old bridge. You'll know it from there. And you can tell me what it's like in Scotland. I've never been.'

Phoebe let herself be led, telling Gwyneth a little about her life before it had all been so cruelly turned upside down. The route seemed impossibly quicker than her meandering outward journey, and all too soon they had arrived. They parted not at the old bridge, which had long since collapsed into the river and been overrun with brambles, but at the more modern wooden structure a hundred yards or so downstream.

'Meet me here again,' Gwyneth said, then glanced upwards at the strip of sky visible where the river split the forest in two. 'But not tomorrow. It's going to be horrid wet.'

And then with a squeeze of the hand and a cheery wave, she turned and strode away.

Phoebe watched, slightly bemused, as the strange girl disappeared into the gloom. A fat drop of rain spattered on her shoulder, and as she looked down she could see dark blotches beginning to appear on the wooden decking of the bridge. Time to head back to Pant Melyn before the promised deluge arrived.

She made it through the back door, hair damp and shoulders soggy as the heavens opened. Phoebe stood for a while staring out into the garden at the sudden ferocity of the downpour. The noise was a roar of overhead jet fighters, and for a moment she recalled the fire that had destroyed her life, the misery of the weeks that had passed since. Then she remembered Gwyneth's smile, her infectious enthusiasm and general oddness. Not tomorrow, but maybe the day after, she'd meet her again. Someone much her own age, who knew the place and was easy to be around.

A lot less miserable than she had been when she'd left that morning, Phoebe closed the door on the storm outside and went through to the kitchen in search of lunch. It was all still horrible and hopeless, but at least now she had found a friend.

14

2023

Police Constable Angharad Fairweather is not at all the person Phoebe had been expecting. She's older, for one thing. Probably not much younger than Phoebe herself. Maybe five foot six in her stout police-issue boots, she has a weathered face and a friendly smile. They meet at the entrance to Bronglais Hospital, up the hill near the library.

'I'm so sorry for your loss,' she says by way of introduction. Phoebe has heard the phrase so often in her life it has lost all meaning, the automatic response to bad news. And yet somehow the constable manages to make it sound sincere. Practice, maybe. Or she has genuine empathy.

'Thank you. It's hard to take in, but Aunt Maude lived a very long life and seems to have left it on her own terms.'

'Would that we were all so fortunate.' The constable indicates the self-opening door, which slides open on cue as if she has the Force. 'Shall we?'

The nurses on reception are clearly no stranger to PC Fairweather, and with the briefest of nods they are past the desk and heading into the depths of the hospital. Phoebe says nothing, listens instead to the echo of their footsteps along the linoleum-floored corridor. It is busy, but quietens as they reach their destination, an anonymous door with the sign 'Bereavement Centre' written on it in English and Welsh.

'There's no need for a formal identification, since she was found in her own home by her home help. I met her myself a year or two back.' PC Fairweather puts on something of a schoolteacher voice as she explains the procedure. 'You don't have to see her if you don't want to.'

It's an odd thing to suggest now that they have come this far. Another rote part of the job, perhaps. Phoebe has been mentally preparing herself for this since first hearing of her aunt's death though. It's not something she can not do, either.

'I'm fine. Not the first dead body I've ever seen. And besides, I want to see her. Say goodbye properly, you know?'

PC Fairweather nods her understanding and opens the door. Beyond is a small waiting room, comfortably furnished and noticeably without the endless health and safety posters pinned to the walls. There's a second, closed, door directly opposite the one they have come through, and standing beside it a nurse half Phoebe's age. She greets them with a tired smile.

'You're here for Mrs Jenkins?'

'Ms Jenkins, yes.' PC Fairweather corrects the nurse before Phoebe can. 'Is she ready?'

Is she ready. The question hangs there, and for a moment Phoebe imagines her aunt on the other side of the closed door, propped up on too many pillows in an ordinary hospital ward bed. She'll have that knowing smile on her face, that mischievous twinkle in her eye. She'll ask Phoebe about all the little things most troubling her; the embarrassing things and the things she doesn't want to confront. Like she has always done, every time they've met up again over the past two score years and more. Always too seldom, and now never again.

'You OK?' Phoebe feels the gentlest of touches on her arm, PC

Fairweather breaking what has probably been an uncomfortably long pause.

'Fine. Yes. Let's just . . .' She's about to say 'get this over and done with' and manages to stop herself. The nurse nods her head once, then opens the door onto a small room beyond. Phoebe swallows back the sudden grief that has formed in her throat and steps through.

At first, she thinks the tiny figure lying on the bed is someone else. Maude was such a large character in life, this small, empty shell cannot possibly be her. But as she approaches, so Phoebe sees that familiar face. The lines have eased, the pain that dogged her later years finally gone. She'd let her hair grow longer since the last time they spoke face to face, how many months ago? How many years?

The nurse and PC Fairweather say nothing, stay in the waiting room, and Phoebe is grateful to them for it as she stands for a last few moments with the dead body. Nothing but a shell. She feels no need to touch her aunt in any way; it's enough to simply be there. And then that's more than enough and she steps away.

'Thank you,' she says as she pulls the door closed behind her, surprised at how level and calm her voice is.

The nurse nods her head again in acknowledgement. 'Have you had a chance to think about funeral arrangements?' she asks.

'Next on my list. Maude left fairly specific instructions, so it shouldn't take too long to arrange.'

'I'll walk you back, then.' Constable Fairweather opens the first door, and together they retrace their steps through the bustling hospital to the main entrance, again silent. The whole procedure has taken less than half an hour, but Phoebe feels a weight off her shoulders for having done it.

'You've got my number if you need anything, but here's a card anyway.' PC Fairweather's smile is a little less strained now. Phoebe takes the card, sees the shield and crown of Dyfed-Powys Police.

'I've put my mobile on the back, see. Just in case. Please don't hesitate to call now. And do let me know when the funeral will be.'

Phoebe turns the card to see another number neatly written in biro. Did the constable do that just now, or have all her cards got this personal touch on them?

'Thanks, I will,' she says as she slips it into her pocket. 'And thank you for being here. It's the sort of thing Maude would have done. She was very much one for helping others in their time of need.'

15

1985

T rue to Gwyneth's word, the rain fell steadily all night and
through the rest of the next day. Phoebe mooched around
the house, quiet whenever she was in the kitchen as her uncle
worked to make up for the time lost the day before. She still wasn't
quite sure what it was that he'd done wrong, or forgotten to do at
all, that had taken a whole day to sort out, but it was clearly not the
first time it had happened. Aunt Maude had apparently forgiven
and forgotten by the morning, back to her usual indomitable self.
Certainly a little rain, or even a lot of rain for that matter, wasn't
going to put her off her beloved gardening, and she'd disappeared
out into the murk shortly after breakfast. At least she'd been wearing clothes this time, Phoebe had been glad to see.

At one point in the afternoon, having made sure that Uncle
Louis wasn't using the extension in his study, Phoebe had tried
phoning Jenny for a chat. It had started well enough, the usual 'hi,
how are yous', and 'when are you going to visits' that all of their
conversations had started and ended on. But when Jen had launched
into her tales of what everyone was up to, who'd been seen with
whom and what all the latest gossip was, Phoebe had found herself
tuning out. It was almost as if the people she'd known had become

less real now, so far away were they. She'd tried to tell her oldest and best friend about the strange barefoot girl Gwyneth, but Jenny tell that Jenny was responding in exactly the same uninterested way that she herself had been doing just moments earlier in the conversation. It had all come to an unsatisfactory end shortly after that, and Phoebe had spent the rest of the day lost in a book.

But now it was a new morning, and the rain had given way to clear blue skies with only the occasional cotton-wool cloud to break up the monotony. Phoebe had managed to pre-empt Aunt Maude's suggestion she help out with weeding the vegetable beds by announcing at breakfast that she was going to spend the morning exploring the woods. Much to her surprise, her aunt had agreed without so much as a counter-argument, which rather spoiled the fun.

As she followed the narrow path through the meadow towards the trees, Phoebe began to have second thoughts. It might have stopped raining, but over twenty-four hours of deluge had left everything soaking wet. The long grass drooped with the weight of water, and before she'd even made it to the trees her trousers were soaked from the knee down, her purloined walking boots squelchy with each step.

It didn't get much better in the woods. Yes, the path was clear, but the undergrowth to either side leaned in, each frond a glistening drop at its tip. Every time the breeze gusted enough to jostle the treetops, yet more water would come cascading down. By the time she reached the ruined old stone bridge and the pool where Aunt Maude had brought her that first day, Phoebe might as well have taken another impromptu swim, she wouldn't have got any wetter.

The wooden bridge a little further downstream steamed gently as the sun hit it where the river cut a scar through the forest canopy wide enough to let the light in. Phoebe stood in the middle, leaned on the railing and breathed in the pure air. The rush of the water, twice as much as the last time she'd been here, blanked out the sounds of everything else, a kind of white noise that took all her troublesome thoughts away with it and left her wonderfully calm.

'You fall in again?'

In any other setting, Phoebe imagined she would have jumped out of her skin. And yet somehow she'd known that Gwyneth was there, even though she'd not seen her approach, felt her weight on the bridge or heard anything until the young girl spoke. She turned her head, not surprised to find her wearing the same old dress as the previous time, feet still bare. She'd tidied up her hair though, her hands and face clean. She was also suspiciously dry compared to Phoebe's drowned rat state.

'How'd you manage not to get soaked coming here?' She pushed herself slowly upright from the handrail and faced Gwyneth. 'You're dry as a bone.'

Something flickered across the young girl's face for an instant. Not quite a frown, but a stray thought she maybe had to suppress with effort. It was soon replaced with a mischievous grin.

'Practice, Feebs. You live in Llancwm long enough you learn how to dodge the showers.'

It was Phoebe's turn to frown. She was about to say, 'But I don't want to live here long,' only her brain caught up with the words before they could spill out. No point ruining things right at the start.

'You were right about the rain though. Don't think I've ever seen so much. Everything's dripping.' Phoebe slapped at her jeans. 'Even me.'

'We should go and see the falls. They're always spectacular after it's rained. If we take the riverside path, you'll have a chance to dry out some, too.' Gwyneth didn't wait for Phoebe to agree. With a slight cock of her head to one side, she set off across the bridge towards the opposite bank. Phoebe watched her for a moment, wondered whether this might be some elaborate prank. It didn't really matter if it was, she realised. Anything was better than helping Aunt Maude in the garden or tiptoeing around Uncle Louis as he typed away at who knew what in his study. Still damp, and with a squelch to every step, she set off after her new friend.

They walked for about twenty minutes alongside a stretch of the river where it ran wide and slow. As promised, the track wasn't overgrown with bushes and the morning sun did its best to dry Phoebe's clothes. They talked of inconsequential things, Gwyneth pointing out the occasional landmark she thought important.

'Don't go that way, it's just a bog now.' She pointed at a fork in the path and what looked like it might have been a promising route to explore. 'Used to be Cerys the fortune-teller's cottage but it fell down years ago.'

Phoebe had no idea who Cerys the fortune-teller was, or indeed how long ago her cottage might have fallen into disrepair. Before she could ask more, Gwyneth had stopped beside an ancient pine tree, tall and straight like the masts on the ships that sometimes came to Dundee. It had clearly been there a lot longer than the trees that surrounded it, many of which were probably its offspring.

'This is Blodwyn's tree. Where she used to wait for Aneurin so they could walk together to the village school.'

Again Phoebe had no idea who Gwyneth was talking about, but the young girl had moved on before she could ask.

The sound of the falls blended in so well with the general noise of the forest that Phoebe didn't at first register it. They'd moved from the wide-open path to a narrower gorge, where overhanging branches threatened to soak her all over again. Gwyneth seemed to have a knack for never brushing the leaves as she passed, and Phoebe found adopting a similar rhythm to her walk helped her do the same. She forgot herself when they finally rounded a sharp corner and she caught her first glimpse, knocking a good half a pint of cold rainwater down the back of her neck. It could have been a gallon for all that she noticed, such was the view.

The forest mostly hid the rock formations that made up the valley, undergrowth smoothing everything so that it seemed to rise evenly from the centre on either side until the trees gave out and the moors began. From here, Phoebe could see that wasn't quite the case. A series of ridges cut diagonally across the way, like stairs for some mythical giant. The river crashed over them in a series of spectacular waterfalls, four in all. With the weight of rain that had fallen in the past day or so, the water burst out into the air before plummeting down to the next level. Then again, and again.

'Good, isn't it.' Gwyneth had to shout over the din to be heard.

'It's amazing.'

'Come on. We can get closer, see.'

Without waiting, the young girl set off along the path towards the base of the lowest waterfall. Unlike the spot further downstream where Aunt Maude had swum and Phoebe had fallen in, the pool at the bottom of this plume had no beach. The banks were formed by solid rock, worn away by aeons of erosion to form almost perfectly sheer sides. Water brown as shaken Coca-Cola churned a foot or so below the edge, whirling and eddying until it finally tumbled away over boulders and on down the valley.

Phoebe edged nervously towards the falls, the noise and motion making her feel giddy, off balance. Tumbling in here would not be a good idea, she knew. Ahead of her, Gwyneth seemed unperturbed by the danger, skipping across the flat wet stone towards the point where the river fell in a great sheet of creamy white. She reached out a hand and let the water splash over it, then, with a cheeky look back over her shoulder, disappeared.

For a moment, Phoebe couldn't work out what had happened. Her heart leapt to her mouth at the thought that her new friend had been pulled in by the flow. She hurried forward as quickly as she dared, her dizziness mixed with alarm to form a queasy sense of vertigo. Damp coated every surface, little puddles in the path to make it slippery, mossy fronds and bracken glistening in the sunlight.

'Gwyneth?' Phoebe's voice came out too quietly, lost in the roar of the falls. 'Gwyneth!' She shouted over the noise, panic rising. And then an instant later she saw what had happened.

Cut in the rock, either by nature or cold iron, the path didn't end at the sheer cliff face ahead of her. Instead, it ducked in under the waterfall. A cave hollowed into the ridge, a smaller stream running through the centre of it, bringing yet more water from deep within the earth. And sitting beside it, one bare foot dangled into the flow, was Gwyneth.

'You scared the hell out of me there. Don't do that.'

The young girl looked up at her, a mischievous grin on her face. 'Sorry,' she said, although she plainly wasn't. 'It's good though, isn't it. I love this place, especially after heavy rain. Nature doing its thing.'

Gwyneth's voice should have been hard to hear over the roar of the falls, and yet something about the acoustics of the cave let it carry despite her not having shouted. She gestured for Phoebe to join her, shuffling slightly to give her a space to sit that wasn't half puddle, half damp moss. Phoebe hugged her knees to her chest and kept her feet out of the stream, but Gwyneth hitched up her dress and dangled both legs over the edge, her feet disappearing into the murky brown water.

'Where does it come from?' Phoebe nodded into the darkness that was the back of the cave. She could just about make out the back wall, rough slate stone shiny with damp and cut through with paler fault lines. The stream seemed to just appear, with no obvious sign of a tunnel, flowing past them swiftly before merging with the falls.

'There's caves and tunnels all over this place. Some are man-made, but a lot's just natural. Water gets in a crack up the hilltop, works its way down through the rocks until it finds a way out. You'll notice we've a lot of water here, a lot of rain.' Gwyneth turned to face her, and Phoebe was struck by that feeling of familiarity again. 'You'd be surprised how much is hidden deep in the earth here.'

Something about the words made Phoebe shiver. Or more likely it was the damp, cold cave they were sitting in and the fact her clothes were practically dripping wet.

'It's brilliant. Thank you for showing me. But I think I need to get back into the sun. Dry out a bit.'

Gwyneth reached out and placed a hand on Phoebe's shoulder. Her touch was light, but it felt strange, almost as if a static shock had passed between them, only slower.

'You're soaked right through, Feebs. You should have said earlier.' The young girl hauled her bare feet out of the river, spraying yet more water over Phoebe in the process. 'Come on. Let's get out of this gloomy cave and back into the daylight.'

The sunlight was a welcome, warming relief as they retraced their steps down the riverside path, but Phoebe couldn't help thinking what she really needed was a complete change of clothes. It didn't help that the morning's small fluffy clouds had given way to something rather more sinister, and the gentle breeze was playing with the treetops rather more forcefully now. Occasional gusts made it down to the riverside, sent shivers goosebumping over her skin.

'I think I might have to head back to Pant Melyn,' she said as they reached the remains of the ruined bridge. 'Getting really cold now.'

Gwyneth stopped, looked at Phoebe with her head tilted at a quizzical angle for a moment. The clothes she wore were much lighter than Phoebe's, hardly proof against the weather at all. But then she wasn't soaked through, and she didn't seem to feel the cold.

'You're right.' The young girl shrugged, her smile not fading. 'It'll be lunchtime soon, and you wouldn't want Maude getting worried either.'

'You want to come?' The words were out of Phoebe's mouth

before she'd even considered them. 'I'm sure it'd be OK. There's always plenty to eat.'

Gwyneth's smile grew, but she shook her head slowly. 'No, but thanks. I've stuff I need to be doing too. It's been fun though, having someone to talk to.'

'Likewise.' Phoebe shivered again as another gust of wind blew lazily straight through her. She couldn't help but notice the edge of loneliness in the girl's voice. 'You want to meet up again some time?'

'Sure. I'd like that.'

'Tomorrow, maybe?' Phoebe glanced up at the ever-darkening sky. 'If it's not raining.'

Gwyneth followed Phoebe's gaze upwards, then she licked a finger and held it out as if that was the most accurate weather forecast available. 'Don't think it will. Come if you can. I can keep myself busy if you can't make it. Who knows what Maude'll have you doing next.'

'Where will I find you?' Phoebe asked. 'Where do you stay?'

'Here and there,' Gwyneth said with a shrug. 'If you wait at the new bridge like today, I'll find you. Only don't hang around too long if I don't come. Probably busy doing something else.'

Phoebe was about to ask what she meant by that, but Gwyneth simply muttered a quiet 'bye, Feebs' and turned back the way they had just come. After half a dozen steps she had almost faded into the growing gloom, a half a dozen more and she was gone.

Not quite sure whether she'd done something wrong or not, Phoebe carried on down the track towards the wooden bridge. She was getting very cold now and hoped that Aunt Maude had made soup for lunch. She could never be quite sure what was in Maude's soups, but they were always warming and usually tasted a lot better than they looked.

As she stepped off the far side of the bridge and took the fork in the path that would lead her back to Pant Melyn, Phoebe had the sudden sensation of being watched. She wondered if it was Gwyneth having changed her mind, but a glance over her shoulder showed no sign of her. Only as she was turning back to her path did Phoebe catch a glimpse of movement off down the track that led to the village. Changing tack, she jogged the short distance to the first bend, reaching it just in time to see a man hurrying away.

'Hello?' she shouted, then immediately regretted her boldness. The man stopped as if he'd been struck, turned slowly to face her.

Stick thin, with a long face and a shock of pure white hair, Phoebe thought at first that he must be ancient. The long overcoat and scarf wrapped around his neck added to the impression of age. Phoebe was cold, but that was more down to being soaked through than the actual temperature. It seemed strange for someone to be so heavily clothed on what was really a warm day.

'Are you local?' she asked, her voice pitched a little louder than usual in case he was deaf.

He still didn't answer, shook his head very slowly. His eyes were wide, his gaze fixed on Phoebe as if she were some kind of apparition. The more she studied him, the younger she estimated his age despite his colourless hair and old man clothes. Younger than Uncle Louis, for sure, although maybe a little older than her parents.

'I'm Phoebe.' She held out a hand despite the two of them standing too far apart for it to be more than a gesture. 'Phoebe MacDonald. I'm staying at Pant Melyn with my uncle and aunt.'

At the name of the house, the man flinched. He turned from her as if to walk away, then turned back again, eyes once more drawn to her face. It wasn't creepy, she found. She had no sense of danger from him at all. Possibly because he looked so frail the wind whipping the treetops would likely knock him over if a gust made it down to the path.

'You . . . you look so like her.' His words came out in a soft croak, as if he was recovering from a bad cold.

'Like who?' Phoebe asked.

He shook his head again, coughed gently as if clearing his throat. If he was, it didn't work, as when he spoke again his voice was just as weak and hoarse. 'I heard about your parents. Little Siân. I'm so sorry.'

'Wait. You know my mother?' Phoebe took a step forward, her wet clothes and the chill momentarily forgotten. The man shrunk back as if she were a snake.

'I shouldn't have . . . I must go. I can't stay. Be safe, Phoebe MacDonald.' He backed up two paces, turned and hurried away. Phoebe might have followed, but the wind chose that moment to whistle down the track, chilling her damp clothes more effectively than any fridge. She shivered, hugged herself for warmth, and then set off for Pant Melyn as fast as her tired legs could take her.

16

2023

The town has changed since last she was here, and yet in many ways it's just the same. It's been the best part of a decade now since her uncle died, but the solicitor's office is still that dull shade of beige, still has that slightly musty smell to it, still the same smiling receptionist at the front desk. Even if she's looking a little older.

'Dr MacDonald.' Her smile has genuine warmth to it, but is short-lived. 'I'm so sorry for your loss.'

That phrase again, perhaps a little less sincere than PC Fairweather's words, or maybe less practised. It is a loss, but now she has seen her aunt's body in the hospital Phoebe finds she can distance herself from the fact of it and focus on the tasks that need to be accomplished. So many things the dead leave behind for the living to deal with.

'Mr Jones is expecting you. Would you like a coffee?' The receptionist guides her to the door at the rear of the reception area as if she is a half-wit. Phoebe supposes that maybe right now she is. It's hard to concentrate on anything much. Lack of sleep from her overnight drive down from Edinburgh, perhaps. The world catching up with her.

'Thank you. That would be lovely,' she finally manages to say as she's ushered into the office of Tom Jones – not that one – solicitor and executor of the estate of Maude Jenkins. His smile is more measured and lasts longer. He has aged less well than his receptionist. In the time since last they met to deal with the death of Phoebe's uncle his hair has given up the fight it was losing even then.

'Dr MacDonald. I'm so sorry for your loss.' He stands, offers a hand to shake across his cluttered desk. Phoebe's mind goes back to another solicitor's office, a lifetime ago. Mr Stearn had always kept everything obsessively tidy, she recalls. Possibly a good habit in a lawyer, but something that's always made her suspicious.

'Thank you, Mr Jones. It's still a bit of a shock, I suppose. But Maude lived a long life. She was ninety-four, after all. And she died in her own bed in her own home, too. I can't imagine her in a hospital, or fading away.'

'Indeed not. Nor would she have ever wanted to be beholden to anyone. You'll not be surprised to find that all her affairs were in order, nor that you are the sole beneficiary of her will.' Mr Jones fetches a slim sheaf of papers out from underneath a larger folder, flicks idly through the pages and then hands it across to Phoebe.

'She said as much when Uncle Louis died.'

'Yes, well. There'll need to be a valuation done on the house and contents. The taxman will have his pound of flesh, but it all seems fairly straightforward to me.'

'Happy to leave it in your hands. You've got my contact details if you need anything. I'll be staying at Pant Melyn for a while. At least until the funeral's done.'

Mr Jones shuffles among his papers again before finding another page. 'Yes, she left a few instructions as to what she wanted done with her remains.' He peers at the words, raises a grey eyebrow. 'Something about water cremation and scattering her . . . ashes? Would that be the right word?'

Phoebe can't help but smile at the solicitor's confusion, even if it is probably feigned. 'Aye, she told me. Actually, she told me every time we talked for about the last eighteen months. I think she was quite keen I get it right.'

'That sounds like Maude.' Mr Jones nods his head. 'Well, if you need any help with the arrangements, just give me a shout.'

'I'll do that, thanks.' Phoebe folds the copy of the will, starts to stand up.

'There was one other thing.' Mr Jones makes a small, embarrassed shrug and picks up the larger folder under which the papers had been hiding. Phoebe settles back into her chair.

'There is?'

'You'll be familiar with the name Tegwin Ellis, I presume?'

A cold prickle across the nape of her neck, Phoebe feels herself tumbling back in time to that fateful summer. 1985. When she was twelve years old and her life fell apart. 'I knew him, yes. He died though. About five years ago, wasn't it?'

'Six years, actually. Terrible business. Maude told me all about it, poor fellow.' Mr Jones pauses a moment, rubs his hands together as if his knuckle joints pain him. 'The thing is, Mr Ellis left no will when he died, and somehow the task of finding his nearest next of kin fell to me.'

'He was related to half the people in Llancwm, wasn't he?'

Mr Jones does that embarrassed shrug again, picks up the folder and opens it to the first page. 'Emphasis on the "was". Tegwin never married, you see. And, well, you know the sorry stories about his brother and sister. Of course you do. It would seem most everyone who was related to his father is dead too. Or can't be traced at all. Except for you.'

'I . . .' Phoebe's mouth hangs open, no more words able to escape.

'So it would seem that as well as Pant Melyn, you have the best claim on Nant Caws Farm too. Quite the inheritance, wouldn't you say.'

17

1985

A week passed, or was it a fortnight? A month? Phoebe gave up counting the days, settling instead into a kind of dull torpor. It wasn't that her new life was terrible, apart from the lack of television, and even then her burning desire to know what was happening in Brookside Close had turned into more of a niggling worry she might be missing out. She could find no enthusiasm for anything, not even mourning. Most of the time she slept, or at least lay in bed and stared at the ceiling, thinking of nothing. Of everything.

The only thing she had was her music. Aunt Maude had found a power adapter that fitted her Walkman, and Phoebe spent all of her time listening to the one tape she had taken with her to Edinburgh and that fateful school trip. Sixty minutes, more or less, of singles recorded from the chart show, complete with tiny snippets of the DJ's voice at the beginning and end where she'd not been quick enough with the pause button. It played on a loop, first one side, then a hissy few moments of nothing before the machine clunked over and played the other.

Hard to believe it was only a few weeks ago she'd made the tape, obsessed by the music and the pretty boys singing it, their outrageous clothes and weird haircuts and more make-up than Phoebe had ever worn. She'd had posters of a few of them on her bedroom wall, creases still showing where they'd been carefully unstapled from the centre pages of *Smash Hits*. Lying on her back and staring at nothing, she could see them now. Paul Young, Haircut 100, Simple Minds, Eurythmics, Strawberry Switchblade with their weird Goth thing that she'd always secretly wished she could get away with. And lurking in the background, abandoned in the corner, the Smurfs and dolls and teddy bears of an earlier age. Forgotten but never quite abandoned. That bedroom was gone now, reduced to ash and rubble. Deep down she knew it was important to hold on to that memory, but Phoebe found it hard to care enough, impossible to muster the energy.

'You there, Phoebe dear?'

Aunt Maude's voice somehow managed to penetrate both the door and the white noise of the song without her actually shouting. It was a daft question, since there wasn't anywhere else Phoebe could be.

'What?' she asked, a bit more aggressively than she'd meant to. As she pulled off her headphones and thumbed the stop button on her Walkman, the bedroom door cracked open.

'Thought I'd find you up here. I need to check up on old Mrs Evans. She's ninety-seven, doesn't get out much. You want to come along and see a bit of the village? You could help me with the shopping.'

It was voiced as a question, a suggestion, but Phoebe was wise enough to know a command when she heard one. With a weary sigh, she levered herself off the bed and shuffled into her trainers as she pulled on an old woolly jumper that smelled of mothballs. It was a change of scene, she supposed. She followed her aunt down the stairs, through the house and then into the kitchen, where a collection of old and much-patched cotton bags lay on the table beside a neatly written shopping list.

'Here, take these. You can go to the shop while I see the old girl.' Aunt Maude handed Phoebe the list and a rolled-up wad of money to go with the bags, then set off towards the laundry room and the back door.

'Are we walking?' She had come this far, but the thought of expending any more effort was too much, surely. Her aunt had already set off across the grass towards the little gate that opened onto the meadow and the forest path. Phoebe almost dropped the bags, turned away, but at that precise moment the sun came out from behind the clouds. It lit up the garden, the meadow, the dark pines and distant valley sides, and felt like someone had flipped a switch in her head.

'You really should try to get out more,' her aunt said as Phoebe finally caught up. She wanted to ask 'and do what?' but managed to keep the words to herself as they settled into a steady rhythm, walking along the slowly descending path through the trees.

'I spoke to Mrs Dalgliesh this morning,' Aunt Maude announced out of nowhere. 'She asked how you were coping, bless her. Said Jennifer misses you terribly.'

Phoebe found that hard to believe, given the short and stilted conversation she and Jenny had managed the last time she'd phoned. There didn't seem to be anything to say. Not like when they'd been living just half a mile apart. But then their phone calls had always been short and simple. Come round to my place; meet at the Merkat Cross; Luvians for ice cream. It hadn't been that long since either of them had been allowed out unsupervised.

'She mentioned the idea of a visit,' Aunt Maude said.

Phoebe stopped in her tracks so suddenly her aunt had to turn and face her to continue the conversation.

'I . . . I can go visit Jen? In Cupar?' The possibility seemed unreal. Like waking up from a long, slow nightmare.

'Ah . . . no.' Aunt Maude let her shoulders slump as if the disappointment were crushing her rather than Phoebe. 'I don't think it would be good for you to go back so soon, dear. It would only make things harder for you, trust me.'

'What?' Phoebe's voice came out as a squeak, her throat tight and tears threatening. 'Why not? Why can't I—'

'It's too soon, Phoebe dear.' Aunt Maude was at her side without appearing to have covered the distance that had been between them. 'Believe me when I say this. Going back will be very hard on you. It will be as if everything you ever knew has changed. You'll be in the place where you grew up, but you won't be able to go home, and everyone will treat you differently whether they mean to or not.'

'I don't care. I hate it here. I just want to go—' She stopped herself at the last moment, almost falling into the trap Aunt Maude had set. Sniffing like a toddler, she swallowed the lump that was threatening to choke her. 'I just want to see my friends.'

'I know, cariad. I know.' Aunt Maude crouched down beside her and swept Phoebe into a hug. She resisted at first, but then relented. It was nice to be held, to know that someone cared at least that much. Even if they were being unreasonable about letting her go away.

'So . . . Jenny can come visit me here?' she asked after her aunt had released her and they were once more walking down the path towards the village.

'Of course she can. Any of your friends can, although maybe not all of them at once. But it's still term time, so it will be a while yet.'

Term time. Phoebe hadn't really thought much about that, but it was true. She'd missed so much school already, when would she ever catch up? Her uncle had suggested she might be home-schooled, and there had been a few half-hearted attempts at what might look like lessons in speaking Welsh, but other than that she'd been left to her own devices. Reading trashy romance novels and wandering aimlessly through the woods. Even Gwyneth had disappeared after their visit to the waterfalls, presumably gone back to wherever it was she lived and whatever school she attended.

Phoebe started to ask whether there were any more plans for her education, but before she could get the words out they had stepped out of the woods and onto a narrow pavement at the edge of the village.

'The shop's up the way, about a hundred yards. Past the garage, but before the chapel.' Aunt Maude pointed towards distant buildings that clung to the steep-sided valley like seabirds on a cliff face. She hefted the one small bag she had been carrying and then gestured towards a narrow driveway on the far side of the road. 'I'll be up here. Shouldn't take long. Meet you in the pub in an hour.'

Phoebe watched her aunt stride up the driveway, then set off in search of the shop. She found the garage with no trouble; a half-dozen ancient cars, rust-streaked and furred with green algae, cluttered the forlorn roadside. The workshop hung wide, showing a mess of oily detritus, bits of motor, shelves of unidentifiable parts. A surprisingly modern car was up on a lift, an inspection lamp glowing underneath it, but there was no sign of any actual activity. Only the fuzzy wailing of a radio not quite properly tuned gave any indication that the place was working. That and an elderly sheepdog attached to a long chain by the workshop doors, which looked up at her as she walked passed, sniffed and wagged an arthritic tail.

The hotel, The Llancwm Arms, was perhaps the second biggest building in the village after the chapel. Not that it was large at all, with no more than four rooms if each one had a single window to the front. A lean-to extension to its far side formed the village shop. Outside, a faded wooden trestle table displayed a sorry-looking collection of vegetables, well past their sell-by date but ever hopeful of finding a desperate buyer. Perhaps after being lost in the hills and tiny backroads for a week or so, the average tourist would fall upon the sight of a yellowing, caterpillar-scoured cauliflower with the hunger of the starved, but to Phoebe it just looked like something you'd feed to cattle. And then only to cattle you didn't much like. Alongside the trestle table, someone had managed to split one of the bags of coal untidily piled up by the door, adding to the generally untended air of the place. If it hadn't been for the modern post box unsympathetically bolted to the wall and the garish WE ARE OPEN sign in the door, she might have thought the place long abandoned.

Inside didn't inspire a great deal more confidence. A high row of shelves split the room in two, with a counter at the far end. An elderly glass-fronted refrigerator clattered away like not-too-distant roadworks, struggling to keep milk, cream, eggs and cheese cool in the unusual afternoon heat. Another, quieter fridge, emblazoned with the Wall's logo, held the promise of a refreshing ice cream, but when she peered inside, all Phoebe could see were unidentified white plastic tubs of suspiciously home-made produce.

'Can I help you, love?' A middle-aged lady had appeared at the counter. Phoebe hadn't heard a bell when she'd opened the door, and wondered how it was her entrance had been noticed.

'I've a list.' She fished out the piece of paper Aunt Maude had given her and walked up to the counter. The shopkeeper took it from her, peered at it a moment, then pulled out a pair of spectacles from beneath her blouse where they had been hanging on a string. She held them up to her face, but didn't put them on, instead squinting myopically through lenses obscured by still-folded legs. After a long moment, she tucked them back in her blouse and turned her attention to Phoebe again.

'So you're Lou Pant Melyn's niece. I'd heard you were coming to stay. Such a terrible thing, you poor dear.'

Phoebe wasn't entirely sure what the shopkeeper meant, not least because her accent rose up and down unexpectedly, and she paused mid-word as if she'd forgotten what she was saying. She'd thought Uncle Lou and Aunt Maude's accents strange, but they weren't half as thick as this woman's. She smiled all the same, and hoped she didn't look too much like an idiot.

'Well, let me see what we can do for you.' The shopkeeper bustled out from behind the counter, still clutching Aunt Maude's list, and set off down the narrow aisle at a fair speed. Phoebe hurried to catch up, just in time to be handed a bag full of pale-looking buns.

'I'm Mrs Griffiths, by the way. But you can call me Bethan. I run the shop here and my husband, Tom, runs the pub and hotel. I'm sure you'll be very welcome in the village . . .' The shopkeeper looked up at Phoebe expectantly.

'Oh. I'm sorry. Phoebe. Phoebe MacDonald.'

'Well, it's a terrible, terrible thing that's brought you here, but I'm sure you'll find a warm welcome in Llancwm. I'm sure you'll fit right in.'

Phoebe was about to complain that she didn't want to fit right in, that she wanted to get away from this place and back to civilisation just as soon as was legally possible. But it would have been rude, and she was interrupted anyway by the door opening. An old man stepped in, pulling off his flat cap as he did so. His head was down as he wiped his boots on the doormat, showing a crown of fine, thinning white hair. The old tweed jacket he wore was beyond the help of leather elbow patches, and grime encrusted both his neck and the collar of his once-white shirt, merging them together in an invisible line. His baggy trousers were faded and rolled up around his ankles. Phoebe half expected him to be using a piece of old rope as a belt, and was disappointed when she saw he wasn't chewing on a piece of straw.

'Shwmae, Mr Ellis,' Bethan Griffiths said as he looked up, but his eyes weren't on her. They were on Phoebe and they were mad-staring wide.

'Gwen bach?' He gasped the words, half question, half accusation. Then clutched at his chest and crumpled slowly to the floor.

Phoebe was moving before she realised she knew what was

happening. Years of training in the Girl Guides kicked in as she checked the old man's pulse, loosened the tight-knotted tie around his neck and moved him into a more comfortable position. When she looked back to where Mrs Griffiths had been, the shopkeeper was still standing, mouth slightly agape, a can of beans clutched to her bosom.

'Phone an ambulance, quick,' she shouted. 'I think he's having a heart attack.'

18

'He said something, I don't know. It's sounded like "get back"? Then he just keeled over onto the floor, poor man.'

Phoebe sat in the pub on the opposite side of the hotel to the shop, a glass of Coke in front of her and Aunt Maude by her side. The place was packed, the sleepy little village suddenly alive with what felt like hundreds of people. She had no idea where they'd all come from; they'd just budded out of the ground like mushrooms on a wet morning. And all of them were jabbering away about Ellis Nant Caws and his heart attack, and how he'd be dead if the young girl hadn't acted so quickly. Phoebe could hear them all, and understand those of them who were speaking English. But none of them were talking to her. It seemed almost as if none of them dared.

'Never you mind, girl.' Aunt Maude took a delicate sip from her glass of red wine. The drinks were on the house, apparently. Some form of reward for saving an old man's life. Phoebe couldn't help thinking, as she sipped her flat, weak Coke, that she'd got the worse end of the deal. She didn't even like Coke.

'But he was staring at me. I don't know, it was almost like he recognised me. And he was terrified. What did he mean, "get back"? I wasn't anywhere near him. It's nonsense.'

'Not "get back". "Gwen Bach". Little Gwen. It's a term of endearment. Usually.'

A young woman, perhaps seventeen or eighteen, dropped into one of the chairs at the table. Shorter than Phoebe, she had jet-black hair cut like she'd come from a party in the 1920s. Her round face was fixed in a permanent smile, one eye slightly lower than the other to give her a faintly comical air. Her clothes were well worn, a heavy black cotton jacket over a grubby black T-shirt, torn black jeans and boots designed with safety in mind more than fashion. Aunt Maude gave her an unfriendly stare, which she ignored. Something Phoebe found unaccountably amusing.

'Angharad,' Maude said eventually. Her tone was almost icy. 'This is my niece, Phoebe.'

Phoebe held out a hand and said, 'Hi.' Angharad looked a little surprised, but then shook, her lop-sided smile growing larger.

'You just visiting?' she asked.

'I . . . well. Not exactly, no. I guess I'm going to be staying with my uncle and aunt for a while.'

'Well, I'll be seeing you around, then, Phoebe. Just wanted to say thanks for helping the old man. There's not many here would have taken the bother.' Angharad pushed herself out of her chair. She nodded at Aunt Maude, said 'Maude', as if they were friends, then started towards the bar.

'Wait a minute, please.' Phoebe found herself standing as well. 'You said the old man said Gwen Bach. But why? My name's not Gwen, and I've never met him before in my life.'

'Well, that's a story would take some telling.' Angharad nodded in the direction of the doorway, which had just swung open to admit yet more strangers, and one familiar figure. 'Why don't you ask Lou about it, eh?'

Phoebe watched her uncle stare around the room, trying to find her. She waved, and when she looked back, Angharad had gone. Sitting down, she could see the scowl still hard on Aunt Maude's face.

'You'd do well to keep away from Angharad Roberts,' she said through a mouth that looked like it had eaten all the soor plooms.

'Why? What's wrong with her?'

But the answer to that had to wait as the recently vacated chair was suddenly filled by the bulk of Uncle Louis. He held a full pint of beer in his hand and wore an expression of amazement.

'Is it true? You gave the kiss of life to old Meredith Ellis?'

'It wasn't like that,' Phoebe said. 'He just had a bit of a turn. It was over in seconds. All I did was make him comfortable until the ambulance arrived.'

'That's not what they're saying at the bar.' Uncle Louis held up his glass, looked at it as if it might suddenly disappear, then took a long swig. 'I've lived in this village all my life and Tom's never given me a free drink once. Nor his father before him.'

'Angharad was here,' Maude said. Her first words since Uncle Louis had arrived.

'Did I miss her? Shame. She's always such fun.' He took another swig of beer. Aunt Maude drained her wine glass.

'We should be getting back. I've supper to cook.'

Uncle Louis raised an eyebrow at that, took another sip and then shook his head slightly.

'Phoebe here needs to have a word with Sergeant Griffiths first.'

'Sergeant . . .?' Phoebe froze in panic. 'You mean police sergeant? But I've not done anything wrong.'

'It's OK, Phoebe. He's not here to arrest you. Quite the opposite.' Uncle Louis put his pint carefully down on a coaster, then looked over his shoulder towards the door. Held up his hand and waved. 'Won't take long. He just needs to ask you a few questions so he can put it in his report.'

Phoebe wanted to complain, but before she could get any words out, their small group had been joined by the man who must have been Sergeant Griffiths. Any fear of the police evaporated at the sight of him, red-faced and slightly out of breath as if he'd run all the way here from Aberystwyth. Phoebe tried not to stare at his enormous nose, but it wasn't easy. That nose must have seen a lot of sun and a lot more whisky. Or whatever spirit they favoured in these parts.

'Maude,' he said, nodding his head at her. Then his attention focused on Phoebe. 'And you must be Miss MacDonald.'

Phoebe tried to shrink from the attention, but there really wasn't any getting away from it. Fortunately Aunt Maude came to her rescue.

'Is this really necessary, Eifion? It's not as if Mered died, after all. He might have done if Phoebe hadn't been there, but she was and now he's fine.'

Given that the last Phoebe had seen of the old man was his unconscious, oxygen-masked body being loaded into the back of an ambulance, which had then set off with the full sirens and flashing lights going, she thought Aunt Maude's prognosis was perhaps a little optimistic. She kept that to herself though.

'It won't take a moment. Just a few questions and we'll be done.' The policeman pulled out a notebook and pen, then sat down before asking, 'Or would you rather I dropped round Pant Melyn later this evening?'

Phoebe could see by the way Aunt Maude bristled at that suggestion that she wasn't overly fond of Sergeant Eifion Griffiths.

'What did you need to know?' she asked, figuring that the sooner they started, the sooner it would be over.

'Well, now.' Sergeant Griffiths stared at Uncle Louis's half-finished pint of beer, paused a moment as he licked his lips involuntarily, then seemed to remember himself. 'You were in the shop, I understand? Talking to Bethan when old Mered came in?'

'That's right,' Phoebe said. 'I was just running some messages for Aunt Maude when—'

'Messages?' Sergeant Griffiths interrupted her, somehow managing to add more syllables to the words than Phoebe reckoned it deserved.

'Aye, messages. You know. The shopping?'

The sergeant cocked his head like a confused dog, then scribbled something down in his notebook. Phoebe decided it was best if she just pressed on.

'The old man came in as I was about to pay for everything. Don't think he saw me at first, 'cause he had his head down. Soon as he looked up, he went white as a sheet. He said something that sounded like "get back". I thought he was frightened by something, but it couldn't have been me, aye? Only, then he clutched at his chest and keeled over.'

'Get back?' Sergeant Griffiths looked up from his notebook. 'That sounds quite aggressive to me.'

'Aye, well. Seems I didn't hear him right. According to . . .' Phoebe paused, unable to remember the name of the young woman who'd spoken to her only a few moments earlier. She looked to Aunt Maude for help.

'Angharad Roberts was here.' The old woman raised an eyebrow as she spoke the name, and Sergeant Griffiths raised both of his in agreement of something. Phoebe didn't give them time to tell her what.

'Angharad, that was it. She said the old man said "Gwen Bach". Apparently that means Little Gwen or something? Only, that's silly. My name's not Gwen, and I've never met that old man before.'

Phoebe was going to say more, but the police sergeant had fixed her with such an intense stare she couldn't help but stop speaking. His face was round, pudgy, an unhealthy pallor to his skin the result of too many pies and not enough exercise, and all centred around that monstrous, red-veined nose. His frown wrinkled everything together until she wasn't sure how he could see anything at all. He shook his head once, very slightly, and muttered something that sounded like 'dew dew' before turning his attention back to his notebook. He scribbled something else down quickly, then snapped the book closed and tucked his pen back into his jacket pocket.

'Well, Miss MacDonald. I don't think I need trouble you any further. That's plenty for my report.' Sergeant Griffiths ground the legs of his chair on the flagstone floor as he stood up, letting out a screech that made Aunt Maude wince visibly. 'I'll be in touch to let you know how old Mered's doing. They've taken him to Bronglais for now. Hopefully he'll make a full recovery.'

With a nod of the head and a curt 'Maude, Louis', the old policeman turned and left.

'Did I say something wrong?' Phoebe asked once she was sure Sergeant Griffiths couldn't overhear her.

'Not at all, Phoebe dear.' Aunt Maude reached out and patted her on the arm, which didn't really help.

'Eifion Griffiths has always been a bit of a strange fellow,' Uncle Louis said, wiping the foam of his finished pint from his lips with the back of his hand. 'Even when he was a boy, long before he joined the police. Thought he'd retired, mind.'

'He did. Then they brought him back part-time, remember. Community policing or something like that.' Aunt Maude pushed her empty wine glass to the middle of the table and reached down for the shopping bag at her feet. 'Now we really should be getting back. I've supper to cook and the day's already gone.'

'You've caused quite a stir, Phoebe,' Uncle Louis said as they walked through the forest back towards the house. Aunt Maude was striding ahead as if she'd left the oven on, and hadn't said a word since they'd stepped out of the pub.

'I didn't really do anything.'

'I'll let you in on a little secret. Sometimes the real skill is just being in the right place at the right time. It's served me well enough down the years.'

'What do you mean?'

'Well.' Uncle Louis slowed his pace, as if the act of thinking interfered with his ability to walk. 'Take my first book for instance.'

'*The Patience of Bees*? I thought it was your only book?'

'Yes, of course.' Uncle Louis stopped in his tracks, a moment-ary look of puzzlement crossing his face, swiftly replaced with his usual smile. 'But it's been republished many times. There's been two anniversary editions, the BBC and ITV adaptations, and of course that rather unfortunate film the Americans tried to make of it. Over the years it's earned me my living, pretty much. And the point is I only managed to get it published because I was in the right place at the right time.'

Phoebe wasn't sure what to make of that. It seemed very unlikely.

'The old farmer. Mr Ellis. Why did he call me Gwen Bach? What does that mean?'

'Gwen Bach? It means little Gwen. The Welsh use the term bach like you'd say love or . . . I don't know . . . hen?'

'I know what it means. Why'd he say it though? My name's not Gwen and I've never met him before.'

'Didn't Angharad say?'

'No, she didn't. She said you'd know.'

Uncle Louis frowned. They were still standing on the path, deep in the woods. The onset of evening had cast everything in deep shadows and a breeze blew up out of nowhere, shaking the pine trees gently.

'Well, I guess you'll hear about it soon enough. Might as well be from me. Ellis Nant Caws, Meredith Ellis to give him his proper name. He had three children before his wife died. Ceredig, Tegwin and Gwen. Ceredig went to London in the early seventies. Worked as a roadie with some band. He died in a car crash up near Cambridge. Terrible business.' Uncle Louis paused as if he'd forgotten what he was talking about. Or maybe a memory had caught him off guard.

'What about the others?' Phoebe prompted. Something she'd learned to do when her father's rambling explanations had stalled in the same way.

'Oh, right. Yes. Well. There's Tegwin, who works Nant Caws Farm with his father. Always been a bit of an odd one, him. He must be what? Almost fifty now? But he never married. Hardly socialises at all, really. He's a bit simple, but harmless enough.' Uncle Louis stopped talking, his gaze focused on something far off, or lost in some long-forgotten memory.

'And Gwen?'

'Oh yes, of course. Gwen. Gwen was a bit of a tearaway, you see. She hooked up with the singer in the band her big brother worked with. Problem was he was English. Meredith couldn't bear that, his only daughter with an Englishman. Especially after what happened to his oldest son. So he tried to stop her. Didn't work of course. They moved into a cottage in the woods here, the singer and her. She was going to have his baby. Then he went off on tour with the band, and when he came back she'd upped and disappeared.'

'Disappeared? Where did she go?'

'Well, that's the thing, Phoebe. Nobody knows. She was never seen again.'

'When did all this happen?'

Uncle Louis puffed out his cheeks. 'Now you're asking, it'd be ten, twelve years ago? More maybe. Maude would know better. She's good with dates and stuff like that.'

'So what's any of it got to do with me?'

'Well, like I said, I didn't really know Gwen. Not well. I was good friends with Ceredig, back when we were both lads, but Gwen was a lot younger. More of an age with your mother, I guess. She'd come visit from time to time, and Maude got quite pally with her before she ran away. But I was travelling all over the place doing publicity work for *Bees*, you know? I'd not really thought of her in a while, but to be honest you do look a bit like her. Like she did when she was a girl.'

'But that's crazy. She'd be, like forty now or something? Same as Mum.' Except that Mum's dead. The unsaid words brought a lump to Phoebe's throat and she realised that for most of the day she hadn't thought about her parents at all. Too much else going on.

'It's OK to cry, you know, Pheobe.' Uncle Louis put his hand on her shoulder and for an instant she saw her mother's feature's in his face. Her concern in those gently smiling eyes. It was almost too much to bear.

'Feebs,' she said, finding the ground at her feet suddenly very interesting.

'What?'

'Feebs. No-one calls me Phoebe. Not even Mum and Dad unless they're annoyed with me. All my friends call me Feebs.'

Uncle Louis took his hand off her shoulder, slipped it around her arm like a gentleman out promenading with his lady. 'Well then, Feebs, We'd better get a move on or your Aunt Maude's going to start shouting at us.'

19

2023

Phoebe always used to snigger at the road sign for the little village of Pant-y-Crug. In Welsh, it was purely descriptive, a reference to the heather growing on the nearby hills, but pronouncing it as English brought a smile to her face even in those dark days after her parents had died. Even now, she can feel the muscles tighten around her eyes as she sees it again.

The village has changed almost out of recognition in the years since she first passed through it. A ribbon development on the road east out of Aberystwyth, modern houses line the street, each set back from the road in what once were green fields but have now been tamed into small gardens, or more often than not, gravelled over for parking off the road.

It takes her a while to find the house she's looking for, an old farmworker's cottage set a little back and with actual plants growing around it. Phoebe pulls off the road as far as she dares, but in the time it takes her to climb out, lock the car and push open the narrow wooden gate, no traffic has come past. Perhaps it's safe enough.

There is a doorbell, but before she can press it, the door swings open. The woman standing in the hallway is a head shorter than her, solidly built. She has pulled back her grey-streaked hair so tightly that it seems to stretch the skin of her face, narrowing her eyes slightly, the effect accentuated by the thick spectacles she wears. The look she gives Phoebe isn't unfriendly, but neither is it warm.

'Mrs Tudor?' Phoebe asks, and with those two words the woman changes completely. Her expression crumples into sadness, the slightest shake of her head as if denying it might make the thing to have never happened.

'You must be Phoebe.' Her accent is broad, local. 'Come in, dear. Please.'

Mrs Tudor steps back, sweeps an arm in the direction of the rear of the tiny house. It takes only a few steps for Phoebe to find herself in a warm living room, cluttered with things collected over a lifetime. Although a lifetime spent not travelling much further than the county boundary.

'I'm so sorry . . .' they both manage to say at exactly the same time. It raises a little smile on Mrs Tudor's face, her cheeks dimpling. Phoebe takes the opportunity to get her own apology in again.

'I'm sorry you had to be the one to find her. And thank you, for dealing with it all.'

Mrs Tudor's face turns sombre again. 'Yes, it's a sad thing indeed. But I've been a nurse or a carer all my working life. Your aunt wasn't my first, probably won't be the last. Would you like a cup of tea?'

Phoebe accepts the offer, even though all she really wants to do is flee this tiny house and this sensible, kind-hearted woman. She has always been this way with strangers, though, and she knows that this is important.

'It was a shock, I'll admit,' Mrs Tudor says once they are both seated and cradling sensible mugs of tea. 'When I left her at four the day before, she seemed fine. Slow getting about the house, but then she'd been that way a while, fair enough. She said she was going to call you.'

'Aye, she did. She always called the night before . . . well.'

Mrs Tudor's eyes go wide as the realisation dawns. 'Oh my dear. I had no idea it was, well, that day. How awful for you. I'm so sorry.'

'It's OK. Bad timing, maybe, but that was a long time ago. A very long time ago.' Phoebe gazes out of the window, through a few scraggly trees to the rolling hills beyond as she gathers her thoughts. 'The hospital said it was painless. She just slipped away in her sleep.'

'She looked peaceful, yes. I thought for a moment she might have been sleeping, but Maude was never one for a lie-in. Five years I've been looking after her, and she's always been up before I get there. Except that day, of course.'

Phoebe nods her understanding, takes a sip of tea to cover the awkwardness. Why did she come here? Well, it wasn't as if she could just ignore the person who had been closest to her aunt in her final days. Her final years.

'She worried about you, you know?' Mrs Tudor says, then does that little shake of her head again. 'Well, to be fair she worried about everyone but herself. But you more than most.'

'How so?' Phoebe feels a twinge of irritation at the thought of being talked about behind her back, but there doesn't seem to be any malice in the carer's voice.

'She thought you were too isolated. Living on your own in the big city. You never talked about any friends, she used to say. Only that one, what was her name? Clare, was it?'

The heat starts on the back of Phoebe's neck, as if someone has turned on a hot lamp behind her. It prickles her scalp and she can feel it in her cheeks like a hot flush coming on. Who is this woman to know so much about her? But then she's not wrong.

'Clare, aye. We separated a while back.' She doesn't add that theirs has been an on-again off-again relationship for over a decade now. 'It's fine though. I'm fine. I like my own company. Always have done. Since . . .' And now she tails off, not really wanting to address since when. Isn't that why she's back in Wales, after all? Why she came here in the first place?

'I'm sure you are,' Mrs Tudor says in a voice that suggests the exact opposite. 'It can be hard, keeping up with people. But it's worth the effort, even if you might not think so at the time.'

Phoebe considers the carer's words as she takes a last sip from her tea and puts the mug down on the table. They echo what Maude told her pretty much every time they talked, as if her aunt is reaching out from beyond the veil and carrying on the conversation. It vexes her only inasmuch as she knows that it's true but also that she prefers the quiet and stillness of being alone with her thoughts. And she has lots of friends anyway. It's just that they're not real. They live in her head, and in the heads of the countless people who have read her books. That's enough, isn't it?

Later, Phoebe sits in her car, stares through the windscreen over a short stretch of pebbly beach and out into Cardigan Bay. Somewhere past the choppy grey water, just beyond the horizon, lies Ireland. She's been there a few times over the years, spent one memorable weekend at a literary festival in Dublin. She'd given a scholarly lecture on the art of ghostwriting, well enough received even if at the time all her knowledge on the subject was second hand.

The before times, she likes to think of them. Back when she was forging a career in academia. When it was still possible to be a lecturer specialising in twentieth-century English literature. When universities still had arts faculties and weren't single-mindedly pursuing foreign students and their deep pockets. When she put herself through the hell of going from Miss MacDonald to Doctor MacDonald, for all the good that had done her.

The meeting with Maude's carer, Mrs Bronwen Tudor, was awkward. The woman had been nice enough, but her directness and candour had unsettled Phoebe. Those same qualities would have endeared her to Aunt Maude, of course. No doubt how she managed to clock up five years looking after the old lady.

Five years. That brings Phoebe up short. Five years, and yet today is the first time they have met. That means it's been more than five years since last she made this trip south, came to Wales to see her aunt. Sure, they've talked on the phone, every week and sometimes more often than that. And Maude came to Edinburgh, when was it? A couple of years ago? No, longer. Everything happened longer ago than she thinks; three years and change lost to the pandemic. But the point is she's not been back here, a place she once called home, in so many years. And for the life of her she can't think why she's stayed away.

Perhaps it's as Mrs Tudor says, as Maude said, she is at ease with her loneliness. And it's far easier to be alone in a crowd than somewhere remote like Llancwm. In Edinburgh she knows people, has friends even, but she doesn't have to interact with them if she doesn't want to. She can hide away in her comfortable tenement flat, write those books that will go out under another woman's name. Never her own; she couldn't cope with that kind of fame. Phoebe knows how lucky she is to have found that niche, to be able to exist that way, even as she knows how self-destructive it really is.

She's driven to this spot on the coast to give her mind a chance to settle after her meeting with the carer. Quite how talking to Mrs Tudor has upset her more than seeing Maude's dead body, talking to the solicitor and making arrangements with the funeral director she's not sure. Perhaps because the carer is the last living link with the past. Or maybe because what she told Phoebe was true.

Nestling in the little space designed for it, her phone gives a single chime. A text from the funeral director, as it happens. Details of the resomation of Aunt Maude's body at a place in the Midlands. Phoebe doesn't need to attend, doesn't much fancy the trip, but it reminds her that there is a mobile signal here above the beach, unlike back at Pant Melyn. She hefts the phone in one hand, the other resting on the steering wheel as she stares unseeing out to sea. There are other things she needs to do, other people she needs to talk to. One perhaps more difficult than the rest, which is maybe why she's been putting it off.

Her mind drifts back to that festival in Dublin as she sifts through the contacts list for a number she should really have on speed dial. That was when she first met Clare, now she thinks about it. Although they didn't get together until a couple of years later. Had she known then? Had either of them?

The dial tone makes her jump, coming through the car's audio system rather than the handset. Phoebe had thought her thumb only hovered over the dial icon, but clearly she had tapped it. Well, she had to break the news eventually. Clare had been fond of Maude, after all. It rings three times, four, and she's preparing herself to leave a short message when the tone clicks off and a voice replaces it.

'This is Clare Shaughnessy's phone.'

Phoebe is about to ask who's speaking. Not Clare, but some other woman whose voice she doesn't recognise. Before she can get a word in, the woman continues, laughing as she does. Almost breathless as if she's run hard to answer the call.

'Clare can't speak right now as she's got her mouth full. Might be a while yet. Call back in an hour when we're done with each other.'

The line goes dead before Phoebe can react. She stares at the handset, its screen blank save for the dark reflection of her face in the glass. Part of her is asking what the hell that was, but another part knows all too well. This is presumably why Clare left the message on her phone at home, the reason she thought there was no future in their relationship. She's found someone else.

For a moment Phoebe wonders who this mystery woman is, but the curiosity fades with surprising quickness. There's a little sadness in knowing that part of her life is over now, but it's lost in the much greater sadness of Aunt Maude's death. Perhaps it's time to let things end, move on and see what happens next.

Slipping the phone back into its cubbyhole, she pulls on her seatbelt, starts the car and sets off for Pant Melyn once more.

20

1985

'We're going to check on the bees this morning.'

Phoebe looked up from her muesli, healthy bran floating like dead insects in a sea of insipid milk. Aunt Maude sat at the head of the table, bowl already licked clean, coffee mug clasped in her weathered hands. It was one of the daily rituals Phoebe was coming to dread, the breakfast planning session. Or not so much planning as being told what she was going to do. She had planned to slip away to the woods again, wait at the bridge in the hope that Gwyneth would come, even though it was weeks since she had last seen the girl.

'Do I have to?' she asked.

'And did you have something else pressing that you needed to do?' Aunt Maude fixed her with a stare, one grey eyebrow arched high. 'Sitting in your room and moping? Really, Phoebe dear. You need to get out in the fresh air, exercise a bit. It would do wonders for your mental state.'

Phoebe withered under that stare. Nothing her aunt said was untrue, but the thought of going outside, being with adults rather than people her own age, was overwhelming.

'Did you speak to Mrs Dalgliesh yet? About Jen coming to stay?' she asked, a half-hope that it might be distraction enough to forestall the day's planned activities. Aunt Maude had gone very quiet on the subject since first broaching it on their way to the village. That had been a week ago, and surely term would be over soon.

'I'll give her a call this afternoon. Once we've checked the bees.'

So much for that idea. Bringing the subject up had reminded Phoebe that she'd not spoken to her best friend all week either, and she felt a pang of guilt at that.

'I need to get going.' Uncle Louis emerged from the book he had been reading. Phoebe was pleased to see that he hadn't touched his breakfast either. It might be healthy, but it tasted like wood shavings soaked in cat pee.

'Going?' she asked. 'Where?'

'Aberystwyth, Feebs. I have to give a lecture to the writing school. Then I was going to spend some time in the library researching.'

'Can I come?' Phoebe looked first at Uncle Louis, then at Aunt Maude.

'Why on earth would you want to do that?' the old lady asked.

'Well, you know how you told me the story? About the old man's daughter, Gwen?'

Uncle Louis raised a puzzled eyebrow. 'Yes. What of it?'

'Well, I've been thinking. Since there's not a lot to do here and I'm missing school, right?'

Aunt Maude made a strange noise in the back of her throat that Phoebe took as disagreement. She knew well enough that the old lady would find things to fill her time if she had the chance.

'So I thought, what if I had a project, like? Something I could research and write up, like a journal or something. That's something me an' Jen talked about, being journalists.'

Uncle Louis's eyebrow raised another notch, but neither he nor Aunt Maude said anything. Perhaps it was surprise at seeing Phoebe even a little bit excited; she was all too aware she'd not been a ray of sunshine these past weeks. With good reason, of course.

'An' I reckoned I could look at that story. About what happened to Gwen Ellis. Only, I'd need to search through old newspapers and stuff. You do that at the library, don't you?'

A silence hung over the kitchen for long seconds after she had finished her suggestion. Phoebe looked from her uncle to her aunt and back again, aware that they were both staring at each other.

'It's . . .' Uncle Louis said, but didn't finish.

'Something to think about,' Aunt Maude added. 'It's good to have a project to work on, but . . .' and she seemed unable to put words to the objection Phoebe knew she had. Perhaps it was just that any project not involving gardens and weeding was beyond her.

'Please?' she tried, but she could see it wasn't going to work.

'Another time, Feebs.' Uncle Louis stood up, grabbed his leather satchel from the windowsill and headed for the door. 'Richard said he'd give me a lift, but he won't hang around at the end of the drive for ever.'

Phoebe was so stunned by the swiftness of his departure, she hardly wondered who Richard might be. In moments she heard the front door close and the sound of hurried footsteps across the gravel outside. And as they faded into the background noise, so her frustration grew.

'Why can't I ever do anything nice?' she asked, without bothering to look up from her horrid muesli.

'Whatever do you mean, Phoebe dear?'

'It's like, I'm stuck here in this horrible old house with nothing to do, and all my friends are hundreds of miles away. There's no telly, just loads of boring old books and an endless list of chores. Dig up these weeds, Phoebe. Clean these pots, Phoebe. Eat your gruel, Phoebe. I'm sick of it.'

She lashed out, anger boiling up from nowhere, undirected and violent. With a sweep of both hands, she knocked her unwanted muesli bowl over, scattering soggy oats, raisins and tepid milk all across the table. To her credit, Aunt Maude barely flinched at the tantrum, which only made it worse.

'Why are you like this?' Phoebe found herself screaming, the rage unstoppable now that it had started. She wanted to break things, but even the upturned bowl hadn't cracked.

'Phoebe dear,' Aunt Maude began, but Phoebe wasn't going to be argued out of this.

'I hate you. Both of you. I hate your stupid gardening and wandering around with no clothes on and not going in the study and . . . and I want to watch telly. I want to hang out with Jen and Char and all my other friends. I want . . .' And all of sudden, as quickly as it had exploded, her anger was gone. 'I want my mum and dad back.'

The words hung in the air, impossible to retract. She covered her face with her hands, elbows on the table as the sobs shook her. And then Phoebe felt a gentle arm across her shoulders pull her into the kind of embrace she couldn't remember either of her parents ever giving her. She made to pull away, the memory of her anger still fresh, but in that same moment it all seemed so pointless. The fight fled from her, leaving only lethargy in its place.

'It's OK, Phoebe dear. Perfectly understandable you should be angry. You never asked for any of this.' Aunt Maude gave her a gentle squeeze before releasing her from the hug. 'I'm frankly amazed at how well you've coped so far.'

She had a cloth in one hand, picked up the bowl in the other and started cleaning up the mess all over the table. Milk had seeped through the cracks where the old oak planks had warped apart with age and use, a few puddles collecting on the flagstone floor. Phoebe knew how bad milk could smell if not cleaned up properly, but a rebellious part of her didn't care. At least not until she felt a dampness on her knee.

'Eww. I've got milk all over me.' She pushed back her chair and stood up, brushing ineffectively at the damp patch on her thigh. Aunt Maude didn't laugh, but Phoebe could see she wanted to.

114

'Well, you've only yourself to blame for that. And I doubt your other trousers are dry from the wash yet, so you'll just have to put up with it.'

'I . . .' Phoebe started to complain, then realised there really wasn't any point. It was all hopeless, and even getting angry didn't achieve anything. Not that it ever had. Aunt Maude carried on cleaning up the mess she'd made, cleared the table completely and then poured hot water from the kettle over the table, letting it spatter on the floor below.

'Fetch the mop from the laundry, won't you,' she said. 'Your uncle's always spilling milk on this old table. Makes a terrible smell if you don't deal with it straight away. And once we're done with that, we'll have to see about getting you kitted out for the bees.'

At least her aunt wasn't naked this time; that was a relief after the embarrassment of breakfast. Phoebe traipsed along the forest track behind her, weighed down by a heavy canvas bag full of mysterious implements. She had put on the white overalls her aunt had given her so that she wouldn't have to carry them as well, but half a mile from the house, she was beginning to wish that she hadn't. They pinched in uncomfortable places, sagged awkwardly around her knees, and while the day had been pleasantly cool when they had left Pant Melyn, the sun had turned the forest into what felt like a tropical jungle.

'Is it far?' She stopped, wiped sweat from her face with the back of a heavy gloved hand and hefted the bag once more over her shoulder.

'Not if you don't keep stopping, it isn't.' Aunt Maude hadn't even turned. Defeated, Phoebe put her head down and struggled on.

It was far, despite what her aunt had said. And brutally uphill. They broke out of the trees after what felt like a whole morning's trek, then struggled through long, spiky grass and tangles of heather. The sun beat down with evil intent, but at least as they climbed

Phoebe could begin to see the whole valley spreading out. The woods climbed up either side like some cancerous growth, a darker line in the middle marking the river's course. Further up the valley, a few fields were dotted with the tiny white figures of sheep. Looking the other way, Phoebe thought she could make out some of the houses in the village, but it was hard to tell in the haze.

'Come along now, girl. There's no time for dawdling.'

Behind her, Aunt Maude had finally stopped and was standing next to a cluster of small wooden boxes, seemingly abandoned in a gentle hollow in the middle of the moor. As Phoebe struggled up towards them, she heard the buzz of the bees long before she began to see the tiny bodies hovering around the various entrances. She stopped a dozen paces or so away, unease creeping into her stomach like insects. Bees stung. She knew this from painful experience.

'Bring the bag over here, won't you. I need the smoker.' Aunt Maude beckoned Phoebe with an outstretched arm. A couple of bees landed on her bare skin, crawling around, their back ends pulsing up and down as they looked for somewhere to sink their stings. Phoebe tensed, knowing what was coming next, but Aunt Maude ignored them, and the promised venom never came.

'Quickly, girl. I haven't got all day.'

'But . . . I'll get stung.'

'You're not a proper beekeeper until you've been stung at least a dozen times.' Maude's shoulders drooped in theatrical weariness. 'Look. They're fine. These bees are quite friendly. I've had some swarms that would attack anything that came near. Put your hat on and you'll have nothing to worry about.'

Phoebe struggled with the heavy cotton helmet, uncomfortable and sweaty and getting more miserable by the second. Aunt Maude busied herself with something made of shiny metal, pumping away at what looked like bellows until thick white smoke spouted from the top.

'Smoke calms the bees and masks the pheromones given off by the guards.' Maude pumped the bellows a few more times as she spoke, her voice the same as every teacher Phoebe had ever known. She knew about the smoke, of course. She'd seen something on telly or read it in a book. She liked honey, but wasn't so sure she needed to know exactly how it was made.

'There we go. Should be able to have a look inside now.' Maude put the smoker down carefully, then fiddled around with the lid of the hive until it came away. Phoebe kept herself at a distance, even though a part of her was fascinated by the process. There seemed to be an awful lot of bees crawling around everywhere despite the smoke, and she couldn't help noticing her aunt hadn't bothered with gloves.

'Will they not sting you?'

'Oh, one or two maybe, if I'm not careful. They're in a good mood today though. And it looks like we'll have a decent harvest of honey this year. No sign of mites, either.'

Phoebe opened her mouth to ask what her aunt meant, then remembered being told about it in class a while back. 'Is that a problem here?' she asked instead.

Maude fiddled around with the hive some more, putting everything back together again before answering. 'Not so far, fingers crossed. There's not a lot of arable land this far up the valley. No spraying with horrible pesticides. And you can see well enough there's plenty heather.' She stood up and swept her arm around to take in the spreading moorland that surrounded them. A few lazy bees tumbled from her bare skin before catching themselves and flying off.

'That's us done for now, I think.' She gently picked the last of the bees from her, placing them at the front of a hive before gathering all the kit back into its bag.

'Is that it?' Phoebe couldn't believe she'd been dragged all this way, lugging heavy equipment, for so little obvious reward. On the other hand, she'd managed to keep well away from the bees and any chance of getting stung, so that had to be a win.

'For now, yes.' Aunt Maude hoisted the bag onto her shoulder and took one last look at the hives, slowly waking up again. 'I needed to check everything was OK, but I also wanted to introduce you to the bees. It's important that they know who you are, and that you're not a threat. They seem to like you fine.'

Phoebe had already stood up and was backing away from the small clearing. She stopped, listened again to the low hum, saw the growing industry as the tiny creatures headed out onto the moors in search of nectar. 'Umm . . . That's good?'

'Very. Nothing quite so cussed as an angry bee. Now, come along. It'll be lunchtime soon, but first I think we've both earned ourselves a swim.'

Phoebe didn't go for a swim. She managed not to fall in either this time. Instead, she sat on a rock at the edge of the small sandy beach and looked around the forest as Maude cooled off in the water, half expecting Gwyneth to make an appearance. It was only as her aunt was standing naked as a wrinkly infant and drip-drying in the gentle midday breeze that she remembered the strange old man she'd seen on the path not far away.

'You never worry people might stare?' she asked, glancing away from her aunt towards the bushes.

'It's very unlikely, Phoebe. Not many people walk in these woods, certainly not this far from the village. And besides, why would I care? I'm not ashamed of my body.'

Phoebe had been trying not to look, but it wasn't entirely possible. Aunt Maude was old, approaching sixty Phoebe reckoned, and everything had long since given up the struggle with gravity. She wasn't fat, but she sagged. Whether that would put off the Peeping Tom or encourage him was another matter altogether.

'There was someone. Last time I was here. Tall, thin man,

untidy white hair all sticking out, you know? Just along the path a ways.' She pointed in the direction, half expecting him to appear. 'He said he knew my mum, but then it was like he was scared all of a sudden and he ran off.'

If Aunt Maude was concerned by the news, she didn't show it. She gathered up her clothes and began slowly dressing. 'That'd be the day you came home soaked through, would it? The day you spent the morning with your new friend Gwyneth up at the falls?'

Something about the way the old lady spoke gave Phoebe the impression Aunt Maude didn't entirely believe her. That she hadn't seen the girl since then only annoyed her more. 'That's it, aye,' she said, perhaps a bit more forcefully than she'd intended.

'Well, I dare say he had every right to be where he was.' Aunt Maude shook her head and hefted her bag back onto her shoulder.

'Do you know who he is, then?'

Aunt Maude had begun to climb the stone steps away from the beach, but now she stopped, a frown creasing her forehead. 'There's quite a few old folk live in the village. Could have been any of a dozen people from your description. There's plenty would remember your mother from when she was your age. Or it could have been someone in one of the holiday cottages, like your friend Gwyneth.'

Phoebe knew a non-answer when she heard one. Her mum had been adept at them, especially when the subject of her pills came up. It was clear that Aunt Maude did know who the white-haired man was, or at least had a very good idea. It was also clear that she wasn't going to tell Phoebe.

'What if I'm down here swimming and he comes by again? Sees me?' she asked.

'Really, Phoebe dear. Apart from that one time falling in, you've shown no inclination towards swimming at all.' Aunt Maude took another couple of hurried steps, then stopped, let her shoulders slump a little. 'But if you do feel threatened, or watched, or if you see anything when you're out and about that you think is wrong, then do tell me. Or tell your uncle, although I can't promise he'll take you seriously. He rarely takes anything seriously after all.'

'That's true. I sometimes wonder who's the most grown up, him or me.'

'You, by a country mile. I love Louis dearly, but he can be hard work at times. Now come on, let's get back to the house and have some lunch, eh?'

Phoebe followed Aunt Maude through the woods, across the meadow and into the garden, lugging the heavy bag full of bee-keeping equipment with her. It was such a relief to be rid of the burden, and to wash her face in cold water from a tap rather than a river, that by the time she'd cleaned herself up and gone through to the kitchen for lunch, she had almost forgotten about the strange old man entirely.

21

2023

It's raining, of course. That's something Phoebe hasn't missed about Llancwm and the valley, the incessant rain. She lies on her bed and stares at the skylight as the dawn turns it from black to a blurred grey. There are plenty of other bedrooms in the house, but somehow it felt natural to tuck herself away up in the eaves where she had always slept as a girl.

The house creaks gently as it moves and settles, the sounds counterpoint to the fading patter of raindrops on the roof. Snuggled in her blankets, Phoebe is warm and relaxed in the unreal state between waking and dream. For once she isn't sweating, that unpleasant night-time reminder of her age.

Two things drive her from her state of fugue: the slow realisation that she's not going to hear the clunk and clatter of water pipes as her aunt and uncle get up and prepare themselves to face the day, and a pressing need to pee. The tiny bathroom down the steep wooden steps from her bedroom is unchanged, possibly since the first time she ever used it so many years ago now Phoebe doesn't even want to think of it. The tongue and groove wooden panelling needs sanding back and repainting, but at least the shower's clean. There's plenty of hot water too; nobody else to use it.

In the kitchen, the old range cooker gurgles away as it's always done, but there's no pot of porridge on the warming plate. Phoebe slices thick chunks from the loaf of bread she bought in town the day before, slides them into the oven to toast just the way her uncle had done on her first morning in this house. There is butter in the fridge, a selection of home-made jams in the cupboard, coffee from a cafetière with an alarming crack in its side. She sits at the ancient table, nibbling at her breakfast with little appetite. Outside, the rain has given way to broken clouds and the occasional ray of sunshine. It might well turn out to be a lovely day.

There is so much to do, so many things to organise, people to contact, bad news to break. But Phoebe can only sit, stare out the window, sip her coffee. She should be sad, she knows. Part of her is sad, but it's been sad for a very long time so she's used to it now. Here in this kitchen, in this house in the woods in the middle of nowhere, she feels more at peace than she has in far too long. Yes, there's a mountain of paperwork to deal with, even without the added unwelcome news about Nant Caws Farm across the valley, but none of it is really that urgent, is it?

It's only as she is clearing up, putting the untouched jars of jam away that she remembers the other thing about her first breakfast here. The image of her uncle spooning honey into his coffee brings a smile to her face, even as she recalls the truly awful taste of those horrible instant granules. It reminds her of that honey, like nothing she had ever tasted before. Aunt Maude stopped tending the bees herself some years ago, too old to make the journey to the hives on foot and too stubborn to drive up the perfectly good farm track. But as far as Phoebe knows, the hives still exist. Maude said she'd found someone local to look after them, so she'll have to find out who. Are they out in the meadow still, their winter quarters? Or have they already been moved up to the moors on the far side of the valley?

Phoebe hurries through the washing-up, leaves everything to

drain rather than dry it and put it away. She pulls on old walking boots and a borrowed coat. Her coat now, her boots, she supposes. Outside the back door, the air is fresh and clean, steam rising off the plants in the garden and the meadow beyond. She breathes in deeply, fills her lungs.

Aunt Maude is dead.

It is time to go tell the bees.

A single hive sits at the edge of the meadow, as empty of life as the body laid out in the hospital. Phoebe notes the trampled grass and ruts made by some vehicle come to take the rest of the bees away. A quick glance back at the house; should she have locked it? With a shrug, she carries on walking into the forest.

She's glad of the coat and boots as she follows the familiar path down to the river. Fat drops of water fall from the tree canopy far overhead, dislodged by every gust of wind. At ground level, the undergrowth hangs over the path, each inadvertent brush with her legs making her trousers that little bit more soaked. It's not cold though, so she presses on.

The river's roar makes itself known long before she reaches the scar that it cuts through the forest. She pauses only briefly at the spot where she can look down to the waterfall and roiling pool. A shiver runs down her spine at the memories of all that has happened here, and she moves swiftly on.

When she reaches the middle of the wooden bridge, she stops for a moment. The structure isn't as sturdy as once it was, but then it's been standing here for the better part of forty years. Once-clean timbers are furred with moss and lichen, grey with age. The railing gives slightly as she leans against it to stare down at the churning water below. She thinks about waiting, just in case, but she has a task that needs doing before she can indulge such fancies.

The climb up from the river to the edge of the forest reminds her of how unfit she has become. Time was, she roamed these woods all day and scarcely worked up a sweat. It's a relief to step from the humid air beneath the trees and follow the winding path as it cuts a steep zigzag through the heather. She hears the bees a little before she reaches the hives, begins to spot one or two as they forage for nectar, scant this early in the season. And then with a last push she is there.

They're arranged in a semi-circle, as they always were. Five hives rather than the six she remembers, but then one presumably didn't make it through the winter. A small cloud of black buzzing bodies cluster around the entrance to each one, individuals breaking off and away or returning laden. Phoebe watches from a respectful distance for a while, but the bees ignore this intruder in their midst. For all her aunt's attempts to encourage her, she never had much enthusiasm for beekeeping. She knows nothing about these particular hives, either. It's been years since last she was here. Longer still since she felt any closeness to the tiny insects.

When she steps a little closer, a few bees break off from their business and bumble over. Perhaps they think she is Maude, since that is whose coat she's wearing. Phoebe holds her arms out as two, then four, then a dozen bees land on the damp waxed cotton. They walk in tiny circles, back ends twitching before they take off again, return to their individual hives. More come, in ones and twos, tens and twenties. Never enough to be scary, not with the experience she has had working with bees in the past. She says nothing; they'd not understand her if she did. It's enough that she has come here. They will understand.

It takes maybe half an hour. Phoebe couldn't say how she knows the bees are done, that they have taken the message and will deal with it in their own way. All she feels is a release from a bond she hadn't known was holding her until it is gone. A nod of the head, and then she turns away, retraces her steps down the hill.

22

1985

Llancwm looked somehow different as Phoebe stepped out of the forest and onto the road. She had finally managed to persuade Aunt Maude to take her shopping in Aberystwyth, and the small backpack she had bought felt good slung over her shoulder. So too did the new pair of jeans and floral-patterned top that were the best Aberystwyth had to offer. Or at least as much as her aunt was prepared to pay for, given that the promised allowance from Mr Stearn had still not materialised.

Phoebe clasped in her hand the shopping list Aunt Maude had entrusted her, determined not to lose it. She'd agreed to run the errand on the hope that she might bump into Gwyneth along the way, but even after waiting at the bridge for half an hour, there had been no sign of the young girl. Perhaps it was as Aunt Maude had suggested the first time, and Gwyneth had merely been staying at one of the holiday cottages. Now she was gone, back to whatever home she had come from. That would be just about Phoebe's luck right now.

Approaching the shop and hotel, she found herself passing the narrow fork in the road and the track that led towards the river. As much out of curiosity as anything, Phoebe wandered down to see where it went. An old stone building, possibly once a mill, stood on a rocky crag directly above the flow, and beyond it, in an area that must surely flood every time it rained, a half a dozen miserable modern semi-detached houses had been built.

If she had thought the cars parked on the main road were old, they had nothing on the wrecks that huddled in a weedy parking area by the houses. Half of them were missing vital things like wheels and windscreens, lending the place the look of a scrap yard. The houses themselves weren't much better. They couldn't have been much more than a decade or so old, but already their harled walls were streaked black and green with mould, their slate roofs speckled with lichen and moss.

'Well, well, well. If it's not the little snail come to see us.'

The voice almost made her jump out of her skin. It was so close, and so unfriendly. Phoebe turned, wondering how it was someone could have crept up on her. The constant noise of the river was the explanation, of course. Not that it made her feel any better, especially when she saw who it was.

'Fancy seeing you down here. Not often the posh folk come this way.'

It was the same twins she had seen in Aberystwyth the day she had arrived. For a moment Phoebe wondered whether they'd been following her all this time, waiting for the right moment to . . . what? Rational thought caught up with her fear and surprise. This was where they lived, of course. What were the chances of that?

'Who are you?' Phoebe finally found the voice to ask.

'Who are we?' the first twin looked at the other and they both broke into broad grins. It wasn't an improvement. They stared at each other for a long while, as if they too weren't sure of their identities. Then the first one turned back to Phoebe.

'Well, where are our manners? Axe and Brue Thomas, at your service. And you would be old Lou Beard's niece, right?'

'I . . . yes. Phoebe MacDonald. How did you know?'

'Heard you saved old Mered Nant Caws's life,' one of them said. Phoebe guessed it was Axe, although she had no real way of knowing.

'Probably better if you'd just let the old bastard die,' the other one added. 'Grumpy old fuck always chasing us off his land.'

'Still, you can give us the kiss of life any time you want, eh?'

'Kiss of life. That's good.'

The two of them looked at each other again, then started to bray with laughter. Phoebe was reminded of the donkey sanctuary near Ceres her class had visited on a school trip.

'I have to go,' she said, sidestepping the twins. For a moment she thought they might try to stop her, but they let her pass.

'Come visit us any time, cariad. You've never had it proper til you've done it with twins.'

She felt the blush creeping up her neck as she hurried away, equal parts scared and angered. Behind her the twins carried on laughing, the sound echoing off the rock sides of the valley like some poor animal in pain. She could hear them all the way up past the chapel and along the street to the shop, the whole reason for her being in the village to start with. Why had she gone down there and not concentrated on the task at hand?

Phoebe didn't begin to feel safe until she was inside the shop and heard the squeaky click of the door as it closed behind her. She hadn't dared look back to see if the twins were following, and neither had she wanted to run, letting them know how much they had frightened her. It had taken all of her willpower to walk away, briskly but not too fast, expecting at any moment to hear the sound of running feet behind her.

'Is everything all right, dear? You look a little flushed.'

Phoebe turned towards the counter at the far end of the shop. The shopkeeper had appeared from the room beyond, and for a moment Phoebe could only stare. She couldn't remember the woman's name. Then it came to her. Mrs Griffiths, Bethan. Her husband, Tom, ran the hotel and pub next door. That was it.

'I'm fine, thank you, Mrs Griffiths.' She tugged her rucksack off her shoulder and searched through the pockets for the shopping list Aunt Maude had given her, before remembering it was still clasped in her sweaty palm. 'Just had a run-in with an unpleasant pair of twins. Down by the river there.'

A scowl marred Mrs Griffiths' face, and she shook it away with little success. 'The Thomas boys? Diw diw. You'd best keep away from them. Nothing but trouble since the day they were born, those two.'

Phoebe shrugged her agreement. 'I wasn't looking for them. Just took a wrong turn, got myself a bit lost.'

'You poor thing. It's easy done when you're new to a place. Give it a few weeks and you'll know where everything is. You're safe enough on the main road here, and up to the chapel of course. But keep away from the old mill and the council houses.'

'Are they really that bad? I mean, it's damp and gloomy down there, can't be the nicest place to live, but . . .' Phoebe trailed off, unsure what she was saying and why she was saying it.

'It's not their fault, really. Well, not all of it. See, those houses were built for farmworkers, foresters and the like, but folk with jobs, a bit of money, they find a place closer to town these days. So the council put the difficult tenants in them, see? Out of sight, out of mind. At least it is if you're sitting in an office in Aberystwyth or Cardigan.' Mrs Griffiths leaned over the counter and plucked the list out of Phoebe's fingers as she carried on. 'We, on the other hand, can't help but see them every day.'

'Have you heard anything about old Mr Ellis?' Phoebe asked, anxious to change the subject. She wasn't sure she liked where it was going.

'He's still in Bronglais,' Mrs Griffith said as she stepped out from behind the counter and set off down the narrow aisle. Phoebe followed, and held out her arms as the woman handed her items from the list, one by one.

'Bron—?'

'Bronglais Hospital. In Aberystwyth. There was talk they were going to transfer him to Cardiff, but I doubt old Mered Ellis has ever set foot outside of Ceredigion in his life. The shock would likely kill him.'

Phoebe only half understood what Mrs Griffiths was saying, but her accent was soothing, and she was a friendly face after the twins.

'Is he going to be OK?' she asked.

'Well now. He must be eighty, if he's a day. Lives up at Nant Caws Farm in a house that's not changed much since it was built two hundred years ago. Him and his boy, Tegwin? Well, I say boy, but the lad must be near fifty now. The two of them are as bad as each other. It's a surprise either's lived as long as they have. But he's a tough old bird, is Meredith Ellis. If anyone can survive a heart attack, it's him.'

Mrs Griffiths took a packet of biscuits off the shelf, looked at it, then put it back again, fetched another from further along before handing it to Phoebe.

'That was a good thing that you did. Helping him. Saving him. There's many in this village would have pretended they'd not seen him fall, or taken their time coming to his aid. But you? You didn't stop to think, you just acted. And you knew what to do.'

'We did first aid at school. CPR, that sort of thing. And I was in the Guides, too.' Phoebe followed Mrs Griffiths back to the counter, and watched as everything was run through an elderly till. Aunt Maude had given her what had seemed like far too much money, but it was barely enough. She packed her goods into her rucksack as carefully as she could manage for the long walk back to Pant Melyn.

'There's a difference in knowing how to do a thing and doing it when the time comes.' Mrs Griffiths reached for a jar on a high shelf behind her, unscrewed the wide plastic lid and poured a measure of sweets into the weighing scales on the counter by the till. Her concentration was total as she expertly transferred the sweets to a paper bag and with a deft flick and twist sealed it closed. A smile, a conspiratorial wink, and she handed it over. 'It's not much, but you'll never get much from a Cardi.'

Phoebe stared at the shopkeeper, uncomprehending. Mrs Griffiths laughed.

'It's a joke, pet. Cardiganshire folk are notoriously careful with their money. Make Scotsmen look positively generous.' There was a pause while her words made their way from her mouth to her brain, then the shopkeeper's face turned white. 'Oh, I'm sorry, dear. That was very insensitive of me.'

It was Phoebe's turn to laugh, although it might have sounded a little manic. Mrs Griffiths smiled back, so at least the peace was restored. As she turned to leave, the shopkeeper spoke once more.

'Take care, then, Phoebe. And we'll see you at the weekend.'

Puzzled, Phoebe looked back. 'The weekend? What's happening at the weekend?'

'What's happening at the weekend? Why, only the Llancwm Show. Did your uncle not mention it?'

Phoebe had to admit that no, Uncle Louis hadn't. And neither had Aunt Maude. 'Unless they said something and I wasn't paying attention,' she added.

Mrs Griffiths shrugged. 'Well, I'll give them a call and remind them. Won't be the same without our local celebrity giving out the prizes.'

Phoebe turned to leave, then remembered the thing she'd been meaning to ask the shopkeeper. 'Mrs Griffiths, do you know a girl in the village by the name of Gwyneth? About my age, maybe a little shorter than me but not much. Likes to run around in her bare feet?'

A look of puzzlement etched itself across the shopkeeper's face, and for a moment she simply stared into the middle distance. Finally she shook whatever thought was occupying her head away.

'Can't say as I do, dear. There's people stay in the holiday cottages all summer long, but nobody your age lives in the village at the moment.'

'And she's not come in here these past weeks?' Phoebe gestured at the branded ice-cream refrigerator that didn't actually contain any branded ice creams.

'Well now, we have all sorts through here. You'd be surprised how busy it can get for a quiet backwater in the middle of nowhere.' Mrs Griffiths paused a moment, then shook her head again. 'But I can't think of anyone matching your description. Although it does remind me of someone, I guess.'

'It does? Who?'

A dark shadow seemed to pass over the shopkeeper's features then, and it took her a while to say what Phoebe had thought she might.

'Your mother, Siân. She was always running about the woods in bare feet when she was a girl. Used to drive your grandparents mad.'

'I never met my grandparents,' Phoebe said. They had both died before she was born, her grandmother first and her grandfather a few months later. That was pretty much all she'd ever known about them. They'd been fairly old when her mum came along unexpectedly, Uncle Louis already well into his teens by then. Even so, it surprised her that she'd never tried to find out more. Something to ask her uncle when she got home.

'Oh, you poor thing. I'm so sorry.' Mrs Griffiths clutched a theatrical hand to her bosom, but offered no more free sweets.

'It's OK, I think. Hard to feel sad about someone you never knew.' Phoebe hefted her backpack again, nodded a final thanks to the shopkeeper and stepped outside. Pausing a moment to check for any sign of the twins, she set off on the walk back to Pant Melyn.

She'd not really thought about it until Mrs Griffiths had mentioned her mother, but it struck her then that Siân Beard had grown up in this village. Run around barefoot in the same woods Phoebe now trod, apparently. True, she'd escaped as soon as she possibly could, but she'd lived here, gone to school in Aberystwyth, had a life in this remote corner of Wales. So why had she not sounded like all these people living in Llancwm?

Phoebe stopped in her tracks, staring at nothing. For a terrible moment she couldn't remember the sound of her mother's voice. And she would never hear it again either. She was gone, and for all that she might have been hiding that fact in a locked box at the back of her mind, there was no escaping it. Her mum and dad. Gone.

'We do love you, Feebs. Always will. Even when you think we don't, we still love you.'

Was it a conversation remembered, or only her mind playing tricks on her. The words formed perfectly, fluently, in her mind, and with them an image of her mother leaning against the island in the kitchen. Back home in Scotland. A silly argument, words hurled in anger, tweenie rage at something long forgotten. And all the while her mother's patient, sad smile. That accent, too. It was there when Phoebe looked for it. A soft lilt, the occasional unexpected inflection. Her mum had suppressed it, trained it out of her voice, but a part of this valley had always stayed with her.

Slowly, the forest began to reassert itself on her. Phoebe saw now that she had reached out and placed her hand on an ancient pine tree close to the path, taking its strength and support when she needed it most. Had her mother once touched this tree? Had she trod this very same path? Perhaps she was here even now, somewhere. A ghost returned to the place where she had first breathed life.

Phoebe wondered at that. She didn't believe in ghosts, certainly wasn't frightened of them. But the thought was oddly comforting, of her mother's spirit roaming the trees, freed from the unexplained sadness that had blighted her last few years. It gave her strength, like the tree she leaned upon. She could do this. She could cope.

Shouldering her rucksack once more, Phoebe wiped away the tears she hadn't until then realised she was weeping, and set off back up the valley towards Pant Melyn.

23

2023

Llancwm hasn't changed in all the years since she first arrived here. At least that's what Phoebe thinks as she parks outside the hotel. The roller doors are still wide open on the workshop across the road, a car up on the ramp but no sign of anyone working on it. The elderly sheepdog on a chain at the entrance is probably not the same one she saw in 1985, but it might be a distant relative. Further up the road to nowhere, the chapel looks even more like a ruin, which doesn't bode well for why she is here.

The hotel has had a lick of paint sometime in the past, but the creamy off-white colour is already streaked with green and grey. Nothing can survive long in the oppressive dampness. The shop is still there, bags of coal and a few sorry vegetables stacked outside under a striped awning tattered by years of wind and rain. But when she approaches, Phoebe sees a closed sign in the door. Is it lunchtime? She checks her watch, shrugs. It can't be easy running a business like that in this age of supermarket deliveries and internet shopping. The tourist season's barely started either, so perhaps it makes sense.

Inside the hotel, the smell of the reception area brings back instant memories both good and bad. How many times has she drunk in the bar here? How many meals has she eaten? Lost in memories, she doesn't immediately see the woman who comes from the back to stand behind the reception desk.

'Can I help you?'

For a moment Phoebe is unable to speak. Had she been expecting to see Tom Griffiths or his wife, Bethan? They must have retired years ago, surely. No children, she remembers now, although this woman would be about the right age. Younger than Phoebe by maybe a decade or so, she has a kind face, just starting to show a few lines around the eyes.

'I hope so,' she says eventually. 'I used to live here, a long time ago. Not here,' she adds as if the clarification were necessary. 'Up at Pant Melyn, in the woods. I'm trying to arrange—'

'Oh, you must be Maude's niece. Phoebe, isn't it? How nice to meet you. I'm Cerys.' The woman holds a hand out, all smiles and friendliness until the reason for the visit begins to sink in. 'I am so sorry to hear about her passing. Such a wonderful old lady. Never afraid to speak her own mind.'

'That sounds about right. Did you know her well?'

'Perhaps not well, no. Rhodry and me, we only took over this place a few years back, see? But Maude used to come in once a week for a drink and a chat. And I don't think she ever missed the pub quiz. Place won't feel the same without her.'

'Well, I'm trying to sort out her affairs. She wanted a funeral in the chapel, and there'll need to be a wake afterwards. I was wondering if that was something you'd be able to do here.'

'Can't do much about the funeral, you'll have to talk to one of the elders about that. I can give you the number right enough.' Cerys reaches for a pad on the reception desk, begins to write something down. 'As to the wake, well, I think we could rustle up something to send the old girl off.'

'I don't know when it'll be yet.' Phoebe takes the paper with the number, a name above it. 'I'll need to speak to them first. And I've got to find somewhere with a resomator, too. Aberystwyth doesn't quite reach to those technological heights yet.'

'Reso . . .? Oh, yes. The water-burial thing. I remember her going on about that. Not sure what to make of it, really.'

'It's meant to be more environmentally friendly than cremation. I don't think she fancied being buried in the old graveyard either. She wants to be up on the moor with Uncle Louis and her bees.'

'The bees, of course. She did love her bees. My Rhodry has been looking after them for her since we first came to the village. He used to keep them when we lived near Merthyr, but there's not much space for hives out back.' Cerys hooks a thumb over her shoulder towards the narrow space hacked out of the steep mountainside where the hotel had been built. Just enough room to stack the bins and pretend it's a beer garden.

'I did wonder who'd taken them up to the moor. They seemed happy enough when I went to see them.'

'Shame about the one hive not making it through the winter. Rhodry said he'd clean it up and see about finding another swarm to use it. I don't really understand all the details of it, but the honey's nice.'

'My thoughts exactly.' Phoebe reaches for one of the cards laid out neatly on the reception desk. 'This is the hotel number, I take it? I'll give you a call as soon as I've got some more idea as to what's happening.'

'You do that.'

24

1985

It might have been sunny, but the heavy rain of the previous few days meant Phoebe was very grateful for the old pair of rubber boots Aunt Maude had found for her. Her trainers were getting worn from traipsing through the woods, but at least those paths weren't ankle-deep in mud. And worse.

'What are we even doing here?' she asked, probably for the twentieth time and not loud enough for anyone to hear. Even so, her aunt turned, her face not so much scowling as a warning.

'Fine,' Phoebe grumbled and shoved her hands deep into her jacket pockets. It was a new jacket, and warm with it, the solid weight of her Walkman reassuring. At least she'd be able to listen to her one tape over again if this outing turned out to be as dull as she thought it would.

The Llancwm Agricultural Show and Livestock Market was, according to Uncle Louis, the highlight of the village social calendar. At least, that was what he'd said after she'd asked him about it. Before that, it might as well not have existed, and she suspected they'd have missed it entirely had it not been for the phone call from Bethan Griffiths the evening after her visit to the shop.

Phoebe would much rather have been anywhere else, but then

that was true of her entire existence right now. Everything here was so screamingly dull. What she wouldn't have given for an afternoon in Dundee going round the shops with Jen and Charlotte. Even Cupar was a hive of activity compared to this dump. You could have fitted the entire thing into one of the Fife Show rings.

It had come as some surprise to Phoebe to find that Llancwm has such a thing as a livestock market at all. Tucked away at the end of the village, past the chapel and the last few desperate houses, it was perhaps the only piece of flat land for miles around. Old slate stone walls made up pens, the gates between them wooden and easily twice as old as she was. Maybe even twice as old as the farmers leaning on them and staring at the sheep, and not a one of them would have to pay their own bus fare. Off to one side, a small marquee housed some kind of bring-and-buy sale. There was even a bouncy castle, although as yet Phoebe had seen no children about, and the thing looked as flaccid as a Christmas satsuma.

The focus of the day's activities seemed to be the livestock show. Phoebe looked around the showground, not something that took a long time or much effort, and could only see sheep. Plus the occasional mangy-looking sheepdog, of course. She liked dogs in the main, but these all looked hungry, filthy and fierce. They slunk around as if expecting to be beaten at any moment, or waiting for the command to round up any errant sheep.

'Reckon Ellis Nant Caws will take the prize ram again this year?'

Phoebe stopped her trudging and looked around to see who had spoken. For a start, it had been in English rather than Welsh, and she was surprised at the mention of the old farmer. Surely he'd be still in hospital, or at the very least at home with his feet up after what had happened in the village shop. He couldn't really be out here showing sheep just a few weeks after having a heart attack, could he?

'Doesn't he always, mind?'

'Well, at least his old man won't be judging this year. Heard they've not let him out of Bronglais yet.'

That would explain it. Phoebe turned away from the conversation, shrugging into her jacket in an attempt not to be noticed as she headed over to the marquee. The last thing she wanted was to be recognised by anyone, called out on what she'd done to help the old farmer. She would have been far happier back at Pant Melyn, hidden away in her room with some books for company. The thought brought her up short, forced a little bark of laughter out of her. Who was she? What had she become, and in such a short time? She needed to get away from this place, back to civilisation. But how?

'Well, if it isn't the lifesaver herself. Hello there, little snail.'

Phoebe froze, but it was too late. Of all the people who might recognise her, these two were the worst. Axe and Brue Thomas, the twins. Now that she'd met them a couple of times, she could start to see small differences between them, although she wouldn't have wanted to guess which was Axe and which was Brue. They dressed identically and both had the same permanent sneer, as if everything in the world was a disappointment to them, rather than the other way around.

'You here for the sheep?' She jerked her head in the direction of the pens.

'Nah. Lookin' for your uncle.'

Phoebe stifled the smirk that wanted to plaster itself all over her face as the twins entirely failed to notice how she had insulted them. 'What you want him for?'

'It's not what we want him for, but what he wants from us, see?' One of the twins leaned in close and tapped the side of his nose. Any doubts Phoebe might have had as to what they were talking about vanished as the stench of weed assaulted her.

'Try the bar,' she said, stepping back and waving her hand in front of her face like a fan.

'Good call,' the closest twin said. 'Come on, Brue, let's go get ourselves a drink. Looks like Lou's paying.'

'Rhaid i ti gadw draw oddi wrth y ddau hynny. Maen nhw'n newyddion drwg.'

Phoebe had been so busy watching the twins as they elbowed their way unnecessarily through the meagre crowd that she hadn't noticed someone coming up behind her. She turned and found herself looking at a man's broad, overalled chest. She had to tilt her head back to see his face, so close was he and unusually tall for a Welshman. There was no mistaking who he was, all the same. And although she'd not understood a word he'd said, the way he scowled at the departing twins gave her some idea.

'You're Tegwin, aren't you? Tegwin Ellis? Meredith's son?'

A frown of puzzlement spread across the man's face, making him look even more simple-minded than before. There was something not quite right about him, although Phoebe would have been hard pushed to say exactly what. Apart from the not understanding basic things like social boundaries.

'Your voice is all wrong.' He switched to heavily accented English.

Phoebe recalled the expression on Meredith Ellis's face, the startled way he'd said 'Gwen bach?' before his heart gave out. Like father, like son.

'I'm not Gwen. I'm Phoebe. Phoebe MacDonald, from Scotland. That's why my voice doesn't sound particularly Welsh, aye?' She may have hammed up the accent a bit for emphasis.

The frown slowly eased from Tegwin's face, but it wasn't replaced by any expression of great understanding. What was it Uncle Louis had said? Tegwin was harmless enough, but a bit simple? That was written clearly across the man's face. He'd be in his mid-forties, Phoebe guessed. Older than her dad, but younger than her uncle.

'You like to walk in the woods,' Tegwin said, a statement more than a question. Was he talking about her, or still fixated on his missing sister? Phoebe wasn't sure there was any great distinction in his mind. Or any great mind to make the distinction.

'There's not a lot else to do around these parts.' She waved a hand at the pens, filling up with sheep now. 'Not unless you're a shepherd.'

'Shouldn't walk in the woods alone. It's not safe.'

'If you mean the twins, I don't think they're likely to do anything. I've met their type before: talk big, but they're only wee inside.'

'Not them.' Tegwin reached a hand towards Phoebe. Instinctively, she drew back, but he stopped himself before he actually touched her arm anyway. She could see his fingers flex as some slow inner process worked its way through his mind.

'There are . . . things in the woods.'

'What? You mean the ghosts?' Phoebe remembered the story her uncle had made up. 'Myfanwy's baby?'

Tegwin went stiff at the name. 'Don't make light of them, Gwen bach. They might pretend to be your friend, but they mean you harm. It's not safe to walk the woods alone.'

'I don't . . .' Phoebe started to laugh it off, but there was an intensity in the man's stare that put her on edge. Uncle Louis might think him harmless, but she wasn't so sure. And he'd called her Gwen again, which was creepy. 'You know what? I think I'll go now.'

She backed away a couple of paces, not taking her eyes off the farmer. There was definitely something not right about him. Not exactly menacing, but perhaps unpredictable, like the mangy sheepdogs slinking around. Phoebe couldn't be sure whether they would beg to be stroked or bite any hand that came near them. She got that same vibe from Tegwin Ellis. He watched her go, but didn't say anything and didn't try to stop her. All he did was stare, with that slightly bemused, slightly vacant expression on his face, until finally she turned tail and fled.

★ ★ ★

Unable to go to the bar tent because that was where she knew the twins were, Phoebe was forced to wander the tiny area of market and showground, doing her best to avoid Tegwin Ellis, and in search of some form of distraction until whenever it would be time to go home. Had it been the Fife Show, she'd not have thought twice about leaving. The ground was only a short walk from home, after all. The Fife Show was a lot more interesting than anything Llancwm could hope to offer though. Unless you found small sheep with large horns fascinating.

It was at least a diversion of sorts to watch, as what to her seemed almost identical animals were paraded around the tiny show ring by elderly farmers in suits that probably only saw use this one time a year. Most of the commentary over the tinny tannoy was in Welsh, she thought. Although going by the occasional word she recognised, it could have been English so heavily accented as to make it unintelligible. Eventually, after much toing and froing, a white-haired man in a tweed suit and bowler hat started handing out rosettes. From her vantage point by one of the stone sheep pen walls, Phoebe saw that Tegwin won first prize, and from the reaction of the old farmers standing nearby this came as no great surprise.

As she was staring across the ring, only half taking in the commotion, something on the far side caught Phoebe's attention. At first she couldn't work out what it was, but then she saw it again. Not a face in the crowd so much as the way one person moved. And then she saw the dress flash past a gap in the wall.

'Gwyneth?'

It was a foolish thing to say, since the young girl was too far away to hear, and Phoebe had barely whispered the name anyway. It spurred her into movement all the same. She hurried around the ring, dodging past Tegwin as he led his ram back to wherever it had come from. Close up, the beast was larger than she had thought. Quite fearsome with its ugly, angry face, weirdly piercing eyes and those almost hypnotic curling horns.

142

Beyond the ring, more stone-walled pens filled the space at the edge of the forest, the stench of hundreds of years of sheep filling the air with a miasma so thick she almost choked on it. There were fewer people milling around here, not that the show was exactly overcrowded. Mostly old farmers looking at sheep, discussing sheep with each other or haggling over the price they expected to pay for their sheep. And there, at the forest edge, that same movement that had caught Phoebe's eye in the first place. A flash of light floral dress, a shake of dirty-blonde hair.

'Gwyneth!' This time Phoebe shouted, getting some angry stares from the farmers for her pains. She looked for a route through the pens that would get her to the edge of the woods, but it was like a particularly smelly labyrinth. One that was part-filled with bleating woolly animals too. She could go all the way round, but that would take too long, surely. She'd never catch up with the young girl.

Only, when she looked up to the treeline again, there was no sign of Gwyneth at all.

'What on earth are you doing all the way over here, Phoebe dear?'

Phoebe looked round from where she had been leaning over a low stone wall in search of a path to the woods. Aunt Maude bore down on her like a steamship. Behind the old woman, the Llancwm Agricultural Show and Livestock Market appeared to be coming to an end, if the slow drift of people towards the road was any indication. There were still a few farmers about, mostly loading sheep into ancient stock trailers, but with the obvious exception of the bar tent, the attractions all seemed to be winding down. Even the bouncy castle had almost completely deflated.

'I was looking to see if I could get to the trees,' she said as Aunt Maude picked a careful route through the mounds of slate chippings and fresh droppings that smeared the scrubby grass. A quick glance down at her borrowed wellies confirmed Phoebe's suspicion that in her haste to catch up with Gwyneth she'd not paid nearly as much attention as perhaps she should have.

'Dear me. I knew you weren't keen on coming here, but that's a bit extreme, isn't it? There's no path that way. You have to go back through the village if you want to go home.'

Home. The word choked in Phoebe's throat before she could say anything. Yes, she wanted to go home. But home was in Scotland, not just the other side of the valley. And there was no path back there either.

'She was here. I saw her,' she said, her voice more squeaky than she'd intended.

'Who?' Aunt Maude had arrived at Phoebe's side now, followed her gaze towards the trees. 'Oh, your young friend.'

Phoebe sniffed, not quite sure where the tears had come from. 'Gwyneth,' she said. 'I saw her in the crowd when I was watching the prize-giving. She came this way. I'm sure of it.'

Only, the more she said it, the less certain she was. She'd seen movement, for sure. A familiar shape maybe, the flash of colour that reminded her of Gwyneth's dress. But why would the young girl still be wearing the same dress, weeks later? Staring back at the trees again, Phoebe could see how they moved gently in the breeze, shafts of sunlight flickering in and out of view. Was that what she had seen?

'Come on now. Let's not hang around these smelly pens any longer than we need to.' Aunt Maude held out a hand, and even though part of her hated being treated like a toddler, Phoebe took it, allowed herself to be led back towards the marquee and bar tent. A last look over her shoulder showed nothing but the forest. No Gwyneth at all.

Phoebe walked alongside Aunt Maude as they followed the path through the woods on the way back to Pant Melyn. A little the worse for wear, Uncle Louis was doing the straight-legged walk

Phoebe had seen so often in Cupar on a Saturday night. He wasn't exactly drunk, but neither was he particularly sober. From what she could gather, he was called upon every year to hand out the prizes at the show, being Llancwm's one and only celebrity. And every year he agreed on the understanding that the organisers picked up his tab at the bar. Aunt Maude thought this equal parts funny and exasperating, Phoebe gathered.

'I bumped into Tegwin Ellis today,' she said when a lull in the conversation demanded something to fill it. 'He called me Gwen too, like his dad did. Jabbered away at me in Welsh for a while. Think it was a warning to stay away from those horrible twins. As if I needed one.'

'Axe and Brue Thomas are best avoided, it's true. Not sure they'd do you any real harm, but I'd not give them the chance if it was me.'

'Aye, I get that. Used to be boys like that at school. All mouth when they're in a group, wee fearties when they're on their own. Only twins are never on their own, right?'

Aunt Maude gave her an appraising look. 'You're wise for your age, Phoebe, you know that?'

Phoebe shrugged. 'I miss school,' she said. And it was true, even if she'd never have believed it before.

'I know. We're working on that, your uncle and me. But it's the holidays soon, Phoebe. End of the academic year. It'll be easier to pick things up again in the autumn.'

'So long?' Phoebe kicked out at a tree root, scuffing the dirt with her shoe. 'I'll have missed like a whole year. I'll have so much catching-up to do.'

'Well, it won't be that bad. We'll help you, your uncle and me. And you can start with your little project if you want.'

'Project?' Phoebe's brain took a while to catch up. 'Finding out what happened to Gwen Ellis?'

In the failing light, it was hard to see Aunt Maude's expression, but from the way her posture changed she was obviously none too pleased. She didn't actually put her hands on her hips, but that was the impression she gave.

'Well, maybe that. Or maybe we can find something better for you to research, yes? Something to catch you up with the school year.'

Phoebe started to protest, but she was interrupted by a shout of alarm from behind. She and Aunt Maude both turned to see Uncle Louis staggering to regain his balance, presumably having tripped over the tree root Phoebe had kicked out at moments earlier. He steadied himself by placing a hand on the trunk, shook his head.

'What?' he asked as he noticed their stares.

'Nothing, dear.' Aunt Maude took Phoebe's arm and gently steered her back on course. Once they were a few paces ahead again, she picked up an earlier strand of the conversation, as if the talk of school and summer projects had never happened.

'If you ever get any bother from those twins, let me know. They've been allowed to get away with all sorts for too long now, but they've not had anyone close to their age to bully. Well, apart from Angharad maybe. And she's more than capable of looking after herself.'

'Angharad . . . from the pub?' Phoebe asked, remembering the girl dressed all in black who'd told her that the old farmer hadn't said 'get back' but 'Gwen bach'.

'You'd do well to be careful around Tegwin Ellis, too,' Aunt Maude said, as if she hadn't heard Phoebe's question. 'I don't think he'd mean you any harm, but he's never been right in the head. They say he was a difficult child, didn't come out right or something. That was before I came to the village, so I wouldn't know the whole of it. He keeps to himself, and that's probably for the best.'

Phoebe wasn't sure she quite understood what Aunt Maude

was trying to say, but she didn't want to press the point. They were almost back at Pant Melyn anyway, having stepped out of the trees into a meadow, cooling down now that the sun had slipped past the edge of the hills. Uncle Louis struggled with the gate, humming a merry tune to himself as he sauntered along behind, seemingly oblivious to the thousands upon thousands of tiny midges that swarmed up from the damp grass. They didn't bite so much as get everywhere, in Phoebe's hair, her ears, her nose and eyes. She batted them away as best she could, rushed to the back door and yanked it open, a cloud of them following her as she stepped inside.

'Boots!' Aunt Maude shouted from a distance, before Phoebe could carry on through to the kitchen in her sheep-shit encrusted wellingtons. She shucked them off, wiping at her hair with both hands to try and dislodge the last of her attackers, but she could still feel them crawling over her skin by the time her uncle and aunt stepped inside, seemingly untouched.

'How . . .?' she asked as Aunt Maude carefully removed her own boots and Uncle Louis sat down heavily on the little stool by the door.

'Practice, Phoebe dear.' Aunt Maude ran a hand through her thinning hair, then flicked away the few midges that had penetrated her invisible defences. 'That and learning to live with them. You can always tell summer's finally on its way when the midges appear at dusk.'

'They're horrible.' Phoebe wiped at her lips where a few had managed to push their way into her mouth. She suppressed the urge to spit.

'Nature doing its thing, dear. And they keep the bats well fed.'

Phoebe wasn't sure if that was a good thing or not. She wasn't overly fond of bats either. Before she could say any more, Aunt Maude was shooing her and Uncle Louis through into the kitchen, warm with the scent of something that had been slow-cooking in the oven all day. Her stomach rumbling in hungry anticipation, Phoebe washed her hands and set the table, and by the time her aunt had begun ladling out thick stew and dumplings into wide bowls, she had quite forgotten all the frustrations of the day.

25

2023

Stepping out of the hotel onto the empty road, Phoebe feels somehow lighter. As if gravity has eased, or a great weight has been lifted from her shoulders. It takes her a moment to understand why, and when she does it brings a smile to her face. The simple, welcoming friendliness of Cerys is something she's found in short supply recently. Back home in Edinburgh, she has allowed herself to become immersed in her work, distanced and ever more reclusive. It's why she and Clare argued so often, and maybe why Clare left. Well, one of the reasons she left, certainly. Seems Clare had as much pulling her away as Phoebe pushing her.

Or is that the guilt talking, her deeply ingrained bad thinking that has taken a lifetime to deal with? That she's still dealing with most of the time. Phoebe stops in her tracks. It's been a while now since last she thought about the guilt, let alone felt it. Time was, she blamed herself for her parents' deaths. If she'd been there, not stuck on a late train, she could have saved them. None of this would have happened. Or she might have died with them, overcome by fumes before she even noticed. Burned to a crisp, and three coffins at the funeral rather than two. She'd woken in a cold sweat many a time, the anxiety gnawing at her when she was at her lowest. It had been a constant companion when she'd been writing her PhD. So much so that she almost fell into the same trap as her mother, seeking solace in a pill. Seeking oblivion.

But Phoebe isn't her mother. She never was. True, the loneliness of her life even before the fire, the sense of abandonment, formed her character as much as the events that followed it. Turned her into the recluse, self-reliant to the point of absurdity. Never asking for help, never wanting to be beholden. All these things she knows about herself, has the expensive therapy bills to prove it. They lurk under the surface like sharks, waiting to catch her when her guard is down and drag her into the depths.

And yet she's not thought about any of it since . . . when? The last time she can remember is sitting in her car and staring at the house where she didn't grow up, a cheap bunch of petrol station flowers on the passenger seat and the niggling question of why she put herself through the ritual every year. If things had gone as they usually did, she would have dreamed a wall of flames that night, woken up dripping even more than the hot flushes made her. But she'd loaded up on coffee and driven to Wales. Because Aunt Maude was dead.

Somehow that had broken the cycle.

Or maybe it was simpler than that. The few people she's talked to since returning to Wales have all been kind and friendly. PC Fairweather – Angharad, Phoebe finds herself thinking – went out of her way to help. Even the young nurse at Bronglais seemed more sympathetic than her job required. And now a five minute conversation with a total stranger has done more for her mental health than any number of hours of therapy. Maybe it's this place, Llancwm.

Without quite intending it, she's started walking again. Her feet have brought her up the road to the chapel. Phoebe pushes open the wrought iron gate and steps through. The doors are closed, locked she assumes, but the graveyard slopes gently away around the back of the building. She's never really thought about it before, but there are few flat pieces of land of any good size in the village, and the church takes up perhaps the largest. An indication of how important it once was to the community. Maybe still is, if the generally tidy state of the graveyard is any indication.

A wall at the far end stops the graves from tumbling into the valley below. A little over waist height on this side, Phoebe knows it is much higher on the other, giving a good view of the river, the ruins of the old mill and the short terrace of council houses. She threads a path past lichen-encrusted headstones, not really paying attention to anything much, still enjoying that lightness of being. She will have to return to the real world soon enough, but for now it's a small oasis of calm here among the dead.

A flicker of motion in the corner of her eye, she turns to see a crow standing on the top of one headstone. It has a stick in its beak and stares at her for a moment before flying off. Phoebe shudders as if it's her grave she is walking on, the moment of calm gone. Time to head back to Pant Melyn and start making calls. There's a mountain of admin to wade through, and Aunt Maude's carer's going to drop round for a chat too. Bronwen Tudor. That'll be interesting.

As she's retracing her steps through the headstones, a bunch of flowers catch her eye. Old and limp, almost all decayed to nothing, they strike a chord all the same. With a little ripple of shock, she sees the names carved into the stone, and in particular the one right at the bottom. It's recent, the chiselled letters uncolonised by lichen as of yet. Tegwin Meredith Ellis was born in 1939, so he was ancient when he died. Phoebe finds herself surprised at that. If he never married, like the solicitor said, then who cared for him in his later years? Who left these flowers?

She looks around the graveyard, as if expecting the answers to be there. They are, in a way. This village, this community. Someone looked after Aunt Maude, so why not Tegwin Ellis? The community rallies round, and so it persists.

A memory emerges as she stands beside the grave, a time many years ago when she stood beside it, sprinkled a little earth onto the lid of a coffin six feet down. There had been a big crowd for that funeral, the whole village turned out, the whole county, to pay their last respects to a man who had been central to the community for the whole of his long life, despite the horrible secret he carried with him.

No, not the whole village. All but one. The memory brings a wry smile to her face, and with it another thought. There is someone else in this village as reclusive as she ever was. Is he even still alive? She would have heard if he'd died, surely. Phoebe turns from the grave, sets off towards the road and her car with a new sense of purpose. She will have to find out.

26

1985

Phoebe was surprised at how much the sight of the sea cheered her up. It was a welcome relief after the endless days of forest and mountains, and put her in mind of trips to St Andrews with Mum and Dad, back when she'd been little. She remembered gazing out over the North Sea as the sun glinted off the wave tops. Ice-cream cones melting all over her hands, seagulls screaming at everything, and sand everywhere. This was Cardigan Bay, of course, and somewhere in the distance lay Ireland, but the effect was much the same. As Aunt Maude drove slowly down the steep hill towards the town, the memories brought a lump to Phoebe's throat, but this time her eyes stayed dry.

'I'll drop you off on the high street, Phoebe dear. Louis needs to go to the library, then I've a few errands to run in town. Shouldn't take more than a couple of hours. We can all meet up at the bandstand on the promenade at one.'

Phoebe looked down at her backpack, clutched between her knees. There hadn't been time to explore all the shops in town the last time she'd been there, and she'd been relying on both Aunt Maude's patience and her money then as well. Her allowance had finally come through a couple of days after the Llancwm Show, in the form of a newly opened bank account, complete with cash card and chequebook and a starting balance that was more than she'd ever seen before. And yet now she had the means, the appeal of shopping had waned. It wasn't as much fun doing it on your own.

'I'd quite like to go to the library myself,' she said, surprising herself with her own words. 'I still want to do that project we talked about, remember? Finding out what happened to Gwen Ellis?'

Aunt Maude peered at her in the rear-view mirror, her expression hard to read. 'Are you really sure you want to do that, Phoebe? We could find something else that works better with your school subjects. A maths project perhaps? Or some biology? You could make a survey of all the wildlife in the forest, learn all the proper names for things.'

'Nonsense, Maude. It's a good project for the girl. And she can learn how to research things properly.' Uncle Louis leaned around in his seat and winked at Phoebe, but she was still concentrating on Aunt Maude's face in the mirror. The old lady's expression was a strange one, for all that Phoebe could only see a part of it. Something like annoyance, but she was used to seeing that. No, Maude was worried as much as annoyed.

'Well, on your own head be it,' she said rather cryptically as she indicated, then pulled in to the side of the road. Phoebe wasn't sure where they were until she saw the station.

'But, the library?' she asked as her aunt indicated she was to get out.

'Is up there on the hill. Big white building.' Aunt Maude pointed out the window at the hillside that flanked the northern end of the town. 'We'll have to get your membership card sorted first, and I've still things to do in town. You can meet us both up there in an hour. OK?'

The town was warmer than Phoebe had been expecting, a windless day with only a few wispy clouds in an otherwise clear blue sky. She wandered down the main street, found the bank and then spent an agonising few minutes trying to remember her new pin number. An impatient queue had built up behind her by the time she'd figured it out, and she withdrew more money than she really needed. She tried to ignore the glares as she hurried away, but she could feel the heat of them burning into her back all the same.

Woolworths seemed as good a place as any to start, and she spent a few distracted minutes looking through cassette tapes for some new music. Not having listened to anything for months except the tracks on her one tape and whatever dull classical dirge was on in the kitchen, Phoebe found the selection both bewildering and oddly trite. This was something she'd loved to do with Jenny, spending hours flicking through the racks in the hope there might be something new from one of her favourite bands. Now it felt a little desperate, and she left without buying anything.

It was the same with clothes. There were a few things she thought were nice, but not having a sounding board made her doubt her own judgement. Would that dress really look so good on her as it did on the shop window mannequin? And more realistically, when would she ever wear it? Jeans, heavy-duty cotton shirts and thick socks seemed like the more sensible option. And a decent pair of walking boots, except that she had no idea where to even start with that. Overwhelmed with her own inadequacy, Phoebe took refuge in a small cafe down a side street with a name she couldn't begin to pronounce. A cup of tea and a biscuit she could manage, and by then it would be time to go and meet her aunt and uncle up at the library.

'Well, well, well. If it isn't Florence Nightingale.'

The voice was close. Too close. Phoebe looked up and two identical faces swam into view, ugly as sin and sneering as they stared at her. Then the smell of weed hit, and she understood. The twins, Axe and Brue Thomas. What were they doing in a cafe? Surely the pub was more their style, even if it was morning.

'What are you doing here?' she asked, the question out before she could stop herself. She remembered Aunt Maude's words as they were walking home from the Llancwm Show, and how she had already decided she wanted nothing to do with them. And yet here they were, like a pair of bad pennies, always turning up where they were least expected or wanted.

'What are we doing here?' one of the two asked the other. Phoebe couldn't be sure, but she thought he might have been trying to mimic her accent.

'I don't know, brother? Have we come into the wrong place?'

Phoebe let out a little snort of laughter at the terrible attempt to sound Scottish, then immediately regretted it. She didn't want this attention, didn't want to know these two stoners on any level.

'Nah,' the first twin said, thankfully reverting back to his normal speech. 'Saw you in the window, didn't we. Sitting there all alone and sad. Thought you might need cheering up, see?'

Phoebe reached out for her cup and drew it reflexively towards her. 'I'm fine. Thanks. Need to be getting on anyway. Got to meet my uncle up at the library.'

'The library? But it's the holidays, love. What you want to be going up there for? Shouldn't be swotting away with books an' stuff when the sun's shining. Much better things you could be doing with your time, right?' This last suggestion was delivered with a leer by whichever it was, Axe or Brue, who had been talking. Phoebe found she didn't much care to find out, despite the fact that she could see some differences between the two of them now. One had a scar just below his lower lip, and his left eyelid drooped slightly, weighed down by the swelling lump of a stye. The other's nose had been broken some time ago and not properly set. He had a habit of rubbing his thumbs against his forefingers while he stood, as if itching for a fight, whereas his brother kept his hands shoved into the pockets of his camouflage jacket. It still didn't help with which one was which though.

'Think I'll pass,' Phoebe said as she edged off the bench seat to leave. Neither of the twins moved to let her past, so she had to get far closer than she wanted, her head reeling with the stench of old cigarette smoke and body odour rolling off them. Had they never heard of washing?

'See you around then, little snail.' The nearest of the two reached up a grubby hand towards her, and for a horrible moment Phoebe thought he was going to touch her. Something of her horror must have shown on her face enough to get through though, as he stopped himself, snatched his hand away. The half-friendly smile vanished to be replaced by the more familiar sneer. Phoebe could almost see the cogs clunking slowly in his brain as he began to form some kind of insult or crude sexual innuendo. She didn't wait to hear what it was. Turned her tail and fled.

Phoebe tried to blank the memory of her encounter with the twins as she stared at the slightly tilted image on the screen. She'd marched up the steep hill to the library at double-quick time, burning off the anger and fear both. Uncle Louis had met her at the entrance foyer and used his own library pass to get her into the main reading room. Apparently she couldn't have a pass of her own until she turned sixteen, the irony of which fact was not lost on her one little bit.

Still, the name Louis Beard seemed to have some clout behind it in the place, and nobody bothered her once she was comfortably seated in front of the grey metal microfiche reader. Signed in with her uncle's credentials meant she had access to far more material than she knew what to do with, either.

The man himself had, perhaps foolishly, left her to her own devices. His assumption that she knew how to use microfiche records wasn't wrong, but he was putting a lot of trust in her not to break something, or worse misfile it. He'd also presented her with a brand-new hardbound book, a crimson ribbon place marker stitched into its spine, its blank pages lined in feint blue, along with the sage advice 'always start every project with a new notebook' and then he'd wandered off to do something else.

It had taken Phoebe perhaps half an hour to work out how to search the library's archive of local newspapers, and another half hour to narrow things down to the relevant year. Gwen Ellis of Nant Caws Farm, Llancwm, had disappeared in the spring of 1973, around about the same time as Phoebe had been born, funnily enough. It didn't take long after that to find the first small article in the *Cambrian Gazette and Advertiser*, under the compelling headline PREGNANT WOMAN MISSING.

'Police have asked that the public keep an eye out for a missing Llancwm woman. Gwen Ellis, 23, from Nant Caws Farm, was last seen driving her green Land Rover vehicle away from the village in the direction of Aberystwyth. Miss Ellis, whose brother Ceredig was tragically killed in a car accident in England last year, is heavily pregnant. She was reported to have been in a relationship with Mr Stephen Lorne, lead singer of the popular music band A Distant Tree, although Mr Lorne, who is currently overseas on tour with his band, has not responded to our request for a comment. Anyone with any information as to the whereabouts of Miss Ellis should contact Police Constable Eifion Griffiths.'

There was a phone number that seemed to have too few digits, and that was it. Not even a photograph. Phoebe flipped to the first page of her new notebook and carefully wrote in the date and page number of the newspaper. She added the name of the reporter who had filed the story, Aneurin Jones, then on the next line wrote 'Stephen Lorne' and 'A Distant Tree'. She ended that with a question mark and then moved on with her search.

The next article she stopped on was a couple of months later. Front page, it included a photograph that at first Phoebe thought might have been Gwen herself, but turned out to be a man with long hair. The headline read LLANCWM SUICIDE ATTEMPT, and it was the name of the village that had caught her attention.

'Llancwm resident Mr Stephen Lorne was rushed to hospital following an attempted suicide. Mr Lorne, lead singer of the band A Distant Tree, was said to have been severely depressed after the disappearance of Gwen Ellis, who was alleged to have been carrying his child. A recent incomer to the village, Mr Lorne has been sectioned under the Mental Health Act and will be placed in psychiatric care once he has recovered from his self-inflicted injuries.'

There was more about the band, but Phoebe had stopped taking it in. She was transfixed by the photograph, her mind filling in details that the newspaper print and subsequent microfilming had removed. There was something hauntingly familiar about the face that stared out from its frame of straight, dark, shoulder-length hair, but for the life of her she couldn't have said what.

'You done there, Feebs? It's time to go.'

She looked around to see her uncle, his leather satchel clutched under one arm, coat draped over the other. Behind him, through the glass door to the entrance lobby, she could see Aunt Maude. A quick glance at the clock at the top of the screen showed she'd been at the microfiche viewer for almost two hours. There was no way she was going to be given any slack, even if she begged. With one last look at the enigmatic Lorne, she switched off the machine and returned the film to its container, placing it on the rack for the librarian to put away in the right place. Newly christened notebook under one arm, she followed her uncle out of the reading room. She hadn't managed to get as much done as she would have liked, but it was a start.

They made it almost as far as Pant-y-Crug before Phoebe's need to ask questions overcame her caution with what she knew was a tricky subject. Given the glacial speed at which Aunt Maude drove, that was a monumental feat of patience in itself.

'You knew her, Gwen Ellis, right?' She didn't direct the question at either adult in particular, but it was Uncle Louis who answered, twisting around in his seat so that he could see her.

'I knew Gwen, yes. Right from when she was first born. Terrible business that.'

'How so?' Phoebe looked straight at her uncle as she asked, but she couldn't help but notice Aunt Maude's pursed lips, the way her hands flexed slightly on the steering wheel, the barely audible mutter of something under her breath. Disapproval flowed off her in waves. Uncle Louis either chose not to notice or was genuinely that lacking in sensitivity.

'Well, I think I told you, didn't I? After you saved old Mered's life? He had three children, Ceredig, Tegwin and Gwen. All three were born at home. Not so strange back then, really, but there were . . . complications when Tegwin was born. That's probably why he's the way he is. Happened again with Gwen, only that time it was her mother, Seren, who got the worst of it, and, well, she died, see.'

Aunt Maude's knuckles had turned white, so hard was she clenching her fists around the steering wheel. It was a miracle she hadn't driven them off the road already. Although they'd hardly come to any harm if she did. Mostly likely just bump to a halt.

'That's terrible,' Phoebe said. 'So Gwen grew up without a mother.'

'Oh, the village rallied round and helped, for sure. And she turned out fine. She was a little older than your mother, but they were thick as thieves for a while. Used to run barefoot through the woods in the summertime, out all day getting up to mischief. I'd gone off to university by then, mind. Only came back in the summer for a few weeks.'

'I read in the paper that she was pregnant when she disappeared. Did you know the man who was the father? The pop singer?'

A darkness passed over Uncle Louis's face at Phoebe's question, and for a moment she thought he was going to shout at her. Aunt Maude slowed the car even more than the snail's pace she had been driving.

'I did say this was a bad idea, Louis. Didn't I?'

'Yes, you did. But I never . . .' Uncle Louis started, then slumped in his seat, facing forward, without finishing.

'What?' Phoebe asked, unsure whether she had done something wrong.

'It's all rather complicated, Phoebe dear,' Aunt Maude said. 'And it all happened a long time ago, too. As for the pop singer, well, you've seen him yourself.'

'I have?' Phoebe tried to think back to the last time she'd seen anything resembling a music video. Not even those pretty boy bands who were turning up on *Top of the Pops* so frequently now. The loop of favourite songs on her one cassette tape.

'Did you not read about him in the newspaper archives?' Maude asked, her gaze still fixed firmly on the road ahead. Phoebe flipped open her notebook and scanned the few lines she had written down. Stephen Lorne. A Distant Tree. Suicide attempt. Mental Health Act.

'There wasn't much about him,' she said.

'No, I don't suppose there would be. He did what he did and they locked him away for ten years and more for it. Finally let him out what? Two years ago? Sad, really. He's still searching for her. For Gwen.'

It clicked then, the face that had looked vaguely familiar but unplaceable. That had been taken ages ago. Of course he would have changed. But that much? He'd looked so young in the photograph she'd seen, and that must have been from around the time Phoebe had been born. She'd thought him at least as old as Uncle Louis, but he couldn't be, could he?

'The old man in the woods?'

'The same,' Uncle Louis finally said. 'Poor old Steve, he never deserved what happened to him.'

'What happened to him?' Phoebe looked at her notes again. 'It said he tried to commit suicide.' She paused for a moment, too many pieces of information vying for her attention. 'Wait, did that happen here? In Llancwm? Why didn't you . . .?' she trailed off as it became apparent without needing an answer.

'It was a long time ago, Feebs,' Uncle Louis said. 'A difficult time, too. We put it behind us. Least, we thought we had. I guess some things never really go away, do they?'

Phoebe looked at her notebook again. She'd written in large capital letters across the top of the first page WHAT HAP- PENED TO GWEN ELLIS? and underlined it twice. It seemed such a simple question, a mystery that needed solving. In her head she was the smart young detective, going over all the evidence and seeing something that everybody else had missed all those years ago. But the reality of it was very different. Gwen wasn't some abstract puzzle to be solved; she was a person. She'd had friends, family, a lover, all of whom she'd walked out on and all of whom were still trying to deal with it as best they could. It wasn't Phoebe's fault that she looked like Gwen, wasn't exactly her idea to come to this forgotten corner of Wales either. But her presence had stirred up old memories, brought back the pain of loss even if that had never been her intention. If Gwen was still alive, her child would be Phoebe's age. What good could possibly come of trying to find her if she hadn't let herself be found before?

'I . . . I'll think of something else to research,' she said as the car drove slowly past an old ruined stone building. 'Maybe the silver mines or something?'

And with that she closed the notebook and slid it into her bag.

27

Soft rain pattered against the rooflights, lending a white-noise background to Phoebe's misery. She sat on her bed, knees tucked up under her chin, and stared at the closed door. Her Walkman lay beside her, the headphone cord wound around the black plastic body. She'd given up listening to the music, no longer able to take any comfort from the meagre selection of songs. On the bedside table, a stack of Muriel Baywater books were equally unappealing. She'd read them all, some more than once, and now the worlds of romantic love, small tragedy and evil vanquished felt trite. There were no happy endings in the real world.

Lying at the end of the bed where she'd thrown it, the shiny new hardback notebook her uncle had given her in the library lay open at a blank page. Two days had passed since the conversation with her aunt and uncle in the car on the way back from town had snuffed the spark of excitement she'd felt when first hearing about the mystery of Gwen Ellis. She'd scribbled a few more questions underneath the sparse notes she'd already written, but like everything else in her life, she had no enthusiasm for the project any more. But neither could she think of anything else to while away the endless dull days.

She had cried for a while, tears marking the otherwise pristine pages. But her tears were all spent now, useless. They wouldn't bring her parents back, wouldn't make her friends remember who she was, wouldn't make this backwards old house in the middle of nowhere any less boring to live in.

To live in. The thought kept whirling around in her head. She was stuck here. This was her home now. Nothing for her in Cupar any more. No drunks spilling out of the pubs after the footie on a Saturday afternoon. No meeting up with Jenny and Charlotte at the Mercat Cross and making plans they'd never carry out. Even the burned-out shell that had once been her house would have been bulldozed by now, the ground prepared for a new building. Who would live there once it was finished? Would they know the tragedy that had happened in that very space?

She sniffed, rubbed the back of one hand across her nose, then went back to hugging her knees, back to staring at the door. She cursed the rain that meant she couldn't go outside, and that brought a hollow, mirthless laugh almost to her throat. Go outside. Walk for miles through woodland and up steep-sided hills. It was the kind of thing she had always hated, always fought against when her father had suggested they jump in the car and head north. Climb Schiehallion or one of the other Munros, just because they were there. What she wouldn't give now for the chance to sit in the back seat of the old Saab as they sped up the A9, see her mum and dad sitting in front of her and the road to the Highlands through the windscreen.

As if mocking her, the sound of a car outside broke through the constant rush of the rain. Phoebe cocked her head, listening as the engine slowed to a diesel tickover, door opened, feet on gravel. She heard the knock on the door and knew that it was a delivery van, maybe the postman with a parcel needing signed for. Would anyone else hear?

She waited a moment, until a second knock. Louder this time. It spurred her to action, even as she knew whatever was being delivered would not be for her. Uncle Louis would ignore the disturbance, and it was possible Aunt Maude was out in the green-house, or even dancing naked in the rain. So it fell to her.

By the time she reached the front door and pulled it open, the postman was almost back at his van. The card he had left lay on the flagstone threshold, already turning soggy in the rain. He must have heard the door open though, as he turned, shoulders slumping in relief as he saw her.

'Thought there was nobody home,' he said as he presented her with a heavy cardboard box addressed to her uncle. It had been battered around in the back of his van, and was half soaked too. So much for taking care of your precious delivery. She staggered a little under the weight of it, then made a scrawling squiggle on the delivery form. Soft rain smudged the ink as the postman whipped the clipboard away and hurried back to his van.

There was no sign of Aunt Maude when Phoebe took the box through to the kitchen. The study door stood closed, which meant her uncle didn't want to be disturbed. He could have his parcel when he came out, even if she was curious to know what was in it. Books, obviously. Uncle Louis never seemed to get anything else, and this parcel had the logo of his publisher printed on the side. What books, though? As far as she knew, he'd not written anything new in a while. At least that was what Aunt Maude had said. No doubt they were more review copies, like the endless Muriel Baywaters she'd lost herself in these past weeks.

Phoebe filled the kettle, sliding it as quietly onto the stove as she could manage. She set about making herself a cup of tea, then decided to make a pot just in case her uncle came out, or her aunt appeared. As she went about her task, she kept looking across the table to the parcel. It really was in a sorry state, and she wondered whether it wouldn't be best to open it, take the books out and let them dry. Or at least prevent them from getting any wetter than they must surely already be.

But it was her uncle's parcel, not hers. She knew better than to open it. Only, as she was pouring herself some tea, the paper tape used to seal the cardboard curled up before her eyes, and one flap of the box sprang open. It was a sign, surely.

Phoebe sat for a few minutes, staring first at the box, then at the study door. She took a sip of tea, fetched a biscuit and nibbled at it. Stared at the box some more. It wouldn't hurt just to look, would it? And if Uncle Louis asked, she wouldn't be lying when she told him it had opened by itself.

When she peered in the top, all Phoebe could see was some brown paper packaging, damp at the edges. She looked over her shoulder at the study door again, straining her ears for any sign that her uncle was about to step out into the kitchen. The house was silent but for the gentle burble of the stove, the tock-clunk of the old grandfather clock and the quiet hiss of the rain outside. All the time she had been making the pot of tea, she had heard nothing from the study, which meant Uncle Louis was most likely asleep in his armchair. She gently eased the paper packaging aside to reveal a shiny book cover. A paperback edition in a familiar style, she couldn't immediately read the title or the author's name. Given the size of the box, there must have been a dozen copies, although Phoebe couldn't tell whether they were all the same or several different titles. Not without taking them out.

There was a letter, too, an A4 sheet folded in half and placed on top. She knew it was none of her business, knew that she would get in trouble if she was caught, but she couldn't help herself from reaching in and gently teasing the letter out, unfolding it, reading.

Dear Lou,

It is my pleasure to send you your complimentary copies of the latest Muriel Baywater - The Soft Touch of His Lips. An excellent addition to the series, I truly believe these are getting better with each one. Buy-in is up across the board, and the mass market orders are like

I have never seen before. The book will even feature in several of the larger supermarkets. The world cannot get enough of Muriel, it seems.

Great to hear that you are almost done on book twenty. I look forward to reading it, as do all the girls in admin. I have had a few more requests for interviews, which I will continue to refuse for now. We may have to rethink Muriel's anonymity soon, however. It is only a matter of time before someone works it out.

The letter carried on, but the words no longer registered in Phoebe's head. She was too busy processing the information she had gleaned from the first paragraph. Her uncle. Muriel Baywater. Twenty books. No wonder he spent all his time in the study, and yet hadn't published a novel in twenty years. Not under his own name.

Noise from the utility room broke through Phoebe's musing. She quickly folded the letter and slid it back where it had come from, pulled the packing paper into place and then closed up the parcel. The tape stayed down when she resealed it. No one would ever know.

'Oh, Phoebe. I thought you were in your room.' Aunt Maude bustled into the kitchen, her hair plastered to her face by the rain. At least she was wearing clothes, even if they were soaked through.

'There was a delivery.' Phoebe pointed at the box. 'Had to sign for it. It's for Uncle Louis. Books, by the look of it.'

Aunt Maude raised an eyebrow, but made no move towards the parcel. Then she spotted the teapot and biscuit jar. 'Is that long made?' she asked, and reached for a mug without waiting to be answered.

Phoebe said nothing until her aunt had poured her tea and settled into a seat at the table.

'Why do they keep on sending Uncle Louis romance novels to read?' she asked.

Her aunt looked at her, then across at the parcel, and Phoebe realised the tactical error she had made.

'Romance novels?' The old woman raised an eyebrow. 'You mean that Muriel Baywater woman, I suppose.'

'She's very prolific.'

'Indeed. And that's partly down to Louis. He first introduced her to his publisher, you see. After she somehow managed to persuade him to read a copy of her first novel. That's not her real name, of course. Muriel Baywater, I mean. She's famous for shunning the limelight, sensible woman. Louis is one of the few people who knows her true identity.'

Phoebe started to say that she knew too, then it occurred to her that maybe her aunt wasn't in on the secret. 'And do you know who she is?' she asked instead.

Maude shook her head. 'Heavens, no. I'm sure Louis would tell me if I asked, but really, that sort of thing's not my cup of tea at all.'

As if to emphasise the point, she took a long drink from her mug and settled back into her chair.

'You've never even read them?'

'Oh, I skimmed the first couple, but they weren't for me. Give me a nice fat biography any day. Or gardening books. You should try something else yourself. Might learn something.'

Phoebe looked at the box, the tape still holding now, no evidence that she had opened it before. There were copies of a new Muriel Baywater novel in there, one she could be the first person to read. Well, the first apart from her uncle, his editor and the girls in admin. But the parcel wasn't addressed to her, so she couldn't open it. Which meant sitting on her bed up in the attic, listening to the same old songs on her Walkman, over and over again.

'I'll think about it,' she said, and went and did just that.

28

2023

It's been a few days now since she arrived at Pant Melyn. Phoebe has dealt with the solicitors, the funeral directors, getting somewhere with organising a memorial service at the chapel and a wake at the hotel. She's told the bees. The fridge is stocked with enough food to last her a month, not that she's intending staying that long. There will be many trips back and forth, she's sure, although right now, as she sits in the kitchen with a mug of coffee, the appeal of her tenement flat in Edinburgh is muted. The recent memories that place holds are too stressed, too unhappy. Pant Melyn's legacy is older. Time has worn down the sharp edges of the pain she felt here.

There is still a lot to do, of course. And then there is her work. She's been avoiding it, the way she always does. Putting it off until the last possible moment. But right here, right now, there's no good reason why she can't get on with it. No good reason at all.

In the quiet moments, she's wandered through the house like a ghost, opening doors and poking her nose into cupboards. There are only two rooms she's avoided, although she's looked into her aunt's bedroom long enough to see that whoever took the body away was thoughtful enough to strip the bed. Or maybe that was Mrs Tudor, the carer. Bronwen.

Which leaves only the door she's staring at now. The door to her uncle's study. It's closed, which to a tiny part of her mind means she must not disturb him. She is twelve again, remembering her very first day here, the sudden rage quickly suppressed, perhaps the only time she ever saw him angry.

But that's foolish. Uncle Louis has been dead for almost a decade now. There is no one in that room at all. Aunt Maude closed it up the day he died, and chances are it's not been disturbed since. Nothing so mawkish and sentimental as a shrine to Louis Beard, but simply closing a chapter in her life and moving on. Coffee mug in hand, Phoebe fights down the instinct telling her not to, walks over to the door and pushes it open.

She remembers a well-proportioned but small room, one window looking out onto the driveway. When her uncle had worked there, it had always been chaotic, books and papers everywhere, a desk that you could only make out by the piles of clutter all over it. Someone has tidied up, and the first thought Phoebe has is how annoyed her uncle will be when he sees it.

The computer on the desk is ancient, but then no one has written in this room for ten years or more. Phoebe pulls out the chair, settles into it, reaches instinctively for the keyboard. Could she work here, with all the memories? Maybe, but she'll have to fetch her laptop in from the car.

Standing, she crosses to the wall, all of two steps. Floor to ceiling bookshelves used to be a jumble in keeping with the rest of the room, a place where you'd find old books of poetry and literary giants jostling cheek by jowl with airport thrillers, epic fantasy and romance. Books in languages Phoebe hadn't known existed, let alone was able to read. Dozens of different editions of *The Patience of Bees*, all piled hither and yon as if her uncle only kept them because he didn't know what else to do with them. And, of course, the complete works of one Muriel Baywater, often multiple copies.

Now the shelves are neat, the titles arranged by some categorisation she can't immediately divine. Phoebe traces a finger over the spines; that first edition hardback of *Bees* would excite a few collectors she knows. She finds Muriel on the top shelf, not quite tucked away out of sight, but relegated to a lesser status, the collection no longer complete. She smiles at the memory of Aunt Maude's eye roll when she finally found out the truth. More hurt at the secret Uncle Louis had kept from her for so many years than at the so-called lowbrow content he had been writing all that time. Phoebe can't agree with that sentiment; she owes too much of her sanity to Muriel Baywater, and a lot more besides.

She leaves the study door open, partly in defiance, partly to let a little air circulate in the slightly musty room. A soft shower of rain catches her unawares as she goes to the car to fetch her work bag. Enough to damp her hair, but not her spirits. She spends a while working out how to disconnect all the pieces of her uncle's computer, a little longer finding somewhere to store it. Finally she settles herself into his old chair again and fires up her laptop. Almost new, very expensive, it opens swiftly and she is soon staring at the document on the screen she last worked on over a week ago. Well, if she misses her deadline, it's not as if she hasn't got a good excuse. Her editor will understand.

The world still thinks Muriel Baywater is alive, still as mysterious and reclusive as ever she was. Some critics noted the change in her style around fifteen years ago, put it down to her age. It doesn't stop the books still being bestsellers though, even if Phoebe has a long way to go before she catches up with the number of them her uncle wrote.

29

1985

Rain had left the forest smelling clean, warm and damp as Phoebe escaped from the house and the threat of gardening. The undergrowth had spread out into the path as it zigzagged downhill to the river, but she had mastered the art of avoiding the vegetation now. Under Aunt Maude's watchful guidance, she had cleaned and rubbed wax dubbin into the old pair of walking boots that fitted her best, and now they were almost perfectly waterproof, even if the thick woollen socks she needed to make them fit properly fair itched her ankles and calves.

The river wasn't as high as she'd been expecting by the time Phoebe arrived at the wooden bridge. She crossed as far as the middle, then leaned against the rail and waited. Gwyneth would surely come today, wouldn't she?

After fifteen minutes or so, she sat down and let her legs dangle over the edge. Staring downstream, she could see how the river cut an almost perfectly straight line on its way to Llancwm, bisecting the valley like a knife slash in the top of one of Aunt Maude's loaves before it went in the oven. No doubt there was a geological explanation for that, for all of the strange and wonderful features around here. Phoebe had enjoyed studying that side of geography, although the social stuff had been less fun. Would she be able to continue with the subject come the autumn, when she went to school? Would she even go to school? Her aunt and uncle had gone quiet about homeschooling, but they'd not mentioned any alternative either. It was a long way to Aberystwyth each morning, if that was where she'd have to go. Very early starts and uncomfortable bus journeys. Quite a change from being able to walk from home, catching Charlotte and Jenny on the way.

Home.

The sob escaped from her like she'd been punched. Tears welled in her eyes, and Phoebe sniffed as she wiped them away on the sleeve of her coat. It had been days, weeks even, since she'd been floored like that by the memories. But they were always there, lurking in the background. Waiting for her guard to be lowered so they could ambush her.

She had to move. Sitting only made the misery worse. She scrambled to awkward feet, realising as she did that she'd been on the bridge well over half an hour now. It was clear Gwyneth wasn't coming. Perhaps she'd never really existed at all.

Phoebe paused a moment, glanced the way she had come. She could go back to Pant Melyn and help Aunt Maude weed the vegetable garden, but that didn't appeal any more now than it had an hour earlier. The other end of the bridge held much more allure. There was the path to the waterfalls, for one thing. Or she might try and retrace her steps from the first time she came out here on her own, to the glade with its massive oak tree. That was where she had first met Gwyneth, after all. Maybe she'd see her again there.

It didn't matter that there was no logic to the thought; it was enough to make her mind up. Phoebe took a swig from her canteen, then set off on what she hoped was the right path.

Half an hour later she had to admit that she was hopelessly lost.

Somehow the track which had led her up beyond the woods before had today brought her back downhill and closer to the river.

It was as if the trees moved around and the forest had a mind of its own, leading her where it wanted her to go, not where she wished at all. At times, she almost thought she heard voices, laughter far distant or only a few yards through the trees, but try as she might she could never quite make them out, never quite find the people who were perhaps no more than a figment of her imagination. Or maybe the ghosts her uncle seemed to think lived here. Did ghosts live?

Looking up didn't much help her find her bearings. The sun shone bright and high overhead, so it must have been close to noon. She could tell which side of the river she was on, both by the orientation of the distant hilltops and because she was fairly sure she'd remember having crossed back over. At a rough guess, she was almost directly downhill from Aunt Maude's bees, and she might have clambered up to them were it not for the steepness of the slope and the thick underbrush. Nothing for it but to carry on the way she had been going.

The path zigzagged slowly down the hillside, bringing Phoebe eventually to a wide clearing, neatly bisected by the river. It flowed more sluggishly here, not hemmed in by steep sides, and she was reassured to see it flowing in the direction she had expected. And there ahead of her, perched above the bank in the centre of the clearing, stood a cottage.

At first she thought it was derelict. Like so many of the buildings in and around Llancwm, it was built of unharled dark grey stone, topped off with a steep slate roof that sloped almost to the ground on one side. At some point a large and ungainly extension had been added to one end, but the whole place had an air of ramshackle neglect about it, not helped by the weedy mess of a garden. A couple of sturdy, stone-built sheds stood a short distance from the house itself, almost large enough to be called barns. As she approached she realised that one was a mill house, although the ancient iron mill wheel would need new wooden buckets if it was ever going to turn again.

There was no sign of any car at the cottage, and the track leading away in the direction of the village had more grass growing through it than gravel. Phoebe approached with caution, curious as to how she hadn't found the place before, but not wanting to be seen snooping around. Apart from the gentle rush of the river and the occasional cry of a red kite overhead, the whole place was silent. Even her feet made no sound as she stepped from long-overgrown lawn onto what had once been a wide, flat turning circle with a single pampas grass erupting from a raised bed in the middle.

Closer to it, the house showed signs of habitation. What she had taken for broken glass in the downstairs windows, Phoebe now saw, was only the reflection of the weed saplings that surrounded the building like an approaching army. There were no lights on, but peering in she could see a small living room at the front, an old leather armchair pulled up close to a wood-burning stove. The front door was half glazed, and showed an untidy hallway, cluttered with old walking boots and a few battered cardboard boxes. Shapeless coats hung from a line of pegs on one wall, and as she noticed a couple of longs scarves dangling to the floor, Phoebe began to suspect she knew whose house this was. If she was right, then she really didn't want to be caught.

Moving away, she was momentarily stopped by the downstairs room that was formed by the extension. Through more modern double-glazed windows, she could see an upright piano, a couple of guitars on stands and a few other bits of equipment she half recognised from the music rooms at school.

Phoebe loved music, had started learning the fiddle at primary school but had to give up when Mum's depression had taken hold. She'd tried to persuade her dad to let her take up the drums, too, but to no avail. Seeing the instruments lined up there, she realised she'd not even thought about playing anything since the fire. She saw the old acoustic guitar in her attic bedroom every time she was in there, but had never felt any urge to pick it up and strum. Of course, that might have been because it was missing a couple of strings, but all the same.

'Can I help you, young lady?'

Phoebe whirled around, taken by surprise. She'd not heard anyone approaching, but then the ever-present rush of the river hid a lot of sounds. Now he stood just a few paces away from her, the old man with the white hair. He wore a long coat, scarf wrapped around his neck, Dr Who-style. His hands were clasped together in front of him as if he wasn't quite sure what to do with them. Close up, Phoebe could see an expression of mixed fear and wonder on those aged features. Except that he wasn't as old as she had at first assumed. That shock of pure white hair exploded from a much younger face now that she could see it closely.

'I'm so sorry. I didn't mean to disturb you. I was just following the path, see?' She shrugged, hoping it would suffice.

'Oh.' The man's eyes went wide as he saw her face. 'It's you.'

His voice was still that strangely high, raspy whisper, as if speaking pained him, and his accent was English, Phoebe noticed. She hadn't the last time they'd spoken.

'Phoebe,' she said. 'Phoebe MacDonald. We met . . .' – How long had it been now? Weeks, wasn't it? – 'before. Down by the river.'

The man continued to stare for longer than was polite. Phoebe was used to adults being in control of things, but this one seemed totally out of his depth.

'I didn't realise this was your house. I hope I'm not trespassing.'

Something like a shudder ran through the man and he finally came to his senses. He held out his hand, thin and long-fingered. 'I'm sorry, where are my manners. Steve. Steve Lorne.'

'I . . . Umm . . . I know. Pleased to meet you.' Phoebe took the hand, surprised at how strong the man's grip was. 'I'm sorry if I gave you a shock just now. And down by the river, too.'

Something that might have been embarrassment spread across

Lorne's face, and he shrugged his admission of guilt as he released his grip, let his hand fall to his side.

'It's my fault, really. Although I have to say you do look extraordinarily like someone I once knew.'

'Gwen Ellis? Yes. So everybody tells me.'

Something like sadness passed over the old man's face as Phoebe spoke, as if the sun had gone behind a cloud even though the sky was clear. His shoulders slumped; not that they had been all that square beforehand.

'I suppose your mother and Gwen were quite alike too, now I think about it. They were best friends growing up, although Gwen was a couple of years older.' He stood up a little straighter, as if something had just that moment occurred to him. 'I've probably got some photographs of them both somewhere, if you'd like to see them. I could pop the kettle on for a cup of tea, too.'

Phoebe started to make her excuses. She'd promised Uncle Louis and Aunt Maude that she would stop looking into Gwen's disappearance, and while they'd not exactly warned her off talking to the man, the picture of him they had painted was of someone potentially dangerous. And yet she got no such vibe from him at all. Instead, all she saw was a deep-rooted loneliness, something she could understand all too well. His earlier actions, when she had thought him spying on her, made perfect sense given that she was apparently the spitting image of his . . . what? Phoebe realised she didn't know exactly what Gwen's relationship with this man had been, because nobody wanted to talk about her. Well, maybe Steve Lorne would.

'Sure,' she said, and was rewarded with a gap-toothed smile. 'Why not?'

30

The inside of the house had that same air of basic neglect about it as the outside. It wasn't untidy, and it didn't smell of anything particularly bad, but it was cluttered in a way Aunt Maude would never have tolerated. There might have been a place for everything, but everything certainly wasn't in the right place.

Phoebe followed Lorne along a wide hall and into the living room she had seen from outside. He gestured towards a comfortable-looking if somewhat saggy sofa, draped in an old tartan blanket.

'Sorry about the mess. I had a cleaner, but she's not turned up for a few weeks now and won't answer the phone. So I guess I don't have a cleaner any more.'

Was he asking her if she wanted the job? Phoebe settled herself down on the sofa carefully, but the expected billows of dust didn't materialise.

'It looks fine to me,' she said. 'I think Aunt Maude would maybe disapprove though.'

'Ah yes. The formidable Maude.' A wistful smile spread across his face, then vanished. 'I'll go pop the kettle on. Won't be a minute.'

Phoebe watched him go, noticing that he had a bit of a limp. As if his left hip pained him. To be fair, he looked like all his joints pained him. She wondered how old he actually was. In all her note-taking she'd never written down when the band had formed, but Gwen had disappeared in 1973, which might have been a lifetime ago, but only if like her you were twelve. If Lorne had been in his late twenties then, he'd only be forty or so now. Not much older than her mum and dad had been. What had happened to him in those twelve years to make his hair go that white? To give him so much pain in his joints? Well, he'd been in a mental asylum for one thing, hadn't he. Somehow in all the rush, Phoebe had forgotten that. Now she wondered how wise accepting his invitation to tea might have been.

A little unsettled, she stood up and looked around. The room was a decent size, particularly for an old Welsh stone cottage. The front window gave a view towards the river and an overgrown grass meadow on the other side. Not so steep sided at this point, the valley was wide enough here that Phoebe could even see a little sky above the tops of the hills without straining her neck. Pleasantly cool and dry on this hot summer day, it would be a comfortable place to sit. In the depths of winter, no doubt the heavy cast iron stove set into a deep fireplace would be kept burning around the clock. A single leather armchair was placed close for maximum comfort, and a little further away, a second small sofa had become the last resting place of all manner of detritus.

An old dresser filled the wall opposite the window, its top heaped with a clutter of papers and other things put down on the first available surface. The rest of the room was lined with bookshelves, reminiscent of the living room at Pant Melyn. Or indeed pretty much every room at Pant Melyn if she was being honest. Phoebe scanned the book titles, finding an eclectic mix of fiction, biographies and a whole section on music theory. There were quite a few art books too, the large format, glossy photograph kind that her mother had loved almost as much as her Muriel Baywater romances. And yes, there were a few of them dotted in among the collection too. The woman got everywhere, it seemed. Or the man, perhaps.

There were a few photographs in frames on the shelves, most of the band in various outrageous outfits. Sometimes it was Steve on his own, or with other people who looked like they might be in the music business. In all of them his hair was dark, his face serious and young. Phoebe studied the pictures one by one, working her way around the room until she came to the fireplace, the stove, and the mantelpiece above. More clutter had accumulated here, including several unopened envelopes that were most likely bills. In the centre, set in a simple silver frame, was one more picture. Steve again, but this time with a young woman. The picture wasn't a big one, and like most of the others in the room it had faded with time, so Phoebe had to lean in close to get a better look. The face that stared back at her was fuller, older, but unmistakably her own. She even had the same hairstyle.

'Oh.' She stood back quickly, the room darkening around her. Everything went quiet, and then a gentle ringing began in her ears. She thought she was going to faint, her legs too weak to hold her up. And then she felt a hand on her arm, steadying her, bringing her back to the real world.

'Perhaps now you understand why I stared the first time I saw you.' Steve Lorne smiled at her, let go of her arm. Phoebe hadn't heard him come in, and yet somehow there was a tray with teapot, mugs, plate of biscuits and jug of milk on it, balanced precariously on the arm of the sofa.

'She . . .' Her voice sounded strange, as if someone else was using it. Not her at all. She pointed at the photograph on the mantelpiece, noticing as she did that her hand was shaking.

'Gwen Ellis.' Steve Lorne walked slowly over, took the photograph from its resting place and ran his fingers over the glass. He stared down at it for a long time before finally looking back up at Phoebe. 'Or Gwen Ellis-Lorne, I should say. She was my wife.'

'You . . . you were married? But everyone—'

'Everyone says we were just together, I know. But we were

married in a church in London. Of course that wouldn't be good enough for her father, but it's true all the same. Here, let's have that tea. I don't do a lot of talking these days. Could do with something to soothe my throat.'

Phoebe almost offered to pour it, then remembered Aunt Maude's strange insistence that it was bad luck pouring tea in the home of someone you'd not known for seven years. She didn't say as much, but remained seated while Lorne busied himself with pot and mugs. It took a while, but eventually they were both settled. Her on the sofa, him in his armchair by the unlit fire. After a couple of sips of tea, he began to speak.

'I first met Gwen in London. Must have been what? Nineteen seventy? Seventy-one? She'd come up to see her brother. Cered was our main roadie back then. Almost the sixth member of the band. I can't remember the gig, there were so many back then it all blurs into one. There was a party after, and I didn't want to go, but Cered insisted. Someone I had to meet, he said. And that was her.'

He paused a moment to sip again from his mug of tea. Phoebe wondered if he wasn't hot, in this warm room. He had taken off his coat and scarf, but still wore a thick jacket, a silk cravat around his neck. There wasn't much colour in his cheeks to suggest he was overheating. Not much colour about him at all, given his shocking-white hair and the pale clothes he wore. Only that cravat, as crimson as spilled wine, and the blue of his eyes.

Tea drunk, he put the mug carefully down. Phoebe expected him to carry on talking, but instead he stared at her, blinking every so often, a strangely wistful look on his face. After long seconds of silence, perhaps even a whole minute, she began to feel a little uncomfortable under his gaze. He wasn't creepy, clearly wasn't trying to hit on her or anything like that. Instead he seemed to have slipped into a kind of fugue state, as if his mind had drifted away to another place. Some other time.

'You said you knew my mother?' Phoebe made it a question,

hoping to break a silence that had become extremely awkward. Lorne didn't respond immediately, but then slowly the life came back to his eyes. And with it a frown of puzzlement, as if he'd forgotten she was there even while he stared at her.

'Your mother.' A pause. 'Siân. Yes. Of course. She was a couple of years younger than Gwen, but they were like two sisters. Siân had gone to university when I first met Gwen. Think that's where she met your father, isn't it? I heard lots about her and of course she came back to Pant Melyn from time to time.' He levered himself up out of his seat with a great deal of effort, teetered on his feet for a moment before finding his balance. He limped across to the dresser, pulled out the top drawer and began rummaging around inside. Finally he came out with what looked like a leather-bound photo album. He carried it over to the sofa, handed it to Phoebe. For a moment she didn't know what to do, then she carefully placed her mug on the floor, balanced the half-eaten biscuit on the rim, and took what was offered her.

'Memory's not what it was, but I think she's in a couple of those.' Lorne shuffled away, dropping himself back into his armchair with a sigh of relief. Phoebe opened up the book to find the pages made of thick card, each one set with two or three glossy colour photographs.

'Summer of seventy-one, I think it was. I'd not long bought this place and the builders were still making it habitable. I was away most of the time, on tour. Gwen oversaw all the work. She was good at that sort of thing.'

The first few pages were indeed photographs of the cottage in a terrible, dilapidated state. A builder's van with 'Dai Jones a'i fab' written on the side was in several of the pictures, often along with a short, round man who must have been the builder himself. Halfway through, the setting changed, and after a while Phoebe recognised Pant Melyn, a series of pictures taken out in the back garden. The pampas grass bushes were there, although somewhat smaller than they were now, and the hedges that turned half the garden into maze were only waist height. Phoebe flicked through several pages showing the young Steve Lorne and Gwen Ellis sunning themselves on a lawn that must have been where Aunt Maude's vegetable patch was now. Every time she saw a picture of Gwen, Phoebe's heart did a little skip in her breast. It was like looking at her reflection, if the mirror aged her ten years. Then she turned the last page and her heart thudded even harder.

Two photographs, presumably taken by Steve himself, showed Gwen leaning back into a swinging bench, her arm around the shoulders of a slightly younger woman. Both were smiling wide, toothy grins, and all Phoebe could think was that she couldn't remember the last time she'd seen her mother smile at all.

31

Although it seemed like she had spent the whole day with Lorne, Phoebe was surprised to find it was only early afternoon by the time she emerged from the woods and let herself in the back door to Pant Melyn. Aunt Maude was nowhere to be seen, but Uncle Louis sat at the kitchen table, the debris of his lunch strewn around him like the casualties of a particularly violent war.

'Oh, hey, Feebs. Didn't know if you'd be back till later, so we went ahead and had lunch without you.'

Phoebe dropped her backpack at the kitchen door, then went to the sink to wash her hands. A half-finished loaf still sat on the bread board in the middle of the table, along with the butter dish and a hunk of cheese. She hadn't been hungry until she saw it, sustained by the biscuits she'd eaten with her tea, but now her stomach grumbled. It must have been loud, because when she turned back to the table, her uncle was already slicing two large hunks from the end of the loaf.

'Thank you,' she said as he passed them to her on a plate.

Uncle Louis watched as she spread butter, sliced cheese and formed the whole into a sandwich that probably wouldn't fit between her teeth without dislocating her jaw. He waited until she'd taken an exploratory bite before asking, 'You find your friend, then?'

'Gwyneth?' she said through a mouthful, then had to stop

speaking as it was impossible to chew and talk at the same time. Eventually she shook her head once, swallowed. 'No. I waited for a while, then went to see if I could find her. Didn't, but I did find the old mill and house up the river a ways. Where Steve Lorne lives.'

Uncle Louis frowned. 'Tynhelyg? That's a long way to be wandering, isn't it?'

Phoebe shrugged, her mouth full again. 'Didn't feel like it. I was just walking, and then the path opened up onto this clearing. Thought the house was derelict, but actually it's in quite good nick. Just the garden that's a bit overgrown.'

Uncle Louis's frown deepened. 'You went up to the house? Was there anyone there?'

'Didn't think so at first, but then he came out and introduced himself.'

'Came out? Who?'

'Steve Lorne of course. Who else would come out of his house?'

'You . . . spoke to him? I didn't think he could talk any more.'

'He does sound a bit strange. Sort of squeaky but hoarse, if you know what I mean. And very quiet. He kept drifting away, too. Like he'd forgotten I was there.'

'You . . . you shouldn't have gone there, Phoebe. He's . . .'

But before he could say what Steve Lorne was, Aunt Maude came bustling back into the kitchen, stark naked save for a pair of green wellington boots. She held a wooden trug in the crook of her arm, filled with an impressive assortment of flowers and greenery that couldn't possibly be edible. Not tonight's supper, then. Phoebe was so used to her aunt's casual attitude towards clothing now she barely flinched.

'Don't eat too much, dear. I'm not going to all the trouble of cooking just for you to leave your plate half full.' She put the trug down on the table and brushed invisible dirt from her palms in an exaggerated movement. 'Been off playing with your little friend again, have you?'

'Actually, I didn't see Gwyneth today, no. But I did see some photos of my mum.'

Aunt Maude's stern gaze morphed into one of confusion, until Uncle Louis chimed in.

'She went to Tynhelyg. Saw Steve there. He spoke to her, apparently.'

'He made me a cup of tea and showed me some photos of Gwen and Mum in the garden here.' Phoebe waved a hand in the direction of the back door just in case neither adult knew where the garden was.

Aunt Maude pulled out a chair and sat down at the table. Strangely, this made her nakedness more apparent. Phoebe wasn't at all sure where to look.

'You went in the house? With him?'

'Just the front room, aye. It was a bit untidy, but he said his cleaner had stopped coming. I offered to go and do a bit of cleaning for him, if he wanted. In exchange for music lessons.'

Silence filled the kitchen. Even the clock seemed to hold its tick, the oven pause mid-gurgle. Phoebe looked first to her uncle, then her aunt, both of whose mouths hung slightly open.

'What?' she asked

'It's out of the question.' Aunt Maude rallied first, her nakedness only making her words more forceful.

'But—' Phoebe began.

'Hang on, Maude,' Uncle Louis interrupted her.

'No, Louis. It's out of the question. Phoebe has chores she could be doing here. And we've got to start on her education too. There won't be time.'

Uncle Louis opened his mouth, then closed it again, his sense of self-preservation kicking in. Phoebe followed his lead, saying no more. She couldn't help wondering what the problem was though. Steve had been a little strange, but compared to all the other folk she'd met since coming to Llancwm, he was a model of sanity. It had been his idea to teach her music; she'd only come up with the offer of paying by cleaning because she felt she had to do something in return for his kindness. And yet Aunt Maude was acting as if he was some kind of axe murderer.

'I should be getting back to my work,' Uncle Louis said after the silence had dragged on a little longer than was comfortable. He pushed back his chair with a squeal of wooden legs on flagstone floor, wincing at the noise that he and Phoebe both knew annoyed Aunt Maude more than most things. He slunk towards his study like a dog that's been shouted at, and the look he gave Phoebe as he stepped through the door was hard to read. Only once it had closed behind him did she turn back to her aunt.

'Why are you both acting so strangely?' she asked.

Aunt Maude stared at her a long while before answering, her lack of clothes making Phoebe increasingly uncomfortable. Not just weird, but unreasonable too. What was wrong with these people?

'The last time you mentioned Steve Lorne, he'd been leering at you in the woods, right?'

'I wouldn't say leering, but . . .' Phoebe shrugged. 'An' he said sorry. Said it was because I look like Gwen. I saw the photos he had of her and it's strange. I mean, she's a good bit older than me in all of them, but it's like looking in a mirror. Only, one that shows you what you'd look like all grown up.'

Aunt Maude raised an eyebrow. 'Look, Phoebe. I know you always see the best in people, and you're probably right about Steve. He's likely harmless, most of the time. But he tried to take his own life. Almost succeeded. They sectioned him, locked him up in an asylum for years. Who's to know he won't relapse? Particularly given how much you look like Gwen. It's just not safe for you to be going there on your own, spending time with him. Not fair on him either, the constant reminder of what he lost.'

'But . . .' Phoebe started, but for all that she wanted to talk to Mr Lorne more, and the thought of being taught music by a bona fide rock star was more exciting than anything, she could also see Aunt Maude's point. She remembered the moment when he had zoned out, an oddly whimsical smile on his face as if he were in a different time and place entirely. She knew exactly where he had gone. Didn't she go there herself almost every day? Back to a time before it had all gone wrong? A time before the hurt?

'I'll have to tell him, at least,' she said eventually. 'That's only fair.'

Aunt Maude conceded that with a slight tilt of the head. 'We can both go and see him soon. I've tried enough times before, but he's always shied away from me. From your uncle too. Don't think he really talks to anyone any more, which is why I'm so surprised he talked to you.'

'Really? He seemed fine to me. A little sad and lonely maybe, and there's that thing with the scarves and cravats, but I've had teachers who've been a lot weirder than him.'

'It was all such a long time ago. Before you were even born.' Aunt Maude placed her hands flat on the table in front of her, stared at them for a while as if wondering why they weren't doing anything.

'Shall I make a pot of tea?' Phoebe asked, keen to keep the old lady talking. Before her aunt could answer, she pushed her chair back more carefully than Uncle Louis, stood up and fetched the kettle to the sink to fill it up. Aunt Maude watched her all the while, only speaking again once the mugs were on the table and the pot stewing.

'When Gwen went missing, there were a fair few in the village thought it was Steve's doing.'

'They . . . what?'

'You have to understand something, Phoebe. It's not as blatant as it was, but there used to be a lot of bad feeling about, well, the English. Coming to Wales and buying the houses for their holidays, pricing the locals out, just being English was enough for some. Grudges come easy and stay a long time. Oh, not everyone felt that way, of course. Your mother couldn't wait to get away. Went off to university and hardly ever came back. And there was Ceredig, too. Gwen's brother? He saw how narrow-minded his father was, left and went to work in London. That's how Steve met Gwen in the first place. Only it didn't work out so well for poor Cered, and quite a few in the village blamed Steve for that.'

Phoebe listened, fascinated. She'd encountered nothing but friendliness since arriving in Llancwm, if you didn't count the twins. But then she wasn't English.

'So you see, when Gwen disappeared, quite a few folk around here thought he'd killed her. Accidentally or on purpose, didn't matter. Rumour was he'd buried her body somewhere in the woods and pretended to search for her to keep up appearances. Well, it would have been suspicious if he'd not at least tried looking, I suppose.'

'But he was so distraught he tried to kill himself, didn't he? He actually went mad, right? They locked him up in a loony bin.'

Aunt Maude tilted her head at Phoebe's outburst, something like a smile on her lips as she reached for the pot and poured tea for them both.

'You have to understand the parochial mindset, Phoebe dear. For those who already suspected him, Steve's suicide attempt only confirmed it. It wasn't sadness but guilt that consumed him until he couldn't bear it any more. A lot of the older folk reckon he should have been tried, not sectioned.'

'But not you. Not Uncle Louis.'

'No, not us. For one thing, I know for a fact that Gwen disappeared before Steve got back from his tour. Last I saw her she was heading up to Nant Caws Farm to speak to old Meredith about something. That was two days before Steve's band arrived back in London. I got that from his tour manager, but it was in the papers too.'

Phoebe sipped at her tea, decided she'd already drunk far too much of it today, put the mug down again. 'So if Steve wasn't to blame, why did . . .?' She found she couldn't finish the question.

'Why did he try to kill himself? Ah, Phoebe dear. He and Gwen were so in love with each other it was sometimes almost painful to watch. They spent a few weeks together here, before Tynhelyg was habitable. Don't think I've ever seen anyone so happy and relaxed. Like the weight of the world had been lifted off his shoulders. But the thing is, all that weight had been on them before, or at least that was how he'd felt. He went back into that world again, left Gwen behind, and the only thing sustaining him was the promise that she'd be waiting for him when he got back.'

'Only she wasn't.' Phoebe understood now. 'And it didn't just break his heart; it broke his mind too.'

'Exactly so. And it's taken all this time to even start to mend. You've seen him, out wandering the woods every day. He's still not right, so you can understand why you must keep your distance.'

Phoebe wasn't sure Aunt Maude was right about that. She had enough in common with Steve Lorne that they could have likely helped each other, and in all the time she'd spent with him she'd not felt any kind of threat from the man. She kept that to herself though. An argument for another time. But as she cleared the table of the mess Uncle Louis's lunch had left, stacked the plates by the sink to wash up, she knew that she would be having that argument soon.

Aunt Maude knocked back the rest of her tea, hauled herself out of her chair and picked up the trug she had brought in earlier. She paused at the door through to the utility room, looked back at Phoebe. 'I don't suppose you fancy digging some potatoes? Need to get on with it, and we'll be eating early tonight.'

'Early? Why?'

'Oh, didn't Louis say? It's pub quiz night. Highlight of the Llancwm social calendar.'

Her uncle hadn't mentioned anything of the sort, and Phoebe

was fairly certain the same thing had been said about the Agricultural Show, but things were looking up if there was the prospect of a visit to the village. Even so, she looked past her to the glass door and out into the garden. It wasn't raining, but everything would still be wet. Digging potatoes sounded like hard, muddy work.

'No, thanks. Think I'll go read a book.'

32

2023

There is no mobile signal at Pant Melyn. Phoebe knows that, of course, but it still catches her out every time she swipes on her phone to do something. At least the house has broadband, although for a very loose definition of broad. It's a good thing she's not desperate to stream a TV series or settle down with a good film. Then again, there's no telly either. Some things never change.

She's been waiting for a call back on the land line for an hour, and what's left in the cafetière is cold now, too bitter to drink. It's as good an excuse as any to get out of the house and leave the answering machine to deal with things. A walk in the woods will help clear her mind.

Red kites wheel and scream overhead as Phoebe strides across the meadow. They no longer sound like wailing babies to her, but there is something about their cry that still sends shivers up her back. It's a relief to plunge into the cool shade of the trees and follow the familiar paths. She pauses only briefly on the bridge, no time to dawdle in the hope of meeting someone. Now she is here, there is something important she must do. Something she has been putting off for reasons she can't quite understand. Or maybe she can. Another piece of the trauma that has been such a huge part of her life.

The approach to Tynhelyg doesn't fill her with much in the way of hope. Phoebe remembers visiting the place plenty of times when she was young. She took lessons in guitar and piano, learned how to sing properly and even had a go at writing her own songs. In return, she cleaned, although probably not as much as she should have done. In all those years, the weed saplings in the lawn grew slowly. Never enough to make her realise how large they were becoming.

Now it is as if the forest is reaching out to reclaim the land carved out of it when the buildings were built. The saplings are full grown, the grass between them giving way to ferns and shrubs. Only the area immediately around the house and mill are clear, a few signs of recent pruning an indication that someone comes here occasionally. Do they live here still?

She stands a short distance from the house for a while, uncertain. Aunt Maude rarely spoke of the man who lived here, despite his having been a friend for many years. An earlier trauma strained their relationship to breaking point, maybe beyond. Strange how it goes. There is kindness and community in this valley, it's true. But there are deep divisions too, built over generations.

There is no movement in the house, no light in any of the rooms she can see. Phoebe would probably stand for longer, but the clouds sweep in overhead and a stiff breeze promises rain. Decades since she moved away, yet she still remembers the weather here, the little signals of what's about to come. With a little shudder, she hurries across the weedy gravel driveway and knocks on the front door.

It opens swiftly, as if the owner has been standing there, observing her through the glass and thinking the same thoughts as she has. His frown knits bushy white eyebrows together as he peers at her for a few heartbeats, and then his face breaks out into a broad smile.

'Feebs,' he says, his voice hoarse and whisper quiet at the same time, and she is suddenly twelve years old all over again.

★ ★ ★

The house is tidier than she remembers, although given how frail Steve Lorne has become that is perhaps no bad thing. The hallway had always been cluttered when Phoebe was young, filled with trip hazards. Not a problem in your forties, but dangerous when you reach . . . how old is he?

'I heard about Maude,' he says in that quiet, strained voice. He still covers his neck with a silk cravat, Phoebe sees. 'Very sorry. She lived a good, long life though.'

For a moment, she wonders who told him. Steve was always a recluse, long before it became fashionable. But someone must be keeping the place tidy for him, the village finally taking him to its bosom, perhaps.

'I spoke to her just the evening before. On the phone.' Phoebe has tried to recall every detail of the conversation, but mostly failed. 'I think she had decided it was time to go.'

'That sounds like Maude. Never one to make a fuss.' Steve has led her through to the music room, where they always used to go when she visited. The guitars are still on their stands, the piano still up against its wall, but Phoebe gets the impression there's not been much music made here in a while. 'Where are my manners? Would you like some tea?'

'I'll make it, shall I?' Phoebe doesn't wait to be told. She takes herself through to the kitchen, again far tidier than when she was the one doing the cleaning. By the time Steve shuffles in behind her, she's already got the kettle on, found the teapot and is searching for the old metal caddy the Earl Grey lives in. There's a conversation they should be having, something she's been avoiding the best part of twenty-five years now. Perhaps it's time to face it full on.

'I'm sorry I've been so rubbish at keeping in touch.'

Steve lowers his head once in acknowledgement. He pulls out a chair and sits at the table, brings his hands together. They're old man's hands, Phoebe can't help but notice. Twisted with arthritis, joints swollen, skin blotchy with liver spots and so thin she can see the tendons beneath. Little surprise the music room has fallen silent in her absence.

'You're young. You have things to do far more important than spending time with me. And besides, I've always been happiest with my own company.'

'Not so young any more.' Phoebe finds the caddy, spoons some tea into the pot. The smell of bergamot and cornflower takes her back so many years. 'I'll be fifty in a couple of months.'

Steve looks genuinely shocked, stares at her in silence for a while before shaking his head slowly. He doesn't say anything, doesn't try to contradict her with platitudes. But then he never talked much before. It pains him, Phoebe knows. And she knows why, too.

'I've spoken to one of the elders at the chapel. We'll have a memorial service for Maude next week, and there'll be a wake at the hotel afterwards. You're more than welcome to come if you want, but I'll understand fine if you don't. I know the locals were never too kind to you in the past.'

'There's very few of them left, you know. From back then. I think Maude was probably the last, and she was always welcoming.' Steve swallows, puts one hand up to his cravat and then pulls it away self-consciously. Phoebe pours tea into mugs, a splash of cold water from the tap into Steve's, and passes it across to him. There is melancholy in the smile he gives her by way of thanks, as if this is a ritual no one else has ever managed to perform correctly. He takes a small sip, swallows again.

'Things have changed here in the past few years, Feebs. Since your uncle died, perhaps long before then. There are more in-comers than locals now, folk from all over. And half the houses are holiday lets these days. The forest is so busy in summer, but it gets very quiet in the winter.'

'I spoke to Cerys at the hotel. Surprised me not to see Bethan and Tom, but then they'd be as old as Maude so . . .' She lets the words drift away, not wanting to admit the inevitable.

'Cerys, yes.' Steve takes another sip of tea, pauses for a long while before continuing. 'She's responsible for all this.'

It takes Phoebe a while to understand that he means the tidiness of his house, and the friendly woman she met at the hotel reception goes up in her estimation another level. With that realisation, she feels a pang of guilt, too. Looking after Steve was supposed to be her task, after all.

'Do you get out into the forest much these days?' She studies his face for a reaction as she asks the question, knowing it means more to him than it would to most people. The slump of his shoulders is more eloquent.

'Not so much. I can walk still, but slowly.' Another pause, and Phoebe is about to say something when he speaks again. 'I don't worry about falling down so much. More I'd feel bad for whoever it was found my body. I'm tired, Feebs. Not as old as Maude, but I know how she must have felt.'

A comfortable silence follows that thought, the two of them quietly sipping their tea. Phoebe always felt comfortable with Steve's silence, and maybe that's where her own love of solitude was born. Here, in this kitchen she's not sat in for far too long.

'She asked me to scatter her ashes up near the bees. Well, I say ashes, but she's not being cremated. I'm told the end result is much the same, but it's some kind of water process.'

'Resomation, I know. Maude told everyone, I think. Still, she'll be happy up there, looking down over the rest of us. And she'll be with Louis again. She missed him, you know.'

Phoebe does, but she's surprised that Steve knows too. Aunt Maude was always stoic in the face of adversity. But then Steve has borne his own loss far longer.

'I will come to the chapel and say my goodbyes,' he says after a while. 'And perhaps you'll come visit an old man again before you go back to Scotland, eh?'

Phoebe doesn't have an answer to that immediately. Not because she won't of course come and visit Steve again, and soon. She owes him more than that. No, the thought that strikes her at that exact moment is how strange the idea of going back to Scotland feels. What exactly is there waiting for her?

33

1985

Time was Phoebe would have thought spending an evening in a pub was the height of adult sophistication. Well, maybe not the height, but something to aspire to all the same. After half an hour of actually being in the pub with adults, the shine had more or less completely worn off that idea.

Perhaps it was because her uncle and aunt lived such quiet, secluded lives, a chance to get out and socialise with people was exciting for them. Uncle Louis certainly enjoyed a chance to drink, but Phoebe was surprised at how much less dour Aunt Maude was as she sat at the table in the corner of the bar in Llancwm, chatting with a couple of old women whose names Phoebe hadn't managed to remember.

They were all there for the monthly pub quiz, apparently, her uncle and aunt eager to get started, having missed the previous month's outing due to Phoebe's unexpected arrival. It was quite the social gathering if the packed room was any indication. Busier even than the bustle of the place after she'd saved the old farmer.

The door swung open with a clatter that barely registered over the hubbub of excited conversation, and Angharad Roberts pushed through the throng to the bar. She was dressed all in black again,

Phoebe noticed as the young woman ducked under the serving hatch, grabbed an apron that was also black, and tied it around her middle before starting to serve the punters.

'You want to be on our team, Feebs?' Uncle Louis had a sheet of paper in front of him, two biros lined up alongside it, their ends frayed where someone had spent industrious hours chewing them. Phoebe looked at the team name scrawled across the top of the page. 'The Patient Beekeepers'. She couldn't think of anything she'd rather less be doing than sitting here with these old people. Even the telly on a shelf high up above the door had been switched off. First time she'd even seen one in months and it wasn't working.

'Do I have to?' she asked, hearing the six-year-old in her voice.

''Course not. But if you're just going to sit there, you can go fetch us all drinks, eh?' Uncle Louis produced a crumpled twenty-pound note and handed it to her. It took only a moment to work out who wanted what, and Phoebe was glad of the opportunity to get away. Even if technically she wasn't old enough to be served in a pub.

'You look as bored as me,' Angharad said when Phoebe leaned against the empty bar.

'Was hoping there might be a few more people my own age.' Phoebe glanced around the crowded room, seeing nothing but a sea of blue-rinse hairdos. 'Is there anyone here younger than sixty?'

'Apart from you and me? Doubt it.' The young woman busied herself with pulling pints, pouring wine and fixing up a gin and tonic, ice and a slice. 'This place is dead most nights, mind. I keep telling Tom he should run more things like the quiz, but he never listens.'

The man himself was standing only a few feet away, and the fact he didn't respond lent truth to Angharad's words.

'You not having another Coke?' she asked once the drinks were all arranged on a tray. Phoebe took a while to understand what Angharad had said.

'Can't stand the stuff. I'd kill for an Irn Bru.'

'Irn Bru?' Angharad's eyebrows raised in question as she made a bad job of repeating Phoebe's words.

'Aye, Irn Bru. You know what I mean, right? You've heard of Irn Bru?'

A slow shake of the head suggested that this was not the case.

'Really? It's only Scotland's greatest export after whisky and haggis. Did you know that we're the only country in the world where Coca-Cola isn't the number one soft drink?'

'No way.' Angharad shook her head slowly in disbelief. 'You're kidding, right?'

'It's the truth. And anyway, Irn Bru's much nicer than Coke. Better for you too.'

'I'll take your word for it. Can't see Tom rushing to get stock in, mind you. Talking of which.' Angharad handed Phoebe more change than she had been expecting and pushed the tray towards the edge of the bar. 'Best get back to serving punters before the questions start.'

Phoebe made her excuses after she'd taken the drinks to the table, and headed out to the little area at the back of the pub for some fresh air. Uncle Louis and Aunt Maude had been so caught up in the quiz they'd barely noticed. She didn't feel any great rush to go back inside.

'Hiding from the grown-ups, now is it?'

She looked around to see Angharad come into the yard from another door. She carried a bag over to the bins and dumped it inside before wandering over to where Phoebe sat.

'Is it always like this?' she asked. There was no need to explain what 'this' was.

Angharad swung a leg over the bench next to Phoebe, rested an elbow on the rough tabletop. 'Pretty much. Place used to be a bit livelier a few years back, but the last family with kids your age moved to town. Now we only see the holiday cottage crowd, and even then it's mostly old folks these days.'

'Come to Llancwm: heaven's waiting room.' Phoebe raised both arms to the sky as she spoke, trying to encompass the entirety of what her world had become. Angharad laughed at her.

'Funny. But not so far from the truth. Sometimes feels like every other week there's an ambulance through the village, and it's not all those mad wannabe rally drivers in their souped-up Subarus losing it on the mountain road either. Too many folk collapsing at home, and by the time any help gets to them they're past saving.'

'It's not that bad, is it?' Phoebe worried that maybe it was.

'Well, you should know. How long did you have to give old Mered the kiss of life before the ambulance turned up?'

'Yeah, I guess.' Phoebe scratched at the table, green algae wedging up under her fingernail. It had felt like hours before the first paramedic had arrived, and even longer until the ambulance got there.

'Seems weird people would want to live so far out,' she said. 'I mean, old folk need to be closer to services, don't they?'

Angharad chuckled. 'There's the thing though. They weren't always old, were they? Your Uncle Lou? He was born in this valley. Same with old Mered and his children. Now even Tegwin's past fifty. But the incomers? Yeah, you're right there. They get this idea of retiring to a cottage in Wales. Maybe been here on their holidays and thought it was like that all the time, see? And then they get here and it's mostly raining. Nearest half-decent shop's in Aber, and when you need an ambulance ...' She left the sentence unfinished.

'So they wander the woods as ghosts for evermore, then.' Phoebe shrugged. 'Could be worse, I suppose. It's boring, sure, but it's not exactly hell.'

'Ghosts, is it? What have you been seeing out in those woods, Phoebe bach? Or have you been listening to your uncle's tall tales too much?'

Phoebe stiffened a little at the 'bach'. Angharad might have been a couple of years older than her, but she wasn't any taller. If anyone deserved the term 'little' it was her. Then again, it was meant to be a term of endearment, wasn't it? That's what Aunt Maude had said.

'Don't think I've seen anything I couldn't explain, but the stories get to you sometimes, you know? Like that one about the abandoned child. When you hear the kites screaming, it could be a baby crying for its mother.'

'True enough. They'd be more likely to eat a baby, mind you. Horrible things.'

'You don't like them?' Phoebe asked, surprised.

'Ach, they're all right, I suppose. Just birds doing what birds do. But they can scare the bejesus out of you. Sounding off when you're minding your own business and not paying attention.'

Phoebe knew what Angharad meant. It could be unnerving when you were lost in thoughts, deep in the silence of the forest, and suddenly something screamed overhead like it was being murdered.

'Anyway, I'd best be getting back to the bar before Tom notices I'm not there and docks my wages, eh?' Angharad stood up, looked briefly at the door where she'd come out before turning back to Phoebe. 'And don't go paying too much attention to your uncle and his ghost stories, right? There's nothing more scary in those woods than Axe and Brue Thomas, and they're more mouth than trouser, if you know what I mean.'

The young woman smiled, winked, then walked away. Perhaps she had meant to be reassuring, but as Phoebe thought about her previous encounters with the twins, she couldn't help seeing the threat as real. No one else she had met since arriving in Wales had put her on edge quite the way those two did. And was it her imagination, or had it suddenly become cold out in the yard behind the pub?

Shrugging her jacket tight around her, she stood up and headed back inside.

★ ★ ★

The light had almost gone from the day as they walked from Lla-ncwm, through the woods and along the track to Pant Melyn. Phoebe had been bored sideways by the pub quiz, but things had livened up a bit after the questions had been asked and Tom the landlord was reading out the answers. There was something very amusing about half-drunk adults arguing over trivia.

'I still can't believe they let Peregrine's team get away with Hedley Lamarr when it's Hedy Lamarr. Hedy, not Hedley. They were wrong.' Uncle Lou walked more quickly than normal, his steps lurching slightly from side to side so that Phoebe had to both hurry to keep up and occasionally skip to avoid being knocked over. Aunt Maude somehow managed always to be out of the way, no doubt used to this situation.

'It was perfectly fair, Lou. And you know it. Besides, we won. Isn't that enough?'

They had won, and judging by the reaction of the rest of the teams in the pub quiz, they always won. The prize had been a bottle of whisky that Maude had snatched before Uncle Louis could get his hands on it, and passed to the other two members of the team. Phoebe had felt a little sorry for her uncle then, but it hadn't lasted.

'How was your evening, Feebs?' he asked as they approached the little wooden bridge where Gwyneth had failed to reappear. They had been walking for a good twenty minutes and it was the first time he'd so much as acknowledged her presence.

'It was OK, I guess. Sat out the back and watched the woods. Talked to Angharad a bit.'

Aunt Maude made an odd tutting noise under her breath at the name, but Uncle Louis didn't seem to notice.

'And what did the lovely Miss Roberts have to say?' he asked.

'Not much. She was busy at the bar mostly. We were talking about the ghost stories, you know? How these woods are filled with the spirits of all the folk who've died here down the centuries.'

Phoebe had meant it as a jest, but as she spoke the air turned

chilly and a breeze sprung up out of nowhere. It took her a moment
to realise that this was because they had stepped onto the bridge,
the water cascading over the rocks a few yards below them,
churning the air up and cooling it down.

'And I suppose she told you they're all bunkum.' Uncle Louis
was halfway across the bridge and he stopped, turned to face her,
blocking the way.

'Well, they are. There's no such thing as ghosts. They're just
stories to scare people. Keep them away from places they're not
meant to go.'

'Oh, to be so young and naive.' Uncle Louis hammed the line
like the worst of actors. He leaned back against the railing, arms
crossed. Aunt Maude had already gone ahead, swallowed by the
gloomy depths of the forest.

'There's no such thing as ghosts,' Phoebe insisted.

'So you said. But haven't you ever felt like you're being watched
when you're alone down here? Haven't you seen things moving
out of the corner of your eye, but when you turn to look at them
there's nothing?'

Phoebe had, but while Steve Lorne might look like a ghost, he
was flesh and blood, alive. The only other person she'd met in the
woods was Gwyneth, and she was real enough. Just a bit strange and
elusive.

'Things always move in the woods though, don't they? The wind
in the branches, small animals on the ground, birds.' She pointed
at the water, only the white froth where it rushed over the rocks
visible now in the ever-deepening night. 'Even the river. There
doesn't have to be anything spooky about it. That story you told me,
Myfanwy's baby or whatever. That was just made up, playing around
with the same sort of things Muriel Baywater does in her novels.'

Uncle Louis flinched when he heard the name, the slightest of
reactions he might have been able to hide had he not been several
pints down and full of bonhomie. Phoebe noticed it all the same.

'Why do your publishers keep sending you her novels to review?' she asked. 'It's not as if they've got anything in common with your own book.'

Uncle Louis pushed himself upright, still a little unsteady on his feet, and looked around the clearing. It was almost completely dark now, hard to see much beyond either end of the bridge, harder still to make out his expression.

'They send me all sorts of stuff, Feebs. Most of it goes to the charity shops, but I write reviews for the papers. The few that still carry reviews, that is.' He set off towards the riverbank and the path that would take them home. 'Now hurry up why don't you, before your aunt locks us both out for the night.'

34

2023

The mechanical clang of a tiny bell sends Phoebe straight back to her childhood. She's become so used to ringtones on her mobile, the occasional electronic beep of the phone in her flat in Edinburgh, that the sound of the ancient handset rattling away in the hall leaves her transfixed. Why neither Uncle Louis nor Aunt Maude thought to change it, she never understood, except that it worked and so clearly didn't need replacing.

She's slow getting up from the kitchen table, still clutching her mug of coffee as she strides through to answer the call. It rings off before she can reach out, and she finds herself staring blankly at the old dial. Not quite able to understand why there's no screen to identify who was there.

And then with a clunk, the answering machine comes to life. Older even than the one in her flat, it whirrs for a few seconds before Aunt Maude's voice echoes into the hallway announcing that she's unable to answer the call and asking whoever is on the other end of the line to leave a message. Hearing that voice pulls her up short. Maude in her still-vital sixties rather than the frail ninety-four-year-old woman Phoebe spoke to the evening before she died.

When the message ends, the dull monotone of a dead line plays out for a few seconds before the elderly electronics catch up with what's happening. Whoever called, it wasn't important enough to leave a message. There will be more, Phoebe knows. Regulars checking in, cold callers trying to sell or scam, perhaps even one or two people trying to get in touch with her rather than her aunt.

Without thinking, Phoebe pulls her mobile out of her pocket, the screen lighting up at the movement. There are no new calls, but then that's hardly surprising given the lack of mobile signal. She's connected to the glacially slow broadband in the house, and there are a few messages showing. Nothing that would demand her immediate response though, and nothing from Clare.

Does that surprise her, after her own attempt at calling ended in such an embarrassing way? Phoebe isn't sure. What surprises her is that she's not upset. Perhaps she's too busy to deal with the emotional fallout. Or maybe there simply isn't any. That part of her life is over, time to move on.

It's an odd thought, that hearing Aunt Maude's voice can bring a lump to her throat, but the certain knowledge that her only long-term relationship is over does not bother her. Phoebe's always been good at repressing her emotions, never letting them overwhelm her like they did her mother. Maybe because of what they did to her mother, now she thinks about it. Siân MacDonald had dealt with her pain by blunting it with tranquillisers, and left her daughter to fend for herself. Abandoned her even before the fire, in a way. Perhaps that's what's made her so self-reliant, so much the recluse that gregarious Clare always found hardest to deal with.

She shrugs, even though there is nobody to see her do so, and heads back into the kitchen as the tapes in the answering machine whirr and rewind. Outside, the morning has brightened, the sunlight painting the treetops in shades of pink and gold. There are endless tasks that need completing, a whole house to sort out, a whole life. But there is time enough to deal with all that later.

She puts her coffee down on the table, goes through to the utility room and stands at the open back door. Cool air washes over her face, but it's not so cold really. A day for being out in the garden, weeding the vegetable beds and sorting out the greenhouse. A memory older even than the ancient answering machine comes back to her, and brings with it a mischievous smile. Why not? It's her garden now, her life.

Phoebe kicks off her unlaced trainers, pulls her hoodie and T-shirt over her head in one movement. The breeze brings goosebumps to her flesh, but the sun on her skin is wonderful as she steps out of her jogging pants and walks naked onto the back lawn. It's taken her a long time, but now she understands what her aunt was on about all those years ago. She closes her eyes, raises hands high and laughs as the red kites wheel and cry above her.

35

1985

'We've a few friends coming round for dinner, Phoebe dear. I wonder if you wouldn't mind having an early night.'

A quick flick of the eyes to the clock hanging on the wall showed her it wasn't quite six in the evening yet, although it wasn't far off. Phoebe had spent the morning helping Aunt Maude in the garden, and then explored the woods all afternoon with Gwyneth. She had been waiting for Phoebe at the bridge as if only a day had passed since their last adventure, and somehow that had seemed perfectly natural. Too wrapped up in the joy of having someone her own age for company, she'd quite forgotten all the questions she had wanted to ask until after they had parted as the sun dipped into evening. Finding her aunt busy at the cooker and ladling stew onto a plate as she came into the kitchen, Phoebe had sat down to eat without really thinking, but now she saw how odd it was to be at the table alone.

'Umm. How early did you have in mind?' She shoved a forkful of stew into her mouth, her stomach grumbling in appreciation at the hot food.

'Well, now. It's a regular thing, you see? The other university lecturers and folk who live nearby. Very informal, but we try to get together once a month or so for dinner. We missed the last one because you'd only just arrived and we didn't think it'd be fair.'

Phoebe wanted to ask why she couldn't join them all, but in truth the idea of a dinner party with a bunch of university lecturers sounded duller even than being stuck at Pant Melyn. She'd listened at the dining room door when her parents had entertained guests for dinner before, and the memory of her father finding her asleep on the stairs, carrying her back up to bed, brought tears to her eyes she had to hide with a sniff.

'What time will they be here?' she asked after she'd wiped her nose on her sleeve. Distracted by the bubbling pots on the stove top, Aunt Maude fortunately didn't seem to notice.

'Well, the colonel's usually first to arrive and he'll probably be here by seven.'

'You want me to go to bed after I've eaten?' What was she, five?

Aunt Maude shrugged. 'Well, you don't have to go to bed. Just read a book maybe. Listen to some music on that cassette player of yours. I don't know.'

Phoebe ate a mouthful, pleasantly surprised at how nice it tasted. The shock of that memory from home fading, she realised that it had been years ago, when she was still only little. Before her mother had started taking sleeping pills and going to bed right after supper. There had been no more dinner parties after that. And just because her father's friends had been dull, it didn't necessarily mean her aunt and uncle's friends would be the same.

'Could I meet them? Your friends. I don't know anybody here.'

Aunt Maude seemed taken aback by the question. 'I . . . Why would you want to meet them? They're our generation. Old, you'd probably say.' She smiled at this last comment, some joke with herself that Phoebe didn't understand.

'I dunno. Just thought it might be nice. Someone to talk to if nothing else.' She set about her food again, using a thick slice of freshly baked bread to mop up the sauce like Uncle Louis always did. Maude watched her for a moment, then went back to the stove and her pots. She hadn't answered the question, but Phoebe had learned not to push too hard. Aunt Maude and Uncle Louis were a lot less strict than her parents had ever been, but they liked to take their time coming to a decision. Nothing in Pant Melyn moved fast.

She had cleared the plate and was chewing the last of the bread when her aunt finally spoke again. Before she could get any understandable words out though, the study door clicked open and Uncle Louis stepped into the kitchen. His hair looked like an explosion in a wig factory, and he had a dazed expression on his face, or at least more dazed than usual. It took him a moment to focus on the scene in the kitchen, a moment longer for it to register in his mind enough to smile.

'You back then, Feebs?'

'Phoebe was just saying she'd quite like to meet our guests,' Maude cut in before Phoebe could answer. A look of panicked horror spread across Uncle Louis's face for a moment.

'She does? Why?' he asked, then remembered Phoebe was there, directed the question at her. 'You do? Why?'

'I hardly ever get to see anyone except you both.' Phoebe was warming to the idea now, a little spark of excitement in what had otherwise been yet another dull day. 'Thought it'd be nice to talk to someone else for a change.'

Uncle Louis's face cycled through a number of expressions, mostly alarm. Phoebe sat there, sweetly innocent, while he thought things through.

'Well, I guess you could help serve drinks when they arrive. You'd be best keeping out of the way though. Some of these folks are ...' Uncle Louis paused a moment, searching for the right words. 'Well, they're a bit old-fashioned.'

'I can do that,' Phoebe said, then turned her attention to Aunt Maude. 'And I can keep an eye on the food if you want. Stay in here, you know? Keep out of the way?'

For a moment she thought it might have worked, and that she'd not be confined to her attic bedroom until breakfast came around. Her uncle seemed to be considering something, but then he shook his head slowly before heading back to his study door.

'I'm sorry, Feebs, but it would really be best if you kept out of the way this time. There is something though. I almost forgot.'

He disappeared into the room for a moment, returning with something clasped in his hand. Two things, Phoebe saw as he came closer. He held out the first one for her, and she saw it was one of the copies of the new Muriel Baywater novel, *The Soft Touch of His Lips*.

'I know you enjoy these, and this one's not published until next month so you'll get to read it before anyone else.'

Phoebe took the book with an unenthusiastic 'thanks'. It wasn't that she didn't want to read it so much as that it seemed scant recompense for being sent to her room for no reason.

'And I found this when I was looking for something else. You said you were interested in music lessons, didn't you?' Uncle Louis handed over what turned out to be a larger book with a picture of an old acoustic guitar on the front. *The Guitar Handbook* by someone called Ralph Denver. It looked like it had never been opened.

'I—' she began to speak, only to be interrupted by a voice shouting 'halloo!' from the hall.

'That'll be the colonel,' Aunt Maude said as she headed out of the kitchen. She paused at the door. 'Come along, then, Phoebe, since you're so anxious to meet him.'

Phoebe had built an image in her head the moment her aunt had first mentioned 'the colonel', and she was almost disappointed when it turned out to be a hundred percent accurate. He was older than her aunt and uncle, she thought, although it might have been a life of active service that had turned his hair white and thin, reddened his cheeks and nose. He wore a tweed suit that strained around the waistcoat and trouser, but he held himself upright, back straight, shoulders square.

'Maude, how lovely to see you,' he said with a deep, English voice toned with genuine affection.

'Likewise, Alastair.' The two grown-ups embraced each other warmly, and for what seemed like an indecently long time before breaking apart. Aunt Maude stepped back and gestured for the colonel to come inside. Only then did he notice Phoebe standing a few paces back.

'Ah, and you must be young Miss MacDonald. Colonel Peterson at your service, m'dear.' He gave a her a mock salute, which left Phoebe uncertain of how to greet him. A handshake would have been easy, but it felt awkward now. He had no coat either, so she couldn't offer to take it.

'Come through to the living room, Alastair.' Aunt Maude pointed in the direction, although the colonel must have known where he was going anyway. Phoebe followed the two of them through, surprised to find that a small fire had been lit in the fireplace. She'd not thought the evening cold, but she couldn't deny it brought a much-needed ambience to the otherwise rather dour room.

'Can I get you a drink, Colonel Peterson, sir?' she asked as the old man dropped heavily into one of the ancient leather armchairs, dust billowing up around him.

'Now there's a damned fine suggestion.' He slapped both hands against the arms of the chair, seemingly oblivious to the yet more dust disturbed by the action. 'Scotch and soda, please. No ice. Tall glass and don't skimp on the Scotch like your Uncle Louis does.'

Phoebe knew where the drinks were kept. There wasn't an inch of the house outside Aunt Maude and Uncle Louis's bedrooms she hadn't poked her nose into over the months since she'd arrived. She went to the little cupboard in the ancient sideboard and clinked aside bottles until she found what she needed. There were a few additions to the selection since last she'd looked. Mixers, mostly, their shiny plastic at odds with the make do and mend ethos that was a hallmark of Pant Melyn.

'Wonderful, thank you.' The colonel barely looked at his drink when Phoebe handed it to him, tipping it to his mouth and taking a long draught. 'Perfect,' he added when almost half of it was gone. 'So, you're the young lady Maude and Louis think they can home-school, are you?'

For a moment, Phoebe could only stare in surprise. Who was this man to know anything about her? Aunt Maude came to the rescue before she could say as much.

'Phoebe dear, could you go and see where your uncle's got to?'

'Yes, of course.' Phoebe tried to smile at the colonel, although it might have come out as a grimace as she bobbed her head once then fled the room.

Across the kitchen, the study door stood open, a faint glow from inside suggesting only the desk light was switched on. Phoebe found her uncle leaning over the chair, poking at the keyboard with one finger of each hand. He looked up at her as she came in, smiled.

'I thought I had a set of these somewhere.' He held up one hand, a bunch of small square paper envelopes in it that Phoebe knew contained guitar strings. 'Not sure about tuning, but it'll get you started, right enough. I'd say you could use the piano, but it's in the dining room and we'll all be eating in there soon.'

Phoebe had seen the piano, ancient and upright. She'd even sat at it a couple of times. When she'd summoned the nerve to poke at its yellowing ivory keys, the sound it had made suggested it hadn't been tuned in many years. Unlikely to be a useful reference for any other instrument. And while she was grateful for any distraction, the guitar tutor book and set of strings felt like a very last-minute arrangement. She'd far rather have taken proper lessons from Steve Lorne.

'Umm ... thanks?' She didn't mean to make it a question, but somehow it came out that way as she took the packet of strings. Uncle Louis made no comment about her lack of genuine gratitude. He straightened, his spine clicking as he stretched the kinks out of it.

'We only want the best for you, Feebs. Me and Maude. Remember that, OK?'

'I . . . Yes. Thank you.' Phoebe managed to make it sound sincere this time, even if she didn't really feel it. The evening was strange. She had thought it would be interesting, exciting even, to meet new people. But now that she had spoken to the colonel, she was beginning to have her doubts about that. Perhaps shutting herself in her room was the best thing to do. She could try to get the guitar restrung, if nothing else. And there was always the new Muriel Baywater to read.

'I—' The distant chime of the doorbell interrupted Uncle Louis, and whatever he had been going to say must have been unimportant. He laid a gentle hand on Phoebe's shoulder for a second, then hurried off to see who had arrived.

36

Phoebe woke to bright sun flooding in through the roof window and painting the far wall in dappled shadows. She lay for a while, comfortable and warm, mind empty save for the echoes of a dream where she'd been playing music in a band. She'd strung the old guitar after a quick flick through the book, done her best to tune it without any note to reference, and spent the better part of an hour trying to make her fingers shape the chords to play a simple tune. In the end it had been more frustrating than rewarding, so she'd given up and started reading *The Soft Touch of His Lips*. Even then the knowledge that her uncle had written the words, not some middle-aged woman with a kindly smile and a twinkle in her eye, took away some of the enjoyment. Eventually, early even for her new life at Pant Melyn, she'd turned off the light and tried to sleep. But the mutter of conversation and occasional peals of laughter filtering up through the floor had made even that elusive.

At some point she must have drifted off, and now she was awake again, far too early for her liking. She struggled out of bed and down the steep steps to the bathroom. It was only as she was splashing water on her face and trying to get some semblance of control over her hair that she noticed how quiet the house was. Pant Melyn was never a noisy place, to be sure, but she had come to recognise the various small noises that defined it. Her aunt pottering around in the kitchen as she prepared breakfast, her uncle's low, rumbling snores or the banging of the pipes as he ran his morning bath. There were little tells that reassured Phoebe the house was lived in, and now they weren't there.

The living-room door stood ajar as she passed on her way to the kitchen, showing a scene of untidiness that Aunt Maude would surely not have left for the morning. Glasses, some still half full, were perched all around the room. The cushions had been pulled off the enormous sofa and now lay on the floor in a heap. A sour smell of stale wine and tobacco smoke tainted the air.

A similar scene of devastation greeted her in the kitchen. The table had been piled high with dirty dishes, glasses, empty bottles. More lined up beside the sink ready to be washed up. Pots and pans were perched precariously on the stove, where whatever remains of food were in them had surely dried out and stuck fast by now. Of her aunt, there was no sign.

Shifting the detritus as best she could, Phoebe hauled the kettle onto the hotplate and set about searching for some break-fast. Clearly the dinner party had been a success, and it had gone on into the wee small hours. Chances were her aunt and uncle were fast asleep, which meant that she would have to entertain herself for the morning at least, if not the whole day. A glance out the window showed blue sky dotted with fluffy white clouds. The trees barely moved in the breeze. It was going to be a lovely day.

Tea and toast, with plenty of Aunt Maude's honey, Phoebe found herself a tiny corner of the kitchen table to sit and eat her breakfast, all the while listening for any sign of life. By the time she was down to just the crusts, neatly arranged around the edge of her plate, there had still been nothing. She cradled her mug in both hands, leaning back in her chair as she contemplated what to do next. Opposite the entrance to the hallway, the door to her uncle's study stood open. It was the only room in the house she'd not really explored. She could go in there and have a bit of a snoop, see if there were any more Muriel Baywater novels to read while everyone was sleeping off their hangovers. Or she could set about tidying the kitchen, doing the washing-up, putting everything away. That would earn her brownie points she might be able to trade for a trip to town later.

Looking at the chaos all around, the idea held less appeal than Phoebe might have expected. The forest was much more interesting, and with luck she might find Gwyneth again. Decision made, she carefully cleaned her plate and mug, leaving everything else as she had found it, and headed outside.

Sitting in the middle of the wooden bridge, legs dangling over the edge, arms resting on the lower of the two rails that ran along each side, Phoebe stared first down at the tumbling, rushing water, then up at the pale blue sky. Summer had come properly to the valley now, she guessed. How long it would last was another question. For the moment she was happy enough to sit and wait and stare at nothing as the forest chittered and sighed all around her.

She waited longer than half an hour, even though she had realised Gwyneth wasn't coming after the first five minutes. It was soothing here, in the middle of the bridge. The point where the valley split apart. Phoebe could take the time to let the inevitable wave of anger, resentment and crushing grief at what had happened pass over her, let it wash away to the back of her mind and take the tears with it. The long weeks since she had walked that fateful night home from the station had begun to soften the edges, but the memories could still floor her without warning. Like the time Morag Carstairs had punched her in the stomach in the playground for no reason. Being still and calm helped, the rush of the water beneath her taking her troubles away to the sea.

Eventually the numbness in her backside became too much to ignore, and Phoebe pulled herself to tingling feet. Leaning against the rail, she looked up at the slice of pale blue sky again as red kites wheeled and screamed for a while before arrowing off towards the mountains. What would it be like to fly over the forest, the endless dark spread of trees, cut only by the narrow scar of the river and the occasional clearings where the few houses, farmyards and the old walled garden lay? For a moment she could almost see it, as if she had swapped places with one of the great birds. The feeling made her giddy, and she had to stand up straight, shake her head to clear it.

As she did so, she thought she saw movement on the riverbank. A lone figure disappearing through a gap in the rhododendron bushes that spilled down the steep slope like a shiny green blanket, she thought it might have been Steve Lorne, opened her mouth to call his name. But as the image faded in her memory, that felt wrong. It couldn't have been Gwyneth; she'd not be lurking, but coming out to say hello and suggest some new place of wonder to visit. Could it have been one or both of the twins? What cause would they have to come this way? No, it couldn't have been them. They'd never shy at a chance to intimidate her, make lewd suggestions or worse.

As the possibilities evaporated, so did the memory of what she had actually seen. Perhaps she was imagining the whole thing. A rush of blood from the head as she stood too quickly. The woods certainly encouraged her to let her thoughts run wild. It was a place to stimulate the imagination. Not like home, where all she had been obsessed about was gossiping with Jenny, lusting after clothes she could never afford and laughing at the pathetic attempts of the boys in her year as they tried to impress her and her friends.

But that was all gone now. And would she really want to go back? She'd be the marked one. Different. They'd whisper behind her back, talk about her among themselves. Touched by such terrible tragedy, who would want to have anything to do with her? Maybe that was why Jenny had stopped calling. Why none of her other friends ever had.

Lost in her melancholy, it was quite some time before Phoebe noticed that she had started walking and that the path her feet had taken wasn't one she was familiar with. She'd had in the back of her mind the idea to visit the bees, but this wasn't the way she had come with Aunt Maude before. It wasn't climbing up the steep side of the valley for one thing, taking an easier diagonal route. And it was heading in quite the wrong direction. Somewhere she'd not been before on her many bored and lonely rambles. She didn't feel lost, though, and going to visit the bees had only been a half-baked plan at best. So she carried on along this new path to see where it went.

The first few buildings she came to were derelict almost to the point of collapse. Some kind of farm sheds, their low stone walls were green with moss and squatted windowless under pitched slate roofs. The trees grew so close some had begun to undermine the walls with their roots, and the doors were more rot than wood.

Poking her head into one, she saw the remains of an old Land Rover mouldering into rust. It had been draped with a tarpaulin at some point, but that had frayed almost to nothing. Even had it been still intact, it would have provided scant protection against the tumble of collapsed beams and heavy slates that had stoved in the roof and smashed the windscreen.

A little further on, the trees gave way to a series of bare paddocks with drystone walls, a few sorry-looking sheep scrabbling for what little grass grew among the rocks. Beyond them stood an ancient sheep fank with rusted metal shedding gates, a couple of barns, larger and slightly more modern than the stone byres, and finally a ramshackle old farmhouse.

As she passed by the fank, Phoebe saw that several of the pens were full of sheep, standing patiently and staring at nothing in particular. Similar to the ones she had seen at the Llancwm Show, they were small and slight, their fleeces a dirty off-white and falling away from speckled black necks and faces. Some had horns that twisted and curled around their ears, others nothing at all.

What breed were they, and why they were all penned up like that with nobody around?

No sooner had the thought entered her mind than it was chased out by a voice, loud and unfriendly. Too close for comfort and directly behind her.

'Pwy dych chi? Beth dych chi'n gwneud 'ma? Tir preifat yw hwn. Dych chi'n tresmasu.'

Phoebe couldn't understand what it meant, but the underlying threat wasn't hard to work out. She turned to face the man who had spoken so harshly, to try and explain herself, but her words died in her throat as she recognised him. Tegwin Ellis towered over her, his angry features turning into a puzzled frown. Phoebe barely registered these details, almost all her attention focused on the thing he held in his arms. An ancient shotgun levelled straight at her.

She froze, arms raised, palms out in supplication, but she needn't have worried. The muzzle of the shotgun began to droop downwards. His gaze flicked briefly away from her in the direction of the house, then snapped back onto her like a searchlight. He shook his head like a man trying to dislodge water from his ear. And then he spoke again, a softer, friendlier, bemused voice this time.

'Gwen bach?'

37

Phoebe recalled several people saying of Tegwin Ellis that he wasn't particularly bright. She'd taken that to mean he was maybe poorly educated, perhaps knowledgeable when it came to farming, but not so good with his reading and writing. The truth she was coming to understand was that he was short of a shilling, as her dad had sometimes cruelly put it. There was something very simple about him. Childlike even, despite his advanced years. He had clearly forgotten their meeting at the show, mistaking her once again for his long-lost sister.

Somehow her wandering had brought her through the woods to Nant Caws Farm, Gwen's former home. How strange it must seem to this man to see her in the yard, so long after she had disappeared. Despite having spoken to her in English before, he now seemed only able to converse in Welsh. Phoebe hadn't learned much of the language, despite her uncle and aunt's best endeavours, but she knew enough to understand Tegwin's invitation into the house for a cup of tea, and recognised the name 'Meredith'. The old man must be home, then.

'Eisteddwch chi 'ma, Gwen bach,' Tegwin said, indicating one of the old wooden wheel-back chairs arranged around the cluttered kitchen table. Then he disappeared into the house, leaving her alone.

The kitchen would have horrified Aunt Maude. It was much the same size as the one at Pant Melyn, dominated by an old cast iron range stove that struggled to chase away the damp. The big Belfast sink was empty and clean, but the crockery had been stacked to dry on the draining board to one side after washing up, rather than put away, and what looked like breakfast was piled up on the other side, waiting its turn. Behind the sink, the window that opened out onto the farmyard was opaque with dust and grime, what little light making it through then blocked by several half-empty washing-up-liquid bottles, a pot full of scrubbing brushes and, somewhat incongruously, a pair of leather boots. The wall opposite the window was dominated by a large dresser, its top cluttered with piles of yellowing papers, bowls of what might once have been fruit, an enormous black leather-bound book that was most likely a bible in Welsh, given the gilded cross on the front. Phoebe almost went to fetch it for a peek, but noise overhead shrunk her back into her chair. Looking up, she noticed for the first time that the low ceiling was made up of bare wooden joists and floorboards, dark with age, cracks giving a restricted view up into the room above where shadows moved.

Voices in Welsh, low and hurried, filtered down from the room, then fell silent. Phoebe listened as someone walked slowly from one side to the other, then followed the sound of them through the house, down creaking stairs and shuffling across stone flags, slow, slow, until finally the kitchen door swung open and the old farmer appeared. She stood up to greet him, watched his face as he stared back at her, the tumble of different thoughts and emotions playing across that wrinkled and sunken skin. It was probably only a few seconds, but felt like hours until he blinked, shook his head once as if trying to dislodge something stuck in it, then managed a tired smile.

'Diw diw,' he said under his breath as he came into the room. 'You really do look a lot like her. Shall we have a cup of tea, then?'

★ ★ ★

'I suppose it shouldn't be all that much of a surprise, really. We are related after all, you and me.'

They sat at the cluttered kitchen table, old Meredith Ellis with his back to the stove. A cracked brown teapot stood between them, alongside a plate of stale biscuits neither had touched. Phoebe hadn't been much of a tea drinker before coming to Wales, but a month or so with Aunt Maude had changed all that. There were precious few fizzy drinks at Pant Melyn, no fruit squash, and Irn Bru nothing but a distant memory. You could drink milk, water, coffee or tea. Wine, beer and spirits were available if you were an adult, but Phoebe had noticed Maude didn't often drink alcohol.

'Related?' she asked as the old farmer's words penetrated through her wandering thoughts.

'Your grandmother was my cousin, see? Something like that anyway. It all gets a bit complicated.'

Phoebe had never known her grandmother. Not her mother's mother, anyway. She'd seen a few photographs, most of which had been burned in the fire. No doubt Uncle Louis had some too. She'd never been struck by any great similarity between herself and the stern-faced old lady in faded black and white. Neither could she ever recall anyone saying 'you're so like your gran'. She didn't even look that much like her mum. She'd always thought she took more after her dad.

'There was something of a feud between the Ellises and the Beards for years, until Branwen Ellis married young Dafydd Beard. I was just a boy back then, so it must have been a very long time ago.'

Phoebe took a sip of her tea, trying not to gag at the mixture of tar-like bitterness and slightly off milk. She hadn't meant to come here, certainly hadn't anticipated talking to the old farmer, but she couldn't deny that he was interesting. His voice had that soft lilt to it that everyone from this valley spoke with.

'My mother never spoke much about her family,' she said, and realised as she did how very true that was.

224

'Well, I'm sure that uncle of yours could correct that. He's always threatening to write about the history of the village. Your family has played its part.'

Phoebe was about to ask what part that might have been, but Tegwin took that moment to stride back into the kitchen. He looked only briefly at her, then asked his father something in swift Welsh. The old man replied, nodding his head towards the dresser. Tegwin pulled open the middle drawer, rifled around inside it for a while, and came out with a handful of cartridges. He shoved them in his pocket, muttered something in Welsh again, then strode out the back door, pausing only to pick up the shotgun on the way. Silence reigned for long moments after he was gone.

'He's always been a bit shy, has my Tegwin,' Meredith said after a while. 'Ever since his mother passed. He was her favourite, I think. And she never . . . Well.' He shook his head, and Phoebe knew better than to press the matter, even though she wanted to. The only sound for a while after that was the slow tick, tick, ticking of an old clock hanging above the doorway through to the rest of the house. Phoebe stared at it a while before realising what the time was.

'I should probably head back to Pant Melyn before—' But before she could say what, the loud blast of a shotgun outside made her flinch and fall silent. The old man barely moved a muscle, then sighed and took a drink of tea.

'It's a sad business,' he said once he'd swallowed. He stared out of the window opposite, even if he couldn't possibly have seen anything through the grimy glass. 'But what can you do?'

'I . . . I don't understand.' Phoebe followed the direction of his gaze. 'Was one of the sheep injured?'

That got her a raised eyebrow, white and scraggly. 'In a way, I suppose. A ram from off the moor got in with some of our ewes last night. One of those foreign breeds, a Texel or something. We can't be having any of that, see? It's a pure-bred Tordu flock, the bloodlines go back hundreds of years. My father bred them, and his father before that. The Ellis Tordus are famous, best in show for generations.'

It was the most animated Phoebe had ever seen the old man, almost as if a light came on in his eyes when he talked about his sheep. She wasn't quite sure where the gun came into it though, or more accurately she wasn't quite sure how to ask the question that would confirm her suspicions. Meredith didn't need to be asked, fortunately.

'That's the second time he's done this. No point putting him back where he's supposed to be. He'll only find a way through the fence again. Tegwin has shot him before he can soil any more of our ewes.'

'Oh.' It was all Phoebe could think of to say. For his part, Meredith seemed to have run out of words too, and energy. He looked paler than when he had first come into the kitchen, his skin grey and clammy, breathing laboured. Phoebe had the horrible feeling he wasn't long for this world, as if she could see an aura of death around him, a shadow growing ever closer.

'I should go.' She stood up this time, even though her mug of tea was still three quarters full, the plate of biscuits untouched. 'Thank you for your kind hospitality, Mr Ellis. I'm glad to see that you're recovering.'

The old farmer made to stand up himself, but then sank back into his seat with a slightly surprised expression on his face. 'Diw diw,' he muttered under his wheezy breath. Phoebe looked at him once more, certain now that it would be the last time she did. Then she turned and left the house.

The bright sunlight hurt her eyes after the gloom of the kitchen. Phoebe squinted, and held her hand up to her forehead for shade. Across the yard she could see Tegwin in the sheep fank, hauling something along the ground. He didn't see her, too focused on his task. She watched as he reached the gate, swung it open and then dragged the ram out by its back legs. Even from a distance she could tell that he had shot it in the head, point-blank. A messy smear of blood and bone was all that was left of one side, and as he dragged the carcass away towards the trees, it left a sticky red trail.

She had hoped to get away unnoticed, but he saw her as she skirted around the edge of the yard back the way she had originally come. He scowled at her, not so much unfriendly as perturbed. His face had a look about it of constant confusion, as if the world didn't make sense and he was done trying to figure it out. At least there was still a wall between them as he fetched a shovel from where it leaned against one of the rusty metal gates. The ewes hurried to the back of their pens as he passed.

'Will they go back to the fields now?' Phoebe found herself asking, unsure quite why she had done so. She didn't want to prolong this uncomfortable meeting any more than necessary, but maybe showing a little bit of interest would help to reassure Tegwin that she was no threat to him. He was the one with the shotgun, after all.

'Not until the lambs come. Must keep an eye on them until then.'

The answer surprised her as much for the fact that it was in English as what for was actually said. Clearly her bafflement showed on her face, as Phoebe had barely begun to formulate the next question before Tegwin spoke again.

'Got to maintain the purity of the flock, you see?' He spoke as if that should have been self-evident, even if it was anything but. Phoebe had a suspicion she might have understood, especially as Tegwin hefted his spade over his shoulder and with little more than a curt nod set off back to where he had left the dead ram. She watched as he found a spot by the edge of the trees and began to dig. The ewes stared at her with terrified eyes, but there was nothing she could do to comfort them.

She looked around the farmyard for a moment, taking in the

dilapidated state of the house itself, the crumbling stonework of the sheep fank and outbuildings. Even the elderly Land Rover parked by the larger shed was probably twice her age, although it was in much better nick than the one in the collapsed barn. The whole place had an air of neglect, and hanging over it all that same indefinable sense of things being close to an ending. From what she had heard tell, and her short interactions with the man, she doubted Tegwin Ellis would be able to look after himself once his father was gone. And yet he was what, fifty years old, hadn't they said? No wife, no children. How would he cope here alone with only his terrified sheep for company? Somebody else's problem, Phoebe turned away and set off for the track that would take her back to the woods and then Pant Melyn.

The voice pulled her up short just as she was passing the last of the tumbledown sheds, about to leave Pant Caws Farm and step into the forest.

'Gwen bach!'

For a moment she thought of ignoring him, but past experience had shown her that sometimes it was best to face the problem head on. Shoulders slumped in resignation, she turned to see Tegwin approaching again.

'I told youse already,' she amped her accent to the max, channelling the North East Fife farm boys she'd known from school. 'Ah'm no' Gwen. Ah'm Phoebe, aye? Phoebe Mac—' But she never managed to get the 'Donald' out, such was her surprise at what she saw.

Tegwin had abandoned his digging, although his hands were still covered in dirt and perhaps a little blood. He still had that perplexed expression on his face that made him look like a toddler in a grown man's body, and he was holding out a bunch of hastily picked forest edge flowers.

'They were always your favourites,' he said, the English words still sounding odd coming from his mouth. Not knowing what else to do, Phoebe took them.

'Umm. Thank you?'

'You be careful in the woods now, Gwen bach. Bad things in the woods.'

Phoebe opened her mouth to explain once again that she wasn't Gwen, but Tegwin had already turned away and was walking back towards Pant Caws. She looked down at the bunch of flowers, a tiny spark of recognition going off in the back of her brain. There was something very familiar about them, but she couldn't for the life of her think what.

Gripping them tight so as not to lose any, she turned away from the farm and set off back for Pant Melyn.

38

Phoebe was still clutching the flowers when she reached the wooden bridge over the river. She stopped in the middle for a while, hoping she might see Gwyneth, but after a few minutes it was someone else entirely who hove into view.

'Oh. Hello there, Phoebe. I wasn't expecting to bump into you down here.'

Aunt Maude looked a little tired, her eyes puffy and hair a little awry. She was dressed wrong for going to the village, or up to the moors to check the bees. Given the side of the river she had appeared from, Phoebe had the distinct impression that her aunt was on her way back to Pant Melyn from somewhere she had been all night. Which would explain the mess in the sitting room and kitchen at least. But why would she have left in the first place?

'Been picking flowers have you?' Aunt Maude nodded in the direction of the bunch. Phoebe had almost forgotten about them, held them up to study a little more closely.

'No. I was given them,' she said as an unidentified small black insect appeared on one of the petals.

'Given?' Aunt Maude's expression was a mixture of disbelief and surprise. 'Who gave you flowers?'

'Tegwin Ellis did. He's very strange. Convinced I'm his sister come back, even though she'd be all grown up now, aye?'

'Tegwin?' Aunt Maude's disbelief turned to something else Phoebe couldn't quite identify. 'Where was this?'

'I went up to the farm. Where Meredith Ellis lives.'

'Nant Caws Farm? What on earth possessed you to go up to that miserable place?'

'I don't know, really. Couldn't find Gwyneth, so I was just wandering around, nothing better to do. Followed my feet and there it was.'

'I'm surprised Tegwin didn't chase you off the place. He doesn't like strangers getting anywhere near his sheep.'

'He was weird, right enough. But he wasn't unfriendly. I felt worse for the ram, to be honest.'

'The ram?' Aunt Maude's initial surprise had begun to ease now, and she started walking again as she spoke. Phoebe told her all that had happened.

'Well, I suppose you did save old Meredith's life, so maybe they feel beholden. And you do look a bit like Gwen, it's true. She was fond of wildflowers, too.' Aunt Maude stopped in her tracks, crossed her arms and gave Phoebe what amounted to a stern look. 'You need to be careful though, Phoebe dear. Tegwin's a bit . . . How can I put it?'

'Simple?' Phoebe offered.

'If he were a child today, they'd say he had learning difficulties. Special needs. But he was born in a time when things like that weren't so well understood. Children like him were put in asylums and forgotten about, not given the help they needed to survive in the world.'

'You reckon he's autistic, then?'

'Oh, most definitely. Not that he's ever had any diagnosis, of course. Mered wouldn't contemplate such a thing. But he's been fortunate in one way, growing up where he did. He's been sheltered from the world his whole life.'

Phoebe wasn't sure quite how fortunate that really was. 'But what will happen when the old man dies? How will he cope on his own?'

Aunt Maude sighed theatrically. 'It's good that you care, Phoebe, but let's just hope that's a problem won't need facing for a while yet.'

Phoebe recalled the sickly aura that had clung to the old man like the oily sheen on cooked meat that has gone past its sell-by date, how he shuffled around the kitchen like something out of a zombie film. She wanted to tell Aunt Maude about the strange feeling, almost a certainty in her mind, that she would never see him alive again. But it was one thing to think such thoughts, another to voice them out loud.

'Perhaps we should be getting home,' Aunt Maude said to the silence that had spread between them. 'I'll be needing to get lunch on the go soon enough. And there'll be a mountain of washing-up to do.'

They set off together, past the old collapsed stone bridge, the falls and pool where Aunt Maude liked to swim. Phoebe said nothing, too many thoughts jostling around in her brain for her to concentrate on conversation.

'You're probably wondering about last night's dinner party. And this.' Aunt Maude waved her hands in front of her to indicate something, or maybe everything, as they began the zigzag climb from the valley bottom. Phoebe kept her mouth shut, knowing there was no good way to answer that.

'Alastair . . . the colonel. He drinks too much, you see. Has his reasons, but . . . well. It's no matter. I usually end up driving him home. Sometimes have to put him to bed, too.'

Phoebe wasn't sure if she was supposed to be shocked by this, but she couldn't see much difference between the colonel drinking himself into oblivion and her mother doing the same with her pills. It was something some adults seemed to do. She hoped she never felt like doing it herself.

'Does he live far away?' she asked after they had walked in silence for a bit longer.

'A bit. The other side of the valley, on the way down towards

Aber.' Aunt Maude stopped walking, put her hands on her hips and did that weird twisting stretch thing Phoebe had sometimes seen leotard-clad women do on daytime telly. 'I like to make sure Alastair's OK before I head home. And it takes me a while to build up the strength needed to tackle tidying the place. Your uncle's . . . not good at the domestic stuff.'

'I had noticed,' Phoebe said, and started to add 'Dad's the same', but the implications of that statement came as another one of those unexpected gut punches, harder by far than anything Morag Carstairs could have managed. Even before the tears had started to flow, she found herself being swept into a warm and welcome hug.

'It's all right, Phoebe dear. Just let it out. Sometimes crying's all you can do, but it's a powerful healer too.'

Phoebe did as she was told; she had no choice in the matter. It was as if she'd been holding back her grief for weeks and now it had breached the dam inside her. She wailed and sobbed and sniffled until there was nothing left, and only then did she reluctantly pull away. Tears, and perhaps not a little snot, had made a dark stain on the front of her aunt's coat.

'See? I bet that feels better already.' Aunt Maude reached a hand out to ruffle Phoebe's hair, then stopped herself and snatched it back. They had reached a fork in the path, and now she looked uphill towards where the trees thinned and the garden began. Not far at all to the kitchen and all that washing-up.

'You know what, Phoebe. It's too fine a day for sitting around indoors nursing a sore head. Why don't we go and see the bees?'

By the time they reached the edge of the forest and the short track up to the beehives, Phoebe was parched. She'd not thought to bring a bottle of water with her, and the tea Meredith Ellis had made had been so disgusting she'd left most of it in the mug. Aunt Maude must have read her thoughts, as instead of heading straight for the clearing, she led the way through the heather to where a tiny rill bubbled down the hillside.

'Cleanest, freshest water you'll ever taste,' she said as she knelt beside the flow and dipped her hands in. The peat-browned liquid that came out cupped in her hands looked more chewy than Phoebe was used to drinking, but Aunt Maude didn't seem to care. She slaked her thirst, then splashed more water on her face.

'Is it . . . Is it safe?' Phoebe asked, then realised how daft that sounded given what her aunt had both said and done.

'Safer than the river down there.' Maude nodded her head towards the valley. From their vantage point, Phoebe could see over the tree-tops to where the river formed a scar through the forest. 'Not that the river water's bad, particularly, but you need to be careful after a flood. There's the old silver lead mines further up the valley, see.'

Phoebe stared past the green of the forest to where she could make out a grey rocky landscape as the valley narrowed towards its head. She'd been up there on one of her walks with Gwyneth, seen the ruined remains of the heavy industry that had gone on in the past. Even if it was all closed down now, who knew what pollution might still be seeping into the river? And yet uphill from where she was the moors stretched away for miles. Nothing but the heather, wildlife and sheep between the rain clouds and the stream.

In the end, her thirst overcame her reticence, even the thought of sheep, and Phoebe joined her aunt beside the burn. Not much more than a foot wide, it trickled and bounced through the peaty soil and exposed rocks in a series of mini cascades. When she cupped her hands under one, the water was wonderfully cool, and when she drank, it tasted almost sweet. She copied her aunt, drinking first and then splashing her face. When she stood up again, she felt stronger, as if she could take on the world. It didn't last long.

'I spoke to Mrs Dalgliesh yesterday, Phoebe dear. About Jennifer coming to visit in the summer.'

'You did? When?' Phoebe couldn't remember there being any phone calls during the day.

'After you went to bed. She wouldn't have known about the . . . party, of course.'

Something shifted in Phoebe's gut. If Mrs Dalgliesh had phoned, then Jenny would have been there too. She could have talked to her friend, but she'd been sent to bed early like some badly behaved toddler.

'Could you not have told me at the time? I'd have liked to have a chat with Jenny.' The petulant whine in her voice was very much how that badly behaved toddler might sound, but Phoebe didn't care. Her mood was all over the place these days, and now it swung towards anger.

'It was quite late. I've no doubt Jennifer would have been in her bed. And anyway, it was a quick call.'

'So when's Jen coming? It must be nearly the end of term now.' Phoebe's brow furrowed into a frown as she realised that she didn't actually know when term ended, wasn't entirely sure what the date was at all. There was so little to differentiate one day from the next, she'd quite lost track of time in this slow, boring backwater.

'Well now, that's the thing, see?' Aunt Maude put on a sombre face that only made Phoebe grumpier. 'Holidays start next week, but the Dalgliesh family are going away for a month the week after that. Something about a trip to America for Mr Dalgliesh's business and turning it into a big family trip. It sounds quite exhausting to me, but what would I know?'

'America?' Phoebe sank to her knees, barely registering the damp through her jeans. 'So . . . so she's not coming to visit, then?'

'Not for a while, at least. But you can call her this evening if you want. I know you miss your friends, and it's not like there's anyone here your age either.'

Phoebe almost said, 'There's Gwyneth', but something stopped her. It occurred to her that Gwyneth should have been at school, shouldn't she? The term times were different between Scotland and Wales, she knew, but not so much, surely. Phoebe herself was only out of school because of what had happened to her parents. What was Gwyneth's excuse? Or maybe that was why she'd not seen her for a while. Phoebe would have to ask her new, perhaps only, friend the next time they met up. And somehow she was sure they would meet again.

'Shall we check the bees, then?' she asked instead.

Aunt Maude considered her for a moment, her head cocked as if a thought weighed it heavily on one side.

'Let's do that,' she said eventually. 'Then we can go home and have some lunch.'

39

2023

It's been a long time since last she visited Nant Caws Farm. Thirty-eight years, if she's counting. Not since that terrible summer that changed her whole life. The place was decrepit even then, and time hasn't been kind since.

The first old stone barn has collapsed entirely now, the forest reclaiming it with admirable zeal. The larger barn still stands, but its roof sags in the middle and there are holes where more than a few slates have lost their battle with the wind. The stone-walled sheep pens look to be in relatively good shape, although several gates are missing entirely and those that are not have seen better days. There are weeds everywhere, poking through gaps in the concrete yard and blossoming out of the old lime mortar. Phoebe remembers the farm as being a little run down, but she hadn't expected it to be quite such a ruin. Then again, it's been six years since Tegwin died, and he can't have been keeping on top of things before then. Not on his own and at his age.

The house at least looks watertight, even if it is as dour and neglected as the rest of the farmyard. Parked up outside it, the solicitor, Tom Jones, is sitting in his car waiting for her. Phoebe suspects he might have been there a while; he's tipped back his seat and appears to be asleep as she approaches from the woodland path. She checks her watch to make sure she's not late, but she's timed the walk across the valley from Pant Melyn almost to perfection.

A shadow, the flicker of movement, or maybe he wasn't actually asleep at all, but he sits up as she comes near, pops open the door and steps out.

'Doctor MacDonald. Good to see you again. You walked over, I see.'

Phoebe glances at the drive that spears up to the farm from the village a mile or so further down the valley. Impossible to see how deep the ruts are, as it is so overgrown with weeds. Branches lean over from the nearby trees too, swooping low and turning it into something of a tunnel.

'I wasn't sure my car would make it without ripping the battery out of the bottom. It's bad enough at Pant Melyn, and that's been looked after.'

The solicitor dips his head in understanding, reaches a hand into his pocket and pulls out a bunch of keys.

'Shall we?' he asks, and without further prompting walks over to the farmhouse door. It unlocks smoothly enough, but needs a hefty shove to open, old wood warped and swollen with damp. Phoebe follows him through a musty-smelling boot room and on into the kitchen.

The last time she was here she'd been a frightened twelve-year-old, doing her best to be polite in a very difficult situation. She remembers the kitchen all the same, its untidiness and general air of a place where no woman had lived in many a year. Apart from the absence of old Meredith with his sickly pallor of death about him, and still young Tegwin with his sheep-killing shotgun, Phoebe's hard pushed to say that anything about the room has changed at all.

'Could do with a bit of an airing,' the solicitor says. 'But it's stood a long time now, and I dare say it will stand a lot longer yet.

Helps that they never put concrete render on the outside in the sixties, like so many of these old houses had done to them.'

Phoebe is only half listening, her eyes darting from the old dresser still piled high with papers, boxes, clutter, to the sink, mercifully clean and clear of washing-up. The table has been tidied at least, the things Tegwin Ellis left arranged into neat piles. It reminds her in a way of Pant Melyn, a mountain of possessions that once meant something to someone but now is just so much stuff. She's been stealing herself to the task of going through Aunt Maude's life, must she do the same with a stranger's too?

'. . . brought a map of the property bounds, if you'd like to see it?' The solicitor's voice finally breaks through her thoughts, and Phoebe turns to face him.

'Sorry. Zoned out a bit there. It's all a bit much.' She gestures towards the rolled-up sheet he had produced from somewhere. 'Map, you say?'

The solicitor carefully unrolls the sheet on top of the neatly arranged items on the kitchen table. Phoebe remembers sitting at it all those years ago, trying not to gag at the bitter, overbrewed tea and the slightly off milk. Another quick look around, but she can't see a fridge. A blessing, probably, given how long this house has stood empty.

'This is the village here, and we're in the farmhouse here.'

She drags her attention back to the map, takes a moment to orient herself. She's seen maps of the valley before, but they've never managed to accurately portray its strange dimensions. This one shows the river running through the vast swathe of trees that makes up the forest, and, cutting across it at the far corner of the sheet, the road that passes through the village. The solicitor has drawn a shape in what looks like red crayon, crudely following field boundaries and for a while the river itself. The lines go up onto the moors too, an area of land too vast for her to make sense of.

'Is . . . Is this the whole farm?'

'Well, yes and no. There's common grazing rights on the moor that are shared with several other farms. What you see here is the land directly owned by the late Mr Ellis. And this house and farm buildings, of course. All told it stretches to about eight hundred acres. A fair size for a Welsh hill farm, but a lot of it's trees, see.'

And Phoebe can see, easily enough. The forest comes right up to the farmyard, but the actual boundary is all the way down at the river. It goes all the way to the road, too.

'I had no idea,' she says, and it's true. Meredith Ellis lived like a pauper. Even looking around this gloomy kitchen, there's no money been spent on anything in decades. She remembers the Land Rover he used to drive, ancient even when she was a girl. And yet he owned a huge amount of land. But then wasn't that always the way with family farms? Asset rich and cash poor?

'With the Pant Melyn estate added, you'll end up owning most of the valley, I expect.' The solicitor echoes her own thoughts as he rolls up the map and offers it to her. Phoebe isn't sure whether she can bring herself to take it, and after a moment he puts it down on the table, gestures towards the far door. 'Would you like to see round the house?'

A shiver runs down her spine at the thought of it. She has never been beyond this kitchen before, and going any further feels like trespass. Daft, she knows. Tegwin died six years ago, his father long before him. They're not here, not even their ghosts.

'Maybe another time, Mr Jones,' she manages to say in a voice that only quavers a little. 'It's all a bit too much to take in. I think I need a little fresh air.'

If he's disappointed, the solicitor hides it well. His smile is warm and sympathetic. 'Of course, of course.' He crosses the room to the door where they entered, opens it and waves for Phoebe to go ahead. 'I'll leave you the keys for now, although it will be a while before all the legalities are sorted. Intestacy proceedings are always onerous, but we'll get there in the end.'

The woods feel different as Phoebe takes the path away from Nant Caws Farm towards Pant Melyn. It's later in the day, true, but there's more to it than that. The track is the same, both familiar and changed with the years, but there's a charge in the air as if thunder is on the way. Looking up through the branches reveals only blue sky and the thinnest wisps of cloud, so it can't be that.

Perhaps it's the meeting with Tom Jones, the solicitor. The growing realisation that she has inherited not just her aunt and uncle's property but a farm of considerable size. What is she going to do with it all? Phoebe has no idea. Sell it, maybe. That would be the obvious thing. She might need to do that anyway if the taxman wants too much. But something she can't quite put into words holds her back from that easy solution.

It's not as if she's ever felt any kinship with the Ellis family. She only met Meredith twice and the first time he had a heart attack the moment he saw her. And Tegwin never quite understood that she wasn't his wee sister. He was always giving her little bunches of wildflowers, picked from the edges of paths like these. Always calling her Gwen bach and gibbering away at her in Welsh she struggled to understand.

She became quite proficient in the language after a few years living with her aunt and uncle, but Louis had escaped Llancwm, gone to Oxford, softened his accent. And Maude had come from further down the valley. The old hill farmers had a way of speaking all of their own, it seemed. Some version of Welsh that a twelfth-century monk might have understood more readily than her. She'd struggle with even a modern Welsh speaker now, her skills rusty after twenty years of disuse. Something she'll have to work on.

The idea brings her up short. Like when speaking to Steve Lorne in his tidy kitchen, there's an idea at the back of her mind that she might not go back to Edinburgh and pick up where her old life left off. But stay here? In Llancwm?

As she looks around, Phoebe sees that she has wandered off the path that would take her back to Pant Melyn. Through the ranks of pine trees she can see the dappled light of a clearing, and she knows where her feet have brought her. Where the forest has steered her steps.

In moments she is there, the sun warming her face as she emerges from the gloom. Ahead, the tall oak tree stands in its own little fiefdom, older like everything else but mostly unchanged. The air is still, not a leaf fluttering at all, and the silence reaches over her like a warm blanket. Like a mother's embrace.

For a long time she simply stands there, soaking it all in. No sound, no thoughts, just that endless moment when nothing matters at all. And then, as if someone is slowly turning up the volume, she begins to hear the low buzz of bees as they busy themselves in the long grass. Once she has noticed them, the other sounds begin to come into focus. Songbirds twitter in the branches and flit around the clearing like flashes of colour. Leaves rustle in the gentle breeze that was always there. High overhead, red kites mewl and cry like abandoned infants. And right on the edge of hearing, more imagined than real, a young girl hums a mournful tune.

Phoebe has to make her own path through the grass to the base of the oak and its massive trunk. That alone should tell her that nobody comes here often, if at all. She can't quite pinpoint the source of the humming, either, but she is filled with a desperate urgency all the same. The shade of the wide canopy is like stepping from summer heat into a cool cellar. The bees turn up the volume, but that almost familiar hum is still there. Almost a counterpoint.

The tree has formed deep bowls where its roots spear away from the trunk and plunge deep into the earth. Phoebe steps around them, one hand reaching out to brush the ancient bark as she makes her way around to the far side. There are no bouquets of wildflowers here any more, fresh or decayed, and when she reaches the far side there is nobody to see. The old dead branch has long since cracked and fallen to the ground, no more the rope she had once thought a child's swing. As she walks slowly into the sunlight where it reaches through this gap in the canopy, so the humming grows louder. Occasional half-heard words, as if whoever is singing has forgotten most of them but remembers one or two.

Further out from the tree, and still Phoebe can't see anyone. The clearing is not so large that a person could hide easily, unless they were lying down in the long grass and small like a child.

'Hello?' she asks, uncertainty turning the word into a question. And then, since this whole episode is strange but not unsettling, she adds 'Gwyneth?'

At the mention of the name, the humming stops. Phoebe's heart does too, for a moment. She half expects to see her childhood friend stand up from wherever she's been hiding, not aged a day in almost forty years. But there is nothing. Only the bees going about their industrious work, the birds flitting across the clearing, a few early butterflies making the most of the sun and the warmth. Her imagination playing tricks on her.

With a shake of the head, Phoebe retraces her steps, following the line she has made in the grass until it brings her back to the clearing's edge and the path. She throws one last look at the ancient oak, so out of place it might be another world living here in the depths of the forest. It occurs to her that this spot might well still be within the boundary of Nant Caws Farm, somewhere in that swathe of forest that was enclosed by the thick red lines on the map Tom Jones showed her in the kitchen. Daft to think that she could own something so huge and magnificent, but she could accept being its custodian. Its protector.

She turns away, steps from sunlight to shade. And as her feet find the hard packed earth of the forest track, the wind plays through the branches high overhead. A sound like a young girl's joyous laughter.

40

1985

Time passed slowly after the dinner party and Phoebe's unplanned visit to Nant Caws Farm. Uncle Louis had not even got out of bed, let alone done any tidying up by the time she and Aunt Maude had returned from their impromptu visit to the bees, and so the atmosphere in the house was a little strained for a day or two. As if someone had turned the thermostat down a couple of degrees. Not that there was anything so sophisticated as central heating and thermostats at Pant Melyn.

Phoebe wanted to go down to the bridge and search for Gwyneth so they could explore more of the valley, or simply wander the woods to keep herself out from under the grown-ups' feet and the air of slight frostiness, but Aunt Maude had other plans. No doubt alarmed at her having been talking to Meredith and Tegwin Ellis, she had set Phoebe a series of tasks that kept her busy for days. Cleaning pots, weeding vegetable beds, helping turn the produce of the greenhouse into endless jars of preserves. There was always something else that needed urgently to be done.

She couldn't have said how many days after the visit to the farm it was when she finally pushed back. Time seemed to have no real meaning in the valley of Llancwm, after all.

'Did you ever speak to Steve Lorne?' she asked as she buttered her toast at breakfast and reached for the honey pot. Neither Aunt Maude nor Uncle Louis had been speaking before she voiced her question, but she could tell by the sudden stillness that she'd struck a nerve.

'He doesn't seem to be answering his phone,' Aunt Maude said after far too long a pause. 'But he's not come looking for you either, has he?'

Phoebe had to admit that she hadn't even spotted him wandering the woods, but then again she'd not had a chance to spend much time there herself recently.

'I'll give him another call today,' Aunt Maude continued. 'If he still doesn't answer, we can both go round tomorrow and speak to him. OK?'

Phoebe nodded her head in acceptance, not so much because she didn't want to speak as because she had just taken a bite of toast.

'So. Are you going to help me with the tomatoes this morning?'

Phoebe glanced at the window. Outside, the sun shone bright and a gentle breeze played with the pampas grass. The tomatoes were in the long greenhouse and a separate polytunnel, both of which would be sweltering. Even the thought of it made her sweaty, and of course Aunt Maude would most likely shuck off her clothes the moment she stepped out the back door.

'Actually, I thought I might go for a walk. See if I can't find Gwyneth again. It's been ages since I last saw her.'

The look Aunt Maude gave her was an odd one, Phoebe thought. Not annoyed at refusing to work in the garden, more a mixture of surprise and suspicion.

'I won't go anywhere near Mr Lorne's house, I promise,' Phoebe added swiftly. 'Probably just go and check out the falls again, since the river's gone down a lot.'

'Well, make sure you don't fall in unless it's on purpose.' Aunt Maude reached for Phoebe's empty plate, stacking it on top of hers in a manner that suggested breakfast was now over and the day's activities needed to be started. 'And don't be staying out all day either. There's lots needs to be done if we're going to get everything pickled and preserved for winter.'

Phoebe wondered at her aunt's words after she'd helped clear the table, washed the plates, tidied up the kitchen and finally escaped out the back door. As far as she was concerned summer had barely started, and since arriving in Wales it had rained more than it had been sunny. How could anyone think about winter when the sky was clear and the air was warm? Now was a time for enjoying life, not planning for dark days and cold nights.

When she reached the wooden bridge, it was empty again. Trying her best to ignore the way that made her heart sink, Phoebe walked to the middle, slid the backpack she had brought with the canteen and a pac-a-mac raincoat in it and sat with her legs dangling over the edge. Even without company, there was something about leaning on the lower rail and staring downstream that helped calm her thoughts. She couldn't hear anything over the joyful babble of the river, tumbling less forcefully over the rocks today, but noisy all the same. Nevertheless, there was something, a change in the air or the lightest of vibrations through the wood of the bridge, that let her know she wasn't alone any more.

'You came.'

Phoebe looked up to see Gwyneth standing a couple of paces away. She wore a different dress today, although still of a style at least twenty years out of date. On her feet, she sported a pair of stout leather walking boots not unlike Phoebe's own, although older and more faded. Bare legs between her chunky woollen socks and the ratty hem of her dress, the ensemble made her look even stranger than usual.

'Would have come before, but Aunt Maude's had me doing endless boring chores. Think she was trying to stop me wandering the woods. Don't know why, really.' Phoebe hauled herself to her feet, then put a swift hand to the rail as the world went dizzy for a moment.

'You went up to Nant Caws Farm, didn't you,' Gwyneth said after a while. 'Shouldn't go there, you know. Bad things happen there.'

'Tell me about it. They killed a ram, just because it was doing what rams do.'

'Tegwin's killed a lot of sheep over the years. Other things too.'

'You know them well?'

'All my life. Try not to go there any more though. Don't much like the place. Too many bad memories. And those two . . .' Gwyneth didn't say who, or what, but Phoebe knew.

'They are weird, right enough.' She considered telling Gwyneth about Meredith and how ill he was, but it was too nice a day to dwell on such things. Instead she changed the subject with a simple 'Where are we going to go today, then?'

Gwyneth stuck her hands in her pockets and stared down at her feet for a moment. 'Did you like the cave? Up at the falls?'

Phoebe had mixed feelings about that. It had been awesome, wonderful to behold, amazing, all those things. But she had been soaked through and cold at the time, which had rather spoiled the fun. Fortunately Gwyneth didn't wait for an answer.

'Only there's a place I know that's like it but much better, see? Thought I might show you. It's not far, and it's brilliant. Come on.' And she set off at speed.

Phoebe had to hurry to catch up, surprised again by how quickly the girl covered the ground. In no time at all the woods thinned a little, ancient trees giving way to smaller saplings and the ubiquitous rhododendron bushes. Soon there was no path at all, but Gwyneth seemed to know where she was going, even if she often managed to slip through gaps in the foliage without disturbing them, while Phoebe had to batter her way through like some graceless, lumbering oaf.

She tripped on the first stone, almost planting herself face first in a muddy puddle. Once she had regained her balance, pausing for a moment to catch her breath, Phoebe saw more of them dotted around. Not random rocks, she realised, but the remains of some old building. Blocks as big as her head, their rectangular shapes disappearing under a soft layer of moss. There were larger stones, too, and the more she looked, the more she saw. What she had taken for tall bushes were half-fallen walls clad with thick ivy. Further towards the trees, more stonework rose almost two storeys, grey and camouflaged by the gloom. A vast old house must have been here years before, only these ruins left to be reclaimed by nature.

'Plas Llancwm. The old mansion house. It burned to the ground almost a hundred years ago.' Gwyneth had been a few paces ahead, but she came back to stand beside Phoebe, pointing out what at first looked like a particularly large bush. 'It had a tower at the front, see?'

'It's huge. How far does it go on for?'

'You've seen the mines, Feebs? Up the valley on the mountain road. These hills are full of silver. Men have always been digging it out. One family made a lot of money out of the mines, came to own almost all the land for miles around here. First of them was Thomas Ap Hywel, Thomas son of Hywel. But they soon became Powells when they wanted to court favour with the English. They built themselves a fine house, laid out all these woodlands, but it wasn't enough. They were greedy, see, the Powells. They wanted more. More land, more silver, a bigger house. Titles and airs and graces. They treated the people who worked down the mines little better than slaves. Oh, it wasn't fair. It never is. They grew richer and richer, and the people of Llancwm grew thinner and thinner, living off the scraps, grazing what few animals they had on the very worst of the hill land. High up on the Ffrydd.'

Phoebe was fairly sure that she had heard this story before. There were shades of her uncle's tale about Myfanwy and her baby in it, the same injustice and exploitation of the poor by the rich.

Still, there was a lilt to Gwyneth's voice as she spoke that was quite lyrical, almost hypnotic.

'Most folk worked in the mines. Men, women and children all. And it was hard, dirty, dangerous work. There's silver, see, but there's lead too. It's poisonous, dulls children's minds. You should go look at the graveyard round the chapel. Half the tombstones are for children who died before they were even five years old.'

'So what happened, then? You said it burned to the ground?' An image rose unbidden in Phoebe's mind, a wall of flame and the roaring noise of jets out of Leuchars. Her knees felt weak, and she had to put a hand out to steady herself. In an instant, Gwyneth was there, an arm to lean on.

'Oh, Phoebe bach. I'm so sorry. I never thought . . .'

Somehow Gwyneth's distress made it easier to cope with her own. Still, Phoebe was glad of her support. She was strong and warm, her touch reassuring. She exuded the same sense of calm as the woods themselves, as if she were ancient and immovable, not just maybe twelve years old. And she smelled of the forest as much as anything else, too. Wildflowers and tree bark and rich, moist loam.

'It's OK. Just brought up some bad memories. I'd not thought about . . . that for a while.'

'Horrible when it hits you out of the blue like that. I should have realised, but this place . . .' Gwyneth raised a hand towards the tallest remnant of building. 'It's something everyone in the village knows about. One of those stories, see?'

Phoebe looked at her friend again. What trauma had she suffered that she was so wise to Phoebe's own suffering? It struck her that she knew very little about Gwyneth at all. Not even her surname, now she thought about it. And she'd never said where in the village it was that she lived. She opened her mouth to ask more about her, surprised when an entirely different question came out.

'So what actually happened, then? To the mansion?'

Gwyneth's smile broadened, more welcome warmth in the cool shade of the trees.

'Well now. There's a story for the telling. The last of the Powells. Old man Roderick. He was mean-spirited, miserly. Nobody liked him, but they did his bidding all the same. Until his money ran out, and he started selling off bits of his estate to pay his debts. That's how Meredith Ellis's grandfather came to own Nant Caws Farm. How your Uncle Louis's great-great-grandmother got her hands on Pant Melyn. Bit by bit Roderick Powell sold off the family silver.' Gwyneth laughed. 'Quite literally, when you think about it. He sold the mines, after all. And then there was just him, and the mansion and a few servants who stayed more out of habit than any great sense of loyalty. Then one winter's evening he sent them all to the village. Gave the butler a handful of coins and said they should all drink his health. Well, I don't suppose they often had such generosity from their master, so they did as they were told. And when he was alone, he set a fire in the main hall and climbed the tower.'

'Why?' Phoebe fought against the image of flames, the slow pulse of flashing blue lights, the roaring pressure that built up behind her eyes. Then she felt Gwyneth's hand take hers, squeeze it gently, and everything was all right again. For now.

'Who really knows? Some say he was lovesick. That he'd been spurned by the only woman he felt was his equal. Others say he knew the end was coming, and wanted to meet death on his own terms. Some say he was haunted by the ghosts of all the folk who've died in this valley down the years. Me? I think he was probably mad as a box of frogs. The Powells never bred far from the family line, and that can't work out well in the end. Whatever the reason, nobody knew what was happening until it was too late. They say one of the servants saw the glow of the fire reflected on the low clouds as he was standing outside the pub taking a piss. That sounds about right, if you ask me. By the time they all reached the house, the flames were past putting out. There was just mad Roderick standing at the top of tower shouting into the wind as the fire took him. Screaming he was, but not in pain. He was shouting curses on the village, the people he blamed for his misfortune even though it was all of his own doing. What was left of him once it had all burned out, they found right about here.'

Phoebe looked down at the ground by her feet, where Gwyneth pointed, then looked back up at the girl whose hand she was still holding. There was a moment's silence, and then Phoebe laughed. Not a little titter, like the girls at school used to, this was full-throated, hilarious, almost hysterical laughter that burst out of her in a wonderful release. Gwyneth started to chuckle too, and soon both of them could do nothing else, each setting the other off. Phoebe sank slowly to the ground, her legs unable to take her weight, the sense of impossible loss that had been gnawing away at her since the night her parents died finally beginning to ease. She leaned back against a sturdy sapling, and Gwyneth dropped cross-legged beside her.

'These woods are full of ghosts,' she said once the chuckling had finally subsided. 'Old Roderick's not the first, and not the last either. The people who have lived in this valley, died here, they leave their mark.'

'I don't doubt it,' Phoebe said, serious now that the hilarity had subsided. The laughter had emptied her, but it had taken some of her pain with it. If she could have held on to that moment for ever, she would have done, but she knew that the black dog would be back.

'Come on, let's go see the caves, right?' Gwyneth sprang to her feet as if she was made of rubber, dragging Phoebe up with her. There was an energy and enthusiasm about her that was almost infectious.

'Aye, we've come this far. Might as well, eh?'

41

At first it didn't look anything like a cave to Phoebe. She followed Gwyneth through the ruins of the mansion until they reached what must once have been the great tower. Walls climbed two storeys high, crumbling tops capped with ivy, ancient plaster turned green with damp, and barely visible through the rubbery leaves. Following a path that was hardly there, Phoebe came upon the remains of a spectacular stone staircase, its steps set into the wall. Close to the ground they were still intact, but after about five they had broken off like rotten teeth, piled in a heap and overgrown with brambles.

'This way. Careful on the thorns, right?' Gwyneth hunkered down under the last whole step, squeezing into a gap barely big enough for her. Phoebe waited, unsure whether she dared follow. The lightness of their earlier laughter had all seeped away, and now she could feel the dark creep back, twisting a knot of fear in her stomach. This wasn't what she had been expecting; she wasn't sure what she had been expecting, but this surely wasn't it.

'Well? Are you coming or what?' Gwyneth's head reappeared, disembodied as if she were a ghost. Then it retracted back into the darkness.

'I can't . . .' Phoebe was going to complain that she couldn't see, but then she remembered the torch, taken from the shelf in the

252

boot room as she was getting ready to leave earlier. She wasn't sure what had made her put it in her backpack. There was no way she could have known she was coming to this place, but she was glad she had it all the same. It took a moment to find, but once she had clicked it on she could see through the gap in the rubble. More steps led down into the earth, narrower than the ones that had risen skywards, but solid enough. She slung her rucksack into the gap, then wriggled through after it.

A dozen steps down, her torch beam showed solid flagstone floor. As she stopped at the bottom, a silence settled over her so profound it was as if she had gone deaf. She hadn't thought the forest to be so noisy, but now there was nothing. Only the sound of her uncertain breath and the faint rush of blood in her ears.

She played the torch around, making out a surprisingly large and well-constructed basement. Time and nature might have destroyed the mansion above, but it seemed to have left the place untouched below ground. Squat pillars and heavy arches held up the structural walls overhead, the whole space mirroring its layout. A central corridor ran the length of the house, with rooms on either side. It was vast, and still.

'Come on, then, slowcoach.'

Phoebe almost jumped out of her skin. She whirled around to see Gwyneth grinning like a loon right behind her. Without another word, the young girl set off towards what must originally have been the back of the house. Phoebe made the mistake of shining her torch up at the ceiling before following, and revised her earlier opinion about the basement being untouched. Roots poked through stonework, dangling down in best horror-movie fashion. Here and there neatly carved blocks had fallen out and now lay in rubble heaps on the flagstone floor. It wasn't safe down here, surely. And yet Gwyneth strode off along the corridor as if it was something she did every day. As if this were the manor to which she had been born.

'Wait,' Phoebe said, her voice louder than she'd intended. Gwyneth stopped, shrugged, and waited for her to catch up.

'Do you know anything about the Picturesque Movement?' she asked as the two of them set off down the corridor again. Phoebe had just ducked under a dangling clump of roots, mis-timed it and ended up with a trickle of dried dirt down her neck.

'The what?' she asked.

'I'll take that as a no, then.' Gwyneth brushed aside more roots, revealing an open doorway in what Phoebe had thought would be the outer wall of the basement. Beyond it was a tunnel hewn from the rock. Her torchlight didn't penetrate the darkness far, but she could feel the faintest of breezes, a scent she couldn't quite place, a sound so quiet it was almost a whisper and yet hinted at distant noise.

'Would have been about two hundred years ago, I guess. Maybe a little more. Rich folk decided that true beauty was in the natural world, the rugged cliffs and towering trees and stuff. You can see it in all the paintings of the time. Lovely landscapes. Bleak, they are. It became very fashionable to visit the wilderness, but nobody wants to trek for days to see it now, do they. They want their comforts, their warm houses and armies of servants. So they built the wilderness closer to home, see?'

Phoebe didn't, but as they walked along the tunnel, she felt the breeze on her face strengthen, the faint noise turn into a distant whistling roar. There was a dampness to the air now, too. More so than she had felt before.

'The Powells were at their richest when the Picturesque was at its most popular. They spent millions on the estate, well, the equivalent of millions today, I suppose. They changed the course of the river, see? Built waterfalls and hacked deep gullies out of the rock. They planted trees everywhere, and made artful little walks through them. The idea was you'd be surrounded by forest as you strolled along, and then suddenly the path would turn to reveal a wonderful vista. Something to make your heart soar. And that was getting close to nature, see?'

'So all these paths through the woods, the bridges and stuff?' Phoebe could see light up ahead now, whiter than the dull yellow of her dying torch. The walls of the tunnel glistened with moisture, and somehow without her noticing, the noise had grown almost too loud to talk, a rushing gurgling sound of a great deal of water moving swiftly through a narrow space.

'They were never meant for the likes of you and me, mind.' Gwyneth stopped, the light picking her out in silhouette now. 'Only the wealthy and influential were allowed to see the wonders. And this was even more private than most. Come on, but watch your feet, right? The rocks can get slippy.'

Phoebe followed, more slowly now, as Gwyneth set off along the tunnel. Enough light filtered in to show rusted iron rings hammered into the rock at waist height. Presumably they had once been threaded with rope to make a handrail. The noise grew to a deafening thunder, almost right up ahead. Gwyneth stopped, turned to one side. Her next step took her out of Phoebe's sight.

'Hold on,' she shouted over the racket, hurrying to keep up. Then she stopped, abruptly, her heart leaping into her mouth. 'Oh shit.'

The passage opened up onto a huge cavern. Light filtered in through a tiny sliver of hole at the top, just enough to show that the drop was both sheer and fatally high. There was no barrier to stop a careless visitor from plunging to certain death. Or even a relatively careful visitor, given the slippery floor. Phoebe didn't have much of a problem with heights, not like her mum, who had panicked at the top of the Walter Scott Monument and needed to be led down with her eyes closed. This was different though, and the biggest difference was the water.

It erupted from another gap in the cave wall, higher up and off to one side, then plunged into the depths far below. Spray and spume filled the air, and the constant motion was mesmerising. Without thinking, Phoebe reached out and grabbed the nearest cast-iron hoop, steadying herself even though she had been standing fast.

'It gets you like that if you're not careful,' Gwyneth shouted. She was standing much closer to the edge, alarmingly closer, and Phoebe began to reach for her, meaning to pull her back.

'Come on. I'll show you something even better.' Before Phoebe could make contact, Gwyneth ducked away, her booted feet slapping in the puddles on the passage floor as she went back the way they had come. Phoebe took one last look at the incredible sight, then followed. Across the passage, she saw a narrow gash in the rock face that she hadn't noticed before. It looked natural, except that it was suspiciously large enough for a person, and someone had carved steps in the floor. They curved downwards, descending through the stone until they emerged directly underneath the waterfall where it hit a pool at the base of the cavern. Uncountable years of water flow had carved away the rock in an almost perfect circle, the flow spiralling around the sides, faster and faster until it disappeared in the middle with a continuous sucking, gurgling sound.

'They made this place?' Phoebe said after long minutes of staring and drinking it all in. 'Wow.'

'No, silly. This place has been here since for ever.' Gwyneth leaned forward until she could hold her hand out to the edge of the waterfall, letting the water splash over her arm. Phoebe felt cold just looking at her, but she seemed not to notice the chill.

'The Powell family had the tunnels made, but this cave, the waterfall and the pool? They're all natural. Time was you could only get down here through the hole up there, see?' She pulled her hand out of the flow, pointing upwards at the sliver of sky so far away and splashing drops across Phoebe's face at the same time.

'Of course, a place like this, people would be superstitious, see?

They called it Pantri'r Diafol. The Devil's Larder. Or sometimes the Devil's Arsehole, but that doesn't make as much sense.'

'Does either?' Phoebe was still awed by the cavern, but the cold had begun to seep into her bones now, and she longed for the feel of the sun on her face again.

'Well, think about it. Many's the wandering sheep has fallen through that gap up there. Some might even have survived the fall, but once they're in here, the only way out is down. And you're not going that way without dying.'

'The bodies must come out somewhere, though. That's what I'd call the Devil's Arsehole.' Phoebe rolled her tongue around the word, and Gwyneth giggled. Her smiling face was suddenly, oddly, familiar, but Phoebe just couldn't place it. And then she had it. Gwyneth looked like her mum. Except that Phoebe couldn't remember the last time she'd seen her mum smile, giggle, have fun. The pills had taken all that away from her.

'It's cold in here.' She shivered, clasped her arms tight to her body and rubbed at them. 'I should probably be getting back or Aunt Maude'll have me weeding the vegetable patch for a week.'

Gwyneth's smile dropped, but only for a moment. 'OK,' she said. 'But you mustn't tell anyone about this place, right? It's our secret.'

Phoebe ran a pinched finger and thumb across her mouth. 'My lips are sealed.' She shivered again, amazed that her companion hardly seemed to notice the cold and damp. 'But I must get going, aye?'

The Gwyneth paused a moment, head cocked at a quizzical angle as if she was listening for something. Not that it was possible to hear much over the roar of the waterfall, echoed around the cavern.

'OK,' she said eventually. 'But I'll have to show you a different way home. Reckon the twins are out and about today, and we wouldn't want to bump into them now, would we?'

42

'Oh, there you are, Phoebe. I was beginning to wonder.'
Aunt Maude stood at the kitchen sink, washing dirt off something that would probably be supper in a few hours, when Phoebe traipsed in through the back door tired and gritty with sweat, hopeful of something to eat a good deal sooner. The route Gwyneth had led her to avoid the walled garden and the twins had been long and gruelling, even if it had given her some spectacular views down the valley at times. To her relief, the kitchen table was set for lunch, and judging by the fresh loaf and lack of detritus around Uncle Louis's place, nobody had eaten yet. She waited for her aunt to make a space before washing hands much grubbier than she had realised.

'Been anywhere interesting?' Aunt Maude asked as Phoebe pulled out a chair and sank into it, only realising how much her legs and feet ached once she took the weight off them.

'Just walking, mostly.' She opened her mouth to ask about the waterfall in the cavern, whether her aunt had been there or even knew about it. But then she remembered Gwyneth's insistence it be their secret, so she shut her mouth again.

'All alone?'

'No. I met up with Gwyneth again. You know, the girl I told you about? She showed me the ruins of the old mansion.' That much seemed safe enough to say, but before the last of her words were out, Aunt Maude had put down whatever root vegetable it was she had been cleaning, turned and wiped her wet, muddy hands on her apron.

'You be careful going up there on your own, Phoebe. It's not safe, and if you hurt yourself. Well . . .'

'But I wasn't alone. I was with Gwyneth.'

Aunt Maude tilted her head slightly. 'This Gwyneth who wanders the woods barefoot? Who lives in the village? About your age? Honestly, Phoebe. I'd have thought you were old enough to have grown out of such things.'

'I . . .' Phoebe started, then her brain caught up with her aunt's words. 'What?'

'There is no Gwyneth in the village, dear. Not your age least ways.' Aunt Maude pulled out a chair and sat down across the table from Phoebe, her face a picture of gentle concern.

'It's understandable, really. I know you're bored, what with the lack of television and nobody your own age to play with. It was probably unfair bringing you here, to be honest. But we didn't have much option. Your uncle's your legal guardian. He's obliged to look after you.' She paused a moment, a frown wrinkling her forehead. 'Not that he doesn't want to anyway. That's not what I meant. We both do. And we both care.'

Phoebe leaned back in her chair, glancing sideways at the closed study door. She couldn't quite work out what it was that her aunt was trying to say. And then it hit her.

'You think Gwyneth is an imaginary friend?' She tried not to let the incredulity show in her voice, although it wasn't easy.

'Is she not?' Aunt Maude kept the question neutral, placing her hands palm down on the tabletop in front of her in a gesture of conciliation. Phoebe crossed her arms, knowing how defensive it made her look.

'I'm twelve, not two. I know the difference between a real person and some kind of . . . I don't know . . . ghost.'

Except that as she said it, she wasn't so sure. There were times when she felt as lonely and bewildered as she had when she'd been little. And she couldn't deny that Gwyneth was a bit strange. On the other hand, they'd laughed together, gone up to the falls and into the caves underneath the ruins of Plas Llancwm. They'd even been to see Aunt Maude's bees. Gwyneth knew everyone in the village, what they were doing, who they were related to, who hated whom and so much more. They'd talked about it at great length as they wandered the woods together.

'Well, as long as you're keeping yourself out of trouble, that's fine.' Aunt Maude stood up, turned back to the sink and began washing the vegetables again. Phoebe watched her for a while, the thoughts tumbling through her head. She knew that Gwyneth was real. There was no way she'd invent someone like that for a friend. And besides, Gwyneth knew too much about stuff Phoebe couldn't possibly know. If she were just some figment of her bored imagination then Gwyneth would never have known about the old mansion, the cavern.

'Do you know much about the Powell family?' Phoebe asked as her aunt began chopping an onion.

'Well. They used to own most of the valley. Built that big old mansion you were talking about. Last of them was old Mad Roderick, so I heard. He died in the fire that destroyed the place, must be over a hundred years ago now.'

'Why do you call him mad?'

'I don't rightly know. That's just what everyone calls him. Way I heard it, there was something dodgy about the fire anyway. Insurance didn't pay up, so the family abandoned the whole estate and never came back.'

Aunt Maude put a pan on the stove, then cut a heavy slice of butter into it before following up with the onions. A delicious smell began to fill the room, covering up the less pleasant odour from Phoebe's damp and sweaty top.

'If you're really interested in it, I'm sure your uncle has books on the subject. You can ask him about it at lunchtime, won't be long now. And if he's not got anything here you can make it your next project when we go to the library again.' She plucked a wooden spoon from the old clay pot by the stove where they all lived. 'But first, I think you'd better go and have a shower, young lady. Change out of those filthy clothes. You fair stink the place out.'

Phoebe heard the low noise of conversation in the hallway as she reached the bottom of the back staircase, her hair still wet from washing. Someone had come to the house, a rare visitor to this middle-of-nowhere prison and a welcome distraction from the endless boredom. She paused, out of sight, to listen in and try to work out who her aunt might be talking to.

'. . . terribly sad, but it's a miracle it didn't happen sooner, really.'

She peered around the corner, hoping not to be noticed. The front door stood open, the afternoon light blocked by Aunt Maude and a figure in shadow on the threshold.

'. . . that last turn. He never really recovered properly. Even with what . . . the girl did for him.'

Phoebe didn't recognise the voice, although the accent suggested it was a local. She knew almost instantly what they were talking about though. Old Meredith Ellis. How long was it since she'd sat with him in his damp old kitchen, seen the aura of death clinging to him like a teenage boy's body odour? Not long, although the days had a habit of blurring into one.

'Well, thanks for bringing us the news. I'll tell Phoebe when she comes down. You'll let me know about the arrangements?'

If the visitor said anything, Phoebe didn't catch it. Moments later, Maude had closed the door and was heading for the kitchen. She followed on behind, entering the room as her aunt was putting the kettle on the stove.

'Did you hear all of that, or just the end?'

Phoebe pulled out her usual chair at the table and sat down. 'Just the end. He died though, didn't he? Old Meredith?'

Aunt Maude raised a grey eyebrow at that. 'Meredith? I didn't realise you were on first name terms.'

'Not really.' Phoebe shrugged. 'I didn't think he looked well when I saw him. It's a shame, but he was very old, wasn't he?'

'Eighty, I think. Your uncle would know better. The Ellises and the Beards are the two families who've lived longest in this valley. Longer even than the Powells you were asking about before.'

As if hearing his name said, or perhaps drawn by the sound of the kettle on the hob, the door to the study swung open and Uncle Louis appeared.

'What's that about the Powells?' he asked, then noticed Phoebe, smiled. 'Hey, Feebs. You back from roaming the hills, then?'

'Meredith Ellis died,' Aunt Maude said as she bent to the stove and brought bowls out of the warming oven. She ladled thick soup into them and passed them round.

'He did? When?' Uncle Louis stared at his soup as if it might have the answer for him. Either that or he couldn't quite believe it was his lunch.

'Early this morning, apparently. That was Tom Griffiths dropped by to let us know. Not sure why he didn't phone, but there you go.'

'He might have tried. I was on a call with my agent for half the morning.'

Aunt Maude raised an eyebrow at that, but said nothing. For a moment there was only the quiet sound of cutlery as they set about the soup, the rasp of the bread knife cutting another inch-thick slice for Uncle Louis to dip. Phoebe knew better than to say anything, and besides, she was famished after her long walk through the woods.

'I suppose there'll be a funeral,' Uncle Louis said finally, through the last mouthful of bread he had used to wipe the inside of the bowl clean. He didn't sound very enthusiastic about it.

262

'Later in the week, I'd expect. It's not as if his death was suspicious or anything.'

'We'd better go, I guess.' Uncle Louis made it sound like the most onerous of chores.

'Of course we'll go. I know you never saw eye to eye with the Ellises, but they're our neighbours. Your cousins, even. Old Meredith was the heart of the village.'

Phoebe paused with her spoon halfway to her mouth, surprised by the vehemence in her aunt's voice, and her uncle's childlike sullenness. 'Where will the funeral be? In the chapel down in the village?'

'It will indeed, Phoebe. And that means Bethan and I will have to sort out some flowers and make sure the place is looking presentable.' Aunt Maude glanced up at the clock on the wall. 'Perhaps you'd be so good as to help me in the garden once you've finished your soup?'

'But I was going to ask Uncle Louis about Mad Roderick Powell,' she protested. Anything had to be better than an afternoon digging vegetables and weeding.

'You were?' Uncle Louis asked. 'Why? I mean, what brought that up?'

'Phoebe's been up at Plas Llancwm this morning, Louis. Perhaps you can talk some sense into her about going so far on her own. It's not safe, you know. There's old mine workings and who knows what in the undergrowth.'

'I . . .' Phoebe began to say that she hadn't been on her own, but that seemed pointless given Aunt Maude's earlier assumption about Gwyneth.

'Well, the family history of the Powells is a fascinating story. You know the derivation of the name Powell, right?'

'Ap Hywel, son of Hywel. It's like MacDonald means son of Donald, only I'm not a boy so I'm nobody's son.'

Uncle Louis stared at her with a slightly disappointed expression.

263

No doubt he'd been hoping to educate her about Welsh names. The moment passed almost before it had come, his frown replaced with a smile.

'That's exactly right. Well, it's a bit more complicated than that, but yes, Ap in Welsh means son of, much the same as Mac in Scots Gaelic. Patronymics, that's naming a child after their father, were very common in ancient societies, so in English you get Johnson, Thomson, Peterson and so on. Scots have the MacDonalds and McLeans and many more. Your point about not being a boy is an interesting one, of course. In the Gaelic, you have Nic instead of Mac, meaning daughter of, so you could be Phoebe Nic Phillip. Except that the patronymic has fallen out of fashion rather. Although not in Iceland, of course, where it's still used. You'd be Phoebe Phillipsdottir if you'd been born in Reykjavik, and he would have been Phillip . . . What was your grandfather's first name again?'

Phoebe sort of understood what her uncle was saying, although he had a habit of going off at tangents multiple times in any conversation. The trick was finding the right way to steer him back on track. Or at least knowing when to give up.

'I don't know. He died before I was born.' She picked up her empty soup bowl and stacked it neatly on top of her side plate, ready to take to the sink for washing up. 'Perhaps I will help Aunt Maude in the garden this afternoon.'

43

Phoebe sat between her aunt and uncle, close to the back of a packed chapel, and tried her best not to fidget. It was only the second time in as many years that she'd been in a place of worship, and the last time had been a funeral too. Her mum and dad. Then, she'd been numb, her mind a blank. Now, she didn't know what to do, but a lingering sense of unfairness made her anxious and fidgety. Why did she have to be here? Why did people keep dying around her? And who were all these strangers with whom she'd been forced to live?

Everyone spoke Welsh, the hymns were in Welsh and even the tunes were unfamiliar. She could read the neatly printed order of service, but apart from the name and the dates on the front it meant nothing to her. Even then, she'd only come across the name Meredith when she'd first met the old man, and his middle names, Eifion and Hywel, she wasn't quite sure how to pronounce. Was that Hywel as in Ap Hywel? She'd thought it was spelled Howl to rhyme with Powell. She could manage Ellis though, that was easy enough. Perhaps rather than wandering the woods and hills for the past couple of months she would have been better served trying to learn a bit more of the language. Or maybe she would have been better off staying in Scotland in the first place. That was her real home, after all. Not this strange, mad place with its too many consonants and not enough vowels.

The dates beneath the name gave her pause, too. Everyone had said the old farmer was eighty or even eighty-five, but he'd been born in 1907. That seemed an impossible long time ago, but Phoebe's maths told her was only seventy-eight years. Still old, but not ancient. Not really.

The chapel was a dour place, despite the efforts Aunt Maude and Bethan Griffiths had made to brighten it up a bit. The windows didn't let in much light, which might have been on purpose or might have been down to the green algae growing on the glass. A single, vaulted chamber, its roof beams and arches made of wood so dark it could have been painted black. The simple, uncomfortable wooden benches sucked in what little light there was too, as did the dark grey suits of the mourners and the slate slabs that made up the floor. Only the white painted walls broke up the dullness, although even they were stained with damp and mould. It was a suitably miserable setting for a send-off.

Not able to pay attention to the tedious and interminable service, Phoebe tried instead to spot people she knew. It was a foolish task, really. Tom and Bethan Griffiths sat near the front, and she thought she recognised the postman a few rows behind them, although she only knew his face, not his name. It seemed odd to her that the postie would attend the funeral of one of the people on his rounds, but then even postmen had families, relations, friends, she supposed.

Towards the back of the church, on the other side of the aisle, Phoebe spotted Angharad and wondered what she was doing there. Her surname was Roberts, wasn't it? Not Ellis, for sure. On the other hand, it seemed everyone in Llancwm was related, one way or another, so maybe the old man had been family. Or maybe she just liked funerals. She looked more like a Goth than a mourner, and as bored as Phoebe felt. She had been staring resolutely at her hands, but Phoebe's gaze must have touched some sixth sense, as she looked up, caught her eye and made a face.

Seeing Angharad reminded Phoebe of who she hadn't seen. The twins were noticeably absent, although that was no great loss as far as she was concerned. But there was also no sign of Gwyneth. She knew everything about everyone in the village; she must have been related to at least some of them. Then again, Phoebe couldn't imagine her young friend dressed in sombre clothes and not grubby from mucking about in the forest. And she'd said before she didn't much like Nant Caws Farm, hadn't she? So maybe not a fan of the Ellis family at all.

No wiser, but grateful for the passage of time her musing had brought about, Phoebe watched as a selection of men from the front of the chapel stepped into the aisle and approached the minister. She only recognised Tegwin among them when they all turned, stooped, and lifted the coffin onto their shoulders. The wheezy organ began to play, and they carried old Meredith Eifion Hywel Ellis out of the chapel to his final resting place. The congregation followed, Phoebe, her aunt and uncle among the last of them.

Outside the sun shone bright and high overhead, much to her surprise. Phoebe had thought it must have been late evening at least, given how long the service had dragged on and how dark it had been in the chapel. Her second surprise was that Meredith's coffin wasn't taken to a waiting hearse to be whisked off to the nearest crematorium like her mum and dad had been. The slow party carried him through the cluttered graveyard to a freshly dug hole near the back. By the time Phoebe reached it, the coffin had already been lowered into the ground. She would have been happy to leave it at that, no great desire to approach the grave, even less to be noticed. Unfortunately for her, Aunt Maude had other ideas.

'Time to pay your last respects, dear.' She placed a hand on Phoebe's shoulder and steered her through the crowd. Nobody complained, far from it. They parted like the proverbial Red Sea.

'I don't . . .' Phoebe protested, but her aunt simply leaned close and whispered in her ear.

'Take a small handful of dirt. Drop it on the coffin. Bow your head and move on.'

Panic gripped Phoebe as she looked around. The only dirt she could see was the heap that lay alongside the hole, partly covered with a lurid green tarpaulin. Was she meant to go and grab some of that? She hadn't seen anyone else reaching for it. Looking around for an alternative source, she noticed that there was already a gravestone at the head of the opening. That seemed a bit premature to her until she saw the names already there. Seren Ellis – 1915 to 1949; Ceredig Ellis – 1935 to 1971. Meredith's wife and oldest son were already buried here. Somewhere under her feet. She felt the ground sway unsteadily beneath her, the hole growing bigger, the coffin lying deep in the ground, dry earth scattered over its shiny wooden top.

'Steady there now.' The voice cut through Phoebe's stupor, and she felt Aunt Maude's hand on her shoulder again, fingers gently squeezing. At the same time, the minister coughed gently, held up what looked like one of the small plastic buckets they used for chicken feed, and shook it gently. Peering inside, she saw more dry dirt and finally understood what she needed to do.

'For a moment there I thought you were going to tumble into poor old Mered's grave.'

Phoebe sat at a table in the hotel bar, next to Uncle Louis. It was the same table, she realised, that she'd sat at after Meredith Ellis had collapsed and she'd saved his life with CPR. For all the good that had done him. The room was fuller now than it had been then, the wake in full swing.

'I don't ever want to have to do that again.' She looked at her hand, rubbed her fingers against her thumb as if she could still feel the dry earth on them. As if it was somehow connected to the old man, dead, cold, lying beside his wife and eldest son.

'You did very well.' Aunt Maude patted her on the shoulder as if she was an obedient dog. Phoebe tried not to wince and shrug off her touch. The whole day was desperately uncomfortable, from the horrible black dress her aunt had found for her to wear, to the sombre faces and impenetrable accents of everyone around her. And behind it all, the memory of the last funeral she'd been too. Not one coffin but a pair of them side by side at the altar. Mum and Dad.

Somehow Phoebe had managed to go several days without really thinking about them. They were always there, of course. Always would be. But she'd stopped having the mini panic attacks when the memories caught her unawares. Mostly stopped, at least. They could still catch her, when the reality of her situation hit while she was in the middle of doing something perfectly ordinary. How long had it been since she'd come home from that school trip to Edinburgh? Since she'd smelled smoke on the air as she walked from the station? Cursing her dad for forgetting he was meant to pick her up. Cursing her mum for being useless and weak, addicted to tranquillisers. That had been the last thing she'd done before finding out they were dead, cursed them both.

'Do we have to stay?' she asked, suddenly cold despite the heat of the day and the press of bodies in the room.

Uncle Louis lifted up his pint, still only a third drunk. 'Why the hurry? It's not every day you get free food and drink from an Ellis.'

'Louis Beard, don't you dare.' Aunt Maude slapped his arm, but Phoebe could see it wasn't really meant. Maude had a glass of red wine, but had insisted Phoebe only drink Coke. She'd have preferred water, tea, anything really.

'We'll have to stay a little longer, Phoebe dear.' Aunt Maude craned her neck as she looked through the crowd in the direction of the bar. 'At least have something to eat, OK? I know it's hard for you, but people notice.'

If that was meant to make her feel better it was ill-judged. The last thing Phoebe wanted was to be noticed. She wanted to slink out the back door, scurry away from the village and into the woods where she felt safe. Maybe she'd find Gwyneth out there too.

A commotion at the far end of the room turned into the twins elbowing their way through the crowd in the direction of the bar. They'd not been at the funeral, but that clearly wasn't going to stop them helping themselves to free food and booze. Phoebe wasn't sure why, but something about them repulsed her more than anything she had ever encountered. Far more than the bullies and loud-mouthed yobs at school. It was bad enough being in this crowded room, but the thought of sharing the same air as them was too much.

"'Scuse me. Need the loo.' She pushed her Coke away, stood and hurried off in the opposite direction before she could be spotted, and before either Uncle Louis or Aunt Maude could say anything. Since she hadn't actually needed a pee, just an excuse to get out of the room, Phoebe carried on past the door marked Ladies and outside.

It wasn't much changed from when she'd last been there, escaping from the pub quiz. The space between the building and the steep side of the hill climbing away from it was small, and filled mostly with empty beer barrels, bakery bread trays and crates. The bins lined up against the end where vehicles could back in behind the shop, and closer to the hotel the small wooden table with two benches huddled under a wide umbrella where she had sat before. Judging by the discarded cigarette buts and half-burned matches at her feet, people had been here recently, which was probably why she carried on walking until she found herself emerging into the street almost directly opposite the chapel.

It was blissfully quiet now, with everyone in the bar. Not knowing quite why, Phoebe crossed the road and pushed through the little iron gate. The graveyard stood empty, silent, not even the noise of someone filling in the grave. Presumably that had been done already; they wouldn't leave it open any longer than necessary, would they? Curious, she started off in that direction, then froze when she realised that she wasn't quite as alone as she had thought.

A single figure stood at the grave and stared at the headstone. Hands in the pockets of his long overcoat, he had his back to Phoebe and didn't seem to have heard her approach. It was easy enough to identify Steve Lorne by his shock of unruly white hair and the scarf wrapped around his neck on what was actually quite a pleasant and warm afternoon. Phoebe almost approached him, but something about the way his shoulders hunched stopped her, his head bowed as if weighed down by the whole world, and looking almost like he might have been sobbing. A friend of the family? Not exactly, if what little she'd gleaned about him from Uncle Louis and Aunt Maude was true. Should she go and speak to him? Tell him she was sorry for not coming back after they'd had tea that afternoon?

Phoebe took a step forward, and at the same time Lorne tensed. He turned swiftly, eyes wide as he saw her. She opened her mouth to speak, almost managed to get out a quiet 'Mr . . .' before he shook his head once, and hurried away. She followed, but not in pursuit. She stopped when she reached the grave and the low mound of freshly returned earth that covered the coffin and the mortal remains of Meredith Ellis. There was an odd smell in the air, and something had scuffed the surface about halfway up from the feet to the head, as if a small animal had burrowed at the ground in search of worms. Phoebe stared at it, puzzled, then realised she'd been gone from the wake too long. Aunt Maude would come looking for her.

She hurried away from the grave, returning to the hotel. And it was only as she was back inside and sidestepping past the Ladies' toilet as another mourner went in, that she realised what that strange smell had been. Steve Lorne had not been crying at the grave of Meredith Ellis.

He'd been pissing on it.

44

'Ah, there you are, dear. I was beginning to worry you might have run out on us.'

Phoebe approached the table where Aunt Maude and Uncle Louis still sat. She noticed that her uncle's pint was finished whereas her aunt's wine had hardly been touched. Much like her glass of Coke, which looked horribly flat.

'Needed a bit of air,' she said as she pulled out her chair and sat down. She briefly considered telling her aunt about Steve Lorne and what she'd seen him doing. A donkey-bray of laughter over towards the crowded bar stopped her, and reminded her of why she'd ducked out in the first place. One of the twins was finding rather too much amusement in what should have been a solemn occasion. Judging by the sour look on Aunt Maude's face, she felt much the same.

'A wise choice.' She pushed her wine glass towards the middle of the table and got to her feet. 'We must go and pay our respects to Tegwin now. And then I think we should all go home.'

Uncle Louis picked up his empty pint glass and stared at it like a child who has unwrapped all his Christmas presents. 'But we've only just started.'

'You can have another when we get home, Louis. You're always complaining about how bad the beer is in here anyway.' Aunt Maude took the glass from him and placed it on the table.

'But it's free,' was all the plaintive excuse Uncle Louis could come up with, but Phoebe could see his heart wasn't in it. On the one hand, she was pleased that they were going to be leaving. She didn't think she could take much more of the wake, and she desperately wanted to get out of the dress her aunt had given her, pull on something more comfortable. On the other, there were so many more questions she needed to ask about Steve Lorne. Sober, it was unlikely she'd get much out of Uncle Louis, and she'd known her aunt long enough now to see how she would shut down the subject if she could. A couple of beers in, though, and her uncle might be a bit more loose-lipped. That wasn't going to happen if they walked back to Pant Melyn before he'd had more than the one pint.

There was also the small matter of speaking to Tegwin Ellis. Phoebe had a muddled memory of the wake after her parents' funeral, and the seemingly endless line of people expressing their heartfelt condolences to her. She had no idea who any of them were, no interest in finding out. But apparently such things were important. Funerals, she was coming to understand, were not about the dead so much as the living left behind, and it was a social minefield she was ill-equipped to navigate.

Aunt Maude had no such reservations. She led them both through the crowd as if it were no more substantial than smoke, arriving at a small cluster of chairs near the bar where Tegwin Ellis sat surrounded by more nameless people dressed in various shades of dark grey and black. Phoebe guessed they must have been relatives, but then she was technically one of those too.

'We're so sorry for your loss, Tegwin.' Aunt Maude bent towards the farmer, taking an unresisting hand in hers as she spoke. It was the first time Phoebe had seen him since she'd first wandered up to Nant Caws Farm. Since she had seen the aura of death hanging around Meredith like a cowl. Since Tegwin had shot the ram and dragged its carcass away to bury. Since he had presented her with that odd bunch of flowers. Back then he had been a barrel of a man, overlarge as if there was the blood of giants somewhere in his distant ancestry. Now, he seemed deflated, shrunken somehow. And the look on his face was a mixture of bewilderment and fear.

'I know this is a difficult time, but if there's anything we can do, you only have to ask.' Uncle Louis stepped up, placed a gentle hand on Tegwin's shoulder for a moment, then said something else in Welsh that Phoebe didn't understand. The farmer looked at him with uncomprehending eyes, then his gaze slid across to where she stood and what little colour there was in his face drained completely. There was an instant's pause, and then he reached out and grabbed her hand.

'Gwen?'

Phoebe struggled with the urge to scream, clenched her hands into fists for a moment and then released them, hoping the irritation would go.

'No. I'm Phoebe, remember? From Scotland?'

The frown creasing Tegwin's brow deepened even further, and he looked away. Phoebe extricated her hand from his, added a quiet 'I'm sorry' and then made good her escape. As she followed her aunt and uncle through the crowd, they went past a couple of trestle tables laid out with food. Piles of white bread sandwiches, sausage rolls, Welsh cakes and more. Enough to feed everyone present twice over. For a moment she was transfixed, unable to move as she stared at the mourners loading their plates high, stuffing their faces as if they feared not seeing another meal for weeks. A couple of men were surreptitiously slipping biscuits and crisps into their jacket pockets. Something for their tea at Tegwin Ellis's expense.

'Are they . . .?' She looked around, thinking her aunt and uncle close by, but they were at the door and beckoning. One more look back at the food table, one more sandwich artfully wrapped in a paper napkin and hidden for later. Phoebe shook her head and made for the exit.

She caught up with her aunt and uncle in the wide passageway that formed a kind of reception area for the hotel. Most of the mourners were in the bar, but a few had found their way to the quieter room on the opposite side. Phoebe looked over her shoulder, pointed with one finger towards the table laden with food.

'Did you see those men back there? Putting sandwiches in their pockets?'

Uncle Louis grinned, patting at his own jacket. 'Of course. It's not a proper wake if there's any food left afterwards.'

'Honestly, Lou.' Aunt Maude rolled her eyes. She began to turn towards the front door, and then something stopped her. 'Ah, yes. Knew there was something else we had to do. Come on, Phoebe dear. You need to sign the book of condolences.'

Phoebe hadn't noticed the table set up at the back of reception, when she had come in. There'd been too many people milling around, chattering away at each other loudly in a language she didn't understand. Now that they were all drinking and eating at someone else's expense, she could see that a table had been placed so as to block the stairs to the hotel's bedrooms. A plain white cover and a vase with lilies in it, someone had placed a couple of photograph frames either side of what looked like a hotel visitors' book. There had been one similar at her parents' funeral, although she wasn't at all sure where it might be now. Uncle Louis must have it, she supposed. She certainly didn't.

As she bent to add her name, Phoebe saw that one of the pictures was of Meredith and a woman who must have been Seren, his wife. Taken on their wedding day, unless she had been in the habit of wearing long flowing white dresses all the time. She looked beautiful in the way all brides do, and much younger than him. But there was a sadness in her eyes too, as if she knew what was coming for her in the future.

'What happened to Meredith's wife?' She pointed at the photograph, then looked around to see where Uncle Louis had got to. He emerged from the bar looking slightly guilty, his pockets bulging more than Phoebe remembered.

'What?'

'Meredith's wife.' Phoebe picked up the photograph and showed it to him. 'What happened to her?'

'Oh, Seren. Yes.' Uncle Louis took his spectacles out of his breast pocket and held them up so that he could get a better look. 'Terrible business. She died giving birth to Gwen.'

'Are we done yet?' Aunt Maude stood at the door, half open and letting the afternoon sun flood in. Phoebe placed the picture back on the table, scribbled her name in the book, and only noticed the second photograph as she was putting the pen down alongside it. A family group, posed at what looked like a rather grander agricultural show than the one held in Llancwm. The centre of the picture was dominated by a large ram, not unlike the one she'd seen shot. Behind it, a proud, and much younger, Meredith posed with two boys and a girl. Phoebe recognised the solid stockiness of Tegwin, which meant the other boy must have been Ceredig. Whip-thin, he had shoulder-length hair that framed a face surprisingly like his mother's. But it was the young girl standing next to him that caught her attention. Welly boots and an old-fashioned dress that seemed quite inappropriate to the surroundings, her mop of unruly dirty-blonde hair framed a face that Phoebe found oddly familiar, but not from looking in the mirror.

'Ah. The Aberystwyth Fair. Champion Welsh Mountain Ram, too.'

She flinched as the photograph frame was plucked from her hands. Uncle Louis peered at the image, still holding his folded spectacles up to his eyes like a pince-nez.

'This must be early sixties, judging by the clothes and Cered's ridiculous haircut.' He handed back the photograph, stabbing a finger at it. 'There you go, Feebs. See the resemblance? Now you know why everyone calls you Gwen. She'd be pretty much your age when that was taken. Looks just like you.'

Phoebe studied the photograph again, but she couldn't see it herself. Yes, there was something of her about the girl. She was slight, like Phoebe, and their hair had the same grubby straw colour. But that was where the similarity ended. No, if young Gwen looked like anyone, then it was surely Gwyneth.

45

2023

It's raining, of course. How could it be any other way? Phoebe enters the chapel expecting there to be very few people in attendance; Maude might have lived in the village for decades, but it is a small community and most of her contemporaries left long before she did. And so it's something of a surprise to find the place packed.

The last time she was here, it was a memorial service for her uncle. That was busy too, but most of the dark-suited congregation were literary types, people from far away, a few journalists. Of the faces that turn to see her walk quickly to her reserved seat at the front, she's surprised to find she recognises more than half. They're not all wearing black, either, although a few are. Plenty like her have chosen colour, as her aunt would have wanted.

Phoebe has never had much time for religion. Her parents weren't regular churchgoers, and their fate long ago cemented the idea within her that she wanted nothing to do with any god who could be so cruel. This service of remembrance is more for Maude than for her though, and at least in her later years the old lady had found some solace in chapel. From her conversation with the Elder, Phoebe understands that was very much on her aunt's terms. More to do with community than worship.

The service is mercifully brief, and everyone joins in with the hymns even if they don't know the Welsh. Phoebe gives a short and heartfelt eulogy, all too aware that most of the people she is talking to have probably seen her aunt more recently than she has. Not counting the visit to Bronglais and its bereavement room. There is no body here, no coffin to take outside and lower into the ground. Aunt Maude has already been to Birmingham to be resomated, her remains returned as a remarkably small box of chalk-white powder. Phoebe will pick a drier day to take them up to the bees for scattering.

The rain is still falling when it's all done, persistent rather than heavy, that soft Welsh rain that even the most expensive outdoor wear can't keep out for long. Phoebe stands in the shelter of the chapel doorway as people leave, some pausing briefly to wish her well, most hurrying across the road to the hotel. Eventually it is just her and a shuffling, white-haired old figure. Steve Lorne has tidied himself up a bit, found a dark jacket that isn't too crumpled. He's read the mood though, wearing a silk scarf around his neck that is a vibrant red and blue Paisley pattern.

'Never been inside before,' he says in his soft, raspy voice. 'Lived in this village half a century, on and off. Never felt the need.'

'You've visited the graveyard though.'

The old man looks at her for a moment, head tilted ever so slightly to one side. Then he breaks into a broad smile that is almost enough to stop the rain. 'Yes. You saw that, didn't you. Thought I was alone.'

'You've every reason to hate Meredith, although I didn't quite understand why at the time. Worked it out not long after, right enough.'

Lorne nods, his focus glazing over for a moment. 'So you did, Feebs. So you did. That was a cruel summer for you.'

'Hard for all of us, harder for some. You coming to the wake?' Phoebe holds out her arm, but she can see the hesitation in Steve's eyes. He's a recluse by nature, and across the road will be a room full of people. Unlike the chapel, they'll be mingling and talking, swapping stories about Maude and Louis or just gossiping while someone else pays for the food and drink.

'I'm not much of one for socialising. The service was nice, but I think I'll be getting home now.'

'You didn't walk here, did you?' Phoebe looks out at the wet tarmac road, the trees dripping everywhere, then back at Steve's rather unsuitable garb. He puts a hand in his jacket pocket and comes out with a keyring.

'Not that foolish, no. But perhaps you could help me to the car. These steps are slippery and my balance isn't what it used to be.'

The road is lined with cars on both sides, stretching away to the end of the village. A rare sight but understandable given how many people turned up for the festivities. Phoebe is about to ask where Steve's car is, but no sooner has the thought occurred to her than she sees it. Sleek, low and probably older than she is, it's surely unsuitable for a man of Steve's age. As she gets closer, she sees the Aston Martin badge. Like something James Bond would drive.

'This is yours?' she asks. 'It's beautiful.'

'Bought it new in 1969. About six months before I passed my driving test.' He unlocks the door and pulls it open. Inside is old leather, a pair of thin driving gloves laid on the dashboard. Steve grins at her as he lowers himself with great care into the seat, winds down the window by hand and pulls the door closed.

'I used to be a rock star, you know. There are standards we have to maintain.'

46

1985

Time seemed to simultaneously speed up and slow to a crawl in the days after Meredith's funeral. Phoebe's hopes of a hot, dry summer were soon dashed by the arrival of dark clouds and endless rain. It put a halt to her plans to find Gwyneth and ask her who she really was, which left her with that half-remembered image in the photograph and a growing feeling that she had simply imagined it all. Uncle Louis had said the girl in the picture looked like her, but Phoebe thought it had looked like Gwyneth, and Gwyneth didn't look much like her at all, did she? Or maybe she did, a bit. Chances were they were related, when she thought about it. Everyone in the valley seemed to be a cousin of some form to everyone else, and Phoebe's mum had come from here, after all. With each passing day, the memory of that photo faded a little more, but she still wanted to find her new friend and ask her a few questions.

There was the small matter of Steve Lorne, too, but Phoebe knew she'd have to pick the right time to broach that subject. And Uncle Louis seemed to be constantly in his study working away at the next Muriel Baywater, which was mostly a good thing since she'd read all of them now, some more than once. When, after a week that felt like a month, Aunt Maude had asked if she wanted to go with her to Aberystwyth for the afternoon, Phoebe had leapt at the chance. Although once there, the town's lack of any great fashion sense and her own disillusionment had conspired to make the visit dull.

It was on the way back to Pant Melyn, a bag full of books her only successful purchase, that Phoebe realised her aunt was driving a different route to usual.

'Where are we going?' she asked as they passed a village sign with no vowels on it at all.

'A little detour, Phoebe dear. We're going to see the colonel.'

'The colonel?' Phoebe echoed her aunt, then remembered the elderly gentleman at the dinner party. 'Why?'

'Because believe it or not, he's a qualified history teacher, among other things. You did say you wanted to study history, didn't you?'

She had, at one point that summer. But now Phoebe wasn't so sure, especially if it meant being tutored by the tweed-suited old man.

'I said I was interested in it when you asked me about all those books I was reading.' Muriel Baywater, mostly, and it hadn't really been the history side of things so much as the romance. The escapism, if she was being honest with herself. Phoebe reckoned she could learn as much about history from her uncle. He'd written those books, after all.

Aunt Maude flexed her hands on the steering wheel in that way she had of showing her displeasure. 'Well, Alastair . . . Colonel Peterson has very kindly agreed to speak to you about your options. I know we mentioned homeschooling, your uncle and I, but there are other alternatives. Better, I dare say, for both you and us. Alastair knows a great deal about the Welsh education system. His advice is sound, for all he might come across as a bit of an old bufty sometimes.'

'Bufty?'

'It doesn't matter, Phoebe. We've left it so far because, well . . .'

Maude glanced briefly at her, then snapped her attention back to the road, causing the car to drift slowly onto the wrong side. 'But anyway, we need to sort something out soon. The new academic year's not far off now. Alastair can help you with that.'

'Is he all right? The colonel?' Phoebe remembered the dinner party, and more particularly meeting Aunt Maude the next day as she walked back to Pant Melyn, presumably from wherever it was they were going now.

'How do you mean?'

'You said he drinks too much. We had a teacher like that at school, only they sacked him because he kept turning up late to his classes.'

Aunt Maude glanced across at Phoebe again, the car following her gaze until she noticed what was happening and corrected their course before they drove into a hedge.

'It's not like that, really. Alastair's wife died a few years ago. Lilly. The cancer got her, poor thing. She was a lovely lady, you know. Always helping out in the village. It was a terrible shock when she went. I think you can probably appreciate that better than most of us at the moment. And Alistair took it very badly. Those first few months were particularly hard. He's a lot better now, but he gets lonely like the rest of us.'

'And the drink helps?' Phoebe couldn't imagine how it might.

'To be honest, I don't think he drinks much when he's alone any more. There's not as many bottles in his recycling as there used to be, for sure. So when he comes to dinner with us, he perhaps makes up for it a little too enthusiastically. Really, Phoebe. He's the sweetest man.'

Aunt Maude slowed the car almost to a crawl, then without indicating, turned suddenly across the road into a narrow entrance Phoebe hadn't seen. 'Anyway, we're here now. Let's go in and have a cup of tea. See if Alastair can teach you anything useful.'

★ ★ ★

Set high up the side of the valley, the colonel's house would have had commanding views towards far-distant Aberystwyth and the sea of Cardigan Bay were it not surrounded by mature trees and a small walled garden. Phoebe unclipped her seatbelt and climbed out of the car, shivering in the cold wind that blew up out of nowhere. The two of them bustled over to the front door, and by the time they arrived it had opened, Colonel Peterson waiting to usher them inside.

Dressed more casually than the first time she had met him, the colonel was a lot less intimidating to Phoebe as he led her and Aunt Maude through to the kitchen. The house was of a similar size to Pant Melyn, but whereas her uncle's place was a rambling, much-extended old farmhouse, this had more of the manor about it. Purpose built to be larger than the cottages dotted around the hills and along the road that ran through the centre of the village, its rooms were well proportioned, and its ceilings reminded Phoebe more of the older Scottish houses some of her friends lived in, almost twice her height and with ornate plasterwork to the cornices.

'This is the old mine captain's house,' the colonel said, noticing her stares. 'It's quite a bit grander than the workers' cottages. A bit big for me to be rattling around in on my own, too. But I couldn't really contemplate leaving. Not now.'

The kitchen was a bright and airy room at the back of the house, with a large dining area and French windows opening up onto the garden. Phoebe's initial impression was of extreme neatness. There was very little in the way of clutter and even the morning's post, placed down on the countertop, was lined up perfectly. A small collection of books had been similarly arranged on the table, placed with the kind of precision that might be expected of a master mason.

'Please, have a seat both of you. I'll put the kettle on.'

'It's all right, Alastair. Why don't I do that, and you and Phoebe can have a little chat, eh?' Aunt Maude bustled past the old colonel, opening cupboards and pulling out tea-making things as if this were her own kitchen. Phoebe could only watch, slightly astonished.

'So, young lady. Your aunt tells me you're interested in studying history.' The colonel pulled out one of the chairs and gestured for Phoebe to sit. Once she had done so, he took a seat for himself directly opposite.

'I'm not really sure what I want to study any more. Not really sure of anything, to be honest.' As she said it, Phoebe realised just how true it was. Her plans, like those of all her friends at school, had been based on their shared interests. She and Jenny had both enjoyed English and thought about maybe going into journalism. It was what Dundee was famous for, after all, alongside jute and jam. But without Jenny to bounce ideas off, she was no longer sure. And where was she going to end up?

'Well, your grades are excellent, as are the reports from all your teachers. So the world is very much your oyster right now.' The colonel lifted up one of the books to reveal a slim folder underneath. Phoebe saw her name written neatly along the dotted line marked on the cover for such purposes. Clearly someone had been doing their homework.

'I don't even know what I'd be best doing next. I mean, I heard that you have to learn Welsh as part of the curriculum. Don't mind languages, but I'll be years behind everyone else, won't I?' Phoebe heard the panic rising in her own voice and managed to stop herself talking. Everything she'd said was true though, and it didn't help that Aunt Maude had bounced her into this meeting. Sure, she'd had time to think about it over the summer, but that didn't mean she'd actually done that. There'd been too much else going on to worry about school.

'Not all schools in Wales require you to speak the language, Phoebe. Set your mind at rest about that. It's true that wherever you go you'll be at a disadvantage for a little while, but then that was always going to be the case, I'm afraid. Your aunt and uncle were thinking along the lines of homeschooling, to make it easier on you. I'd be happy to help with that, and there's plenty other people in and around Llancwm with the knowledge and experience.' The colonel leaned his elbows on the table and clutched his hands together as if in prayer, paused for a moment before adding, 'But I can't help thinking you would be better off, happier even, with people of your own age.'

'So I should go to school in Aberystwyth, then?' Phoebe felt a little flutter in her chest at the thought. Making new friends, yes, but also early mornings and long bus rides. Or being driven by Aunt Maude, which was even worse.

'Possibly there, yes.' The colonel reached for an A4 envelope that had been lying underneath the folder, opened it and pulled out a glossy colour brochure. He slid it across the table towards her. 'Or this might be an option.'

Phoebe picked up the brochure, scanned the cover quickly. It was for a place called Llandod Hall, which appeared to be a large mansion house somewhere near Llandrindod Wells, wherever that was. Photographs showed girls playing hockey, sitting in airy classrooms, studying in a high-ceilinged library stacked with shelves of old leather-bound books.

'A private school?' She flicked through the pages, seeing yet more images including one of a smartly dressed girl about her own age standing in front of a narrow bed in a room with a desk under its sash window and a rather incongruous poster stuck to the wall. 'A boarding school? But who would pay for it?'

The colonel looked past her, up to where Aunt Maude was standing. 'The money isn't a problem, Phoebe. And as I say, this is only one option. It's a very good school though. I've known the headmistress for years.'

Phoebe turned in her chair, looking to her aunt for confirmation. The old woman nodded once. 'It's not so far. You could weekly board to start with, come back home to Pant Melyn at the weekends.'

'There's no need to make a decision straight away,' the colonel said. 'Take that home with you. Read it through. We've a few weeks yet before we'll need an answer.'

Phoebe looked at the brochure, up at the colonel, down at the brochure again. She hadn't really given her education much thought since her aunt had first told her they would be homeschooling, and the sporadic Welsh lessons with Uncle Louis had given her a taste of what that would be like. Now there was a tantalising, almost unbelievable alternative. A posh private school in a big mansion. And all she could think about was the look on Jenny's face when she found out.

47

More days of rain followed on from Phoebe's visit to the colonel's house, keeping her locked up inside until she was ready to scream. She'd studied the scant information on Llandod Hall a dozen times, switching between excitement at the thought of going there and certainty that she could not on an almost hourly basis. One moment she wanted to go, eager for the challenge and the new friends she might make. The next she imagined snooty posh girls from rich families looking down on her provincial accent and making fun of her. She'd be arriving at a new school at the wrong time and wrong age. Her contemporaries would already have formed their cliques, established their pecking order. It would be too hard to fit in.

But that was just daft. She'd be the same going to secondary school in Aberystwyth, with the added worry that they'd all be talking to each other in Welsh too. Aunt Maude had assured her that wasn't the case, that the town was very cosmopolitan due to the university, and a lot of the children there came from all over the place. It hadn't really helped.

There was the other pressing question too, she thought as she stared out the window at the endless rain. Who was Gwyneth, really? Aunt Maude had thought her an imaginary friend, but Phoebe knew that wasn't true. Gwyneth was real, not some kind of apparition. But she was strange. She knew the valley like a native born and bred, had all the gossip on everyone. She'd even known Phoebe's predicament when they'd first met up in that glade under the old oak tree. And yet she looked remarkably like Gwen Ellis when she'd been Phoebe's age. Even sometimes wore the same style of dress. Phoebe longed to get out into the woods, track down her friend and find out the truth. But the rain kept on falling, as if someone up there had started running a bath and then been distracted for a week.

And so the days blurred into one another. The stack of Muriel Baywater romance novels was long since finished and read again. Phoebe had even given *The Patience of Bees* another go. She'd abandoned that after the first couple of chapters, still not really sure what it was supposed to be about. Before the fire had so cruelly upended her life, she would have dealt with the boredom by spending hours on the phone with Jenny. It had been a while now since last she'd called her oldest friend, and that hadn't been as much fun as it should have been. Phoebe might even have whiled away the time by asking her uncle about the history of Llancwm, something she felt might work as a new project. But apart from brief breaks to eat, he'd been locked away in his study, apparently hard at work.

'What is it Uncle Louis spends all his time writing?' she asked one damp afternoon, as she helped her aunt prepare tiny cucumbers for pickling. She knew the answer, of course, but she wanted to know if her aunt did too.

'Who knows? He might be marking essays for the university. Or reviewing for the papers, though there's not so much of that goes on any more.'

'Do you ever read it? His writing?'

'I read *Patience* a long time ago. He's not really done much since then. Doesn't seem to have to. The money keeps coming in. What publishers call a long tail, that one. It'll still be selling thousands of copies a year when both of us are in the ground.'

Phoebe shuddered at the expression, recalled the feel of the dirt as she'd sprinkled it onto Meredith Ellis's coffin. Mum and Dad had been cremated, and it occurred to her then that she wasn't entirely sure where their ashes were. It seemed oddly indelicate to ask.

The sound of the study door opening broke the silence that had fallen on the kitchen. Phoebe looked around to see her uncle step out. He'd pulled on his old jacket, and held his leather satchel in one hand like an elderly schoolboy. Off somewhere, probably into town although she knew better than to ask if she could come too.

'I need to get something to the Post Office before collection. Promised Phil he'd have it tomorrow.' He held up the satchel, that familiar, plaintive look on his face, then glanced at the window where the rain bounced off the stone sill and clattered against the glass.

Aunt Maude let out a sigh that could be heard above the roar from outside. There was a post box in Llancwm, but the nearest Post Office was Devil's Bridge. Normally Uncle Louis would either walk or take his ancient sit-up-and-beg bicycle. Today, he needed to be driven. It occurred to Phoebe that Uncle Louis never drove, it was always Aunt Maude. Perhaps he had never passed his test, although that seemed unlikely given where he lived. She glanced up at the clock on the wall. They'd have to go soon, too, if they wanted to catch the afternoon collection.

'Fine.' Aunt Maude rinsed her hands under the cold tap, drying them on a tea cloth which she then handed to Phoebe. 'But don't complain to me if your pickles aren't crunchy enough.'

For a moment Phoebe thought that might have changed Uncle Louis's mind for him, such was the look of indecision on his face. It only lasted for the length of time it took Aunt Maude to cross the kitchen and exit to the hall though. Then he shrugged at Phoebe, turned and followed.

Leaving his study door wide open behind him.

★ ★ ★

Phoebe had hardly ever entered her uncle's study in all the time she'd been at Pant Melyn. Perhaps that first mistake, so early on, had marked it as a place never to go. Or most likely it was simply that her uncle was always in there, churning out Muriel Baywater romance novels at a prodigious rate. She was nothing if not curious, though, and here was a golden opportunity. The way Aunt Maude drove, it would be at least a half an hour before they were back. She could have a good look around, and maybe find out how far along the next book had come.

She approached the doorway cautiously, ears straining for any sound of an early return. Peering in, she saw a mess that looked like a small bomb had gone off. She'd only had brief glimpses before, but this seemed like the room's default state. How anyone could work among such clutter was beyond her.

A soft whirring sound came from the desk, and as Phoebe picked a clear path through the papers she saw that her uncle's computer was running. She didn't know much about computers for working, although Jenny's brother had been given something for playing games on the previous Christmas, and she'd had a go on that. This looked far more businesslike, boxy and square and with a little logo on it that looked like a half-eaten apple in rainbow colours. Clearing aside a pile of printed sheets, Phoebe saw the words Macintosh SE written on the beige plastic casing. The screen had been blank, but she must have nudged something as it popped into life before her eyes. She almost fled, worried she'd broken it, and then the words across the page caught her attention. Tiny letters forming a page of manuscript, the familiar prose, and at the top of the screen a title: *Will I See You in the Next World?*

Not the catchiest, and from what little Phoebe could read, it would need a lot of work. She didn't want to touch anything in case she accidentally deleted it, so there was no way to read any more. As she was carefully putting back the sheets of paper so nobody would know she had been in there, two names almost leapt out of the print at her. Philip MacDonald and Siân Mac-Donald (née Beard).

Phoebe scanned the page, seeing now that it was a letter from the solicitor, Mr Stearn. She didn't much understand it, other than that there had been some problem with the insurance on the house, but that had all been sorted now and the estate would be held in trust until Phoebe reached her majority. For a moment she wondered at the word 'estate'. It brought to mind rolling country-side and a big old mansion. But of course it only meant the sum total of her parents' worldly goods and possessions. Hers now, or at least when she turned sixteen.

Idly, she flipped through the pages to see what else there was. She half expected to see figures, some breakdown of the value put on those two lives. What she found was far more troubling. A poorly aligned and slightly out of focus photocopy of the procur-ator fiscal's report into their deaths.

Phoebe flicked through the pages, the computer forgotten as she half read the words. A little voice deep inside her head was telling her to stop, to put it down, that such things were better off left unknown. But she'd never been much good at listening to herself.

All the time she'd been at Pant Melyn, the weeks before when she'd stayed with Jenny, ever since she'd walked home from the station to find the cul-de-sac filled with police cars, fire engines and the neighbours in their dressing gowns, she had wondered how it could be that neither her mother nor father had noticed the fire before it got so bad that it was too late.

And now she knew.

Tests on the remains of her mother had determined that she had been out of it on tranquillisers when she died. That didn't sur-prise Phoebe much. Her mum had been numbing herself for years, even if Phoebe didn't exactly know why. It was something to do with wanting more children but not being able to have any. More than that she'd never managed to get out of either of them. And now she never would.

She stared at the final page for a long while, not quite understanding why it was so much more blurred than the rest until the tears overflowed and began to run down her cheeks. Phoebe wiped them away, sniffed, and stared at the final paragraph, the results of the tests done on her father.

He'd been much more badly burned than her mother, apparently due to being close to the centre of the fire. From what they could tell, he probably fell asleep in his chair while smoking. And how often had she pleaded with him to give up the cigarettes? Phoebe could almost scream.

It struck her then that if the school trip had gone as planned, she would have been home. Probably in her bedroom listening to music. Or on the phone chatting with Jenny about the trip they'd both just got back from. She'd have smelled the fire long before it got out of control, maybe even heard the fire alarm if it had gone off. She knew where the fire extinguisher lived, and she could have got them out, raised the alarm.

Mum and Dad would still be alive.

48

2023

The house was always quiet when she was growing up, but now
Phoebe feels its silence is different somehow. The creaks and
groans as the joists swell and shrink seem muted, the slow breathing
of the stones stilled as if in anticipation. She's put the radio on in the
kitchen, the occasional sound of music or snippet of conversation
reaching her as she goes from room to room, not so much surveying
the contents as mentally preparing herself for the task ahead.

It surprises her how little the house has changed since she first
set foot in it, all those many years ago. Uncle Louis and Aunt
Maude were well set in their ways when she was dumped uncere-
moniously upon them by cruel circumstances. Theirs was a simple
life of slow routine, and even the arrival of a soon-to-be-teenage
girl couldn't shake that. She only managed to coax a few conces-
sions to modernity from them in the years before she, like her
mother before her, fled the valley for university, and most of them
were quietly tidied out of the way not long after.

If there was one word to sum up the whole of Pant Melyn, it
would be books. If there were two, it would be books and gardening. Every room in the house contains at least one bookcase, and
every bookcase overflows. Good insulation, Phoebe supposes, as

she runs a finger over cracked leather spines and shiny paperback covers. So many words committed to paper, could anyone possibly read them all?

In the living room, poorly labelled since hardly anyone ever used it, Uncle Louis's ancient record player and collection of LPs still fill the lower shelves. They're probably worth a fortune now, but Phoebe can't imagine selling them. She crouches on stiff knees, sifts through the rows until she finds one in particular and slides it out. The eponymous first album by the band A Distant Tree. She remembers finding it not long after Steve Lorne started giving her music lessons. On the back of the album cover, the four band members each have their own photograph, and Steve looks very serious, very young. He's autographed it, as have the other three. Phoebe hasn't listened to their music in years, and she almost goes to play it. Something stops her, perhaps the thought of breaking the peace and quiet, perhaps the musty dampness of the room that puts her off lingering there. She slides the album back into its place and stands up again, letting out an audible 'oof' as she does so.

There is far more of her uncle in the place than she had been expecting so long after his death. Ten years have passed since his funeral, or is it more? For a moment Phoebe can't remember. The house isn't a shrine to him; Aunt Maude was never so sentimental. But neither was she one to change things around for no good reason. The house worked fine as it was, so she let it be.

The only changes are ones of necessity, like the handrails in the downstairs loo and in the bathroom opposite Maude's bedroom. There is WiFi that reaches most of the house, and Maude had an emergency alert bracelet in case she fell, although as far as Phoebe is aware she never did. Not like poor old Uncle Louis in his final years.

The door to his study stands open. Her study now, Phoebe supposes. She remembers that visit, what was it, fifteen years ago? More? When she realised he wasn't going to be writing any more, and the sadness that brought him only slightly cheered by his delight in the work she was doing. She'd been her uncle's first reader for a while by then, greedily devouring each new Muriel Baywater novel, then going back over it more slowly, methodically, with her editor's head on. At what point had she started rewriting them for him? Not just suggesting changes but making them too? Looking back, she can see how he had gently eased her into becoming his successor, becoming Muriel. And then he had started to fall, become clumsy, struggle with the keyboard. He'd stopped sending her novels and instead sent outlines, then a few ideas, and finally left her to get on with it on her own. A slow, thoughtful handing over of the baton.

Phoebe pours herself coffee from the pot keeping warm on the stove, settles into a chair and stares out of the window at nothing in particular. She's not really thought about her uncle in a while, not properly. Oh, there's not a day goes by she doesn't remember something about him, same as Aunt Maude. That mischievous twinkle in his eye, perhaps, or the feel of his hand on her shoulder. But she's not thought about what it must have been like for him, taking on the responsibility of raising her after her mother had died. His little sister had died. Of seeing Siân's face in hers every day. How that must have pained him. And still he had been kind, generous, warm. He had steered her to a career in literature, but only because he'd seen how much she loved words.

Phoebe smiles at the thought. Her love of words came from him, after all. Those early days at Pant Melyn, when she railed against the lack of television and found solace in books he had written. He'd been a good replacement parent, in the end. And Maude had risen to the challenge too. This house had seen its share of arguments, of anger and resentment, but it had been a home too. Perhaps it could be again.

49

1985

'It's Thursday, isn't it?' Phoebe asked over breakfast. For once all three of them were eating at the same time, although judging by the way Uncle Louis had dressed, he was about to depart on one of his regular trips.

'I hope so,' he said. 'That's when the ticket's booked for.'

'It is indeed Thursday, Phoebe dear. Any particular reason for asking?' Aunt Maude pulled some slices of toast out of the oven, juggled them across to the table and waiting toast rack with asbestos fingers.

'Just lost track of the days. It's been so wet and miserable.'

'We had noticed your mood. Feeling better now?' Uncle Louis grabbed one of the slices of toast and stretched for the butter. Phoebe wondered what he meant by his question, the slightly knowing look on his face as he asked it. The reasons for her sullen mood were twofold. The endless rain that had finally stopped that morning, keeping her locked up indoors with only old books and her thoughts, and the report into her parents' deaths that had been the source of most of those thoughts. But Uncle Louis didn't know that she had seen it, or at least she assumed he didn't know. He'd certainly not mentioned it in the days since. So he must have been referring to something else. She blushed as realisation dawned. Well, it worked for her if he thought it was that time of the month. Men didn't seem to be particularly comfortable around the subject, which made it a useful weapon. A handy excuse.

'Much better, thanks.' She squirmed in her seat a little for emphasis. 'Thought I'd go for a wander in the woods today. Since it's finally stopped raining.' She was about to mention her plan to try and find Gwyneth, but stopped at the last moment. Aunt Maude had started looking at her in an odd way every time she mentioned her new friend. Outside, the sun had already cleared the distant ridge line that marked the point where the valley gave way to the moors beyond. The blue sky and occasional fluffy cloud promised a hot day.

'Fine, dear. I have to take your uncle to the train in Carmarthen anyway, so I'll be gone until late afternoon, maybe early evening. You can make yourself a sandwich and take it with you if you want. And if you're up near the bees you could maybe check they're OK?'

'Carmarthen? I thought the station was in Aberystwyth?' Phoebe almost asked if she could come too, but then she remembered how slowly her aunt drove, how narrow and twisty were the Welsh roads. And she really did want to get out and wander the woods. Being cooped up indoors for a few days had made her realise how much she missed the freedom to simply roam wherever her feet took her. And hopefully she wouldn't be alone.

'Only going as far as Cardiff. Then a flight from Barry. There's a literary festival in Paris this weekend and I'm the guest of honour.' Uncle Louis looked insufferably smug as he wiped toast crumbs from his face.

'You'll be the absent guest of honour if you don't get a move on.' Aunt Maude slipped off her apron and hung it on the pantry door, then shooed Uncle Louis to his feet as she headed for the hall.

★ ★ ★

Phoebe sat at the table, listening until the noise of Aunt Maude's car as it struggled up the track to the road had faded away to nothing. She glanced briefly at the study door, but in truth there was nothing behind it that interested her much. It would do her no end of good to get outside, fill her lungs with fresh air and stretch her legs a bit.

Not quite sure who she was any more, she tidied up the kitchen, made herself a couple of sandwiches for lunch and filled the battered old canteen with water. Without a backward glance, she stepped out of the house and strode through the garden to the woods beyond. It had been an anxious week, cooped up inside while enough rain had fallen to drown an army. She had been haunted by the words of the report into Mum and Dad's deaths, but as she passed from the warm sunshine and into the cool air under the trees, Phoebe began to feel the tension ease from her neck and shoulders. It was as if the forest welcomed her with an embrace that smelled of tree sap, damp underbrush and rich loam. The place was full of life, all the creatures, great and small, that had been hunkered down for the duration of the storm now come out to forage and frolic. Insects buzzed; butterflies sunned themselves on leaves glistening with water droplets; birds zipped about under the canopy and chittered higher up in the treetops. It lifted her mood so much she almost laughed out loud.

The roar of the river came to her much more quickly than Phoebe had been expecting. When she reached the old ruined stone bridge she understood why. Swollen by the rains, it ran in full spate, crashing through the narrow gullies and exploding over the waterfall. The pool where her aunt had swum that first day was now twice its normal size, the beach gone and a couple of the stone steps with it. Upstream, the water fizzed and frothed, aerated by the cascade, but it soon smoothed and darkened into deceptive calmness before tumbling over the rocks at the far end. It was just as well she wasn't there to swim.

Phoebe followed the path to the wooden bridge, hoping to see that familiar figure waiting for her. There was no sign of Gwyneth, so she walked to the middle and stared downstream. She might have sat down, were the rushing waters underneath not so high that the spray had made the walkway sodden. The noise was deafening too. What might the falls further upstream be like? Too dangerous to approach, that was for sure.

She waited for what felt like half an hour, but was probably only ten minutes. Even so, Phoebe knew that her friend wasn't going to come today. She had plenty of time to kill though, so maybe she would try and retrace her steps to the glade with the oak tree where they had first met.

But first she had a task that needed attending to, up on the edge of the moor. Aunt Maude might have made her request sound like a suggestion, but Phoebe knew well enough what the old lady expected of her. She climbed the steep path through the trees, then followed the track as it zigzagged through the heather until finally she arrived in the little hollow where the beehives stood.

She wasn't quite sure what to do, once she actually arrived. She had none of the kit needed to inspect the bees, and wouldn't have known what to look for even if she had brought the heavy protective overalls and netted hat with her. It was enough to sit nearby, listening to the drone, the buzz as the workers left in search of nectar or returned from their forays heavily laden and bright with pollen.

All the hives were busy, the bees unconcerned by her presence as they went about their patient industry. Warmed by the sun and lulled by the gentle hum, Phoebe must have dozed for a while. She woke with a start, the memory of some loud noise, or perhaps a scream, still lingering. Red kites wheeled overhead, their occasional mewling cries cutting through the busy hum, so maybe it had been one of them. Phoebe glanced at her wrist before remembering that she had left her watch in her tiny bathroom when she'd had a shower that morning. Judging by the sun high overhead it must have been near enough midday.

She struggled to her feet, brushing bits of heather and insects from her clothes. The bees paid her no attention as she walked slowly around the hives. All of them still busy, the entrances a bustle of activity that must surely be a sign of good health. She would report as much back to Aunt Maude, even if that meant tomorrow would probably involve lugging all the heavy equipment up here from the house. There was a track that a Land Rover or tractor could easily negotiate, which was presumably how they had brought the hives up in the first place. Too much to expect her aunt and uncle to own a four-by-four to make life easier for them. Aunt Maude was most definitely the kind of person who believed honey was sweeter the harder you worked for it.

As she set off away from the hives, Phoebe took the opportunity of being above the treeline to try and spot the great oak under whose shade she had first met Gwyneth. The mass of green canopy marching down the hill made it hard to be sure. There were several grand trees that stood head and shoulders above the rest, like responsible adults on a school outing. She wished she had brought a pair of binoculars with her, but it was too late now to go back and fetch them. Instead, she tried to make sense of the undulations, clearings and thinning trees. The long scar of the river was easy enough to see, and she thought she could place the ruins of Plas Llancwm. Pant Melyn and Tynhelyg would be over the far side of the valley, lost to the midday heat haze, but another clearing beyond the old mansion site would be Nant Caws Farm.

And then she had it, she was sure. A great mound of leaves just a shade lighter than the pines that surrounded it. Phoebe did her best to set the direction in her mind, picturing it in relation to places she had some idea of how to get to, and then once more descended into the welcome cool shade of the forest.

It took far longer to reach than she had thought, the paths conspiring to turn her back on herself several times before she was sure she must be in the right place. How big was this forest? It must be vast, a miracle she hadn't become hopelessly lost many times before. And yet as she walked between the trees, pausing occasionally to touch an ancient trunk or listen to the constant hum and bustle, Phoebe never felt afraid. Not like the time when she was very small and her parents had taken her to the Highland Show outside Edinburgh. So many people, towering over her like these trees, but also moving, jostling. She had gripped her mother's hand tight as they went to see the cattle being judged, but something had happened to make her let go. Years later, she could still taste that panic, that utter terror of being alone in a sea of bodies, for all that it had been only moments before her mum had found her, scooped her up and carried her to safety.

Here, though the trees reached so high into the sky and crowded so close together, she felt only peace. And as she emerged from the gloom into the oak clearing, that feeling only deepened.

It was as if she had stepped into another world. The noise of the wind dropped away almost to nothing, a gentle rustling of the oak leaves the faintest of white noise in the background. Here the birds chirruped and tweeted, flitting from branch to branch with little brrp brrps of their wings. Butterflies and bees filled the clearing, waist-high grass and meadow flowers a veritable feast for the insects. Phoebe followed the narrow path someone else had worn in a gentle curve to the base of the great tree, felt the temperature drop several degrees as she moved into the shadow of its vast canopy.

Nothing much had changed since her last visit, her first visit. The grass was longer, the leaves of the great oak a little darker. The mound where she had first spied Gwyneth was all but invisible under a riot of wildflowers, red poppies, white dog rose, yellow ladies bed straw, tiny forget-me-nots and others she would need a book to name. No sign of the young girl though.

302

Phoebe slipped her pack off her shoulders, and sat down with her back to the old trunk. Despite her snooze up at the bees, she was tired. Hungry too. As she was eating her sandwiches and wishing she had something a little more thirst-quenching than tepid water, she noticed an odd shape out of the corner of her eye. Turning, she could see now the last few rotting remains of the bunch of flowers she had seen before. No doubt whoever they had been left for had never come to collect them. An assignation missed, an affair that never got off the ground? Or had she been reading too much Muriel Baywater?

By the time she had finished her lunch, Phoebe was certain that she wasn't going to see Gwyneth that day. She was so infuriating sometimes, and yet Phoebe felt more sad than annoyed. She enjoyed Gwyneth's company, and not just because she was the only person within a five-mile radius anywhere near her own age. Shouldering her pack again, she heaved herself up, one last glance at the long-dead, discarded flowers, and set off for Pant Melyn.

It was as she was stepping back into the shade of the pine trees that she heard the footsteps. For a moment, Phoebe thought it might be Gwyneth come to see her after all. But then she realised the tread was all wrong. Too heavy, the time between each footfall too long. Someone large and tall was coming, and Gwyneth was neither of those things.

Despite her earlier sense of peace and calm, Phoebe found that she didn't want to be seen here, didn't want to interact with anyone. She stepped off the path, hiding in the shadows where she was sure she would not be seen, and waited for whoever it was to pass. But when she saw who it was, she could only stop and stare.

Phoebe hadn't seen Tegwin Ellis since the funeral. He'd looked a state then, pale, shrunken in on himself as if his entire world had just collapsed. In a way it had, she supposed. If anything, now he looked worse. There was nothing left of the great bear of a man who had accosted her at the edge of Nant Caws farmyard only a few short weeks earlier. He was still tall and broad for a Welshman, but he carried himself like a scared little boy. He walked like a man condemned, too. Slow strides as if his boots were filled with lead. That was how she had heard him coming. Head down, he didn't see her lurking in the shade, carried on up the path and into the clearing. And that was when Phoebe saw that he had something in his hand. Something that made her almost choke in surprise.

He was carrying a bunch of flowers.

Unsure why she did it, she picked a slow, careful route through the undergrowth so that she could watch him unseen. Tegwin followed that same well-worn path through the meadow grass up to the old oak tree, barely looking at it as he ducked under the canopy. Phoebe couldn't tell what he was doing until she edged around a little further. The spot where the old branch had died let enough light in that she could see the farmer kneel at the trunk. He picked up the old flowers, long dead and decaying. Shoved them in the front pocket of his overalls. Then he carefully placed the fresh bunch in their place.

At first, Phoebe thought the sound she could hear was just another of the forest noises, but a gentle shift in the breeze brought it more clearly to her. Tegwin spoke in a low, soft voice, his Welsh rising and falling like the wind through the trees. He was too far away for her to catch the words, and she wouldn't have understood much of it even if she had been closer, but she was fairly sure that she heard the name Gwen a couple of times.

When the old farmer finally stopped his muttering and stood up, Phoebe had to shrink back into the shadows. For a moment she was convinced he had seen her, so intense was his stare in her direction. But his gaze was unfocused, as if what he looked at was somewhere in the past. He took a couple of strides forwards, one hand reaching for the trailing rope that dangled from the branch, its end frayed to thin threads. Then he stood at the mound where

Phoebe had first seen Gwyneth, crossed his hands over his waist and dropped his head as if in prayer.

Phoebe backed away slowly into the dark of the forest, her head full of questions for which there could be no logical answers. When she was sure she was far enough away not to be heard, she hurried back to the path and along it in the direction of Pant Melyn. What had just happened? What was it she had witnessed?

It was only as she was descending the zigzag path towards the river and the old derelict bridge that she remembered the last time she had seen Tegwin with a bunch of flowers. He had given them to her, hastily picked from the field edge at Nant Caws Farm. But he had thought her Gwen, intended them for his little sister. So why was he taking similar flowers and leaving them in that clearing?

The spark of an idea began to form in Phoebe's mind, the dots joining up in a manner that should have been obvious from the beginning. She almost had it as she stepped onto the riverside path, when a piercing scream of terror ripped through the rushing noise of the water.

50

Phoebe almost jumped out of her skin. The scream had been so terrifying, so terrified. It was clearly human, not the cry of a kite high overhead. Not even an eagle could have made that noise.

The path had brought her to the point where the old collapsed stone bridge would once have crossed the river. It was possible to make out the remains of the original path, slowly losing the battle with the brambles and bracken. Someone appeared to have hacked a path to the edge, and while Phoebe couldn't understand why anyone could have been so daft, especially with the river running so fast and high, she still made her careful way through to try and see what was happening. Once she reached the start of the stone bridge, it all made sense.

The twins stood, one on either side of the gap where the stone arch had collapsed into the raging torrent below. Phoebe still couldn't have said which was Axe and which was Brue, although she had found out that they were both named after rivers in Somerset, but not why. Whichever one was on the other side must have been the one who had screamed, presumably as he jumped across on some stupid dare. Now he was beckoning his brother to join him, goading him on with taunts of cowardice and sweeps of his arm. Phoebe was about to shrink back, hopeful she'd not been seen, but the far twin stopped his waving, stood up straight, shouted over the roar of the river below.

'Well, look who's come to see us. If it isn't the little snail.'

The second twin, still on her side of the river, turned to see what his brother was on about. Phoebe watched it play out almost in slow motion as he put one foot down too close to the moss-covered edge. She saw the way his boot slipped out from under him, the sudden widening of his eyes as he both saw her and real-ised what had happened at the same time. Then he let out a curiously high-pitched squeal of surprise, and he was falling.

Without a thought, Phoebe rushed forward, one hand out-stretched as if to save him. A little part of her mind that understood physics knew that if he did manage to get a hold of her he would take them both over the edge, but she was too far away. His brother, looked like he was going to try and leap back across, but some small nugget of sense stopped him, teetering on his own edge.

Still rushing to get to him, Phoebe watched as the hapless twin slithered and scraped over the edge. He grabbed at the rocks to try and stop his fall, but the moss simply came away in his hands. By the time she reached the edge he had almost managed, hanging on by the most tenuous of grips. She flung herself to the ground, reaching out as far as she could.

'Take my hand!' It shouldn't have needed saying, but the young man was almost senseless with fear, operating on reflex only. Beneath him, the river surged and boiled, a treacherous flow that would surely suck him down and break him on the rocks. The noise was deafening, an echo of that roar as the flames devoured Phoebe's house, destroyed her life.

'Grab my hand, you idiot!' She stretched further, and now the twin looked up at her, surprise adding to his fear. She could see he was the one with the stye, although that still didn't help with whether this was Axe or Brue. A quick look up showed his brother still standing on the other side, paralysed.

'Get round here and help,' she shouted, her voice hardly audible over the water. He raised both hands in the universal gesture of being a useless waste of space.

'It's too dangerous. Can't jump.'

'The wooden bridge.' Phoebe pointed downstream with one hand, the other still reaching down. 'Run!'

For a moment she thought he wasn't going to. He stood and stared at his brother, dangling above the ferocious waters, and Phoebe could almost see the sluggish thoughts working their way through the drug-addled morass of his mind. Then, as if someone had shoved a cattle prod up his arse, he sprung into action.

'Don't let him fall!' he shouted, then lumbered off through the undergrowth towards the path. How long would it take him to cover the distance? Phoebe hoped it wasn't long.

'You Axe or Brue?' She turned her attention back to the remaining twin, still clinging with all his strength to the narrowest of handholds. He didn't answer, probably wasn't capable of anything more complicated than holding on.

'Come on. Take my hand.' Phoebe felt the damp from the moss and weed seeping into her top as she lay as flat to the ground as possible. Hand outstretched, open wide, it would have been simple for the twin to grab. True, she wouldn't have the strength to pull him up, but she could hold him until his brother arrived. She was fairly sure of that. As long as he hurried up.

'I . . . I . . .' The young man looked slowly around, head twisted so he could see the rushing water below. It wasn't a long drop, but far enough. And it was clear that the current would overpower even the strongest of swimmers, snap arms and break open heads, or simply pin them to the bottom until they drowned.

'Look at me. Axe, Brue, whatever your name is. Look at me!' Phoebe shouted, and something in her voice must have cut through, as the twin snapped his head back around to look at her. Unfortunately for him, the movement loosened his grip, fingers of one hand slipping off the crack of rock to which they had been clinging. Phoebe lunged down to catch the hand as it flailed past her fingers. They touched for a moment, madly scrabbling for a grip. And then with a horribly silent wail of despair, the other hand gave up and he was falling.

She half expected to hear the impact as the twin hit the water, certainly thought there would be a splash. But it was as if the river simply swallowed him whole in an instant. One moment he was there, falling. The next he was gone.

Phoebe stared, followed the flow downstream where the water roiled and churned around rocks and through the deep, narrow channel, breath held as she waited for the twin's body to surface. It was probably only seconds, but felt like long minutes before his head briefly appeared, one arm bursting from the surface with it as if he was waving. Then the current took him under again, and he was gone.

She scrambled to her feet, pushed through the brambles back to the path with scant regard for the pain as thorns dug into her legs and hands. There was no sign of the other twin as she ran flat out down towards the wooden bridge, and by the time she got there he was only just arriving at the other bank. He stopped when he saw her, one hand clutched to his side and bent double as if he was about to puke. What was it, a hundred yards? Two? Certainly not any more than that.

'Wha—?' he tried to ask as she hurried over the bridge.

'He went in. Couldn't reach him.' Phoebe didn't wait to see if she was being followed, but ran back upstream, headed for the small waterfall and the pool where she had swum before. With luck, the current would bring the unfortunate twin over the falls and she'd be able to fetch him out as the waters slowed. Whether he was still alive by then was another matter, and of course it was always possible he was wedged against a rock somewhere, drowned.

Waves lapped at the bottom of the steps, cream-coloured foam spiralling around in eddies at the edges, while the main flow moved swiftly down the middle. The falls under which aunt had washed her hair would drown a person now, even if they were able to stand up to the deluge. All around was the raw power of nature, the pent-up force of days of rain spilling down this narrow cleft that formed the centre of the valley. Phoebe paused at the lowest step, scanning for any sign of the missing twin. She couldn't tell how deep the water was, but there was no sign of the beach. How far could she wade into that current before getting swept off her feet and carried away to the unforgiving rocks downstream?

No sign of any bodies, she paused for long enough to pull off her boots and socks before stepping carefully into the water. When she felt the gritty sand under her feet, the level came to the top of her calves, a gentle tug of force not yet threatening to topple her. How far out had it been before the shallows had given way to deeper water? She couldn't remember, and anyway the river was twice as wide now as it had been back then.

'Where is he? Where's Brue?' A voice behind her as the other twin finally caught up. He stayed a couple of steps above the surface, eyes locked on Phoebe, expression hard to read but not friendly. He was Axe, then, at least she had that much sorted.

'I don't know. He can't have—' Phoebe started, and then something slipped over the waterfall and crashed into the pool. It disappeared under the foam and spume before she could work out what it had been, but played back in her memory she was almost certain it had been a human body. Limp like a puppet thrown down the stairs.

'Brue!' The other twin screamed his brother's name, but didn't move from his dry step well above the waterline. Phoebe figured it was best to ignore him, and turned her attention to the swift running current in the middle. The river was so high it surged like a standing wave over the rocks that normally formed the downstream end of the pool, so if the body did resurface, she'd not have much chance to catch it before it was swept away beyond her ability to do anything.

It. Why was she thinking of the body as it? As if Brue were already dead.

'Brue!' his brother screamed again, but judging by the volume and direction, he still hadn't moved. Phoebe was about to shout at him to get his feet down here and help, when something large and body-shaped bobbed to the surface a few yards from the fizz around the waterfall. She recognised the camouflage jacket, but Brue's head was under water, face down, as the current bore him swiftly towards the surge.

Without much thought for her own safety, Phoebe waded out towards a point where she might possibly be able to intercept him before he was carried away. It was difficult going, the water up to her thighs, the bottom of the river soft and threatening to trip her. She could feel the tug of the current grow stronger too, and a shiver of fear ran through her as she realised how monumentally stupid this all was. Brue's body was close now, coming at her fast. She dug her toes into the soft sand, reached out and grabbed at the soggy material of his jacket.

For a moment she thought she had made a grave mistake. He might have been floating, just about, but Brue Thomas was still heavy. His momentum almost pulled her off her feet. She dug in with her heels, leaned back and pivoted, letting his bulk swing slowly round and out of the fast current. Only once she was sure he was not going to get dragged away again did she slowly back up, pulling him with her towards the bank.

'A little help here,' she shouted at the useless brother. When she looked around, he was still standing on the same step, his mouth hanging open like the half wit he so clearly was.

'Jesus, could you be more useless.' She hauled Brue's limp body as far into the shallows as she could before his dangling arms and legs fouled on the bottom, then rolled him over to bring his head clear of the water. He wasn't breathing, which was hardly a surprise, but more worrying was the gash to one side of his head, washed clean by the churning waters and not bleeding much at all. For a moment she froze in panic. This was far more than she had ever covered in First Aid at Guide Camp. How long had he been in the water? How long could he survive without breathing? What if his heart had stopped? This was so much worse than old Meredith Ellis. He'd not needed anything more than loosening his tie and making sure he was comfortable. But she'd done that. She could do this. And if it was all for nothing, well, at least she'd tried.

With the last of her fading strength, Phoebe hauled Brue's limp body until it was half in the water, half on the bank. She felt for a pulse, sure at first that the clammy, cold body was dead. Then she had it, weak, but there. Doubtless the twin's lungs were full of water. How was it you were supposed to clear them?

Movement beside her, and she was about to say to Axe to help her get his brother completely out of the water, up to somewhere flat where they could turn him over. But at the same time as she felt a hand on her shoulder, another hand reached past her to gently prise open one of the twin's eyes. A hand older and thinner than the great hams both twins had, fingers long and delicate. She turned then to see Steve Lorne crouched beside her. A quick glance up showed Axe still stuck on his step, mouth open to any flies that might come past.

'Is he . . .?' Lorne asked, his raspy, quiet voice barely audible above the noise of the falls, despite him being right at Phoebe's side.

'Pulse. Weak but there. Not breathing.' Phoebe realised as she said it just how exhausted and out of breath she was too. She'd not noticed the cold, but now it seeped through her, making her sluggish.

'Get him on his side.' Lorne didn't wait for her to help, just grabbed Brue's shoulder and heaved him around with surprising strength for his slim frame. As he did so, a great gout of water spewed from the twin's mouth. Lorne worked Brue's arm as if it were the handle of an old well pump, and surprisingly enough yet more water began to spew out of the young man's mouth and nose. After what seemed enough to fill the pool twice over, the young man convulsed, spewing and choking reflexively, sucking in ragged breaths between each body-spasming cough. He let out a low, painful groan, opened one eye that stared, brief and unseeing, at Phoebe and Lorne before the pupil fluttered upwards and he fell into unconsciousness.

'He needs an ambulance.' Lorne checked the twin's neck for a pulse, then leaned in close to see if he was breathing. Phoebe pushed herself to unsteady feet, still in the water up to her knees. If she didn't get out soon she was going to collapse, but she summoned the energy to shout at the useless waste of space still standing two steps up.

'You. Axe. Go to the village and call an ambulance. We need to get him to hospital.'

Axe stood motionless, save for the wringing of his hands. 'Is he . . .? Is he . . .?'

Phoebe decided she'd had quite enough. 'Run!' she bellowed with all of her might. And to her considerable surprise, he did.

51

2023

The burbling rumble of ancient engine is still echoing in her ears as Phoebe steps into the hotel. For a moment she is twelve again, following along behind Aunt Maude as her uncle heads straight to the bar for a free drink. In front of her, the reception table has been set out almost exactly the same as for Meredith Ellis's funeral, with a book of remembrance flanked by a couple of photographs and some lilies in a vase. There's no photograph of a family proudly posing beside their prize ram at the Aberystwyth show, although if that picture still exists, Phoebe supposes it belongs to her now.

Through in the main lounge, all the tables have been pushed to the walls and laden with food. The room is full of people chattering away to each other, a few small children clinging to a parent's leg or wandering around as if they own the place. Phoebe watches from the door for a while, more people than she has interacted with in a very long time. A village come together to remember and celebrate the life of one of its own. This is what belonging feels like, she understands then. It's something she had forgotten.

'It's very heartwarming to see so many people turn out to something like this.'

Phoebe turns at the voice, takes a moment to recognise the woman coming out of the bar on the other side of the reception area. She's holding two cups of tea, and proffers one. Angharad Fairweather, the family liaison officer, looks very different in tidy dress and jacket. She's gone for a dark shade, but late-autumn forest green rather than black or grey. It matches her eyes.

'Almost didn't recognise you out of uniform. That's a lovely colour.' Phoebe takes the cup from her, grateful she doesn't have to fight through the scrum to get one of her own. She hadn't realised how thirsty she was until she takes a sip.

'Thank you. Don't often get a chance to put my glad rags on, but it was worth the effort, I think. A good turnout, and that was a nice service too. You did well, with the eulogy.'

'Never did like public speaking, but it was one of the things drummed into us at school.'

'Didn't go to Penglais, then.' The family liaison officer means it as a joke, but the look on her face as she makes it shows the thought processes running to catch up. 'Oh, I'm sorry. Of course you didn't. I heard the story, about what brought you to Llancwm.'

'It's OK. All happened a long time ago. And I might have gone to school in Aber. It was an option. In the end they sent me to a posh boarding school outside Llandrindod Wells.'

'Where they taught you public speaking. That must have been nice.'

'It was fine, I guess. I got a decent education, made a few friends there.' None of whom she's spoken to in twenty years. 'Never was all that good at keeping in touch with them though. Not like Maude. She was always on the phone, checking in on people and making sure they were all right.'

'It's OK to miss her, you know.'

Phoebe is surprised by the woman's tone, so like her aunt's. She's more surprised by the light touch to her arm, a simple connection she had not been expecting. Almost as swiftly as it's done, the family liaison officer takes her hand away, and Phoebe is surprised to find that bothers her too.

'You met her, my aunt?' she says, unsure how to keep the conversation going, aware that she should be greeting the collected mourners. 'You must have, otherwise how would you know what brought me here all those years ago.'

'Once or twice, yes. I live a little way down the valley, not quite as remote as Llancwm, see? But this is my beat, if you like. A few times I've been called in to help out a family who've been recently bereaved, only to find your aunt had got there before me.'

'That sounds like her. Always trying to help everyone else, never too bothered about herself.' Phoebe glances around at the people in the main lounge. Is that a line forming? Do they all want to speak to her? 'She'd probably be horrified at the thought of all these people making a fuss over her.'

'Horrified, maybe, but quietly pleased too. I've seen enough miserable funerals in my time to know that this is a celebration of someone much loved.'

'Thank you. And thank you for coming, too. I'm sure it's more than your job requires.'

'It is, really. But like I said, I met your aunt a couple of times. She was a character, and there's few enough of them left these days. She told me some stories you wouldn't believe.'

'Oh, I probably would. Still, I'd love to hear them some time.' Phoebe glances around again. That's definitely a line. 'Perhaps we could meet for coffee in Aber some time. You can tell me all about it.'

'Well, you've got my number. Give me a call.' PC Fairweather holds her hand up to the side of her head in the universal gesture. 'Now I'd better stop hogging you and let all these other good folk have a word.'

52

1985

Phoebe didn't think she had ever been so tired. Her whole body ached, and she was shivering with cold. It didn't help that she was also soaked through to the skin. Even her backpack dripped horribly as she dumped it on the step and reached for the door.

It had taken over an hour for a paramedic to arrive. An hour in which she and Steve Lorne had sat with Brue Thomas as the young man clung to life with surprising tenacity. Not a young man, really, but a boy, Phoebe had come to see during that time. She wasn't sure how old the twins were, but unconscious, helpless and injured, Brue looked more sixteen than eighteen. By his behaviour she wouldn't have put him any older than that.

Steve Lorne had said very little as they sat vigil with the injured boy. Talking obviously pained him, and Phoebe suspected that simply looking at her brought mixed memories of Gwen, the good times and the bad. There had been too much going on since she'd first heard the twins screaming at each other for her to gather the thoughts she'd had up at the clearing, but as she sat with him for that long hour, the ideas had begun to coalesce in her mind. Every time she thought she had it though, something stopped her from speaking.

It was only once the ambulance crew had arrived, hefting a stretcher up the path from the nearest point they had managed to reach in their vehicle, that she had finally tried to stand up and realised quite how close to collapse she was. Lorne must have noticed it too, as he had steadied her, helped her up the steps to the path and finally insisted on accompanying her back to Pant Melyn.

Which was why, when the door opened before she could reach the handle, Aunt Maude's half-angry, half-worried tirade had come to an abrupt end.

'Phoebe, where on earth have you . . . oh.'

'Hello, Maude. It's been a while.' Lorne stepped forward, his trousers clinging to his thin calves where they had soaked at the bottom as he stood in the river. Phoebe watched as Aunt Maude looked him slowly up and down, then switched her attention over, first to the backpack oozing a small puddle onto the flagstones, and finally to her.

'Been swimming again?' She raised an eyebrow, preparing some other arch comment before realisation dawned and she changed tack. 'What happened? No. Come in, both of you. Then you can tell me what happened.'

Phoebe was surprised not to be asked to strip off in the laundry room, and expected Aunt Maude to insist that Lorne at least take his boots off, but after seeing both of them close up, she hurried them through to the kitchen and bade them both sit. She noticed Lorne glance briefly at the closed door to Uncle Louis's study, then direct a questioning expression at her aunt.

'He's away in France until next week. Sit down before you fall down.' Aunt Maude hauled the filled kettle onto the hotplate and busied herself with teapot, milk jug and biscuit jar. When Lorne did as he was told, sinking into one of the chairs and cupping his face in his hands, Phoebe understood that telling the sorry tale was going to fall to her now.

'It's Brue Thomas. He fell in the river. I managed to drag him out, but . . .' Phoebe shivered a great shaking from head right down to her damp toes. 'I don't know if he'll survive.'

'What . . .? How did he even . . .?' Aunt Maude asked, for once lost for words.

'They were doing that stupid dare thing, you know? Trying to jump across where the old bridge has collapsed? Only with all the rain, the river's in spate and everything.' Phoebe found she couldn't say any more. Lorne took that as his cue, carefully pushed back his seat and made to stand up.

'I should go now. I just wanted to make sure she was safely home. She's had a terrible shock, but I don't think I've ever seen someone so selflessly brave.'

'Nonsense, Steven. You must stay here. Warm yourself up and get dry. I'll drive you back to Tynhelyg after.' Aunt Maude's voice brooked no argument, and Lorne, half standing, settled himself back into his chair.

Time passed slowly, Phoebe barely registering anything until it had happened. Somehow she had tea, milky and sweet as promised. Her coat was gone, a warm, soft towel wrapped around her neck and shoulders. She was vaguely aware that Steve Lorne had stayed, still sat at the table staring into the middle distance as if he too was lost in his own world.

'I hope he makes it, even if him and his brother are the bane of my life sometimes.'

It took Phoebe a moment to process the words, understand that it was Lorne who had spoken them and turn to face him. He had a mug held between two hands, steam rising gently from the surface of his tea. Hunched over, his face looked haggard, hair even more unkempt than usual. But as he turned to face her, his eyes were bright and shiny with tears. He also had a towel around his shoulders, and he had taken off his coat and scarf. This close, Phoebe could see a mark around his neck like an old scar or weal.

319

She saw him notice the direction of her gaze, go to cover himself up, then slump as the effort proved too much.

'Does it . . . does it hurt, Mr Lorne?' she asked.

'I think you can call me Steve, wouldn't you say, Phoebe? After all that we've been through?' Lorne reached a slender hand up to his neck, long fingers playing around the scar but never quite touching it. He started to pull the towel around his shoulders to conceal the mark, then stopped, looked straight at her.

'This is the mark the rope left. The same rope that did so much damage to my voice box I struggle to speak. Won't ever sing again.' A wistful expression clouded his features, his eyes losing their focus for a moment, seeing something that happened long ago. Then he came back to himself with a snap. 'The rope I tried to hang myself with when I finally knew that my dear Gwen was never coming back to me.'

Phoebe saw him then, but she also saw something else in the front of her mind as if she were there at the same time. As if it were still afternoon and Brue Thomas had never fallen into the river. The great oak tree in its peaceful glade, the low mound in the grass where she had first met Gwyneth, the frayed rope hanging from the branch she had taken for a long-abandoned swing. The pieces of the puzzle slotted into place so neatly she was surprised she'd not seen the picture before.

'She died like her mother, didn't she. Giving birth to your child. But why was she at Nant Caws . . .? Oh.'

Something like sadness clouded Steve Lorne's face, but it was mixed with a heavy relief. As if this was a secret he had kept bottled up all these years, but now he could release it.

'She went to see her father one last time before the baby was due. Always trying to build bridges was Gwen. She wanted the stubborn old bastard to know his grandson would be born in Wales, would be as Welsh as any of them. That much I know. The rest, I can only guess, but I'm fairly sure it's true.' Lorne paused, took another sip of tea, swallowed with a little wince of pain. Phoebe spoke before he could go on.

'She went into labour though, didn't she. Up at the farm. And instead of calling an ambulance, they tried to have the baby at the farmhouse. And then it all went wrong like it did when she was born, like it must have done with Tegwin too. I suppose the poor baby didn't survive either.' Phoebe shuddered suddenly, not from the cold that still reached into her bones, but the memory of Meredith's words when Tegwin had shot the ram: how important it was to him to keep the bloodline of his precious pedigree sheep pure. What would they have done with the baby if it had lived?

'Even then, the old man would rather cover it up than admit what had happened. Tegwin, well he'd always done what his father told him to.' Lorne's voice had become little more than a hoarse whisper. 'That old oak tree was her favourite place. Fitting, I suppose, that they chose to bury her there. For them it was probably more that it was remote. Then Meredith got his cousin to start spreading rumours about me to throw everyone off the scent. Wasn't hard, the man always hated me.'

'Cousin?' Phoebe took a moment before her brain came up with the nugget of information from an earlier conversation. 'Sergeant Griffiths? The policeman?'

'Eifion Griffiths shares a lot of Meredith's prejudices, particularly about the English. And he had a crush on Gwen that was as creepy as it was inappropriate. He's a good bit older than her, and they were too closely related for anything to have ever come of it anyway, even if she hadn't loathed him. But still, he hated me. Hates me, I should say.'

Lorne took another sip of his tea, then a longer gulp. His Adam's apple bobbed, stretching the shiny scar on his neck, but this time he didn't wince.

'It drove me a little mad, as I'm sure you know. Bad enough Gwen was gone and I didn't know where. But the whispers, the accusations, the looks from half the people in the village. And with each day the panic only grew worse. I searched those woods from top to bottom, out in all weathers, stopped eating, barely slept. Months it was, although the whole thing just feels like a nightmare after I've woken now. When I finally worked out what had happened, where she was, I guess my mind just snapped.'

So many questions Phoebe wanted to ask then, but the first one to pop out surprised even her. 'How . . . how did you not die?'

Lorne fixed her with a stare that wasn't unfriendly so much as sad. 'How did I not die? Well, that would be your uncle's doing. He found me, you see? Cut me down, loosened the noose. Brought me back from somewhere I never wanted to leave.'

'Wh—?' Phoebe started to ask how her uncle had known, but the look on Lorne's face stopped her.

'I never forgave him for it, you know? For saving me. That's why I couldn't come back here. Couldn't bear to face him.' Lorne looked down at his hands, now resting on the table either side of his tea again. 'And of course I was mad with grief. Or just mad, if you believe the doctors.'

A movement in the corner of her eye caught Phoebe's attention, and she looked up to see Aunt Maude standing silently at the door through to the hall. Lorne didn't appear to have noticed, or if he had he didn't seem to care.

'It's like I've been asleep for all those years. The drugs they gave me at the asylum dulled the pain, and everything else with it. When I came back here, it was enough just to survive at first. I knew the locals didn't much like me, so I've kept to myself.' He looked up then, fixing Phoebe with a stare that might have been threatening had she not spent the past couple of hours in his company. Had they not stood vigil together until help arrived for Brue Thomas.

'And then you came to Llancwm, Phoebe. You are so like her. It's uncanny. It was unsettling at first, but it also woke me up. Seeing you. Here.'

'I'm so sorry, Steven. We have been terrible friends.' Aunt Maude stepped fully into the room, her face sombre as she pulled out a chair and sat down opposite Lorne. He almost flinched when she reached out and took one of his hands in both of hers, Phoebe noticed, but he stopped himself at the last moment. She could see how uncomfortable he was here, almost frightened. But then what else would he be, coming back to a place filled with such painful memories? She felt a little twinge of guilt at the way she had prodded that wound with her questions.

'I hurt you all. Louis particularly. Don't blame anyone but myself.' He gently withdrew his hand, then pulled the towel from his shoulders. 'I should go.'

'I'll drive you there,' Maude said, but Lorne waved her offer away.

'I'm fine. It's not far. And you should stay here with Phoebe. She needs to get herself warm and dry. Get her strength back. There'll be lots of questions to answer, I fear. Hopefully the boy will make a full recovery, but if not . . .' He shook his head, rubbed at his throat as if to ease the pain. He'd probably said more in the past half hour than in the previous ten years, so it was understandable. As he stood, so Phoebe pushed her own chair back, as quietly as her tired muscles would let her.

'Thank you, Mr—Steve.' That got her a smile. 'I hope he's all right, even if it was his own stupid fault.'

'Me too, Phoebe. Me too.' Lorne nodded his head at her aunt. 'Maude, please tell Louis I'm sorry.' And without another word, he turned and left.

53

Phoebe slept badly, despite her exhaustion. Her mind was too much of a whirl at everything that had happened, everything she had learned. Whenever she closed her eyes all she could see was Brue Thomas, pale as a ghost, lips blue, eyes closed as the ambulance men stretchered him away. It made a change from the wall of flame, she supposed, but she'd far rather the oblivion of deep sleep.

She had no idea what time it was when she heard the quiet sounds of Aunt Maude getting up. Phoebe knew her aunt tended to rise with the dawn, if not even earlier. The skylight over her bed showed the palest of skies, wispy high clouds painted in pink and orange pastels. She considered getting up herself, but the bed was warm and comfortable. She snuggled down for a few minutes more, and sunk finally into the deep oblivion that had eluded her all night.

'Thought you might need a bit of a lie-in,' Aunt Maude said as Phoebe went into the kitchen much closer to noon than she had thought. The smell of porridge permeated the air as a pot gently bubbled and burped on the stove.

'Aye, a bit, but.' Phoebe pulled out a chair, yawned and rubbed at her eyes.

'Your uncle phoned last night after you'd gone to bed. Just checking in, but I told him what happened. He's getting an earlier flight back, so I'll have to go to Carmarthen and meet him off the train this afternoon.' Aunt Maude glanced up at the clock. 'Which is to say soon.'

'Oh. He didn't have to do that, surely.'

'No, he didn't. But he wanted to.' Aunt Maude slopped some porridge into a waiting bowl and put it down on the table in front of Phoebe's place. 'I think you should come with me to the station.'

'Do I have to?' The words came out rather more childish and petulant than Phoebe had intended, but Aunt Maude didn't seem to notice.

'I won't force you, Phoebe. But I don't like the idea of you being on your own again. I'll most likely be gone until evening.'

'I'm fine, really.' She reached for the milk jug, knowing that there would be thick cream on the top, and spooned a load of it onto her porridge. 'I won't get myself into any trouble.'

'You had plans, then?' Aunt Maude glanced across the kitchen to Uncle Louis's study, the door still hanging slightly ajar.

'Actually . . .' Phoebe was about to say she was going to look for Gwyneth and let her friend know what had happened, but it struck her that her aunt might not be so keen on her wandering the forest again after the events of the previous day. 'I was hoping I might walk over to Tynhelyg and see how Mr Lorne's doing. He got just as soaked and cold as me, and he's no' so young any more.'

Aunt Maude's gaze narrowed, as if she could read Phoebe as easily as one of Muriel Baywater's romances. She probably could; there wasn't much got past her. Except who actually wrote them, of course.

'That's very noble of you, Phoebe. But do you think that's such a good idea?'

'You still think he's mad and dangerous? After what he said last night?'

'That's not what I . . .' Aunt Maude began to say, then stopped herself. Presumably because that was exactly what she. A little shake of the head, and then she went to the pantry, came back with a loaf of fresh baked bread, a slab of home-made butter wrapped in greaseproof paper, and a pot of honey. She put them all in a hessian bag with the logo of Muriel Baywater's publisher printed on it, and placed it at the end of the table.

'Take him that, as a peace offering.' She glanced up at the clock, clearly anxious to get on the road, despite the fact that she had hours to spare yet. 'And tell him I've spoken to Louis. It's time to let bygones be bygones.'

Phoebe still wasn't sure what it was that had gone between them, but she was determined to make the most of it. 'Does that mean I can have music lessons?'

Aunt Maude's smile was broad and bright, almost a laugh. 'Yes, Phoebe. I reckon you can have music lessons. Now eat your porridge. It'll be a long time until supper.'

Phoebe had set out from Pant Melyn, not long after her aunt had left, with the express intention of going straight to Steve Lorne's house further upriver. And yet as she followed the track first past the spot where last she had seen Brue Thomas, and then on down to the wooden bridge, she found herself drawn along a different path. In what felt like no time at all, she was climbing the far side of the valley, as if the forest was bending itself to her will. Far sooner than she would have thought possible, she was stepping from the gloom and into the glade of the ancient oak tree. Gwen's last resting place.

She followed the winding path through the wildflowers and waist-high grass until she reached the trunk. Lying in the gap between two roots, each as big as her torso, lay Tegwin's floral tribute to his long-dead sister. Were these the same flowers Phoebe had seen him bring the day before, or a new bunch, freshly picked from the field edges at Nant Caws Farm? They looked too vibrant to have been left out overnight, so maybe she had just missed the farmer.

If so, that was a relief, although it posed the question why had he brought fresh flowers so soon after the previous bunch? The ones he had replaced last time she'd seen him had been there for weeks, if not months. Phoebe had a suspicion that she knew, and it wasn't a happy thought. Tegwin would be struggling, now that his father was gone. Not with the farm: he knew how to deal with the sheep, how to mend broken fences and rebuild the drystone dykes, probably even managed to keep himself fed and occasionally do his own laundry. But he would struggle with the other tasks, the ones that involved dealing with people. How long would it be before someone came round asking why the bills hadn't been paid? How would he cope shopping for new clothes, or even food? He was fit and strong, still relatively young, but a few years would soon change that, and what would happen to him then? And so here he was, reaching out to his little sister for help. His little sister who lay buried a few yards away.

'Thought you'd work it out sooner or later.'

Phoebe turned slowly, unsurprised at the voice, but at the same time chilled. Or maybe not chilled, that wasn't the right word. But then again, how did you describe a mixture of fear and joy?

'You're her, aren't you,' she said to the girl standing in the long grass where the low mound sat. 'You're Gwen.'

'I'm Gwyneth, silly.' Gwyneth raised one hand, then pointed it to the ground beneath her feet. 'Gwen's down there.'

'How do you know that? She disappeared before either of us was born.'

Gwyneth shrugged, then walked through the long grass to where Phoebe stood. 'You had the right of it yesterday, Feebs. Poor Gwen. Went to see her dad up at Nant Caws. One last try at per-suading him to accept his grandchild would be half English. Only she wasn't expecting to go into labour there in the kitchen, was she? Told old Mered to call an ambulance, but he wouldn't have none of it. Never did like hospitals, that man. Stupid really, but he

327

always was a stubborn old bastard. Pretty much everything that could go wrong went wrong. Mother and child both died, upstairs in the single bed in her old bedroom.'

Phoebe stared, her mouth slightly open in surprise. She wanted to touch Gwyneth just to be sure she was real, but something stopped her. Instead, Gwyneth reached out and took her hand, her grip warm and dry. With her other hand she gently touched the bark of the old tree.

'It was Tegwin's idea to bury her here. Well, bury them both, I suppose. She had a daughter, you know. Be the same age as you. If she'd survived. Would most likely have called her Seren after her grandmother, but that wasn't to be. Tegwin knew how much Gwen loved this old tree. She used to climb right up into the top of it when she was our age, you know?'

She looked up into the canopy, and Phoebe followed her gaze. She'd never been much of a tree climber, had never really had the chance.

'But you're clever and you worked it all out for yourself, didn't you.' Gwyneth nudged Phoebe in the ribs with one elbow. Not hard, not painful, but enough to push her a little off balance.

'How do you know so much about me? About everything?' Phoebe studied the young girl's face again, more closely this time, trying to see through and into the thoughts behind it. Her hair was unkempt, a few bits of leaf tangled in it as if she had been climbing the oak tree herself. She wore a different dress from the one in the photograph of Gwen, but it was a similar style and just as old-fashioned. Glancing down, she saw that her feet were bare again, toenails rimed with dirt. Standing so close, holding hands, it occurred to Phoebe that Gwyneth didn't smell bad. In fact, she didn't smell at all. Not of dirt or the forest, and certainly not of soap or shampoo. It wasn't something she'd noticed before, but then why would she have done?

'Who are you, Gwyneth?' she asked. 'Who are you really?'

The young girl looked down at the ground, then raised her eyes almost coyly to meet Phoebe's gaze. For a moment, it seemed like she might be about to tell some big secret that made everything clear. But then her gaze lost its focus, her face turned sombre, and when she spoke her tone was very serious indeed.

'You need to go, Feebs. Before he gets here.'

'What?' Phoebe looked around the clearing but couldn't see anyone. 'Who?'

'Axe Thomas. He's on his way here and he's very angry. Thinks you pushed his brother into the river yesterday.'

'I . . . But that's mad. I *saved* his brother from the river.'

'I know that, but he's persuaded himself it's your fault, see? Best not let him catch you now.'

There was something odd about Gwyneth's words, and it took Phoebe a moment to work out what it was. How could she possibly know anyone was on their way here, let alone why? She opened her mouth to say as much, and at that same moment a very different voice shouted from the far side of the clearing.

'There you are. Gonna fucking kill you!'

Phoebe whirled around to see Axe Thomas emerging from the woods at a laboured run. His face was red, although whether that was from anger or exertion, she couldn't tell. Probably both. Either way, she didn't want to hang about and find out. She squeezed Gwyneth's hand and whispered 'you're right, we'd better run.'

But when she turned to face the young girl, nobody was there.

54

If it hadn't been for the twin's lumbering, slow gait, he might have caught her, such was Phoebe's surprise. She looked at her hand, still feeling the touch of Gwyneth's grip even though she was clearly not there. Half stupid with the shock of it, she even gazed up into the canopy of the old oak tree, wondering if Gwyneth had somehow scrambled up there without her noticing. Only Axe's incoherent bellow of rage brought her back to the present.

Phoebe couldn't go the way she wanted, towards the path and eventually home. The long grass would slow her down too much to get past the twin, even if she was fairly confident she could outrun him unhindered. She darted away from the tree trunk, flinched as the dangling, frayed rope end brushed at her face and hair, then struck out across the clearing past Gwen's grave and on towards the pine trees.

'You hurt my brother. Fucking kill you!' came from far too close behind for comfort as she pushed through the low hanging branches and into the gloom. Phoebe wasn't completely sure where she was going, but thought it was in the direction of the forest edge and the track that would lead up to the bees. Beyond them, she could loop down and round to Tynhelyg, hide out there. She still had the hessian bag over her shoulder, even if the butter would be getting rather soft now, the loaf a little battered.

Axe Thomas might have been slow and unfit, but he was strong. As Phoebe tried to slip through the trees without snapping branches or making noise, he crashed along like some rampaging animal. She sped up as best she could, heading for the slope where she could see the trees begin to thin again. But what had happened to Gwyneth? How had she slipped away so completely, and why had she left Phoebe all alone?

Distracted by her thoughts, she almost ran into the old fence that marked the edge of the woods and start of the moor. The rusted wire blended with the brown of the heather, the old wooden fence-posts barely distinguishable from long-fallen branches. Phoebe felt a sharp pain as she caught her arm on a barb, but it was short-lived. Soon she was over, hoping Axe would suffer a similar fate, or ideally worse.

Out in the open she was better able to get her bearings, although the thick heather made the going even slower than her flight through the pines. The hillside rose steeply to a long ridge, the bees off to the east, which meant somewhere close by there should be the wide track to the site. Phoebe struck a diagonal course up the hill away from the point where she had left the forest, cheered by the scream of half pain, half anger that came from further behind than she'd expected. Axe had found the fence, then.

When she reached the bees, Phoebe paused to catch her breath. The wind whistled around the ridge line higher up the hill, but this spot was well sheltered. She couldn't hear any noise of Axe Thomas approaching. Had he given up? Collapsed from a heart attack? Too much to hope, but at least from here she could outrun him to Tynhelyg.

The hives hummed with activity, although the bees paid her no heed. Would they feel differently if they knew she was carrying a jar of their honey in her bag? She hoped not.

Moving slowly and keeping an eye on the track, she edged around to the far side of the hives, putting them in between her and Axe should he arrive more quickly than expected. She hoped maybe to talk him down, rather than have to run for it all the way to Tynhelyg. And what if Steve Lorne wasn't there? She could carry on to Pant Melyn, but Aunt Maude and Uncle Louis wouldn't be home for hours yet.

As if reading her anxiety, the hum of the bees began to grow. They still ignored her, but more flew out of the hives, buzzing backwards and forwards across the little hollow. Overhead, the clouds had thickened yet more. They raced across the sky like startled sheep, blown by a wind she was sheltered from here, but which would be harsh once she left her sanctuary. Of all the things that might happen to her in the next hour, getting caught in a downpour was the least of Phoebe's worries, although she rued coming out with only a lightweight fleece. But surely the threat of rain would see the bees all heading into their shelter, not out from it?

'You're fucking dead, little girl.'

Looking past the bees, Phoebe saw Axe Thomas approaching up the track. Worn out, shoulders slumped, face red with anger and exertion both. And yet for all he looked ridiculous, there was nothing funny about his voice or his threat. She shrank back behind the nearest hive, ready to turn tail and run should she need.

'What did I ever do to you?' Phoebe shouted the question over the growing hum of the bees. Axe eyed them with suspicion before answering.

'You fucking know what you did. Thought it'd be funny, didn't you, pushing Brue into the river.'

'I didn't push him, you idiot. I tried to save him. If you'd no' been playing that stupid game, none of this would've happened.'

Something flickered across the twin's features then, although whether it was doubt or constipation Phoebe couldn't be sure. It didn't last long though, the sneer turning into an angry snarl as he ran at her.

'Gonna fucking kill you, bitch,' he shouted as he sped up far more quickly than she had expected, barging past the furthest hive so close it seemed to rock. Phoebe backed away, caught her over-large boot on a rock and before she knew it she was falling. The heather and Aunt Maude's freshly baked loaf cushioned her, but she was still struggling to get up when Axe reached the middle of the hollow. Scrambling on all fours, she tried to get away, but too quickly he was through the rest of the hives and upon her.

The first kick came out of nowhere. It blasted the wind out of her lungs and sent a shock of pain through her entire body. Phoebe let out a scream, pulled her legs up to her chest as Axe kicked out again. This time he caught her arm so hard she thought he must have broken bones. She tried to roll away, but the next kick caught her in the side. She vomited watery porridge, coughing and gasping as she gasped for breath, but the blows kept on coming, heavy boots thudding into her arms, her legs, her back. She couldn't see for tears, couldn't hear anything over the roar in her ears.

A rough hand grabbed her hair, pulled it back, lifting her head and exposing her throat. She caught a blurry glimpse of something glinting in the light. A knife? It looked long enough to be a sword. Then the twin's ugly face moved in close, the stench of him enough to make her want to vomit again.

'Gonna cut you up and chuck you in that hole in the woods. Ain't nobody gonna find you.'

Phoebe tensed, waiting for the killing blow. She could barely see for the pain coursing through her whole body, and all she could hear was that roaring in her ears.

No. Not roaring.

Buzzing.

She squinted through her tears and realised that the reason she couldn't see much was because the day had turned black. The bees were swarming so thickly they blotted out almost all of the light, so loud even Axe Thomas in his blind rage couldn't ignore them.

He held his knife hand high, and as she watched it disappeared in a writhing mass of black insect bodies. They crawled up his arm, some disappearing under the sleeve of his jacket. More of them settled on his head, crawling in his hair, over his cheeks and nose and eyes.

Phoebe felt the pressure on her neck ease as he let go of her hair, then a thunk in the ground beside her as he also dropped the knife, both hands reaching up to his face now covered in bees.

'Get them off!' he screamed, then fell to silent spitting as yet more bees crawled into his open mouth, up his hairy nostrils. More and more landed on him, crawling over his shoulders, his torso. He swiped at his face, dislodging handfuls at a time, but they were soon replaced by more, hundreds more, thousands more.

When he stood up, they covered his legs too, smothering him in a furry insect bodysuit that buzzed angrily as he flailed and stumbled. He didn't scream, but instead let out soft, terrified whimpering sounds as he staggered away from Phoebe, desperately trying to wipe the tiny creatures from his face. She lay on her side, every breath agony from his earlier onslaught, and watched as he careered from side to side, always in the general direction of away from her, never quite hitting one of the hives.

He made it almost fifty yards, halfway to the point on the wide track where it disappeared around the shoulder of the hill, then collapsed. First onto his knees, then he dropped forward onto his face and lay still.

Moments later, the bees lifted from his body like a black mist, spiralling up into the air. For an instant they swirled into a shape that could have been a face, gazing down on its work in satisfaction. And then before Phoebe had even registered the image, they split into different strands that flew swiftly back to each of the hives. The noise of them quietened from the angry roar back to the quiet, industrious hum of before. In minutes, it was as if nothing had happened at all.

Phoebe lay perfectly still for long minutes as the pain from Axe's kicks slowly began to ease into a dull ache. Only inches from her face, a foot-long hunting knife was stuck pointy end into the ground. She rolled away from it, groaning as her bruises made themselves known, then sat up and hugged her knees to her chest. A single bee buzzed past her head, landed on the sleeve of her coat, as if checking that she was OK.

'Thank you,' she croaked, throat still raw from vomit. The bee ignored her. It turned around a few times until it was certain her fleece wasn't an enormous flower and nectar jackpot, then flew off in search of more appetising fare.

Phoebe picked up the knife and placed it in the hessian bag. The loaf was ruined, the butter an odd shape, but the jar of honey had somehow survived. When she stood up, the world spun around for a moment before settling. Walking wasn't easy, her legs stiff with bruises that were going to be fun to explain to Aunt Maude when she got home. But the more she tried, the better it got.

She approached Axe Thomas's prone body with a mixture of caution and trepidation. Was he dead? Had the bees killed him? Had what she thought she had seen actually happened? Because bees didn't attack like that, did they?

As she came closer, she saw movement, the faintest sign that he was breathing. He lay on his front, one hand stretched forward, the other tucked under him as if the bees had put him in the recovery position after warning him off. She bent down beside him anyway, checked he really was still alive. And that was when she noticed that the skin on his hands and face was clear. No red blotches save for the acne scars he had worn before.

The bees had not stung him at all.

55

2023

When she reaches the dip at the edge of the moors, Steve is sitting there waiting for her. Phoebe wasn't expecting him, has no idea how he's managed to make the climb up the steep, winding track from Tynhelyg, but she's glad of the company all the same. The bees fly out to greet her as she approaches, or maybe they're just doing what bees do. None of them seems bothered by the old man sitting on a coat folded out over the heather.

'I'd forgotten how peaceful it is up here,' he says as Phoebe takes off her backpack and settles down beside him. Together they look out over the forest as it spreads across the valley beneath them, neither saying anything for a long time. Finally, Steve points a slender finger at the pack.

'Maude?' he asks.

By way of answer, Phoebe unzips the top and pulls out the plastic container her aunt's remains have been placed in. A surprisingly small amount of fine white powder, she's glad the old lady didn't want to be scattered somewhere overseas. That would have been an interesting conversation to have with airport security.

'If you want some privacy . . .?' Steve starts to struggle to his feet.

'It's fine, really.' Phoebe stands swiftly and then helps him up.

She bends to fetch his coat, shakes the creases and bits of old heather from it before helping him to put it on. 'A bit of company's nice for a change. I'd kind of forgotten how to be with people, you know?'

Steve gives her a curious look and she realises how foolish her words are. The man's been a recluse for most of his life, tucked away in a corner of the forest.

'I'm talking to the wrong person, I know. Still not sure what I'm doing with this though.' She holds up the plastic pot, then points to a spot beyond the hives. 'We scattered Louis there, so I suppose that's as good a place as any.'

In the end, Steve keeps a reasonable distance as Phoebe steps between two hives and climbs a little way into the heather. She feels she should probably say something, but can't think what. A simple 'goodbye, Maude' seems enough. As she sprinkles the powder, a light breeze picks up some of it, dancing around in the air like a happy ghost. And then it's done. She snaps the lid back onto the pot, stows it away in her backpack and slings it over her shoulder. One last look at the bees, and then she joins Steve at the head of the path down to the woods.

'Will you be leaving soon? Heading back to Edinburgh?' he asks as they walk at an old man's pace towards the trees. There's a slight catch in his voice, as if he's not the recluse he has always made himself out to be.

'I'll have to at some point. Probably soon, although I'll be back again just as quickly. There's a mountain of stuff to sort out, and I can work from Pant Melyn as easily as my flat.'

'Muriel Baywater. Yes. I suppose you can. Easier now there's half-decent broadband to the valley, too.'

Phoebe only half catches the last of Steve's words as she's stopped walking in surprise. He stops a couple of slow paces further on when he realises.

'You . . . you know?' she asks. Another stupid question.

'Louis told me, a few years before he died. Round about the

337

time he handed the mantle on to you, I think. If you ask me, the later novels are far superior.'

Phoebe can't help herself from laughing at that. 'I'll be sure and get you an advance copy of the next one, then. She's been good to me over the years, has Muriel.'

Steve nods, says nothing more, and they continue their slow journey down the side of the valley. Only when they reach the first of the trees does he speak again.

'I think he told me because he thought I'd worry you weren't making something of yourself. He wasn't wrong, and I'm glad to have been in on the secret. I'll be sad when you go away again, Feebs.'

'Oh, don't worry. I'll be back, and soon. It's not just Pant Melyn that needs sorted; I need to work out what to do with Nant Caws Farm.'

It's Steve's turn to stop in his tracks, although Phoebe's a little swifter in her reactions and so barely takes a step beyond him. They are in the trees now, and he reaches a slightly shaky hand out, lays his palm gently against the bark. For a moment she thinks it's the shock of being reminded of the existence of the place, but his eyes are wide with a different kind of wonder.

'Nant Caws? But Tegwin left no will. Or so I was told. Poor man was always a bit simple. But . . .' he looks straight at Phoebe, lets his words fade to nothing.

'Apparently I am the closest living relative. I was surprised as anyone when the solicitor told me. I always thought if you went back far enough everyone in this valley was related, but apparently not.'

'So Nant Caws belongs to you now, does it? And Pant Melyn too. Well, now. Diw diw, as the old locals would have it.' There is a light in Steve's eyes, and he stands a little straighter, shoulders back as he takes his hand off the tree. 'In that case, Doctor MacDonald, I wonder if I might ask you a favour.'

56

H e must have seen her limping down the path from the woods.
Steve Lorne stood at the front door of his cottage as she
approached, a look of horror on his face. He had pulled on his coat
and wrapped a scarf around his neck, but wore a rather incongruous pair of baffies on his feet.

'Phoebe? What's happened?' His voice was still faint, that odd
mixture of high-pitched and hoarse that sounded as painful as
she felt.

'Met Axe Thomas in the woods. He doesn't much like me.
Feeling's mutual.'

'Are you badly hurt? Come inside. Let's have a look at you.'

Phoebe allowed herself to be led through to the front room. It
was just as cluttered and untidy as the last time she had been there,
but it felt safe. She found a space on the sofa and sat down, wincing
as she put pressure on some of her bruises.

'I'll be fine,' she said to Lorne's look of concern. She held out
the hessian bag. 'Aunt Maude sent me over with this as a peace
offering, only I'm afraid it's got a bit bashed about.'

It was only after Lorne had taken the bag from her that she
remembered she'd put Axe's knife in there. He took out the loaf

and the butter first, his eyes lighting up at the sight of the jar of honey. Then he hefted the knife and raised a white eyebrow.

'Sorry. That's not from Aunt Maude.'

'Indeed, it's not.' Lorne placed the knife carefully on the mantlepiece, away from the photograph of Gwen, then turned back to face her. 'Tell me what happened.'

'Axe Thomas happened. Seems he's persuaded himself I pushed his brother into the river.'

Lorne nodded once, as if that made all the sense in the world. 'Shock often brings out the worst in people. Or the best. Is there news of the young man?'

'Brue? Aunt Maude phoned the hospital this morning, but all they'd tell her was that he was still unconscious. That's not good, is it? Don't they say the longer you're out, the less likely you'll make a good recovery?'

'They do indeed. Although they may be keeping him that way to help him heal. That he's still alive is a good sign.'

'I don't know. The way Axe was, you'd have thought his brother had died.' A little shiver ran through Phoebe then, as the implications of that possibility played out in her mind.

'I'll not try to make excuses for him. His actions are too extreme for that. But the bond between twins is a strong one. I dare say Axe Thomas is feeling very scared and alone right now. And scared bullies always lash out.'

Phoebe thought of her own experience of bullies in school, Morag Carstairs and her gang, who she could almost blame for her parents' deaths. Almost. 'Aye, they do. An' I could see there was no arguing with him. So I ran up to the bees, was going to come here since there's no one at Pant Melyn right now.' She paused then, as a little pang of guilt twisted in her gut. Seeing how frail Steve Lorne looked. What had she been thinking, leading a brute like Axe Thomas to his home?

'He caught you though?'

340

'I tripped.' Phoebe lifted one of her aunt's heavy boots as if that explained her near-fatal clumsiness. 'My shoes are still wet from yesterday, so I borrowed these. Fine for walking, but . . .'

Lorne merely nodded, a reminder that talking pained him if he did too much of it.

'He kicked me when I was down. Was going to use that.' Phoebe pointed towards the mantlepiece and the evil knife, then with a growing sense of incredulity described how the bees had come to her rescue. To his credit, Lorne didn't dismiss her as delusional, didn't even interrupt. And when she'd finished he let the silence between them grow for a while before speaking.

'It is a magical place, this valley. It gets into your bones. I knew the first time I came here that part of me would never leave. Even when they locked me away, I was still here.'

'I never asked yesterday, but how did you find out? About Gwen, that is?'

Lorne tilted his head a moment as if considering the question, and Phoebe wondered if she wasn't being a bit impertinent. Rather than being angry with her, or dismissive, her curiosity seemed to bring him alive. As if the secret had been eating away at him all these years and the thought of releasing it was blissful. He'd always seemed ancient to her, with his shock of pure white hair and thin, almost starved face. But in truth he couldn't have been much older than Phoebe's mum and dad. In his forties, not his sixties. And as he spoke, the years seemed to melt away from him.

'It was Tegwin, I suppose. He loved his little sister, still does in his infantile way.' Lorne stared out of the window, eyes unfocused. 'I almost feel sorry for him now. He'll struggle to cope with life with his father gone. He's a child in the body of a man over fifty years old. Must be very frightening.'

'I saw him leave flowers at the base of the tree. The same flowers he gave me when I visited Nant Caws Farm before Meredith died.'

The mention of the old farmer's name brought a flash of anger across Lorne's face, but he smoothed it away with a little effort. 'So he still takes them, does he?'

'I think he's desperate for her to come back. It's like you said: he's lost without someone to look after him.'

'I followed him once. Quiet as I could, don't think he knew I was there. I'd tried going to the farm, confronted . . . Gwen's father.' He shook his head, unable to say the man's name. Phoebe could understand that now.

'This would have been a few months after she'd gone missing. I wasn't in a good place. Hadn't been eating properly, out in all weather and at all hours. Just walking by then, not really searching any more. I knew in here she was gone.' He touched his chest briefly, then turned to face Phoebe. 'But when I saw him striding along that path, clutching those flowers he must have plucked from the forest? They were the sorriest-looking bunch of flowers I'd ever seen, but they were the ones she loved. So I followed him, and he led me to her.'

Phoebe was about to say 'to her grave?', but in that moment she understood. It was as her uncle had told her; the ghosts of everyone who had ever called this valley home still haunted these woods. Some broken by the lives they had lived, some waiting patiently to be reunited with those they had loved. Some befriending the lost and lonely and grieving.

'You wanted to be with her. That's why you . . .' she paused.

'Tried to hang myself?' Lorne nodded, slowly. 'There, where I knew I could find her. We could be together, for ever. Only, part of me must have known it wouldn't work. Or wanted to live even in my misery. I don't know which it was. That's the only reason I can think of why I left a note.'

Phoebe said nothing. She knew what was coming next, and it finally made sense. Of a sort.

'Your uncle. Louis. He'd never been anything but kind to me, unlike all the other locals. Maude had told him I wasn't well, so he

342

came round. I don't know if he wanted to talk, get me drunk, or just keep an eye on me, but it was too late. I'd already gone up into the woods. But I'd left a note and he worked it out. Clever of him.'

'Lucky he found you in time. It's quite a ways from here up to . . . you know.'

'Have you not noticed how sometimes a walk in the woods takes hours, and sometimes it's only a few minutes?' Lorne shook his head slowly, as if even he couldn't bring himself to believe what he was saying. 'This place didn't want me dead, so it sent your uncle to save me, sped him from this cottage to that glade in an instant. But lucky?' He made a sound that might have been a chuckle. 'Neither of us thought so at the time, but you're right. I don't think Gwen would have wanted me to kill myself any more than the forest did. Perhaps they are one and the same. She'd have told me it wasn't my time yet. Be patient.' He shook his head one last time and let out a long, rasping sigh. 'Doubt I'd have listened to her then, but I can listen to her now.'

'You see her, in the woods,' Phoebe said. 'When you're out walking.'

It wasn't a question, and Lorne simply nodded.

'Gwyneth told me the woods are full of the spirits of people who have lived and died in this valley. Uncle Louis said something much the same, but I think he thought it was just a story. I guess everything's a story when you're a writer.'

Talking of her uncle brought her back to the present. She glanced at her watch, and while it was probably hours yet before Aunt Maude returned from Carmarthen, it would take Phoebe a lot longer than normal to walk back to Pant Melyn.

'I should be getting back.' She winced as she went to stand, managed to push through the pain. Sitting had been a relief, but it had allowed her muscles to stiffen up. Lorne was on his feet more swiftly, a helping hand extended although he didn't actually touch her, Phoebe noticed.

'Are you sure? I have a car. I can drive you there.'

'Thank you.' She took the hand, felt a surprising strength in Lorne's grip for a man who looked so frail. 'But I think I need to move before I seize up entirely. I'll be fine, honest. I have a feeling I'll not be hearing from Axe Thomas in a while.'

Lorne considered her words for a moment before nodding once. He released his grip and led her to the front door. She thanked him again as she stepped outside into an afternoon turned much sunnier than she had expected. The wind had died down, the clouds breaking to let patches of blue sky slip through.

'Go carefully, Phoebe. And please thank Maude for her gifts. I will come round soon. Time indeed to let bygones be bygones.'

Phoebe thanked him again, then set off for the woods. When she reached the treeline and turned back before entering the forest, he was still standing by the house, watching her go.

57

The shade of the woods brought a welcome coolness to the air as Phoebe walked the path alongside the river. Everything ached, but moving helped to ease the stiffness and bruising. She didn't stop, didn't even glance at the fork in the path where the track led to the old stone bridge. Neither did she tarry at the pool, although it occurred to her she would probably never swim there again. Not with the memory of Brue Thomas's deathly white face and blue lips in her memory, the pale, bloodless scar across his forehead washed clean by the water.

She wasn't sure why her feet had brought her this way. There was another path from Tynhelyg that would have taken her to Pant Melyn without passing the scene of the accident. And it was an accident, she kept on telling herself that. She had done everything in her power to stop the twin from falling in, and then put herself in danger to get him back out again. How could his brother think she'd done anything else?

Her feet were on the first board of the wooden bridge before she realised where they had led her, but she knew as soon as she saw it why she had come this way. It was a bit more of a struggle to sit down in the middle, her legs and back not as supple as they had been before Axe had tried to kill her, up by the beehives. As she leaned on the railing and stared into the distance, she found herself reliving the attack. His rage had been so total, so brutal. She would have said animal, except that no mere creature would have been quite so sadistic.

Where was he now? Still up there unconscious, or had he woken while she'd been talking to Steve, gathered himself and slunk away like a beaten dog? Would he remember what had happened to him the next time they met, or would he paint a different picture in his mind like he had done with what happened to his brother? Phoebe had no doubt there would be another time, but she'd be ready for him. She wasn't going to be driven away from her home that easily.

A quiet descended over the forest as she rested her chin on her hands and watched the water crashing over rocks, the sunlight dappling the pale green brackens that dangled from the slate cliffs; the brief flashes of colour as tiny birds dipped and dived after insects. It wasn't silent; there was noise everywhere. It wasn't still; the motion was constant. But there was a peace and tranquillity in this place that made it easy to forget all the trauma that had happened here too.

How long she sat there simply staring, Phoebe couldn't have said. Her thoughts bounced between the panic she'd felt while trying to save Brue Thomas, the terror at Axe's horrific attack and the calm of this perfect moment. Slowly, the first two grew quieter, their hold on her loosening as she allowed herself to relax. And then the thought struck her. Home. She'd considered Pant Melyn home. Logically that was what the ramshackle old house was now, with her aunt and uncle in loco parentis until she was old enough to look after herself. But she was far from ready to face the world alone; the events of the past few days had proved that to her.

Instead of making her want to flee back to Scotland, Phoebe found that the trauma had made her oddly proud of this place. She was a part of these woods now, this strange secluded valley with its even stranger inhabitants. It was her home. There were problems with it, of course. Being taught by Aunt Maude, Uncle Louis and a few crusty old lecturers from the university sounded like a real drag; making the trip to Aberystwyth and back every day even more so. Perhaps she would enrol at Llandod Hall, like the colonel had suggested. It would mean leaving Llancwm every week, only returning at the weekends. But she'd looked it up on the map; Llandrindod Wells wasn't so far, and even if the other girls she met there would be total strangers at first, maybe those strangers would some day become friends. And maybe her old friends would come and visit from time to time too. Jenny, Charlotte and a few others. She'd enjoy showing them the valley and the woods, the waterfalls and the hidden caves. There was more to life than ogling pop stars and staring through shop windows at clothes she neither needed nor could afford. And anyway, she was friends with a pop star now. He was going to teach her to play the guitar.

'You decided to stay, then.'

The voice brought her abruptly to her senses. Phoebe looked up sluggishly to see a familiar figure at the end of the bridge.

'Gwyneth?'

The young girl padded over to her and sat down, back to the railings and her shoulder touching Phoebe's. She was warm and smelled of sunshine, barefoot and dressed in those old-fashioned clothes. Her hair was still unkempt, tangling down about her ears and onto her shoulders in a dirty-blonde cascade. She even had the same slightly smudged cheeks, the streak of mud across her forehead where she'd wiped an itch away with a dirty hand. And yet she was also different somehow. She looked older, perhaps. Less like Phoebe in a grubby mirror, more like the old photographs.

'Gwen.'

She smiled at that, a bright, innocent, full-on smile that seemed to lighten the day even down here in the depths of the woods.

'I've waited so long,' she said. 'But I knew you'd find me.'

'I . . . But . . .' Phoebe found she had no words, and neither could she move.

'It's OK, Feebs. It was never your fault. None of it. Not what happened to me, and certainly not what happened to those terrible twins.'

Something clicked in Phoebe's mind then. 'It was you. The bees. That's why they swarmed like that.'

'No, that was their idea. They like you, and they don't much like people picking on their friends.' The young girl shifted slightly, as if trying to get comfortable, and now she wasn't about Phoebe's age. Now she was maybe fifteen years older, her belly swelling with the child she carried. Hers and Steve Lorne's. And was it Phoebe's imagination, or could she see the leaves behind her, through her?

'I'm so sorry. What happened to you. It was terrible. And so stupid too. One old man's blind prejudice causing so much pain.'

'Ah, Feebs, that's kind of you to say, but it's ancient history now. Part of the warp and weft of this valley. I'm glad the truth is coming out though. There's been a darkness hanging over Llancwm ever since it happened, but now it feels like the sun's coming out again, you know?'

Phoebe looked up as the sun did, indeed, come out from behind a cloud, bathing her face in warm gold.

'Will you go now?' she asked.

'Why would I want to leave? I have everything I need here, don't I?' Gwen, or was it Gwyneth, laughed. Or was that the sound of the water tinkling over rocks?

'But you're—'

'Dead? A ghost? A spirit roaming free now. This is my home, Feebs. I'll always be here. And besides, I'm not the only one. Not even the most recent.'

Overhead, a lone kite screeched into the sky. Myfanwy's baby calling for its long-dead mother.

'What do you mean?' Phoebe asked, although she had a suspicion she knew. But Gwyneth or Gwen or whoever she was just shook her head slowly in reply. And she was fading, there was no denying it now. The smudge on her forehead was a leaf in the bushes on the far side of the track, the floral patterns on her dress flowers on the riverbank.

'Keep an eye on Steve, Feebs. For me. He's been through so much, but he has a good heart. That's why I loved him so.'

Phoebe looked around, expecting to see Lorne's shock of white hair, the man himself half hidden by the undergrowth. But the path was empty. And when she turned back again, so was the bridge.

58

2023

She parts with Steve at the fork in the forest path that will take him home to Tynhelyg. He might walk slowly, but for his age he is remarkably fit. Then again, he's spent the past forty years and more walking these paths, a life tied to the forest and the tragedy that took place within it.

Phoebe considers the favour he has asked as she follows the track downhill towards the river. It's a simple enough thing given what she has just done, although it leaves her sad to think about. And it makes perfect sense, too, in a nonsensical way. When his time comes, he would like to be with Gwen, his ashes scattered beneath the great oak tree that stands on land now belonging to her. And who is Phoebe to deny him that?

Of course, she hopes it will be many years yet before she has to perform that final act for him, and she has a horrible feeling that she might end up owning even more of this valley by the time it happens. Almost as much as mad old Roderick Powell. The thought brings a smile unbidden to her lips. She a girl from a housing estate in Cupar ending up owning half a Welsh valley. No idea what she's going to do with it all.

But that's a problem for another day.

The white noise roar of the river brings her back to herself. Phoebe sees first the mist-like spray from the waterfall as it rises through the trees. Closer still, the overgrown path that leads to the broken stone bridge. She shudders at the memory it brings, so sharp it might almost have been yesterday that Brue Thomas went off the edge and into the maelstrom. Both twins avoided her after that summer, left the village a couple of years later, and that suited her just fine. She wonders idly what became of them, and then finds that she doesn't much care.

The sun has broken through the clouds by the time she reaches the wooden bridge, steam rising gently from the damp timbers. Phoebe walks slowly to the middle, tests the railing for strength before leaning against it. New and strong when she was twelve years old, it's showing its age now. Like her. Beneath it the waters tumble and roil, not full spate like that fateful afternoon, but wild enough. Above her, in the gap between the trees, a pair of red kites circle on the warming air. Untamed and wild, she wishes she could be as free. But then why can't she?

The car is packed, fully charged and ready for the trip back to Edinburgh. She has known she would be leaving this place ever since she set out to come here. Home is the empty flat with its one bottle of white wine in the fridge, the collected bric-a-brac of a failed relationship. Home is the tiny bedroom she converted into an office, where she can stare out of the window at the tenement across the street as she dreams of improbable romances and writes those dreams down. Home is the annual pilgrimage to a town she hardly knows, to stare through the windscreen at a house she never lived in.

Home is these woods, where she made her first real friend.

A change in the air, the slightest vibration through her feet and her arms. Phoebe doesn't turn, doesn't dare. She keeps on staring out over the water as the lightest of footsteps treads the old planks. She feels the presence as a closeness, someone leaning beside her, matching her gaze. A warmth against her shoulder that smells like sunshine. And then a voice unchanged in all these years.

'So you've decided to stay, then,' Gwyneth says.

And yes, Phoebe realises. She has.

Acknowledgements

This book has been a long time in the making. I first thought of writing about the memorable characters I had met while visiting Welsh farms and smallholdings almost twenty years ago. Those early ideas were soon shelved, but I am still hugely indebted to the people of Ceredigion, Carmarthenshire and Pembrokeshire in whose kitchens I sat and drunk tea and chatted. Too many to name, and not a one of you like Meredith Ellis at all. Diolch yn fawr pawb!

I am always indebted to my wonderful agent, Juliet Mushens, but for this book even more so. Her feedback on multiple redrafts shaped my somewhat random thoughts into the book you have in your hands now. I doubt I would ever have finished it without her constant encouragement. Thank you, Juliet, and my thanks to all the team at Mushens Entertainment, too. A more talented, dedicated and helpful bunch you couldn't hope to have representing you.

Thank you to Alex, Jack, Areen and all the team at Wildfire for so enthusiastically taking on this book, so different from everything else I've sent you. Who knows what I might come up with next?

A huge thank you, and an apology, to the people of Cwmystwyth, Pontarfynach, Pontrhydygroes and the Hafod Estate, and my friends and colleagues at the Pwllpeiran research farm. You may see reflections of those places in this tale, although I have taken monstrous liberties, for which I apologise. I walked those hills and forests for over a decade, and was inspired by them and all the people I met there. If you ever have the chance to visit, I cannot recommend it highly enough.

And last, but not least, thank you, Barbara. If you hadn't taken that job in the middle of nowhere, I might never have gone to Wales in the first place.

With thanks to everyone who worked on the publication of
Broken Ghosts:

Editorial
Alex Clarke
Jack Butler
Areen Ali

Copyeditor
Federica Leonardis

Proofreader
Sarah Coward

Audio
Ellie Wheeldon

Production
Rhys Callaghan

Design
Caroline Young

Marketing
Katrina Smedley

Publicity
Federica Trogu

Sales
Rebecca Bader
Isobel Smith
Jess Harvey
Eleanor Wood

Contracts
Helen Windrath

Finance
Will Blight